Queen of the Lost Boys
THE NEVERLAND CHRONICLES
VOLUME III

T.S. Kinley

Queen of the Lost Boys, by T. S. Kinley

This is a work of fiction. Names, characters, places, and incidents are either the product of the author's imagination or are used fictitiously. Any resemblance to actual persons, living or dead, events, or locales is entirely coincidental.

Copyright © 2023 by T. S. Kinley

All rights reserved. No part of this book may be reproduced or used in any manner without written permission of the copyright owner except for the use of quotations in a book review. For more information, address: TSKinley@TSKinleyBooks.com

First paperback edition June 2023
ISBN 979-8-9859074-5-2

Book design by T.S. Kinley
Editing by Elizabeth M. Danos
Cover design by Moonpress www.moonpress.co
WWW.TSKinleyBooks.com

To our beloved readers. Who turned our dream into reality… It's been an awfully big adventure. You followed us down the rabbit hole, and allowed us to bring the wonder of Neverland back into your life. It is to you, the soulful dreamers, the unabashed romantics, that are the heartbeat behind these ink-stained pages. From the very depths of our heart, thank you all for believing in us, even when it was hard to believe in ourselves.

Now be a good girl/boy and spread these pages.

AUTHOR'S NOTE

Queen of the Lost Boys is a why choose spicy romance. All characters in this book are above the age of eighteen. The content in this book contains sexually explicit depictions. Please be aware of the following possible trigger warnings and read at your own discretion. Lewd NSFW depictions of sexual acts, bondage/restraints, BDSM, knife play, breath play, drug and alcohol use, graphic violence, gore, mutilation of corpses, abduction, assault, hostage situations, mind control, self mutilation, anxiety and depression, terminal illness/cancer, suicide, and death.

Before you go. Follow T.S. Kinley on social media. Let's be friends! Check out our Instagram, Facebook, Pinterest, and Tic Tok pages and get insights into the beautifully, complicated mind of not one, but two authors! Have questions? Something you are dying to know about the amazing characters we've created? Join us online, we love to engage with our readers!

Neverland

MAROONER'S ROCK

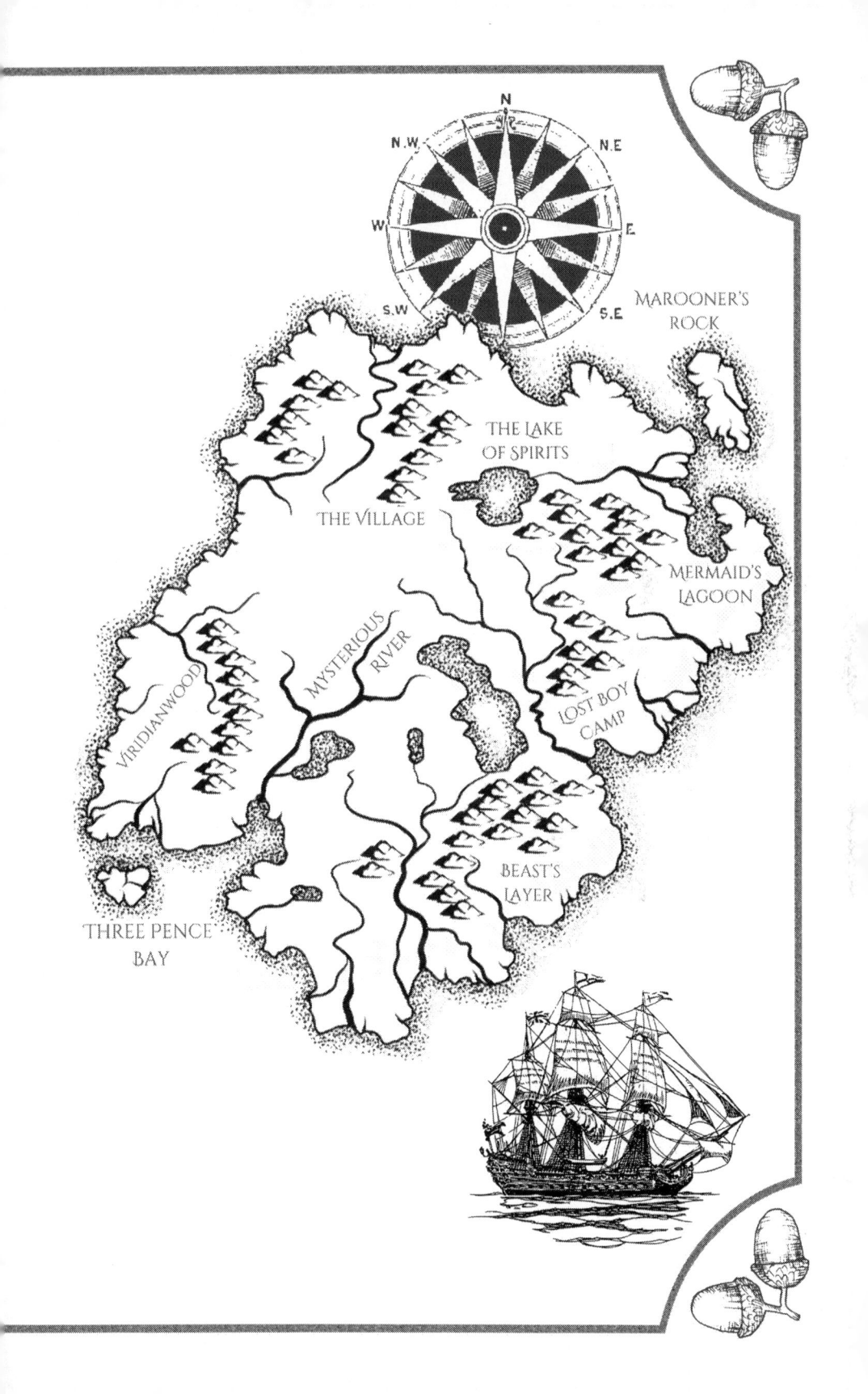

THE LAKE OF SPIRITS

THE VILLAGE

MERMAID'S LAGOON

MYSTERIOUS RIVER

VIRIDIANWOOD

LOST BOY CAMP

BEAST'S LAYER

THREE PENCE BAY

"I'll follow thee and make a heaven of hell, To die upon the hand I love so well."

-William Shakespeare A Midsummer Night's Dream

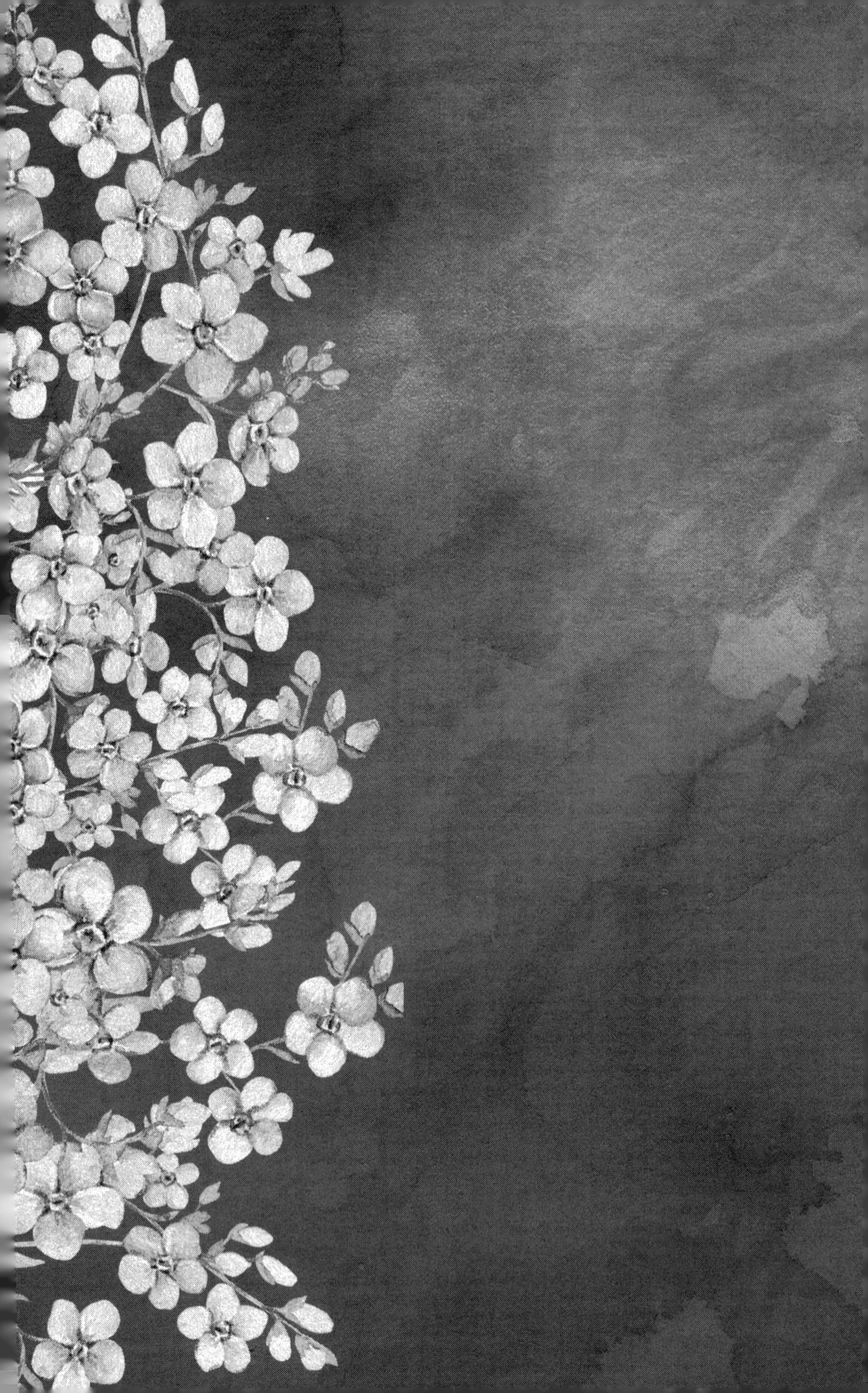

PROLOGUE
-MICHAELA-

The shock of the cold stole my breath away. I flailed in the frigid water as the hole in the ice I'd fallen through grew bigger and bigger. "Mum!" I screamed for help, but I knew it was useless. She'd never hear me. After all, I'd gone to the pond on my own when she'd forbidden me to go. But I was eight years old, which meant I was big enough to make my own decisions. And I'd wanted to go skating. I felt the weight of the skates threaten to drag me down as I kicked. My limbs quickly grew heavy and my joints felt stiff in the icy embrace of the water. Panic began to set in, forcing tears from my eyes and blurring my vision.

"Mic! Mickey!" My little sister's voice broke through the terror of my distress. She must have followed me here. I could see her pink pom-pom hat bobbing up and down as she crawled along the ice to me.

"Go back! You'll fall in too! Go get Mum!" I called to her, frantically waving at her to go back. Mum would kill me if I let my little sister drown because of my foolishness.

"Nope. No time. Don't worry sissy, I've got you." Gwen dismissed my order to go get Mum and kept crawling toward me, not a hint of fear in her voice. She held my stare, her brown eyes solid in her resolve, a courageous fire burning brightly within them as if she already knew how this whole thing would turn out. "Take my hand!" she called, reaching her pink mittened hand to me. A wave of calm washed over me as I reached for her. A spark of warmth radiated through my whole body as my hand grasped hers.

THAT SAME SPARK of warmth penetrated my frozen soul, jolting me from a childhood memory that my mind had all but suppressed. Gwen's little body had miraculously pulled me from my icy death that day, and it was then that I knew she was something altogether different— special. Now I found myself in the same struggle between life and death. The only difference was the frozen prison that I found myself in. Since Tiger Lily had captured me, I'd found sanctuary in a cozy place deep inside my mind. It was a familiar place. I'd retreated there often enough when the pain from cancer had been too much to bear. But I was pulled from my refuge when a wave of her energy penetrated my defenses and washed over me like electricity. I didn't need to open my eyes to know that she'd come for me. And my sister's wrath was so tangible I could feel its presence radiating in the surrounding space.

The room came back to me, and I found myself on my knees. My return to consciousness brought a wave of the pain I'd been suppressing and it stole the breath from my lungs. When I could finally focus, she filled my vision in all her vengeful glory. My sister... my Gwen. The authentic version of her. Not the broken, submissive version of her that had been masquerading around, snuffing out her inner light with the weight of grief and crushing obligations. Neverland had restored her. Her boys had led her down the path that she'd been so afraid to follow. Now she'd come for me, as I knew she always would.

"Let her go, Tiger Lily. It's me you want, not her," Gwen demanded.

My mind went fuzzy, and I could feel my mortal body shutting down. I'd lived on the edge of death for so long that I knew its cold caress well. I didn't have much time left. The words of the people around me sounded muddled, and I put all of my energy into focusing on what was being said.

"Enough! Or she dies!" Tiger Lily shrieked. I felt the weight of her icy blade as it rested on the back of my neck, the harsh metal digging into my skin. "Touch my mate again and I'll part her pretty little head from her body."

"He's not your mate!" Gwen said through gritted teeth. This was it. This was the end of the line for me. It was time.

"Gwen," I called out, managing to raise my head and look at her. I took in those soft brown eyes and my heart leapt to see the fire had returned to them. "Gwen, listen to me. Take Peter and go. She's going to kill us both if you stay. I was dead a long time ago."

"No Mic, don't you dare. It's not your time. This journey proved that!"

"This journey gave me the chance to have my death mean something. I get to save my little sister. What greater honor is there in life than dying for the one you love? I've made up my mind."

I felt a pressure inside my head and Lucius's voice radiated into my conscious thought, *"No! Don't do this. I won't let you die."* Before I had a moment to contemplate the fact that I was truly losing my mind, a loud boom shook the room, dust and plaster fell from the ceiling. The walls continued to shake, taking blow after blow, the sound deafening in the chamber. The attention shifted from me. Tiger Lily and her guards took up defensive positions just before the walls came crumbling down. Chaos ensued, but I could no longer hold myself up. I collapsed on the floor, fading in and out of consciousness. The beasts surrounded me protectively. Their roars reverberated against the walls, challenging the Fae.

My mind nagged at my waning body, attempting to coax it into action by sheer will alone. I needed to get to Gwen. I needed to be sure that she survived this. She was owed a beautiful life, and I refused to die before I could ensure her happily ever after. But my body was a useless traitor and I couldn't bring myself to move. I must have blacked out because the next thing I remembered I was in Lucius's arms, cradled against his chest as he ran full speed behind his brothers, who were still in their bear forms.

"Gwen, I need to get to Gwen! I need to—"

"Shh… don't worry dove, she'll be fine. Her boys will make sure of that. I just need you to rest. We'll make everything better." I could feel a warmth radiating into my body. A tingling energy that pooled at my center before I lapsed into unconsciousness again.

"Give her to me, Lucius. She needs more magic and you're tapped out." A strong voice broke through the darkness that enveloped me. I felt a deep rumble against my cheek as Lucius growled before he shifted my body to another. I was still too weak to move, but death's sweet caress was no longer stroking my soul. My eyes fluttered open to find Nico's dark eyes staring back at me. His face was lined with concern as he looked me over.

We were in a cave of sorts and all the brothers surrounded me, no longer in their bear forms. Lucius, I knew, but the other two I'd only just met. They, too, stared at me with worried looks. Luca and Jase. Their names surfaced out of the fog that still clouded my mind. I inhaled deeply as I settled into Nico's warm body, his scent was ambrosia. I knew in the depths of my soul that I was safe here with these beasts. Just before I was swallowed back into a dreamless abyss, I felt the ground tremble beneath us. A distant roar grew ever louder until a shock wave collided into us. Nico clutched me tighter as we were thrown to the ground with the force.

"What the fuck was that?" Lucius grumbled as he picked himself off the ground.

"It means a chosen is dead," Nico breathed.

"A chosen?"

"One of Neverland's chosen is dead. My guess is either Peter Pan or Tiger Lily have gone to answer to the Divine today." A silence fell over the brothers. I was barely holding onto consciousness, but my heart broke for Gwen if Peter truly was dead. The concern radiating from the beasts was palpable as they shared knowing glances.

"It's time we made plans to get her out of Neverland. That release of power will have sent shock waves to every realm in the cosmos. Every power hungry Fae will make their way to lay claim to the island. War is coming to Neverland."

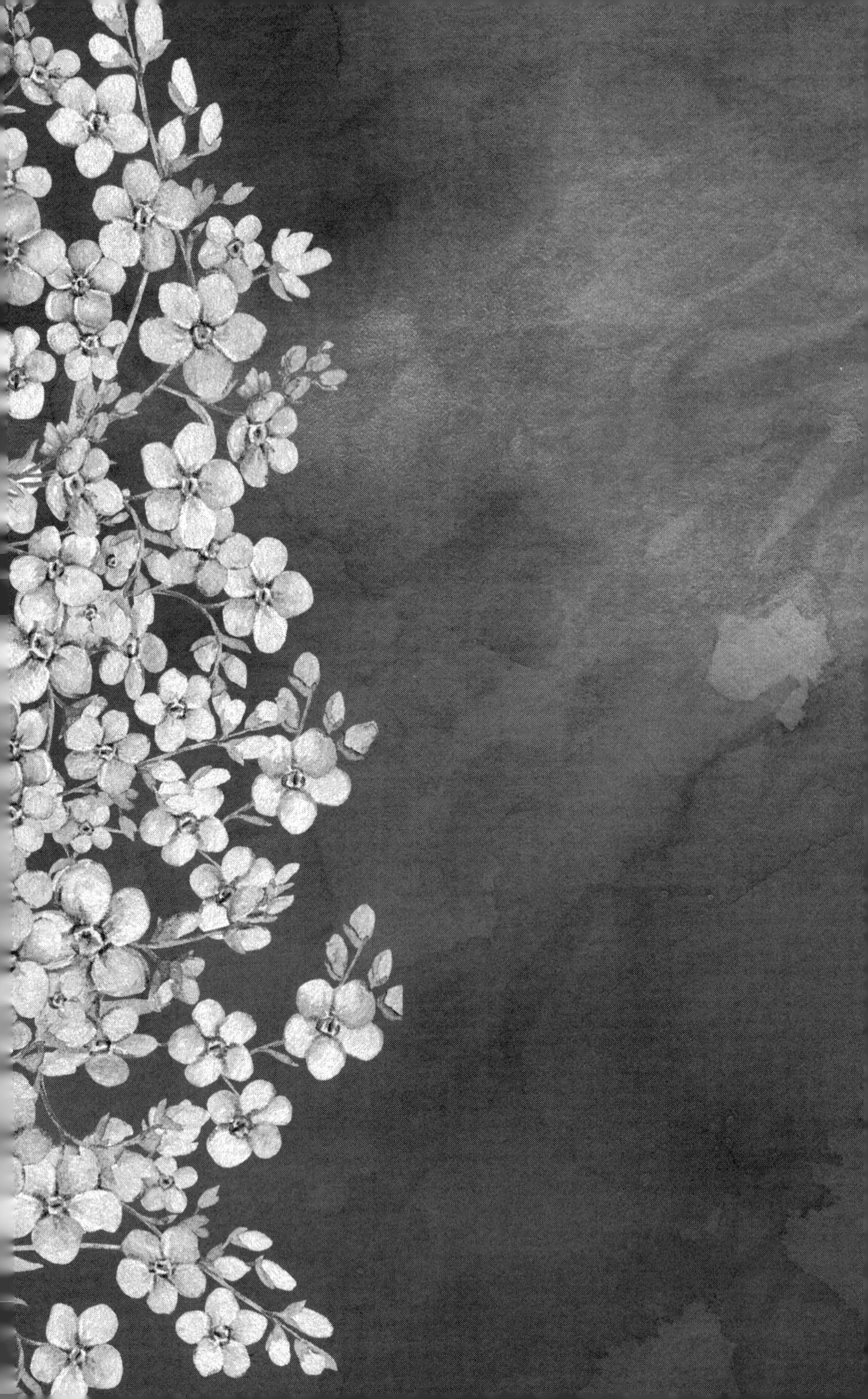

CHAPTER I
CHOICES
-HOOK-

My life was a collection of the decisions I'd made. One wrong move, one altered course and I would have been residing in Davy Jones's locker centuries ago. I'd trusted in fate, that seductive temptress, to lead me on the proper course. She had been a vindictive bitch at times, and I cursed her name on many occasions, but she had never steered me wrong. It was with that deep rooted trust that I found myself at the entrance of the caves below the Temple Mount.

The ivory walls loomed like an ethereal beacon, luring

me into darkness. It called me down the path that was now in the hands of fate. Damnation seize my soul and banish it to hell if I am wrong. But I'd made my decision and I committed to it with every fiber of my being. I had to tamper down the desperation rising in my chest.

Gwendolyn occupied my every thought and these feelings were foreign to me. I was completely unprepared to deal with them. I could feel the weak spot in my soul that ached only for her, and I knew in that moment how foolish I was. I would do absolutely anything for this girl and I was a dead man if anyone found out. The need to get to her was overwhelming, but I did my best to compose myself. It was crucial that I had all of my wits about me tonight. Her life depended on it. I needed a level head, and maybe just a bit of luck. Once the decision had been made, I'd stopped just long enough to flip a gold coin into the Mysterious River. A symbolic payment. A promise of my soul for hers if it should come to that.

The familiar sounds of battle carried on the frigid wind, beckoning me— the clashing of steel, the grunting of men as they fought for their very existence. It had always been a captivating symphony of life and death, but now it sent a shiver of panic down my spine. Was I too late? Had I stood, indecisive, at the crossroads for too long? Had I been complicit in her death by simply not showing up when she needed me? I had learned a long time ago that we were all merely pieces in the Divine's game. "Were we no better than chessmen, moved by an unseen power, vessels the potter fashions at his fancy, for honour or for shame?" Oscar Wilde's poor Lord Arthur Savile had been shaped into a murderous pawn by mere suggestion alone. But surely I was not so naive, but then again I was a man with a tainted soul. And now I couldn't help but wonder if I was already in checkmate. I swallowed hard and picked up my pace, my men fanning out behind me.

"Smee, I think it's high time you let Johnny Corkscrew out to play."

"Aye, Captain," Smee croaked in response before I heard the audible click as he drew the hammer back on his favorite pistol.

"Men!" I called out to the loyal band of pirates who would follow me to the pits of hell if I asked it of them. "Keep to the shadows and only engage at my signal." The hoard grumbled their approval. If I was too late, I wasn't about to sacrifice my men for the likes of Peter fucking Pan. I was here for my girl and my girl alone.

The ivory walls of the temple soared above me as I descended into darkness, the cave swallowing me up. The battle sounds guided me forward. My heart beat double time in anticipation for what I might find. I reminded myself that I would have known if she now rested with the Divine. I calmed myself with the notion that I would have felt it if her resplendent soul had left me. One more bend in the path and I arrived at the melee. Torchlight cast ominous shadows over the Lost Boys who looked ragged and seriously outnumbered in a fight to the death. Peter's second in command was crumpled on the ground, unmoving. Tiger Lily was at the center of it all, propping herself up as blood ran down her arms.

"I told you, he's mine," Tiger Lily seethed. "He's always been mine. Now you'll die at his hands, knowing how little he cared for you." She was obviously wounded, but it did nothing to temper the condemnation in her voice.

I shifted my position quickly, keeping myself hidden in the shadows. As I peered past her, I saw Peter. His large frame hovered over Gwen. Her legs kicked out, trying to find purchase to buck him off. I could hear my blood roaring in my ears as my anger boiled over. The enchanted tattoo on my forearm burned like a brand, its magic fueling the flames of my fury. The magic that had been embedded within my mortal soul very rarely came to my aide, but when it did, the odds were always in my favor. Once upon a time —centuries ago now— I had been in love with a woman, and Peter had taken her from me. I wouldn't let him do it again and neither would the magic that I'd bartered my soul for.

I'd always prided myself on my restraint. My ability to meticulously analyze every situation even in the most dire of circumstances. That all went out the window as I watched Peter smother her light out of existence. I charged past Tiger Lily, catching her shoulder, sending her sprawling as I raced for Gwen. This triggered my men into action. Their battle cries were deafening as they filled the caves, taking on Tiger

Lily's guard, fighting side by side with their sworn enemies, the Lost Boys. I reached Peter in a few long strides, giving no care to the chaos surrounding me. I felt a wave of satisfaction wash over me as I ripped that fucker off of her. I could feel the need for bloodshed feeding the monster within me.

He slammed into the solid wall of the cave, the chains still surrounding his neck clanked against the rock. The blow barely phased him as he whirled around to face me. Only this wasn't the Peter I'd known for centuries. This was a void of the man I knew all too well. A black veil cast dark shadows over his eyes. His typical cocksure expression was replaced by a vacant mask. The thrill of the fight began to diminish. This wasn't my worthy opponent; taking him out now didn't seem like vengeance for the history of wrongs he'd committed against me. Peter deserved every ounce of my wrath. But the idea of finishing him now felt bittersweet because this wasn't Peter. I wanted to look into his eyes when I finally ran him through. He would know that fate had finally caught up to him when the tip of my hook pierced his heart.

But this was no longer about Peter and I. I wasn't the same man anymore. She had irrevocably changed me. I looked at Gwen laying on the floor of the cave and the feud I'd stoked for so many years seemed insignificant. That fucker had crossed the final line. He'd tried to take my girl away from me, the very light in my futile existence. As much as this fight wouldn't live up to my selfish vendetta, I could never allow anyone to threaten my queen and live to see another day.

I leveled a deadly glare at the void of a man before me, engaging him and pulling his attention from Gwen. Peter charged, barreling into me at full speed. He didn't hold back an ounce as he threw the full weight of his shoulder into my gut. My back slammed hard against the confining rock wall. The wind was properly knocked from my lungs and bile rose in my throat. He wasted no time wrapping the chains around his fist before landing a blow solidly on my chin, whipping my head to the side. The silver taste of blood filled my mouth and I smiled as the pain fed my dark soul. Peter's body remained strong, but he fought with no spirit, lacking his usual finesse as a fighter. He pulled me off my feet and we scuffled on the ground, each of us trying to get the upper hand. I refused to pull my sword. Peter was unarmed. I may have scraped the bottom of the morality barrel, but I still had some sense of honor within me. I refused to end our epic feud in such a cowardly way. However, it was absolutely delightful when I felt the crunch of his nose under my fist when I finally landed a blow.

That was enough to lay Peter out for the moment. Blood gushed from his broken nose, pooling in the hollow of his neck as he sprawled on the ground. I managed to wipe his blood from my heavy rings, and focus my attention on Gwen. She remained on the ground, her limbs moving slowly as she came to. I left Peter behind and went to her, pulling her limp body into my lap. She groaned as I pushed back a strand of hair clinging to a bloody gash in her lip. Her eyes flickered open.

"Not enough time. The power... it's left me. Left me before I could have my revenge." An otherworldly voice came from my beautiful girl. Her pupils were blown out and the flicker of foreign magic danced in her eyes briefly before it went out and she slowly began to focus on me.

"Gwen... my love?" I asked tentatively. Terror ripped through me. Her soul felt wrong... tainted somehow. My mind raced with every vile possibility. It was dark magic for sure.

"You came," she breathed, pulling me from my deteriorating thoughts. Her voice returned to her own and a beautiful smile lit her face.

"My love, didn't I tell you not to question my word? Remind me to punish you for that later," I said, a smile tugging at my lips as I masked the horror of what I'd just seen.

"Hook!" A desperate voice demanded my attention. "Get her out of here!" A bruised and bleeding Eben called to me as he took on three of Tiger Lily's guards. He looked resigned, accepting the fact that he would never leave this cave alive. He was using his final stand to give me enough time to save her. I'd always known this Lost Boy was different from the rest. I'd been biding my time, knowing he would be a valuable ally once Peter inevitably grew tired of his insubordination. This man was destined to be so much more than a mere Lost Boy. I felt a growing respect take root in my mind, and I knew if he were to survive this day, it was time to let him know the truth.

"Peter, listen to your mate!" A broken and battered Tiger Lily shrieked, the sound carrying over the savage fighting. She crawled to Peter and shook him violently. She pulled a bottle from her belt and attempted to pour its contents into his mouth. The black liquid ran out of his mouth as he choked on it. This was the Black Lethe she'd been using to entomb his soul. "Finish her!" she screamed at him. "Finish her now or I will not be pleased." She slapped him solidly across the face before she pulled him to his feet. Peter shifted his vacant gaze back to Gwen. I was running out of time. I needed to make a choice, end Peter here and now or tuck tail and run, bringing Gwen to safety. My eyes focused on Peter and my hand shifted to my sword. As I pulled it from its scabbard, her small hand reached out to stop me.

"Please… James." Gwen's weak voice pulled me from my predatory gaze. "Don't hurt him. Spare him… for me. Please! You need to get to Tiger Lily."

"Love, I—"

"You have to. She won't stop coming for me, for my sister. I'm not leaving here until one of us is dead." I could hear the resolve in her voice. My hand loosened on the pommel of my sword. Her plea cracked the ice of my frozen heart. This girl would be the death of me. I reached for my pistol instead. I gently shifted her off of my lap and stood to meet Peter's charge.

"No James, don't!" Gwen cried behind me. I raised my pistol toward Peter and in a perfectly timed strike, I crashed the butt of the pistol into his temple. He fell into me and his unconscious body slid down my chest to the floor.

"Peter!" Gwen pulled herself to his flaccid body, wiping away the blood pouring from the gash in his head.

"He'll be alright, love," I promised her. I had to work hard to keep the venom from my voice. Only moments ago he'd been trying to kill her and yet her obvious devotion to him was unwavering. What was his thrall over her? Maybe if she knew the real Peter, what he was capable of, she might think differently. I turned from the two of them, giving Gwen the space she needed. I turned my attention to Tiger Lily. I would prove to Gwen that I was the better man, and I would start by laying her enemy's corpse at her feet. I pulled a dagger from my belt and placed it in Gwen's hand, wrapping her fingers around the hilt. "If he wakes before I get back, you run him through." It wasn't a request, it was a clear command and she nodded slowly. "Good girl." And with that I turned to the hunt.

I scanned the darkened cave, but Tiger Lily was nowhere to be found. She'd abandoned her fighting men to save her own skin. The cowardly bitch had knowingly sent Peter to his death so that she could escape. And she'd had the audacity to paint me as the villain. She'd used me as a distraction to avert attention from her truly dark soul. Her lackeys tried to stop me, still devoted to their deceitful princess. But they were no match for me. They barely slowed my pace, merely delaying the inevitable. I would find her.

I stalked her into the bowels of the mountain. My borrowed magic guided me every step of the way, alerting me to her presence in the absolute blackness of the caves. I could feel her presence as I approached— the fear radiating out of her in waves. I dragged my hook along the icy walls. The grating sound filled the air. My dark soul purred when I heard her whimper echoing through the hollows. I always had a flair for the dramatic.

"Bones, speak to me! Don't abandon me!" she pleaded as she whirled around, desperately searching the darkness for the evil that was chasing her. A dim ball of Fae light filled the darkness as it flickered over Tiger Lily's palm. I reveled in the fear that danced in her eyes as she took me in. She could barely keep the light aglow, which spelled it all out for me, her magic was tapped out and my grin grew even wider.

"Hook, I would reconsider if I were you. I can offer you a position of power at my side. My top advisor." She attempted to bribe me, stay my hand with her empty promises, because she knew she was no match for me. "It's that girl. She's poisoned your mind just like she did with Peter. She's no good for you. She'll use you and then leave you for the Lost Boys."

"I suggest you shut your fucking mouth Tiger Lily. You're not proving your case," I growled.

"If you let me leave I will owe you a favor— a very valuable favor."

"You have made your own bed, now I think it's time you sleep in it, eternally," I hissed. She turned then and started to run from me, her scream echoing against the rock walls. The predator in me smiled with delight. I loved it when they ran, it made it much more entertaining. I let her get a bit ahead of me just to fuck with her, but I finally caught up to her as she neared the mouth of the cave. She ran directly into Smee, his hulking form blocking her exit. She backed away from him, trying to change course, but it was too late. I grabbed her long, ebony hair, jerking her backward until her slight frame slammed into my chest.

"You'll regret this, Hook. I am a chosen. The Divine will make you pay dearly."

"When you see the Divine, you tell her if she wants me, she'll have to pluck my soul from the 9th Realm of hell," I whispered in her ear before I plunged my hook into her neck. Time slowed in that moment. I closed my eyes, feeling the rhythmic beating of her pulse, her very life source, chiming in my hook… and then I ripped her throat out in one violent motion. The hot splatter of blood coated the ground before me as she took her last gurgled breath. Her power exploded out of her and my world tipped on its axis as chaos ensued until a comforting blackness enveloped me.

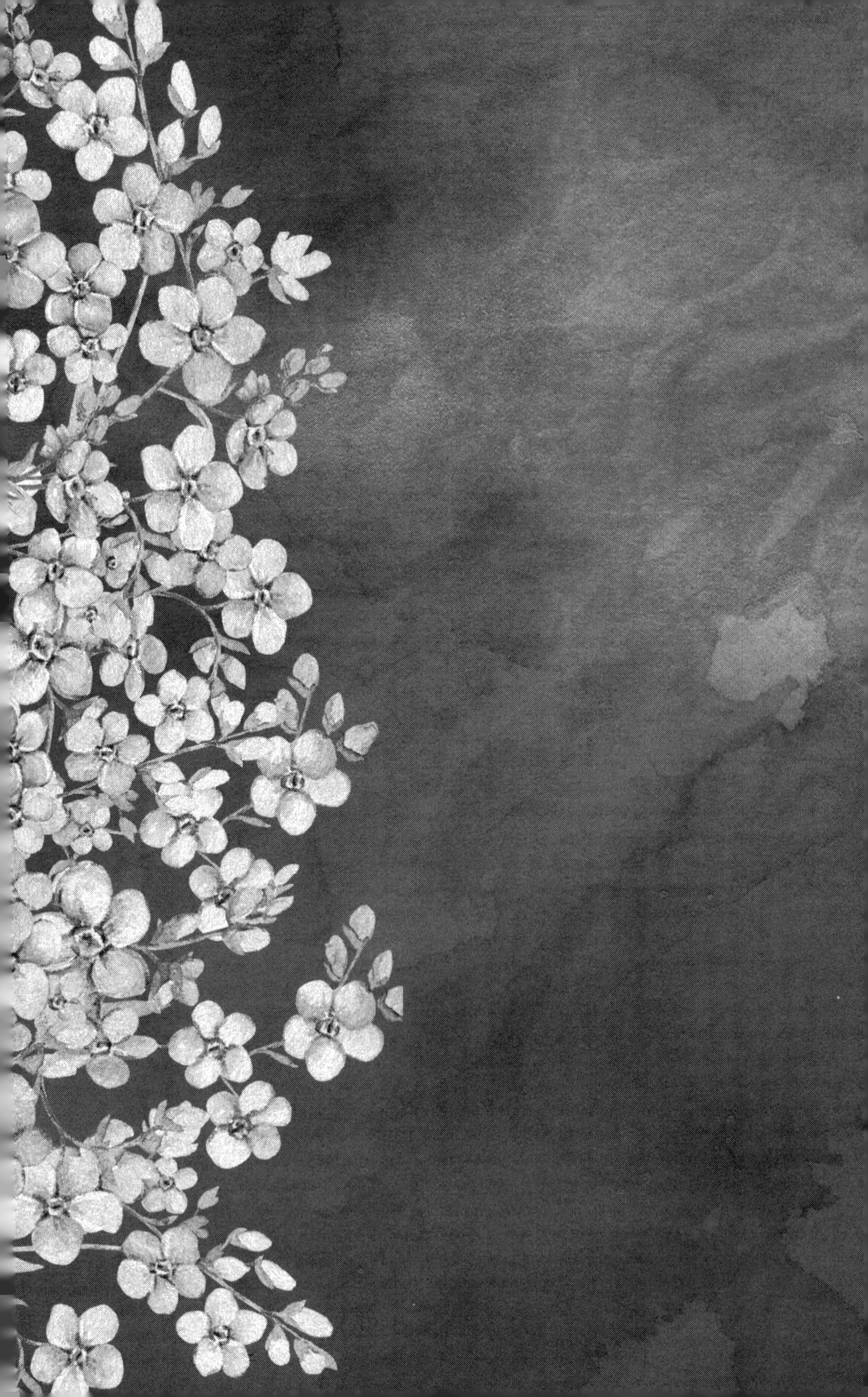

Chapter II
Consequences
-Gwen-

The first thing I remember was the loud buzzing in my ears, as if a swarm of flies had taken up residence in my head. I couldn't remember where I was. What had happened? I tried to pull in a deep breath, but a heavy weight constricted my chest, threatening to suffocate me. I opened my eyes to find a torch laying on the ground beside me. Its flickering flame entranced my recovering mind, and I stared, absently, into the light as it sputtered in the thick haze of debris that swirled in the air.

Memories came flooding back to me. I was still in the

cave. One minute I'd been trying to stifle the bleeding from Peter's head wound, and now I was lying on the ground. The deathly silence finally gave way to the sounds of pained groans. I wasn't the only one who'd been struck down. I began to take inventory of my body, flexing my fingers, trying to detect any serious injury. Staying here on the ground only made me vulnerable. I had to get up. I tried to shift my body to ease the pressure on my chest. I could barely pull in a shallow breath. My lungs burned for air. Something was pinning me down. I managed to turn my head enough to see that the weight crushing me was Peter's lifeless body.

"Peter," I whispered his name as I tried in vain to push him off of me. He couldn't be dead. I wouldn't allow myself a moment to entertain the idea, but I could feel my heartbeat pick up and anxiety bloom in my chest. "Peter… you have to get…" I gasped before pulling in another quick breath. "Please wake up!" Relief washed over me as a slight groan parted his lips and I felt the warmth of his exhale on my neck. "Yes.. that's it… Peter, wake up!" His body moved slowly, his cheek grazing mine as he pulled his weight off of me. I sucked in a deep breath and quickly fell into a coughing fit as the dust coated air filled my lungs.

"Gwen?" The sound of my name coming from Peter's lips was the most beautiful thing I'd ever heard. He pushed off of me just enough so that our faces were mere inches apart. I drank in the sight of him. Of the man who I thought had been lost to me forever. And his eyes… they were that perfectly warm shade of umber as they stared down at me with adoration and just a hint of confusion. Tiger Lily's thrall was gone. Did that mean she was dead? James... my mind drifted to James and a whole new panic began to rise in my chest.

"Is it really you? Because if this is just a dream, don't ever wake me up," he said as he cupped my cheek.

"It's really me. I'm here. I came back." I pushed a lock of his auburn hair from his face, losing myself in his eyes all over again. Words seemed to fail me, as they always did in the pivotal moments of my life. Maybe because words could never do justice to the feelings that were coursing through me.

"I need to tell you... If you'd just let me... I think I can explain..." He stumbled through half-finished sentences.

"Peter, we don't have to do this now. There'll be time later. I think we both have some explaining to do."

"But this can't wait... I need to tell you that I'm sorry and I—"

"Hen?" Ryder's weak voice pulled me back to reality, bursting the momentary bliss of our reunion. "Hen! Where are you?" His voice was thick with concern.

"Ry, I'm here!" I called to him as I attempted to shift myself out from underneath Peter. My vision blurred as I sat up and I fought to keep the contents of my stomach in place.

"Are you alright?" Peter pushed my hair back and rested

his forehead against mine, offering me support as I tried to compose myself.

"I'm fine... really. We need to find the others. Tripp was unconscious the last time I saw him." I had to push down that nagging thought that was lingering in the recesses of my mind. What if Tripp was dead? What if James was dead? I couldn't shut out my worst fears, no matter how hard I tried. The abhorrent thoughts played on repeat inside my head. I needed to be doing something. The panic must have been clear on my face, because Peter got to his feet quickly and offered me a hand, pulling me to my feet.

"Come on, beautiful. Let's get our boys and get out of here," Peter said as he grabbed the torch from the cave floor. It was the only light in the engulfing darkness as we made our way through the rubble. Stones and boulders littered the floor. We could barely see more than a few feet in front of us from the dust lingering in the air. We found Ryder first. He was still on the ground, his beautiful face covered in dirt. Lines of blood cut tracks down his cheek from a gash under his eye. My heart broke as I saw the pain etched into his features.

"Hen, oh thank fuck! You're alright," Ryder breathed out. I raced to him, wrapping my arms around him, relieved to feel him against me. He winced as I squeezed him too tight, but made no move to pull away from me.

"Ryder, are you alright? What can I do?" I pulled away from him, looking him over until my eyes landed on his leg, or rather the large stone that now rested on top of his left leg. Another wave of nausea washed over me as I took in the severity of his situation.

"Peter, help me get this off of him," I commanded. We struggled in vain to move the stone. We managed to move it slightly, only to have it fall back into place. Ryder screamed out in pain, and it brought tears to my eyes.

"Don't worry about me, Hen," Ryder panted. "I'll be alright. Go find the others."

"I'm not leaving you here," I huffed in frustration.

"I'll find a way out of this. Come on, Hen, it's me we're talking about. Nothing can keep me down." Ryder did his best to sound chipper and put his positive spin on things, but I could see the sweat beading on his forehead, the haze of pain clouding his indigo eyes. He was only saying it for my benefit.

"I said I'm not—"

"She's not going to let you get out of this that easily, Ry." I whirled at the familiar voice to find Eben's handsome face emerging from the darkness.

"Oh my god, Eben!" I breathed as my heart stuttered at the sight of him, alive and whole. He cocked a teasing smile at me and I ran into his arms, almost knocking him off his feet.

I stifled a sob as his warm arms embraced me. "Whoa, baby, it's okay. I'm okay. I got you," he whispered in my ear, settling my volatile emotions with his calming words.

"If you're about done, Eben, maybe you can help us get

this rock off of Ryder's leg," Peter interrupted, irritation clear in his voice.

"You can fuck right off, Pan. I'll hold my girl as long as I want," Eben snarled in response. There was definitely some bad blood between the two of them. Their relationship had always been tenuous, but they'd always had a mutual respect for each other that seemed absent now.

"He's right, Eben. We need to help Ry," I agreed. The last thing Ryder needed now was for the two of them to get into it.

"See, Ry, I told you she wouldn't let you get off so easily. Dying might be a lot less painful than this. Brace yourself." Eben nodded at Peter and the three of us bent down to move the stone together. It took every ounce of strength I had to help Peter and Eben move the stone from Ryder's leg. Peter sucked in a breath as we both looked in horror at the wound. Fuck!

"We need faerie dust for this. If we don't do something soon, he'll lose that leg or he'll bleed out," Peter said, laying out his grim prognosis.

"Pan, you better let me fucking die before you take my leg."

"Lill… Lill was in your pocket back in the temple," I blurted out. I pawed at Peter's belt, looking for the pixie. Even if she hadn't survived the blast, I'd shake the faerie dust out of her corpse if it meant I could heal Ryder. Before Peter could stop me, I reached into his belt. My fingers brushed against delicate wings and I pulled her tiny, limp body from his pocket.

"Lill?" Peter's voice sounded shattered as he looked at the lifeless pixie in my hand. Damn it! I needed her to be alive. The small coating of faerie dust she left on my hand wouldn't be enough to heal Ryder. I began to rub her tiny body between my palms, trying to massage the life back into her like a newly born kitten. I closed my eyes, focusing on the feel of her between my hands. I tried to find the spot at my core where I'd felt my own magic. If I had even a grain of power left from the Inalto, I needed to tap into that now. I could feel my hands warming and the faint chiming of bells pulled me out of the deep meditation I'd fallen into.

"Holy shit, Gwen! How did you do that?" Ryder's voice was incredulous. I opened my eyes to find a bleary-eyed Lilleybell staring up at me. A faint tinkle of bells came from her perfect little lips and I knew she was saying, thank you. It wasn't lost on me that it was probably the first pleasant words she'd ever spoken to me. I nodded briefly because we didn't have time to deal with our old bullshit.

"Now help me with Ryder," I demanded. I carried her over to him because even though she was alive, she looked in no shape to fly. Ryder's face was as pale as a sheet and the stain of blood beneath him was growing larger with every passing moment. I placed her on his knee. She began to vibrate so fast that she appeared as a blur, and a flurry of faerie dust cascaded out of her, pooling on Ryder's skin and migrating to his wound. I cringed when the bone popped as it reset itself. Ryder held it together, but his whole body trembled with the pain of it. It took only a few minutes for the faerie dust to work its magic and return Ryder's leg to perfect condition.

"Good as new! Thanks to Lill and Gwen. Dynamic duo… who would have ever guessed!" Ryder said in feigned surprise as he raised his eyebrows at me. I couldn't help but smile back at his antics. He always had a way of making me smile in the most unusual circumstances.

"Eben, have you seen Tripp?" I refocused on the task at hand. The panic bubbling in my chest refused to be eased until I knew all of my boys were safe.

"The last time I saw him on his feet, he was going after Tiger Lily, but he's been down for a while." The doubt in Eben's voice was clear as day. He was not expecting a good outcome when it came to Tripp.

"Let's fan out and search. We're not leaving here without him." I swiped the torch from Peter's hand and turned from the rest of the boys, determined to find him and prove Eben's fears were wrong. Lill managed to flit up to my shoulder and settle herself there. Apparently, we'd struck some kind of truce between us, and I wasn't about to break it. I knew Tripp would need her help once we found him. I tried to remember where I'd seen him last. He'd saved me from Tiger Lily. She'd been in the process of killing me with the power of the Osakren and Tripp had stopped her, taking the lethal magic into himself. *"I only hope that when it's my time, I'll die at your service."* Some of the last words that Tripp had said to me rang in my ears. But fuck that. I wasn't going to allow him to be a martyr for me.

We fanned out, all of the boys remaining close to me. The cave was full of carnage. Tiger Lily's soldiers littered the ground and I stumbled over the bodies on more than one occasion. The ones my boys had missed, had been crushed by falling debris when the blast hit. I tried to focus on finding Tripp alive in a sea of death. I felt an urgent tugging on my hair and a flutter of wings against my cheek as Lill demanded my attention. I turned, the torch casting shadows over the torn fabric of his shirt hanging limp from his bloodied back. His large frame laying on his side was utterly still in the darkness.

"Tripp," I breathed out. "He's here! I found him!" I called urgently to the others as I raced toward him. I grabbed his shoulder and turned his body toward me, his arm falling slack into my lap. "Tripp! Tripp, I'm here. It's going to be okay," I rushed out in a flurry of words, pulling his cold hand into mine.

"He deserved it," a strange voice hissed in my ear. I whirled around, ready to protect Tripp no matter what, but the only faces I saw were those of my boys.

"Hen... how is he? Is he good?" Ryder's voice cracked with all the emotions he was trying to hold back.

"Lill, we need more faerie dust." I turned back to Tripp, forgetting all about the voice I'd heard, focusing all of my attention on him. I lifted Lill off of my shoulder with shaky hands. This time, she managed to fly over Tripp's body. A cascade of glittering dust poured out of her, landing on his chest before it trickled off him like water. I heard the boys let out a collective groan behind me.

"No, no, no! Not fucking Tripp," Ryder shouted, his voice raw. He was beside me in an instant, attempting to pick the dust up and place it back on Tripp's chest, but nothing was happening.

"Ry," Peter said his name gently. "We're too late, man. He's gone."

Gone?

My mind wouldn't process the word. I blinked at Tripp's lifeless body, not believing what I was seeing, what Peter was saying.

"His death tastes so sweeeet," the eerie voice hissed in my ear again.

"Who said that?" I got to my feet, my eyes scanning the darkness, but all I could see were the grief stricken faces of my Lost Boys.

"Baby…" Eben put his hands up as he approached me, as if I was crazy. A frightened deer, about to run into oncoming traffic. "Everything's going to be alright. We'll get through this."

Death. Gone. The two words repeated over and over in my head, but I felt numb. The weight of what they were trying to tell me, I couldn't accept it. Wouldn't accept it. I sank back to my knees before Tripp. My savior. My knight in shining armor. The Prince Charming that I'd waited my whole life for. It couldn't end this way. I started picking up the faerie dust, repeating Ryder's vain attempt to get it to do something, anything. Big, fat tears ran down my cheeks, landing in soft patters, displacing the glittering dust on his chest.

"Old and gray… those were my orders. You can't leave me until we're old and gray!" My heart teetered on the brink. There would be no coming back from this if I couldn't fix it, if I couldn't save him.

"Gwen, baby, it's over." Eben's hand rested on my shoulder as he tried to comfort me. I closed my eyes and focused on my love for Tripp. Gathering every feeling I'd ever felt for him, pulling it into my core. I let the small seed of my infantile magic bathe in the enormity of emotions that pulled me to him, connecting us in ways that only the Divine could know.

I shrugged out from under Eben's hand. "It's not over!" I screamed the words so loud it hurt my ears as it rang off the rock walls. I slammed my palms into the pile of faerie dust over Tripp's heart. A loud rumble of thunder cracked, and the cave lit up as though a bolt of lightning coursed through its passages, blinding me momentarily. It was absolute chaos for a moment in time, and then it was deathly silent.

I opened my eyes, blinking rapidly as I slowly adjusted to the dim light, only to find a pair of moss green eyes staring back at me.

"I always knew you were a goddess," Tripp breathed, his voice low and reverent as he held my gaze. I flinched when I felt his fingers caress my cheek; his touch bringing me back to reality. A reality in which he did exist. And then the tears came, I couldn't hold back the tidal wave of emotions, grieving for what I'd almost lost. I could barely make out Tripp's soothing words, his big hand stroking my hair. I lost all track of time wrapped in his arms.

"It's time to go, my queen. You've shed enough tears for me. Now let me get you somewhere safe, where I can take care of you properly," he whispered. I managed to pull myself together and before I knew what was happening, Tripp was on his feet, sweeping me into his arms.

"Tripp, I can walk." I tried to protest. After all, I'm pretty sure he'd been dead only a few minutes before. But he held me tight as my own body gave out.

"Just rest." I peered out from his arms and all of my boys stared at me with astonished looks on their faces. I couldn't explain what had just happened, but I could feel that the bonds between us had strengthened. Securely tucked into Tripp's arms, the five of us walked out of the darkness, and into the breaking dawn of a new day. As we reached the mouth of the cave, my weary eyes landed on a familiar form.

"James?" I tried to turn in Tripp's arms to see him better. He was sprawled on the ground, covered in blood. "Oh my god, James!"

"James?" Peter snarled when his eyes settled on Hook.

"Let me make sure he's okay," I pleaded with Tripp as I squirmed to get out of his iron grip.

"The Divine's given me a perfectly good opportunity. I shouldn't let it go to waste." Peter sneered as he pulled a dagger from Eben's belt.

"No, Peter! Wait!" I was desperate. So much had happened since I'd last seen Peter. I had no idea how I was going to explain everything that had happened with Hook. But before I could spill my secret, Eben stopped him.

"Look" —Eben nodded, ignoring the death glare he was getting from Peter—"over there. Looks like Hook did you a favor. He broke the thrall by taking her out." My eyes followed Eben's and landed on Tiger Lily. There was no question. She was dead. Her throat was completely ripped out, her eyes stared lifelessly into oblivion.

"Looks like you owe him one." Eben glanced at me briefly. I nodded my silent thanks to him. He and the other boys knew about my growing relationship with Hook, and I knew he'd only spared his life for my sake.

Hook let out a groan, and a wave of relief washed over me. All of my men had survived. Against the odds, we'd all made it. "My love?" he mumbled and my heart leapt in my throat.

Tripp reached for Lill, "Get some dust. We need to get out of here."

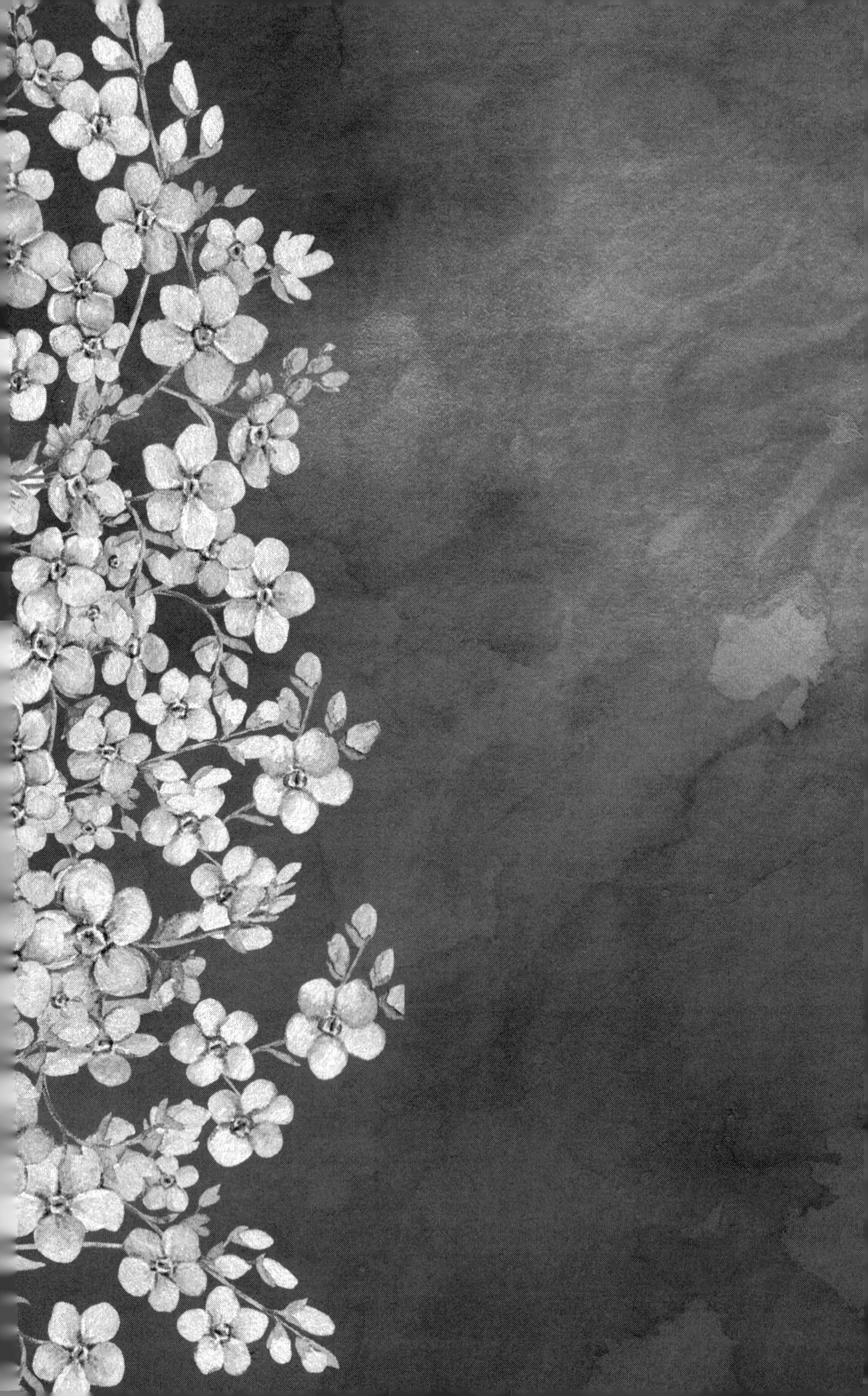

Chapter III
Confessions
-Gwen-

We made our way silently back to Peter's cabin. I reveled in the warmth of Tripp's arms. I shamelessly allowed him to carry me the entire way. I needed to be close to him. Believing he had died had shaken me to my core. And it confirmed what I hadn't yet admitted to myself— I wasn't going back home, ever. I couldn't leave them again. I was hopelessly bound to them. Our strings forever entwined in the stars. I'd gotten my boys back, and I wasn't going to let them go so easily this time.

Eben and Ryder were just ahead, each supporting one

of Peter's shoulders. We were all broken, not just on the outside, but on the inside as well. Neverland would never be the same and we— no *I*— was to blame.

"You know, we are going to have to talk about Hook," Tripp whispered as we approached Peter's door.

"Help me get Peter settled in." I ignored his words. He was right, and I wanted to tell them all what was happening with James. I just didn't know how I was going to do it. Hook was their nemesis. And I was sleeping with the enemy. What if they weren't okay with it? Would I be able to walk away from James? I didn't want to face that choice.

Peter's cabin was in shambles. His table was overturned, its contents strewn about the floor. The broken remains of an old liquor bottle glittered as Tripp lit an oil lamp, illuminating the scene. Books and trinkets that once lined Peter's shelves were littered on the floor, as if the place had been ransacked.

"What happened in here?" I asked.

"Tiger Lily," Ryder replied.

"This wasn't Tiger Lily. This was my doing," Peter confessed. "I was drinking rum before she showed up." His brows pinched together as he remembered the events. "I was reading Gwen's letter. I was in a bad place."

I began mindlessly picking up Peter's belongings as they all watched silently. I couldn't begin to understand what he had been through. The truth was, I never considered what consequences my actions had created. That the boys would carry the same hurt and feelings of betrayal that I had. Tripp placed a chair beside me.

"Sit." The command was gentle but firm. "We have some things to discuss before we leave you to catch up with Pan." My heart sank. I knew what was coming, and I wasn't ready. After the last few days, all I wanted was to crawl up next to my boys after a hot bath, nurse our wounds and revel in each other's presence. We had succeeded against Tiger Lily. Peter was no longer under her thrall. Tripp and Ryder had been healed. Mic was with Lu and his brothers. I had to believe she was safe. Couldn't we have a moment of peace before jumping into the heavy stuff? I sighed as I sat in the chair. The weight of their eyes was heavy on my conscience.

"What's going on with Hook?" Tripp's question was straight to the point.

"I… " I froze. I could see the hurt and confusion on each and every one of their faces. I owed it to them to be honest. I wasn't going to walk away from James. They deserved to know.

"Don't try to deny what we all saw," Eben chided. Disappointment plastered on his face. "He knew about your injury. How?"

"You were injured?" Peter looked me over before looking at Eben, confused.

"She almost died. You missed a lot while you were Tiger Lily's bitch. She can fill you in later."

"She kissed Hook. We all saw it. She didn't even try to hide it," Ryder finally broke his silence.

"Excuse me? What the fuck is going on?" Peter looked at his boys for answers.

"It's true. I kissed Hook. I… " They all stared at me, waiting for me to finish. "Something happened while I was with James."

"Hook?" Peter interrupted. "You kissed Hook?"

"Yes, I did. I… I have developed feelings for him."

"Feelings! Hook is a savage." Peter glared at me. His disgust showed through his bruised and battered face, breaking my heart.

"How did he know about your injury, Gwen?" Eben repeated himself. Clearly irritated by my avoidance of his question.

"Smee brought me to him while I was recovering at Amara's camp. Lu must have sent him word of the attack. He wanted to be sure I was okay."

"Hook doesn't care for anyone but himself." Peter's anger was building. The wind outside was beginning to pick up, causing an eerie howling to pass through the tiny cabin.

"He cares for me," I said bluntly. "He couldn't bear the thought of me in agony so he made an elixir… to numb my pain."

"You didn't take it did you? Tell me you didn't, Gwen," Peter pleaded.

"I did. I'm fine, it wasn't poison."

"Hen"— Ryder dropped to his knees gently grabbing

my face —"*never* do that again. I just got you back. I can't lose you again. Hook is dangerous."

I leaned down and placed a kiss on Ryder's forehead. "I'm not going anywhere."

"I won't lose you." Ryder placed his head in my lap and wrapped his arms around my legs. I felt a smile creep across my face and I began to stroke his tousled hair. Having him this close soothed my nervous energy.

"So let me get this straight," Eben chided. "You secretly met with Hook. While I was sleeping." His jaw clenched as the pieces of the evening began to take shape. "You were with me after…" Eben's face turned red as his fist hit the wall. "I can't do this right now. I need time to think. Sharing you with the enemy…" He shook his head in silence as he stormed out of the cabin.

"Eben, wait!"

"Let him go Gwen. Give him time to process." Tripp's ever calm demeanor began to waver. "Is that what you want? To be shared with Hook?"

"To be shared? I'm not a piece of property to be passed around. What I want is the choice to explore all sides of me. Even the pieces you may not like. Maybe I'm asking too much." I sighed. "I didn't plan on developing a connection with James, it just happened."

"I, for one, don't understand." Ryder's brows furrowed. "I don't think I will ever understand. But, if sharing you with Hook is what I have to do to be with you, I will do so and grovel at your feet for the opportunity." Ryder pulled me up from the chair. "I'm not worthy of your love, Gwen. I will do anything it takes to keep it." He bowed his head and gently kissed my lips. "I love you Gwendolyn Mary Darling Carlisle. All of you."

The breath I was holding released as the weight of Ryder's words sunk in. I leaned forward, resting my forehead against his. He had told me he loved me on more than one occasion, and I'd selfishly held onto my feelings. Because I'd known that I loved them for a long time now, but I'd been afraid. Afraid of what it meant to say those words aloud. Afraid that if I admitted it to the universe, it would find some way to take that love away from me.

But after everything we'd just been through, the idea that I could have lost any one of them back there made everything clear to me. I couldn't waste the time we'd been given and I wouldn't let Ryder go one more minute without knowing exactly how I felt. I traced my fingers along his jawline and curled them into his hair. His deep indigo eyes met mine, nothing but reverence staring back at me— a look that I'm not sure I truly deserved. Caught in his eyes, the entire world seemed to disappear around us. "Thank you," I whispered. "Thank you for loving me exactly the way that I am."

He cocked a smile at me that lit my soul on fire. "You know that I'll always—"

"Wait, wait… I'm not finished," I interrupted, placing a finger over his lips. "I've wanted to tell you this for a long time, and I'm so sorry it's taken me this long. But you have to know, with every ounce of my being, every cracked piece of my soul... I love you." I grabbed his face. Holding his gaze. "All of you."

A smile lit his face, a look of awe and wonder in his eyes. "You love me? Seriously? Oh my Divine... say it again!"

"Yes! I love you." His arms tightened around me, crushing me to his chest and lifting me from the ground, spinning me around.

"Did you hear that, boys? She fucking loves me. Best day ever! Well, aside from Tripp almost dying. But still, best day ever. I think you and Pan need some time alone to talk things over, but I call first dibs afterwards. The two of us have some *love* making to do." He waggled his eyebrows at me, and I laughed at his antics before he cut off my giggles with a scorching kiss. He pressed his forehead to mine for a moment before turning to Tripp, returning us to the tension in the room. "She's answered your questions. Make your peace or take the time you need. Either way, it's time to go. Let's give the two of them some space. Gwen's been through enough. We owe her that."

Tripp approached me, taking my hand. "I'm not thrilled about the idea. You deserve more than a dirty pirate who can offer you nothing but carnage and deceit." He dropped to one knee. "I'll spend my days worshiping you like the goddess you are. Showing you that you are worthy of more." He bowed his head. "Maybe then you'll realize he's not worthy of your affections."

I pulled him to his feet and gently kissed his lips. "Thank you, Tripp. I know it's complicated. I never meant—"

"Don't try to explain. I'll never understand how you could choose to be with him. I don't like it, and I never will. That's something *you* will have to accept. We'll go talk with Eben, and leave you to Peter. He's going to need some convincing. Be honest with him."

Peter paced, silently huffing with frustration. "How did I screw up *so* badly that you fell into the arms of James fucking Hook?"

"This was never your fault. Like you, Tiger Lily played me. She lied to me, she showed me Tinkerbell's journals. Peter, she made me question everything."

"What exactly did she tell you?"

"She made me believe I was a mere replacement for something you could never have. That the Lost Boys wanted me gone." I bowed my head in shame. "That I was a plaything, to be used and discarded."

"And you just believed her? Took her for her word? Did the time we spent together mean nothing?" His broken and bruised face contorted into a painful mask.

"It's not that simple. Peter, she had evidence… Her words destroyed my heart. She crushed my soul. James was the one who reminded me that I was needed back home. That my sister was dying, and that time moves differently here." Remembering the details of that evening caused unhealed wounds to ache. Anger began to bubble under the surface.

If we were ever going to be able to put this behind us, I needed answers. "Why didn't you tell me time was moving faster for Mic? You knew she was dying, Peter. You knew she was everything to me. My only surviving family."

"It's true. I wanted to keep you here for myself. I wanted us, the Lost Boys, to be your family. I was afraid if you knew time was moving differently, you would leave, and I'd never get you back. It was wrong... I made a mistake."

"That wasn't your decision to make." A single tear fell from my eye. To hear that he wanted me, so much so, that he kept me in the dark to keep me from leaving... Although a truly selfish act, it warmed my heart.

"You asked in your letter for forgiveness. For 'the lengths you went to' get it to me."

"Peter." I pleaded silently with my eyes that he wouldn't ask me to share what had happened.

"What did he make you do, Gwen? Did you sell your soul to the devil?"

"I was lost. Everything I was sure of had been taken from me. I wanted to say good-bye. I wanted some kind of closure."

"Did you like it?" Peter stood up and closed the distance between us. The lines of his face taut with anger.

"Why didn't you come for me?" I whispered the words. Afraid of his answer.

Peter's eyes darkened, and lightning flashed in the windows. Like a ravenous wolf stalking his prey, he slowly made his way across the room. "What was the price of closure?"

I'd never seen Peter behave this way. There was a darkness in him I had been blind to. My heart began to race. I instinctively stepped back, losing my balance. In a rush, Peter grabbed my arms and righted me, pinning me against the wall— his touch stoking an ever burning ember.

"You think you're just a cheap replacement?" He leaned in, savoring my scent, sending a shiver down my spine. "Just a plaything?" His brow furrowed as he slid his hand up my arm and wrapped it around my neck, pushing me harder against the wall. "To be used and discarded?"

My breath hitched as his hand gripped my throat tighter. My heart was racing. His thumb caught my chin, tilting my face for his inspection. Warmth pooled between my legs.

"You think I did this to Wendy?" He buried his face in my hair and nipped at my ear. His tongue teasing the tender flesh there. A breathy moan spilled from my lips, and he shifted his attention to my eyes. Closing the gap between us, grinding his excitement against my now throbbing core. "That she made me feel like this?"

I tilted my hips, greedily seeking more. "Peter, I—"

He slapped his hand over my mouth, silencing my plea for atonement, and I became drunk with lust. "Was he rough with you?" he growled. "Did you like it?"

I felt my nipples harden as panic began to mix with need. I shook my head and mumbled no into his palm.

Peter grabbed my breast roughly and trailed his hand to

my waistband, pausing briefly to run his tongue from my collar bone up my neck, stopping just behind my ear, before slipping below my waist band and dipping his warm fingers in my wetness. I moaned shamelessly, grinding into his assault.

"Your body doesn't lie, Gwen." He stared at me, his eyes becoming obsidian as he licked my desire off his fingers. He slid his grip to my jaw and claimed my mouth with a brutal kiss. The taste of my excitement was thick on his tongue as I kissed him back, hard. I needed him now in a way I couldn't explain. I was lost in the sensation, fulfilling a carnal need that had lingered for weeks in his absence. Peter gripped my ass, lifting me up and wrapping my legs around his waist. "You're mine," he growled, claiming me with his words as he carried me to his bed.

I stripped off my clothes while Peter stood watching my every move. "Lay down and spread your legs. I want to see just how excited you are."

I quickly obeyed his demand, sliding my hands down my naked body, spreading myself wide for him to see. I let my fingers glide over my swollen clit and watched as a sinister smirk crossed his face. His eyes were glued to my core.

"Good girl," he purred as he stripped his shirt off and climbed up between my legs. Placing his hands on my thighs, he spread me even wider. He began to tease me with his breath. Blowing directly on my clit, drawing out a cry of desperation. The sensation driving me wild with need. I could feel my excitement pooling beneath me, creating a wet spot on the bed.

"Peter," I cried out. "Please." I writhed about, trying to find some friction. Some release of the tension building in my core.

He gripped my legs even tighter, holding me still, pinching the delicate skin and flooding me with desire. "Please, what?" With the tip of his tongue, he ever so softly circled my clit and pulled away.

I moaned in protest and began to beg. "Peter, please. I need you now."

"But you wanted closure. You didn't want me to come back for you." He slowly dragged his tongue up my slit as he inserted a finger, pushing me further into delirium. "Did you change your mind? Do you want me now?"

"Yes! Yes! Please, Peter. I've always wanted you. I need you *now*."

He began to pump his finger slowly in and out before possessing me with his mouth— his tongue masterfully bringing me to the edge before stopping again to drop his pants, freeing his massive erection. My body was alive with sensation, caught on the edge of orgasm. He slowly crawled back on top of me, teasing the tip of his cock at my opening. He stared into my eyes as he increased the pressure between my legs. "You are mine." He spoke the words as he thrust into me. "Now and forever." He held still, buried to the root for a moment before grinding his hips into mine, giving my clit the attention it so desperately wanted. Our breathing became ragged as our bodies took over, grinding and pumping until I spilled over the edge. My orgasm claimed me as bolts of lightning flashed outside the windows. I cried out as the waves of ecstasy washed over my body and the world around us disappeared. Sins of the past were forgiven as we remained lost in the moment. Peter's rhythm quickened as he cried out— his own pleasure taking hold. We laid still in each other's arms, surrounded by the sound of our ragged breathing.

"Peter." He lifted his head. His eyes had returned to their rich umber. "I'm sorry… for everything." I reached up grabbing his face in my hands and kissed him softly. All my feelings came flooding back.

"Gwen," he said my name as if it pained him, "I'm sorry, too." He kissed my forehead. "I never want to lose you again." His hand went straight to my thigh and gently caressed my scar. "What happened here?"

"Tiger Lily's guards were sent to kill me. They would have succeeded if it weren't for Eben. He is the reason I'm alive today."

"I'll have to thank him for that." Peter continued his inspection, trailing his fingers along the curves of my body. "You have changed."

"I've been training." The changes in my body were subtle. I hadn't been kick boxing for long. Yet he noticed. "I needed an escape. I was tired of being a weak little girl."

"Whatever you've been doing looks good on you." He grabbed my hand, gently turning it over. The black veins had begun to creep further up my forearm. "And this?" he questioned.

"I made a deal with the bone faerie. To save you from Tiger Lily."

His smile quickly fell from his face. "What was the deal? The bone faerie is not one to be trifled with."

"I need to return the Osakren to her. Only I'm not sure where it is at the moment."

"We'll find it. I swear to you, on all I hold dear. I found it once, I'll find it again. We'll return the Osakren and fulfill your deal." He trailed his fingers across my pebbled nipples, sending goose pimples down my body. "I tried to come for you. Hook had already sent you home by the time I found him."

"Peter, there was so much deceit behind everything that happened. Can we…" I paused, making sure I really wanted to say the words. I wanted to forget the emotional torture Tiger Lily had caused. Put an end to the pain and move forward with my Lost Boys. "Can we just put the past behind us?"

Peter reached up to caress my face. "Before we can move forward, I have to set one thing straight. You were never a stand in for Wendy." I felt my eyes prick with tears. Of all the things Tiger Lily had said, this one hurt the most. "Wendy *was* special, but I was thirteen then. She was a crush. I didn't know what love was. This kind of love, what I feel for you… is like no other. Losing you confirmed what I was afraid to admit." He paused, staring into my eyes. "I love you, Gwen." He gently wiped a tear from my face as it spilled down my cheek. It was exactly what I needed to hear.

"I love you too, Peter." I pulled his face to mine and kissed him softly. We spent the night making love and catching up before drifting off into a blissful sleep., m worries evaporating like mist in the early morning sun.

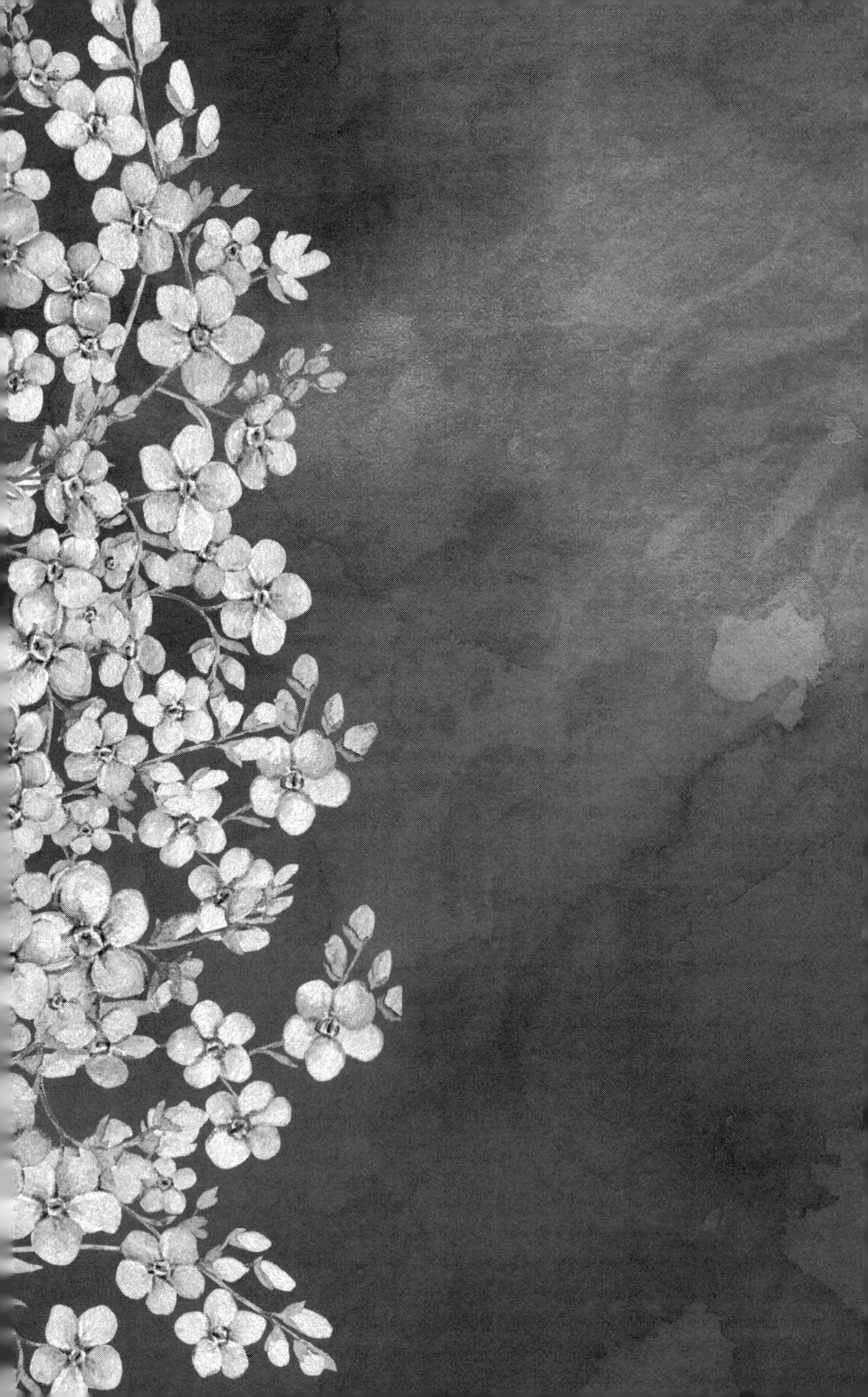

CHAPTER IV
THE DAWN OF A NEW ERA
-PETER-

My eyes popped open, and I sucked in a breath. Panic had my heart pounding in my chest. I raked a trembling hand through my hair and over my face, trying to wipe away the lingering nightmare. My eyes focused on the familiar beams of the ceiling above me. I knew this place. I was home. I was in my cabin. Not stuck in the internal prison Tiger Lily had banished me to. Unwelcome flashbacks played inside my mind. I'd never longed for the forgetfulness of Neverland so much. If I could just bury what she had done to me long enough, it would eventually fade into oblivion and I'd be spared from reliving the nightmare of being Tiger Lily's mate.

I looked down at Gwen as she slept peacefully beside me and I let out a deep sigh, intentionally slowing my breathing. Just the sight of her calmed me and strengthened my resolve. I'd deal with my inner demons on my own. She'd been through enough. There were plenty of other things to focus on. This whole mess with Hook was front and center. And I'd be lying if I said it wasn't fucking with my head. I'd have to prove myself the better man. Remind her I was her perfect match until this ridiculous infatuation with Hook subsided. He'd gotten into her head. Seduced her. And it happened on my watch. That was something I'd never forgive myself for.

Gwen needed a distraction. Neverland had been nothing but a nightmare for her since May Day. I needed to remind her why she had to stay this time. A celebration was exactly what we all needed. Tiger Lily was gone, and that was reason enough to celebrate, but the party would serve multiple purposes.

Neverland's politics were a disaster. The island was no doubt divided. The native Fae had lost their princess to darkness, and she'd left no heir to replace her. I could only imagine the uncertainty that gripped the island in the wake of her death. We all needed a way to come together and celebrate the dawn of a new era.

As much as it killed me to leave Gwen, I had a lot to do. I needed to start planning. It was time to remind my girl that good times were on the horizon, and establish control over the splintered Fae. They needed a clear leader now more than ever. And who better to provide that for them than Neverland's chosen son?

I gently kissed Gwen's forehead. "Mmmm," she sighed, and a smile tugged at her lips. She was so fucking beautiful, and she was mine. My heart clenched at the sight of her. Nothing would ever keep me from her again.

"Sleep, my beautiful girl. I've got some work to do, but when you wake up, I'll have a surprise for you," I whispered to her, pushing an errant lock of hair from her face. I momentarily questioned whether I should stay and sink my cock into her all the way to the root. Reaffirm that I now owned a piece of her soul. Visions of last night flashed in my mind, tempting me further. My cock sprang to life, ready to claim her again. But I'd have to wait. I had an eternity to satisfy my desires with this girl. We had plenty of time.

The sun was just beginning to shed its light on the island and the day was dawning warm, finally awakening from her frozen slumber. Neverland was alive again. The camp was still quiet, save for the birds that were greeting the dawn with me. I climbed up to the crow's nest. It was the perfect spot to plan out the grand feast I had in mind, but I quickly realized that I wasn't the only one who had come up here to think.

"What are you still doing here? I thought I made it clear that you weren't welcome here anymore."

"Fuck off, Pan. Gwen's forgiven me," Eben shot back at me.

"Yeah, well I haven't."

"Her forgiveness is all that matters to me. Plus, once a Lost Boy, always a Lost Boy."

"And why should I let you anywhere near her? You've already proven that you can't keep her safe. You walked out on her yet again last night." Eben slammed me against the wooden railing of the crow's nest, forcing a grunt of pain from my lips. He'd caught me off guard and I still hadn't fully healed from my time with Tiger Lily. His hand wrapped tight around my throat.

"You. Don't. Know. Anything!" he growled. Violence danced in his black eyes. A muscle ticked in his jaw. I'd touched a nerve.

"Prove it then," I challenged. His crushing grip faltered, and he pulled away from me.

"It doesn't bother you? That she wants Hook?" he asked. Obviously, Gwen's confession was eating away at him.

"Hook? You think she's going to choose that bastard over us?"

"You've missed a lot, Pan. You didn't see them together. You didn't see her kiss him. Hook's just as enamored with her as we are."

"I fucked up," I admitted, baring my soul to him for probably the first time. "I should have done more. I should have seen Tiger Lily's deceit. I never should have left her safety in the hands of someone else." He glared at me for the dig, knowing I would never forget how badly he'd fucked up with Gwen. "The Divine is punishing me. I know I deserve it. But if you think I'm just going to roll over and let Hook have her, then you've lost your damn mind. I made mistakes, but I'll prove myself to the Divine. I'll show Gwen that I'm the better man and she'll forget all about that sick fuck. Gwen will be my mate. Now the Divine is making me prove I am worthy of her."

Eben raised a brow. "Mate? You intend on making it official?"

"Of course. Don't you?"

"I don't think that's necess—"

"Do you love her?" I interrupted.

"Love is a poison. What I feel for her is so much more than that."

"Would you ever want another?"

"No," he sighed at that admission.

"Well then, you're already mated to her. You're just too much of a coward to make it official with the Divine." Eben punched my shoulder, sending a shock of pain down my arm.

"Gwen knows how I feel."

"Does she? Does she really know? Have you professed your undying love for her? Do you think you proved yourself when you walked out on her... again? The first hint of trouble and you left her all alone."

"You really are a bastard, aren't you? I'm starting to see

why Hook hates you." Eben smirked a bit, breaking the tension between us.

"We've been given a rare woman. It's up to us to find a way to be worthy of her. We've done a piss-poor job of it so far. I had a lot of time to think while I was Tiger Lily's pet, and all that time I was thinking of Gwen. She deserves a perfect life and I plan on giving her a happily ever after, with or without you. You just need to decide if you're with me or not." I stared at him curiously as he mulled over my words. Every emotion was etched into his face. He'd never intended to fall in love with anyone, let alone Gwen. The vulnerability of it all was something completely new to him. But this was a test. I'd agreed to share her with my Lost Boys, but only if they were worthy of her. If any of them had ill intentions, if any of them hurt her, I wouldn't hesitate to take them out.

Eben turned to me— resolve clear on his face. "I'm with you."

"Good. Let's get the others. We've got the feast of all feasts to plan."

I SPENT the morning meeting with emissaries from the different Fae factions around the island. I'd sent word to every corner of Neverland. An open invitation had gone out to come and usher in the dawn of a new era. Some remained fiercely loyal to Tiger Lily, but I placated them with half truths. I'd never consented to the mating between Tiger Lily and I, making it an invalid union, but they didn't know that. It made them a lot easier to deal with if they believed me to be her next of kin. That and promising them Hook's head on a platter for killing their beloved princess had sealed the deal. That part would be a bit more difficult, but there was time. Now that I had Gwen at my side, all I had was time, stretching out like an endless sea before us.

"Pan, you have a guest that's requesting a private audience," Tripp informed me. He'd reluctantly remained at my side all day. He was eager to get back to Gwen, but I'd sent her to the Fae springs for a day of indulgence with Mira and Fauna, and he was still pissed that I'd chosen Ryder to keep watch over her instead of him.

"Who is it?"

"Lucius."

I perked up at the news. Gwen was desperate for an update on her sister, and I'd sent Eben out first thing this morning to track down the beasts.

"Where?"

"He's waiting for you in the arms cellar."

Tripp accompanied me, and we slid down the hatches into the subterranean cave. My eyes adjusted to the dim light of the torches and settled on Lucius who took up the lion's share of the space. His size alone was an intimidating presence. Massive arms crossed in front of his chest, every inch covered in elaborate tattoos. His face was set in a scowl and dark shadows cast an ominous look on the young prince's face. Fuck… I hated dealing with the beasts.

"Lucius, thanks for coming on such short notice."

"I came of my own accord. I was asked to deliver a message." The beast of a man couldn't meet my gaze, and it piqued my curiosity. If he hadn't come on Eben's request, what was he doing here?

"I see, but before we get into any business, I need to know how fares the other daughter of Wendy?"

"She is none of your concern," he snarled, instantly on edge at the mention of Michaela.

"But Gwen is very much my concern, and she needs to know that her sister is safe in the care of the beasts."

"Tell Gwen she's fine," he growled. "No thanks to her. And let her know it's probably best if she keeps her distance. These are extraordinary times and disaster follows that woman everywhere she goes."

"What the fuck did you just say?" I pulled my dagger from my belt and took a step toward him as my anger threatened to consume me.

"Pan"—Tripp grabbed my arm—"don't." I met Tripp's eyes and noted the stern warning I saw there. Losing my temper with a beast prince was not wise while I was attempting to put the pieces of Neverland back together.

"All these years and you still can't control that temper of yours, Peter." A familiar, rough voice came from the darkness of the cellar and my nemesis stepped from the shadows and into the torchlight.

"How dare you show your face here?" My hand clenched around my dagger as my body tensed. The only way Hook could have made his way into my arm's cellar was with Lucius's help. I started to reconsider running the beast prince through.

"Easy, boy. No need to get your feathers in a bunch," he huffed as if he was addressing a petulant child and I struggled to keep from charging at him then and there. The bastard always knew how to get under my skin. He pulled a white handkerchief from his sleeve and tossed it on the center table. "A momentary parley, if you will. We have things to discuss."

"Discuss? We have nothing to discuss. Not now, not ever." I spat at him.

"We have a mutual interest in protecting Neverland from the darkness that's coming for her."

"When have you ever been concerned about anything above and beyond your own self interest? Neverland doesn't concern you. The only darkness that plagues the island is you."

"Don't be obtuse, boy. That shockwave would have been felt in every corner of the cosmos. A beacon for any Fae, man and beast looking to fill the void of power. Neverland is ripe for the taking. A darkness is coming for her. Without a native born ruler—"

"I will be Neverland's ruler. I am one of her chosen. Fate brought me here for this very moment."

Hook chuckled as he ran a hand down his beard. "Your hubris will get her killed."

"Don't you dare bring her into this," I seethed. The familiar sound of thunder rattled the shelves in the cellar. A clear testament that I had a fragile hold on my temper. I wasn't sure I could keep it together.

"How is Gwendolyn?" he asked. The raw emotion in his voice when he spoke her name took me off guard.

"Don't ever say her name! Don't speak about her, don't think about her. She doesn't exist to you." The edges of my vision blurred as rage took over.

"You will not keep her from me, Peter. If you try to, I will pull a valuable favor to gain access to her. I must speak with her."

"Favor?" I asked, confused. Never in my entire life had I ever owed a favor to Captain James Hook.

"The terms are null and void," Tripp cut in. "You had no antidote."

"Under Fae law, it is binding. You wanted an antidote, and I brought you to one. We achieved your desired outcome. You will not deny me my favor," he growled as he slammed his polished hook on the table.

"I'd send her back across the Veil before I let that happen," I threatened.

"I've already proven that I can thrive back on Earth,

while you… you'd never survive outside of Neverland. So go ahead, send her back. I'll follow wherever she goes."

"You cannot have her," I snapped.

"You cannot stop me."

"Oh, but I can. My fate is set. I *will* come into great power. I'm on the verge. And when I do, I will rip you out by the root, like the weed that you are, and return you to the pits of hell where you belong."

Hook picked up the white handkerchief that he'd tossed on the table and tucked it into his sleeve as he sauntered over to me, appearing amused by my threat, which only served to piss me off further. I held myself in place as he leaned in to me. "I'll take that challenge, Peter, because you know all too well what she is. Your soul burns for hers, just as mine does. And I'll no sooner let her go than you will. But be warned, I have no appetite for power and my only allegiance is to her. You've been in bed with Neverland since the moment you set foot on her fertile shores and mark my words, she is a jealous mistress. One day you will have to choose." I pushed him away from me as the reality of his words punched me in the gut.

"Start preparing the island, Peter. The war is just beginning," he trailed off as he walked away from me and out of the arms cellar. Lucius made to follow, and I grabbed hold of his shirt.

"Tell Nico about the feast, ensure he is there, and make sure he brings the girl with him."

"Fuck off, Pan." He shrugged out of my grip.

"After what you just pulled, you owe me. And it would be a shame if I were to start poking into your private affairs until I uncover why you're Hook's little bitch." He let out a feral growl, but said nothing further before leaving me alone with Tripp.

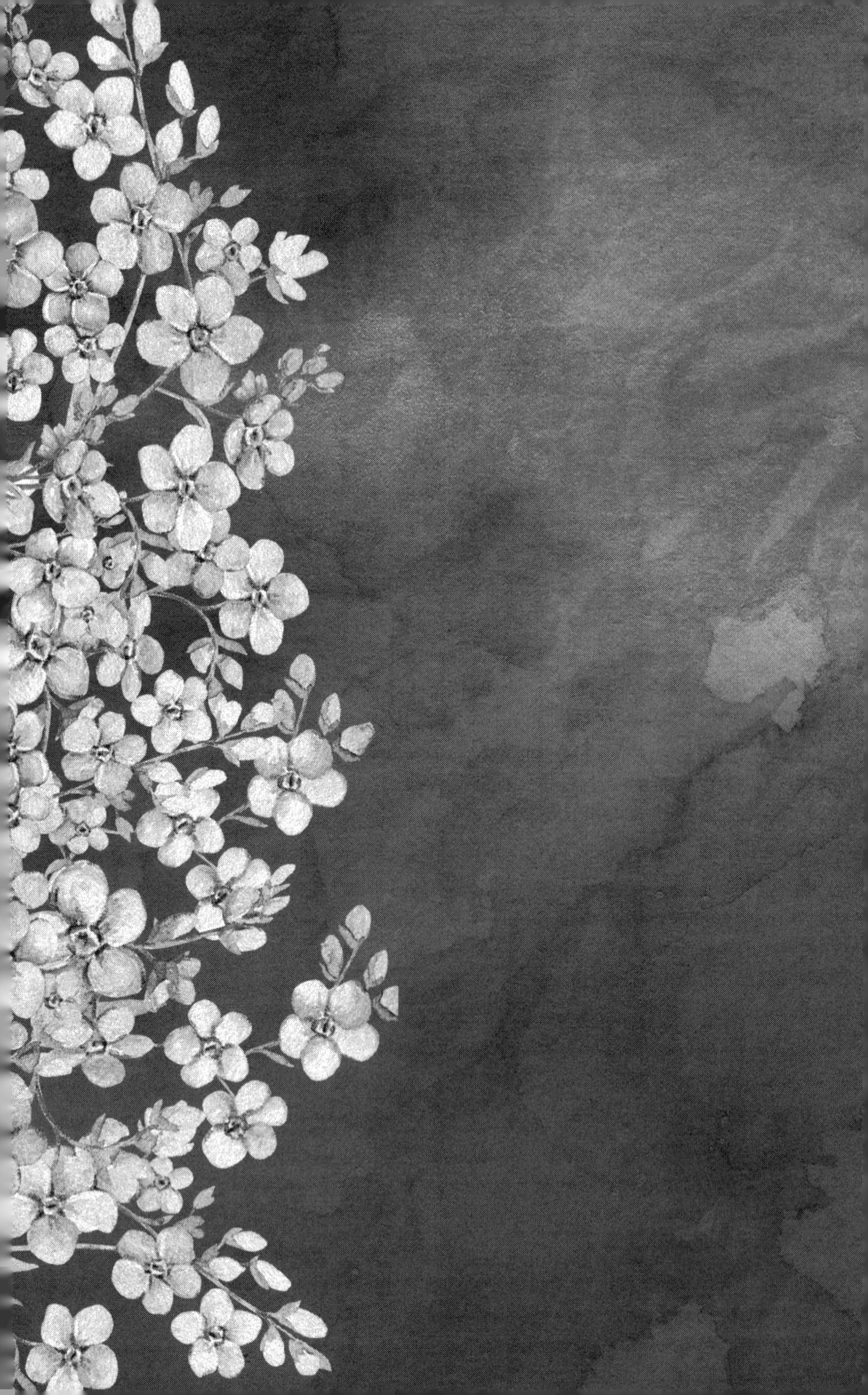

CHAPTER V
AMBROSIA
-GWEN-

"I've had just about enough!" I yanked the hair brush from Fauna's hands, failing miserably to hide my irritation. She was only trying to be nice, but I couldn't handle the "pampering" any longer.

"Oh, but Gwen, I'm only at 380 strokes. I need to get to 444! It's good luck you know… helps to ensure you're on the right path in life." Fauna pouted and crossed her arms over her chest in disapproval.

"I'll be bald by the time I get to that path if you continue to brush my hair."

"Quite the contrary. Have a look." She placed a bowl full of water before me and once the ripples settled, I could see a perfect reflection of myself. Peter had shipped me off to the Fae springs with Mira and Fauna first thing this morning. They had spent all day scrubbing every inch of me as if they were Mother Teresa in a valiant effort to wash away all of my sins.

She was right about my hair. It hung in thick waves around my face, shining brilliantly in the afternoon sun. I almost didn't recognize myself. It had been a while since I'd looked in the mirror— really looked. I'd avoided them back home. I couldn't stand the sight of the broken, melancholy girl I'd become when I returned from Neverland. Now I looked… different. My skin was silky smooth and had a healthy glow for a change. No smudges or dirt anywhere. I reluctantly pushed up the silken robe I was wearing and peered down at my wrist, hoping that the black stain from the bargain I'd struck with the bone faerie had somehow washed away in the springs. But I knew I was being foolish.

I swallowed hard when I took in the extent of it. The black veining now encompassed my elbow and was working its way to my shoulder. It looked like a macabre tattoo, black cobwebs attempting to claim my soul for the bone faerie. I couldn't wait much longer. I had to find the Osakren to fulfill my end of the bargain. She'd given me the means to cure Peter from Tiger Lily's thrall, but in the end I'd failed and if it hadn't been for James, I'm not sure where any of us would be now.

Peter had assured me we'd find the Osakren. It would be our main priority as soon as the feast he was planning was over. I had enough things to worry about. Why not add a magical curse to the pile? Yet more evidence that I was on some cosmic shit list. I pulled the sleeve back in place. Out of sight, out of mind, I thought to myself as I let out a sigh.

"Peter will be pleased. I've picked the perfect dress— fit for a queen," Fauna continued. Neither nymph had made any mention of the markings curling up my arm. They'd initially stared in abject horror for several minutes, but had successfully ignored the black stains for the rest of the day.

"Thank you, Fauna, but I don't need a dress. I'll just clean the clothes that I have."

The side of her lip lifted in disgust as she stared at me for a long moment. "Darling girl, I disposed of those... clothes. They were not salvageable. And if you're planning to be at Peter's side, you must present yourself accordingly. The embodiment of femininity, grace and abundance."

"I don't embody any of those things."

"You will if I have anything to do with it. And you can start with the dress I've picked for you." She disappeared for a moment before reappearing with a shimmering dress draped over her arm.

"What do you think? Isn't it lovely?" she gushed.

The delicate dress was a pale celadon, with a tight bodice, and full-length sleeves, which conveniently would cover the dark mark of the bone faerie. Gauzy skirts fanned out to a detailed edge. The hem was embroidered with leaves in varying shades of green and gold. I was speechless.

"You like it! I knew you would like it," Fauna squealed as she jumped up and down in excitement. Her exuberance was contagious, and I couldn't help but smile back at her. She reminded me of my sister Michaela. I felt a twinge of nagging panic pull at my heart at the thought of her. Peter had promised to find the beasts and get news about her welfare after we'd parted ways at the Temple Mount and I reluctantly conceded the task to him. As much as I wanted to confirm her safety, I knew Peter was better equipped to find answers than I was. While I was washed away with consuming thoughts of my sister, Fauna and Mira stripped me down and dressed me in the elegant gown.

"Look at you! I knew I picked the right dress. You'll be absolutely radiant on the night of the feast. It even pushes up your little breasts. They look deliciously perky. Peter won't be able to keep his hands off of you."

"Agreed," Mira chimed in. "The way the skirts flare at your hips, it accentuates your ample backside. Hips like that, and she'll have no problems giving Peter an heir," she mused to Fauna.

"Whoa, there will be no providing of heirs. Not me. Not this girl." I rushed to shut down that line of discussion. The idea of children was best left to a much more mature, and, well... older version of me.

"You know, we could get Posey to give you a fertility tattoo. She does the best work in camp," Fauna added.

"Yeah... um, no. I think I'll pass on that."

"You must know that Peter intends to take over the island in Tiger Lily's stead. He'll disband the council and become the next King of Neverland. You'll have your role to play if you're his chosen mate," Mira said matter-of-factly.

I stared at her in disbelief. Peter hadn't told me he planned to take over as ruler of Neverland. I guess it was the obvious move after everything that had happened with Tiger Lily, but where would I fit into that life? How would I walk that path with him?

A loud crowing interrupted my brooding. Peter had insisted that Ryder accompany me, adamant that I needed a bodyguard to flush out any curious satyrs while I bathed. Mira and Fauna had shooed him away, relegating him to the forest to keep watch at a distance.

His warning call piqued my attention. I scanned the surrounding forest, my eyes catching on a dark figure emerging from the shadows.

"Eben," I breathed. I was beyond relieved to have an excuse to end this pampering session and take a much needed break from the overbearing nymphs.

My heart stuttered at the sight of him. He was sinfully handsome, his dark hair casting shadows over his fathomless eyes. He hesitated at the edge of the forest, as if he was unsure of himself. A lump began to form in my throat. He hadn't taken my confession about James very well. But could I really blame him? I'd asked him to overlook the fact that I expected him to share me, not only with his brother's, but with his arch nemesis too. I'd pushed him too far, and he'd left. I didn't know what to do from here. It felt like Eben was slipping through my fingers and my heart clenched at the idea of losing him altogether.

"Ladies, if you'll excuse me," I said politely.

"Do be careful with that dress," Fauna cautioned. "We must keep it pristine until the night of the feast!" I nodded absently, brushing them off as I left them behind. If Eben needed me to meet him in the shadows, then that's exactly what I'd do.

"You came back," I whispered. I felt my cheeks heat. An odd sense of shyness washed over me as we stood awkwardly at the edge of the springs, the surrounding forest shrouding us in darkness. We'd been through so much in our fledgling relationship, but I had to remind myself that this was all new. In reality, we barely knew each other.

"You clean up nice." His eyes raked over my body as he bit his lip. His stare felt so intimate that I had to shift my eyes from his to compose myself.

"Thanks. I think I still prefer jeans and my sword."

"How about just the sword? Nothing else." His voice came out in a low grumble. He continued to stare at me predatorily. It was easy to let our primal needs take over. A whole hell of a lot easier than trying to work through our feelings. But I was done hiding behind sex.

"Will you walk with me?" I asked, changing the subject as I continued to avoid his come-fuck-me glare. I know he'd planned to wait, prove himself to me before we were intimate, but I could tell Eben wasn't himself. The more practical side of me began to cycle through the countless questions that had been eating away at me. It was at war with the part of me that wanted to rip his clothes off, give him the best fuck of his life, and forget all about our problems.

"There's a sacred grove of trees not too far. It's supposed to be a favored spot of the Divine. Some say if your case is particularly worthy, the Divine will grant your wish."

"What would you wish for?" I asked. He stepped closer to me, invading my personal space. I swallowed hard, finding it difficult to concentrate with him this close.

"Maybe I'd wish to have you all to myself," he whispered in my ear.

"Eben, I—"

"In order for that wish to come true,"— he interrupted, holding a hand up to allow him a moment to explain— "the Divine would have to change the fabric of your soul. Change the very thing that draws me in and binds me to you in ways I can't explain. I may be selfish, but I would never wish for that." His hand came up tentatively, and he brushed his thumb along my cheekbone. I found myself drowning in his dark eyes, letting myself relish in the words he'd just said. It wasn't quite an approval to continue my relationship with James, but it was an acceptance of who I was, and I think that was as close as I'd ever get. "Do you still want to go for that walk with me?" he asked, changing topics so seamlessly that my mind was still reeling.

"Yes, I would like that very much. Let me just grab my sword before the girls try to dispose of it with the rest of my things." I ran back to the eavesdropping nymphs, who had instantly jolted into action the moment I turned to face them, bumping into one another in the process. I couldn't help but laugh at the sight of them.

"Serves you two right for spying," I giggled as they tried in vain to pick themselves up from the ground as if nothing had happened. "Now, what have you done with my things?"

"They are over by the fire," Fauna said, distracted as she tried to pull leaves from her dress. I hurried to the flaming pile that smoldered just a few feet away. Realizing as I got closer, that my dirty clothes had become tinder. The damn nymphs had burned my favorite pair of knickers, the black lacy ones. I huffed exaggeratedly, hoping to convey my irritation, but I'm pretty sure it fell on deaf ears. I scanned the area, looking for my sword, hoping it had been spared a better fate. I found it half buried in the surrounding leaf litter and rolled my eyes. Next time I spend the day with Mira and Fauna, I'll have to set some very clear boundaries.

"I'm ready," I said as I adjusted the sword on my back, feeling oddly complete now that it was in its rightful place.

"Are you trying to tease me on purpose?"

"Me? What did I do? I thought we were going for a walk."

"That dress, that sword, you're my perfect fantasy come

to life," he said almost mournfully, as if he was about to lose something precious. He turned on his heels, walking off into the forest, and I followed. Not at all sure how I was going to bridge this growing chasm between us.

"You know the sword doesn't do much good. I don't know how to use it. Maybe we could have another date at the practice fields? You could teach me how to use this properly."

"If I remember correctly, you're a good student and a fast learner. I have one request."

"And that is?"

"That when you practice, you practice nude." My jaw dropped, and I gaped at him. He was smirking at me, obviously pleased with himself. I promptly elbowed him in the side and laughed when he overly exaggerated his discomfort.

"Fine, fine, you've beaten me into submission. I'll teach you, but clothes are optional if you change your mind."

"I get the feeling we wouldn't get much practice if I trained naked."

"I'd most definitely give you an A though."

"Not helpful." I glared at him through half-lidded eyes. "Stop trying to distract me. You promised me the truth when I came back. We can't fix everything with sex. I want more from you than just the physical. That's the easy part. I need to know if my relationship with James is a hard limit for you."

"Hook," he corrected. "He's not good enough for you.

But are any of us, really? I can't think rationally when I envision the two of you together. But maybe it has nothing to do with him and everything to do with me. He's unapologetic, wearing his darkness as if it were a badge of honor and you fell for him anyway. Jealousy has sunk its jade claws so deeply into me I can't see straight. I am trying to be everything you want me to be, and I am petrified that if you truly knew me, you wouldn't like what you see."

"I want to know you. Know your stories, your secrets, your fears. Tell me something I don't know." Eben scratched the back of his neck, looking visibly uncomfortable at the turn this conversation was taking. "Come on," I said, "give me something. You know so much about me, and I know nothing about you."

"Okay, I'll give you something real, but you may not like it once you hear it." I stopped walking and turned to face him. This deserved my undivided attention.

"I don't want to fall in love with you." He paused after that statement and I literally felt like my heart had stopped beating and would fall out of my chest at any moment. "I didn't want you to come here. I even tried to stop you from coming altogether. Before I met you, I hated you. Hated what you meant to Pan. I knew in my gut that everything would change. But you came anyway and everything shattered to pieces the moment you kissed me in the rain. All my resolve washed away. I was bound to you in that very first kiss and I fucking hated it. In all of my life, nothing good ever came out of love. It was an excuse that covered up all the vile things that he..." He stopped mid-sentence, realizing that he was letting his guard down. He cleared his throat, and I could feel him retreating from me again.

"Please, keep going."

"I'm falling in love with you anyway, Gwen. I tried not to, but against my better judgment, here I am. I'm incapable of leaving you alone. But I'm plagued with this notion that I deserve to be punished for those thoughts. That maybe I don't deserve you at all."

"Just because you're afraid of love doesn't mean you don't deserve it."

"The only love that I've ever known has been cruel."

"Can you tell me what happened?"

"Neverland has woven her spell around my memories, but I can still peer through the cracks. I think some memories are so ingrained in our minds that no amount of time or Neverland magic can rid you of them," he sighed deeply before continuing. "My mother died bringing me into this world and my father punished me for it every single day of my life."

I felt the twinge of tears prick my eyes at his admission. He looked so young in that moment, his vulnerability showing for once as he bared his soul to me. No one ever prepares you on how to react, or what you should say in times like these, but I knew the last thing Eben would want was my pity. I pushed him further, hoping he would continue to reveal his story.

"How did you end up here in Neverland?"

"Pan's not the only one in our realm who can cross the Veil. There are others.."

"Others, you mean the sentries?"

"The sentries seem tame compared to some of the Fae that prey on our realm. We seem to attract the scum of the cosmos. They run a type of black market, where you can barter for magical items, favors, anything you can think of."

"How does a small boy find and barter with a reclusive Fae?"

Eben smirked at me and leaned over to place a kiss on my temple. "Come on, the wishing trees are right over here." He effectively shut down the conversation, avoiding my question altogether, and pulled me forward. We arrived at what appeared to be a wall of leaves, towering above us with no possible way through. The wind picked up, the leaves shimmering like silver as the breeze whipped by.

"Where do we go from here?"

"Silly girl, don't you remember? Things in Neverland aren't always what they seem." Eben reached his arm to the wall of leaves, sliding his hand through easily, pulling back a curtain of thick branches, exposing a veritable wonderland beyond.

"Ladies first." Eben waved me into a secluded sanctuary. Three massive trees stood at the center of the grove, their smooth white trunks rose impossibly tall. Thousands of branches, thick with leaves, hung all the way to the ground like a weeping willow, completely secluding us from the rest of the forest. An unusual fruit hung heavy from the branches. Shaped oddly like a human heart, they were a vibrant orange, standing out in stark contrast amidst the lush emerald canopy of the grove. The glow of fireflies winked on and off, setting a warm ambience to the darkened space. Brightly colored butterflies flitted about from one mushroom cap to another, a glittering trail in their wake. I could see why the Fae deemed this as a sacred site. It was so beautiful that it almost didn't seem real.

"Oh my god, this is amazing." I whirled around, taking everything in. Eben stood with his arms crossed, ignoring the beauty around us and staring only at me. "Thank you for bringing me here. It's the most beautiful place I've ever seen," I said as I ran a finger over the velvety skin of the fruit hanging from the trees. "What kind of fruit is this?" I asked.

"It's ambrosia. The fruit of the Divine. It's known to heal the sick, impart great wisdom, expand your mind… it's even known to be a potent aphrodisiac." He lifted his brow suggestively. "But mostly it's been known to grant wishes, hence the wishing trees. But if you eat it and the Divine doesn't find you worthy, it will make you deathly ill."

"Well, maybe you should try it. See if you get your wish," I teased. Eben smiled at me, but the smile didn't reach his eyes. I instantly regretted my words. My relationship with Eben was teetering on the precipice. One wrong move, one wrong statement, could spell out complete demise for us. I could see his internal battle raging behind his eyes. He was still trying to keep me out.

"Don't do that. Don't keep pushing me away."

"I'm not good for you, Gwen." His voice was husky with emotion. "I keep running away, leaving you when you need me the most. Maybe I'm subconsciously keeping that distance, knowing what fate has in store. Maybe staying away is the most loving thing I could ever do for you."

"If anything, it's me who isn't good enough. I should go home, but I can't. I should leave before I ruin everything, but I'm not strong enough to do what's best. Honestly, I'm tired of doing 'what's best.' I'm starting to realize there's pain down either path I choose. So I'm choosing to be selfish. I want you Eben, and I will not let you go so easily."

"There are stains on my soul. What if I'm just like my father? What if I have a warped sense of what love is? What if I hurt you?"

"My soul is scarred and stained, too. But they will never go away, and the more you try to deny it, the more broken you'll be. There is a fine line between pain and pleasure. We can learn to skirt that line and please both sides of your soul."

"It could be more than your soul that's scarred." Eben strode toward me until he stood, nose to nose with me. "Take a close look." He pulled his shirt off revealing his all too familiar tattoos. I looked up at him, confused, unsure of what he wanted me to see. "Look!" he commanded, and I jumped, quickly shifting my gaze to the ram's skull on his chest. The closer I looked, the more I noticed the raised skin that was artfully covered by the beautiful tattoos. I traced my fingers over the lines, now noticing the feel of the countless scars perfectly hidden under his tattoos.

"Oh, Eben. I'm so sorry." My heart clenched in my chest as the evidence of Eben's tragic life was right before my eyes.

"I didn't show you for your pity. I showed you as a warning."

"You would never do that to me."

"Wouldn't I? I bet my father never thought he could do it to his own son, and yet here it is."

"If that's who you are, then why cover the scars?"

He shrugged his shoulders, not wanting to answer me. I waited, the silence growing hostile between us. "Because I wanted to put something beautiful over something so ugly."

"You know, you can't just put something beautiful over something that's broken and expect it to be fixed."

"It's worked with you. You've started to put the pieces of my broken soul back together." A wave of emotions washed over me: love, awe, devotion. Feelings I couldn't put words to. All I knew at that moment was that I needed to be touching him. I needed to be one with him. I closed the small space between us and my lips met his with the fierce passion of my convictions. Eben was mine and I would show him we belonged together. My hands fisted in his hair and he met my kiss with his own fevered passion.

"I can't, Gwen," he breathed, pulling away from me. I needed to prove that this thing between us was real and it was right. I walked backward until I brushed up against the partition of leaves that hid us from the rest of the world. I absently reached behind me, pulling a fruit from the tree, my eyes glued on Eben's as he consumed me with his gaze.

"The Divine knows that you belong to me, so my wish is for you to show me your worst, right here, right now, in this sacred space, and then we will know what you're capable of."

"Don't, Gwen," he growled at me, stepping toward me. I brought the fruit to my lips, sinking my teeth into its soft flesh before he could stop me. An explosion of sweetness filled my mouth as the juices dripped down my chin. The skin of the fruit was a dark orange while the flesh was a deep aubergine. I'd never tasted anything so delicious. Truly the fruit of the gods. I felt a heady rush, my cheeks flushing as I waited in anticipation, unsure of what to expect next.

Eben stalked toward me, desire burning in his dark eyes. He slapped the half eaten fruit from my hand, grabbing my arm and pulling me forward. "Why would you do that?" he snapped.

"Because seeing is believing for you."

"Fuck, Gwen. You don't mess with magic."

"Are you angry with me?"

"Yes! I'm pissed."

"Good, be angry with me. You're not a monster, Eben. Even at your worst, you could never be your father."

"You have no concern for your own mortality, and if anything happened to you..."

"So punish me," I challenged.

Eben's glare burned into me. It was a look I'd never seen on his face before. In an instant, his hands were on me, ripping the beautiful dress open. The sound of seams and fabric giving way echoed in the small space. My breasts popped free of the ruined bodice as it hung from my body. My chest was heaving as a twinge of fear tried to worm its way into my mind, but this is what needed to happen. I trusted Eben to give me only what he knew I could take. His hand whipped out, and he grabbed one of the long, hanging branches from the tree, easily snapping it. He spun me around, wrapping the sinewy branches around my wrists, binding me in place.

"You want to play with me, Gwen? Don't say I didn't warn you." He pushed me forward and I stumbled. Without my hands to catch myself, I landed face first at the base of one of the massive trees. The mossy ground absorbed my fall like a sponge. I twisted around until I was able to flip to my back, scooting backward and propping myself up on the massive tree trunk as best I could with my hands still bound. Eben towered over me, not looking at my eyes, but lingering on every inch of my exposed skin. He walked backwards, keeping his eyes on me as he pulled another fruit from the tree.

"You want to play with magic? Get the attention of the Divine? What kind of man would I be if I let you do it all alone?"

He grabbed my ankle, pulling me toward him. He got down on his knees, straddling me. The sight of him alone in all his dark glory, not knowing what to expect next from my broken prince, brought on a rush of wetness between my legs. I shifted under him, shamelessly seeking some friction between us. He met my eyes, disarming me with his dark gaze as he sunk his teeth into the fruit, the dark purple juices running down his chin and over his chest. His eyes flared with something more than desire, as if I could see the magic manifesting there.

He held the fruit over me, squeezing it until the juices dripped over my chest. The soft patter tantalized my already sensitive skin. He tossed it aside and proceeded to lap up the juices with his skillful tongue, working his way up until he reached my breast. He paused briefly, pulling in a deep inhale before sucking my erect nipple into his mouth. My back arched off the ground, sending a surge of pain into my bound wrists, but I didn't care. His hand grasped my other nipple, pinching it hard, a sharp contrast to the sweeps of his tongue. A needy moan escaped my lips and my mind was swimming with the pleasure of it all. My body was overly sensitive, every touch creating an explosion of pleasure. I wanted more. I wanted him to touch every part of me.

He ripped the rest of the dress off with a growl. The beautiful garment was reduced to shreds. Eben's movements were quick and needy. He shifted between my legs, glaring up at me with his dark eyes, still dancing with magic.

"It's your fruit that I crave. You taste finer than any ambrosia," he purred and then buried his face in my dripping pussy. He took his time to savor me, running his tongue through my sweet wetness and then finding the center of my pleasure and working it mercilessly. I writhed on the ground beneath him, the motion causing my bindings to dig painfully into my wrists. His big hands gripped my thighs, pulling them wide and pinning me to the ground so I couldn't move.

"Stop moving, or I won't let you cum," he warned and I stilled instantly. I didn't need to give him any more reason to torment me. "Good girl."

He released my thighs and slowly ran two fingers through my wetness, teasing me before he plunged them deep inside me, my cunt clenching around him. I pulled in a quick breath through gritted teeth as he started to work me with his fingers while his tongue pulsed on my clit. It was a heady rush, and it had my mind swimming with the onslaught of sensation. I let out a moan of pleasure and tilted my hips to meet him, feeling on the verge of climax, and he abruptly ceased his actions, pulling away from me.

"I told you to stop moving. You didn't listen."

"No, please! I didn't mean it. Don't stop," I pleaded as he got to his feet. A pining need ached in my core, and I was desperate for him to touch me again. He continued to stare at me as he unfastened his belt. Palming a single blade before letting the belt fall to the ground, still heavy with his other weapons. He kicked off his boots and pushed his pants down slowly, giving me a show. First exposing the deep V cut lines at his hips, then the dark patch of hair as he got lower, finally pushing them down his muscled thighs, revealing his massive cock, standing to attention. I bit my lip as I drank him in, the size of him making my already fluttering heart pound like a jack-hammer in my chest. I shifted on the ground, rubbing my legs together, shamelessly looking for some friction.

"Get on your knees," he commanded. I struggled, incredibly undignified with my hands behind my back, until I was kneeling before him. I watched in rapt interest as he twirled the small blade in his hand while he stood naked before me.

"Do you remember the first time I held a blade to your throat?"

I nodded, not sure if I could get the words out coherently at that moment.

"That small drop of your blood. It tasted like sin. It took every ounce of restraint not to fuck you right then." He reached for my chin, tilting my head up, slowly laying the cold edge of his blade along my jawline. His hooded eyes were full of his own need. He wanted this as badly as I did, and he couldn't hide it from me.

"Mark me," I whispered. I don't know what possessed me to say it, but I knew I belonged to him, just as all my other boys held a piece of my soul. I wanted him to claim me as his own. His expression morphed from shock to awe as he processed what I was asking. I thought for a moment he was going to deny me, but then he pushed my thick hair aside and concentrated on a spot just behind my ear. I focused intently on what he was doing. I could feel his knife as he slowly cut the letter E behind my ear. The pain was exquisite. He ran his thumb over his initial, coating it in my blood, and it was done. He pulled it to his mouth and sucked it off, a soft groan escaping his lips.

"Now put your pretty little mouth around my cock and maybe I'll let you cum." His hands fisted in my hair, and I eagerly opened for him. He pushed himself to the back of my throat. The girth of him was so wide, I could feel the corners of my mouth sting as I stretched to fit around him. He wasn't slow, and he wasn't gentle. Once he was coated in my saliva, he started to fuck my face, driving down my throat. His hand twisted in my hair, guiding my movements, taking what he needed from me. My eyes watered but I fought to keep them open. Watching him take his pleasure from me was the hottest fucking thing and I could feel my own arousal dripping down my leg.

I could tell he was getting close, but he stopped short. With his hand still in my hair, he pulled me to my feet and kissed me hard.

"I taste good on you," he growled as he pulled away from me. "That little mouth of yours is so sweet. I think you deserve to finish now." He reached behind me with his knife and cut the binding from my wrists. My fingers had long since gone numb and I flexed them as they started to tingle.

"I want to feel your nails down my back when I make you cum." He lifted me off the ground, my arms and legs wrapping around him. He laid us on the moss covered ground and lined himself up and slowly pushed his way inside me.

His eyes focused where our bodies met, watching as he buried his massive cock inside me inch by inch. "You take it so good. You're so tight. Fuck!" His voice was feral as he finally sheathed himself inside me. He sat still for a moment, reveling in the feel of me with his eyes closed, and then he was moving. A punishing rhythm, losing control as he buried himself inside me. He traced his fingers up my body until his hand rested around my throat. He slowed his pace as he looked at me with his head cocked to the side. He increased the pressure around my neck until I couldn't pull in another breath. It was the oddest sensation. His cock was hitting all the right places. I was teetering on the brink of a mind shattering orgasm, all the while my lungs burned, desperate to pull in a breath.

"I could end it all right here," he whispered as he continued to fuck me. Dark spots danced at the corners of my vision. I was desperate for the air, desperate for the orgasm that was tantalizingly close. "Your very existence rests in my hands and you could do nothing to stop me. Better yet, you welcomed me in, a demon in a handsome mask. You brought me to the edge of my own hell and jumped from the cliff with me," he purred the words softly. "If that isn't love, then it truly doesn't exist. Now cum for me, baby." He released his grip, and I pulled in a ragged breath. The feel of his cock, the sweet relief as the air filled my lungs, it was an intoxicating mix, and I came apart. My orgasm ripped through me. I sank my fingernails into his back as I cried out, completely taken over by the passion as it coursed through me. Eben groaned out my name, his body tensing against me and I knew he'd fallen over the edge too.

He collapsed on top of me. The only sound in the grove was our labored breathing. He propped himself on his elbows, his eyes meeting mine with his cock still buried deep inside me. The magic of the Divine still surrounded us, but it was gone from his eyes. It was just Eben and I. We'd laid ourselves bare to one another. It had been raw and emotional, but it was exactly what we needed.

"I guess wishes do come true," he said as he cupped my face in his hands. "You make me feel whole again. I am yours and you are mine. No strings attached. No exceptions. I love you."

CHAPTER VI
PAYMENT IS DUE
-TRIPP-

For the first time since I could remember, life in Neverland had begun to show promise of a happily ever after. We all basked in the joy of simply being together. Eben had begun to teach Gwen how to properly use Gage's sword. He was meticulous in his training, but I'd seen the look of pride creep across his face when he thought she wasn't looking. And Gwen had been spending countless hours teaching Ryder how to read. Somehow, he'd convinced Eben to supply him with romance novels from his library. He spent more time staring at her than he did the pages, but the fucker reaped the benefits— cuddling up with Gwen every evening as they read love stories together.

Peter believed things were going to be easy from here on out. Neverland had chosen him, and he would rule with his Darling queen and his Lost Boys at his side. But something was amiss. I couldn't shake the nagging feeling something big was coming our way. Hook's words continued to replay in my mind. *"Neverland is ripe for the taking. A darkness is coming for her."* He was right. Neverland was in a vulnerable position and Pan was too proud to heed Hook's warning.

Neverland was a valuable commodity and others would seek to control her. Word of Tiger Lily's passing would spread like wildfire and without a crowned ruler, usurpers were sure to come seeking opportunity. Plus, Gwen's debt to the bone faerie was quickly coming due. The black veining was spreading up and over her shoulders and the last thing we needed was a distraction keeping us from finding the Osakren.

Nonetheless, we carried on as if our future was set in the stars. We had been spending our free time secretly building Gwen her very own cottage on the Never Cliffs. There wasn't much to it yet, just four walls. But it was hers. A foundation to build her future on. I had hoped to have it finished before tonight, but Pan had me busy with the council and planning his accession.

After the celebration, we planned to present it to her. The beginning of her happily ever after. I wanted her to feel at home here. She had given up everything to save her sister.

With Mic safe and thriving, she could focus on her future here in Neverland. She deserved a sacred space. I also didn't feel like fighting my brothers over where she was going to sleep for the foreseeable future. We all wanted her in our bed. That was never going to change. With her own place, Gwen could decide who she wanted to share her space with.

Peter's celebration had become quite the event. This was his opportunity to publicly lay claim to the land that chose him to rule. All of Neverland had been invited. And it appeared as though all of them had shown up. The forrest was abuzz with excitement. No extravagance had been spared. The camp had been completely transformed. Lill and her fellow pixies had spent hours decorating the grounds. Faerie lanterns hung from the trees by the hundreds. Illuminating the typically shadowed forest. Pixies were flitting about, leaving a glittering magic to the entire camp. Colorful blooms of every kind adorned the grounds, gently perfuming the air. A feast fit for kings had been laid out, as well as enough faerie mead and Lush tea to seduce even the most crotchety fae. Pan had pulled it off. Neverland was lost in celebration. The loss of their beloved Tiger Lily was a mere memory in their drunken minds. All that was left to do was to claim the proverbial throne.

Those who had gotten into the Lush at the start of the party were beginning to show the effects. Fae were engaging in drunken orgies. Pixies were flying around naked, flinging faerie dust everywhere. Nymphs and satyrs were chasing each other around, completely blind to anything other than their conquest. Others were fucking against the trees. Lush was a potent drug. Before Gwen came into our lives, I would have been one of them. Rutting in the woods like a wild animal. Fucking with reckless abandon. But I'm not that boy anymore. I have eyes for no one but her. My body and all its pleasures belong to her and only her. Plus, the night was still young, and we had our own plans for our beloved.

"Do you think my sister is here yet?" Gwen was pacing, looking through the crowds of Fae. She was a vision in green silks. The fabric draped over her body in sinful waves, accentuating her perfect figure. A deep V at her neckline exposed the gentle swell of her breasts, while the corseted back showcased her petite frame. Her legs peeked through the slits in the gown, offering a little taste for your imagination. She was temptation personified. And she was ours.

"Hen, we have pixies on the look out. We'll know when they arrive." Ryder tried to assure her. "Plus, the beastie boys are not small. They're kinda hard to lose in a crowd."

Gwen giggled. "I'm sorry. I just need to see that she's okay. I miss her so much."

I reached out and grabbed her tiny hand. "They'll be here soon."

"There are so many things I want to show her. She was so sick when we arrived. We never had the chance before—I promised her mermaids."

"And she'll get to see them," Peter boasted. "I'll escort you both myself."

Eben stood silently scanning the crowd. He was still on edge after the incident at May Day.

"Peter! Peter!" One of the pixies we had on surveillance came in hot, flitting about Peter's ear. "They have arrived. The beasts are here."

"Thank you, Clovis. Tell the others they can leave their posts and enjoy the party."

Gwen stood frozen, staring at Pan, holding her breath. Her tiny hand gripped mine tightly. Patiently waiting for him to translate the flurry of bells.

"She's here."

Gwen squealed as she quickly scanned the crowd. I'd never seen her so excited. She was simply radiant. Her smile was pure and uninhibited, no longer hiding within the corners of her mouth. Her happiness was contagious. You couldn't help but smile looking at her. I wanted her to feel that every day of her life. Mark my words, I will spend my days trying to keep that smile on her beautiful face. May the Divine have mercy on those who seek to destroy that bliss. I'll end them swiftly and without remorse.

"There she is!" Gwen quickly took off running toward her sister.

I grabbed Peter, holding him back as he tried to follow her. "Give her some space, Pan. This is their moment."

"The last time I left her at a party, we almost lost her."

"We are *right* here. We'll keep a close eye from afar."

"I don't like it," Peter said, shaking his head.

"She needs to know we trust her. She's not our possession."

"Well, well Peter, If I'd known your party was going to be filled with drunken debauchery, I'd have planned to stick around. The views are starting to get… interesting." Hook's gritty voice snapped our attention away from Gwen.

Eben rolled his eyes, the air around him thickened with tension as he turned his back on Hook, reverting his attention to Gwen and her sister. Effectively ignoring his presence. He was more like Hook than he cared to acknowledge. I think that's why he was having trouble accepting Gwen's attraction to him. They both had an indelible darkness within them. The difference was Eben chose to bury his darkness, where Hook chose to embrace it.

"Speak of the devil," Ryder snarked.

All of Neverland had been invited to celebrate, but I never thought Hook would show his face. Although he often found himself dragged into Neverland's politics, it wasn't his scene. He never attended public events unless he had something to gain. Then again, Gwen was an addictive creature, and Hook was as intoxicated as we were.

"You'd be wise to make yourself scarce," Pan snarled back. "Gwen is with her sister, and I won't allow you to interrupt their reunion."

Hook chuckled. "Oh, that's cute. I won't allow you to interrupt," he mocked, laughing again. "I don't need your permission to see Gwendolyn. I'll do as I damn well please." He paused to take a pull from his cigar, exhaling thick white plumes in Peter's face. "I'm aware of Michaela's arrival. She's provided me with the perfect diversion."

"Diversion for what, Hook?" I interjected. He was up to something. Though we were all trying to accept Gwen's relationship with him, he was still our nemesis. If I knew anything, it was that Hook could not be trusted.

"I'm here to collect my debt."

"What do you want?" Peter repeated my question. I could see his anger beginning to surface. I placed my arm on his shoulder, silently pleading with him to keep calm.

"In three days' time, you will deliver Gwendolyn to the Jolly Roger. I'll be anchored just east of the Mermaid Lagoon."

"I'll do no such thing." He huffed at the boldness of Hook's demand.

"You will, or you will suffer the consequences of reneging on a deal with Captain James Hook." He drew off the cigar again. "Gwendolyn will be able to return to you when she decides to. I'm not her captor."

I was quickly losing my patience. "You may not be her captor, but the bone faerie's prophecy predicted you would kill her and if you think we are just going to forget that, then you are clearly unhinged." I'll never forget hearing the bone faerie spit out those words. "*Should you succeed in killing her.*" My blood ran cold at the thought. I wanted to end him right there. Stop fate in its tracks.

"Tripp, I thought you were smarter than that. Clearly

the '*her*' she was referring to was Tiger Lily. And since you couldn't finish the job I did it for you."

Pan growled under his breath, "You can't use Gwen as a payment for our debt."

"I can, and I will. She doesn't belong to you. She is not yours to keep. I'll collect today if I have to. Do I need to make a scene at your *'celebration'*, Peter? I do love a good brawl."

Peter's jaw flexed as he swallowed his pride. "In a gesture of faith and trust for Gwen, I will fulfill our debt to you. If you harm one hair on her perfect little head I will end you once and for all. I don't care if Gwen begs for your life. I will finish what we started all those years ago and feed the rest of you to that *thing* you call a pet."

A sinister grin slid across Hook's face. "Three days' time, Peter... or I will come seeking payment." He turned and sauntered off, heading straight for Gwen.

Peter growled, "I should have ended that bastard years ago."

Hook and Peter's history was shrouded in mystery. I'm not sure if it was the nature of Neverland and its ability to make you forget the past or if it was intentional. But there was something between the two of them lurking below the surface. They were both accomplished fighters. If either one of them truly wanted the other dead, it would have happened by now.

"We can't just deliver Gwen to Hook without her

consent," Ryder spoke his words carefully. Peter was on edge.

Eben huffed. "I doubt she's going to have a problem with it."

"But can we trust Hook?" I looked to Peter for confirmation. He knew Hook better than anyone.

"You can never really trust Hook. You have to learn to play his game. I have him out-smarted this time. Trust me, I have a plan." He turned and headed toward Gwen.

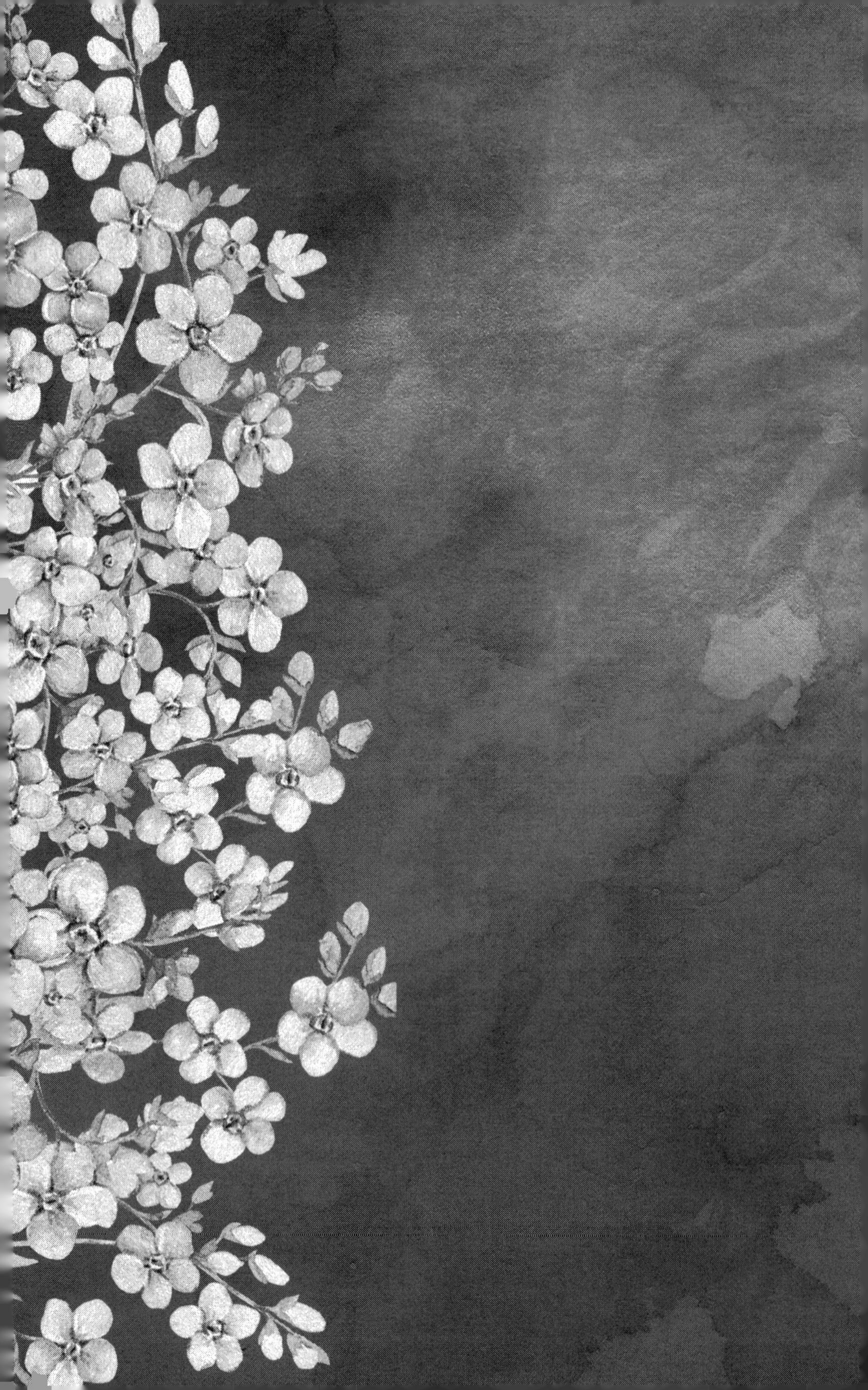

Chapter VII
Sisters Only
-Gwen-

Relief washed over me as I wrapped my arms around Michaela. Her body felt solid against mine. She was now a picture of health. Her long hair hung in lustrous waves, tickling my cheek as we clung to each other. This wasn't the woman I was used to seeing, wasted away to nothing more than skin and bones. Everything the cancer had taken from her had been restored. Tribulation was what the Fae had called it. The manifestation of magic awakening in mortal bodies that were too weak to handle it.

The beast's magic had brought her back from the brink, healed her in ways that no earthly medicine could.

I reveled in the momentary satisfaction. I could count on one hand the wins I'd had in life, and this one topped all the others by far. I'd known all along that Mic was destined for more than a premature demise. It had been that blind faith that had gotten us here, and we'd succeeded against all odds. The elation was indescribable. Mic pulled away, holding me at arm's length, looking me over. "There you are. I've been waiting for you for a long time," she whispered as she pushed a stray tendril of hair behind my ear.

"I tried to find you sooner, I—"

"I know you did, sweetie," she interrupted. "But that's not what I'm talking about. I'm talking about the girl you once were. The sister I knew as a child. She's been gone a long time. Buried under depression, obligation, and fear. But now I see that you've found her. And you have no idea how happy that makes me."

"I'm… I'm sorry." I didn't know what else to say. I knew I felt different. Neverland, this journey, these men, had irrevocably changed me. But I never expected anyone else to realize the enormity of the changes taking place within me.

"You don't have to be sorry, sweetie. I only wish I could have helped you find your way back sooner."

"What doesn't kill you makes you stronger," I said lamely. I swear it was a curse, to never say the right thing in truly poignant moments. She laughed at me, saving me from an awkward pause.

"Guess that means I'll live forever," Mic said as she peered, almost longingly, over her shoulder at her entourage. The entire beast court, all seven of the beast princes, had escorted Mic to the feast.

"Unable are the loved to die, for love is immortality," James's gritty voice reciting Emily Dickinson melted my heart as he came toward me. The sight of him here, at Peter's ascension, shocked it back into an irregular rhythm. "Ms. Michaela, it is an honor to finally make your acquaintance. Captain James Hook, at your service, milady." James bowed to her gracefully.

"Gwen didn't tell me you were a poet," Mic said, her eyes raking over him appraisingly.

"Dickinson was far beyond her time. I could say the same about Gwendolyn." He turned to me then, and I felt weak in the knees from his loaded stare. His arrival complicated things. I was thrilled to see him, a part of my soul came alive with his very presence. But I'd been hoping for more time to figure everything out. I had no idea how I was going to navigate my way around all these alpha males. But if I was being honest with myself, was there even an answer? It was all but inevitable that I'd have to bumble around in the dark, making a mess of things and apologizing profusely, hoping it was enough until I figured it all out.

"Michaela, so glad you could make it." Peter joined us and

the trance James had put me under instantly dissolved, anxiety promptly filling its place. "Welcome to your forever after here in Neverland," Peter said, hiding any hint that James was affecting him. He flashed her a winning smile, ready to welcome her into whatever crazy fucked up family we were trying to put together. His tone was sweet and sincere, but his posture, the slight tick in his clenched jaw, belied his words. Having James so close was eating away at him. "You're welcome to stay here in the camp with Gwen as long as you like."

"Pan, about that. I have some news to share," Nico started, the two men crashing our little reunion.

"Nico, just look at my sister. Isn't she beautiful?" Mic asked, sidetracking him with her random question. "This dress, it's stunning."

"It's a pleasure to see you again, daughter of Wendy, and I second Michaela's observations. It appears that Neverland agrees with you," Nico said as he bowed to me.

"How about you let my sister and I enjoy the party before you jump into politics," Mic said with a certain sense of authority. As though she knew she held some kind of sway over the beast princes.

He bowed to her slightly, a faint smile tugging at the corner of his perpetual scowl. "Of course, as you wish." My eyes darted between the two of them. What in the name of Neverland was going on here? It was at that moment that I realized all the masculine eyes focused on the two of us and I instantly felt like prey being hunted.

"Come on, Mic. Let's go enjoy the party." I affirmed her request. I had more than a few questions for my sister, and I knew I wouldn't get a word out of her with all of these men eyeing us down. I tucked her arm into mine, eager to have a moment away from all the tension.

"Gwen, my love, this is where I leave you for the evening." James stepped directly in front of Peter, completely oblivious to the death glare he received. He bowed slightly, his old-fashioned mannerisms pulling a smile at my lips.

"But you just got here. Are you sure you have to leave so soon?"

"There is altogether too much faerie dust floating around, and you know where I stand on that. But don't fret. I plan on arranging some time for the two of us. A fine glass of rum and intriguing conversation awaits us, along with other *things* I have developed a particular taste for." His brow raised suggestively as he grasped my hand and planted a soft kiss along my knuckles. My cheeks heated as his eyes met mine, conveying dark, lusty promises in their forget-me-not blue depths.

"Not a fucking chance in hell." Peter's growl came out low and measured. My eyes darted to Peter, a moment of embarrassment rushing through me, followed quickly by panic. His jaw was tight, fists clenched at his sides. He was doing his best to hold it together. Decorum alone was the only thing staying his hand. I needed to find a way to walk the fine line between these two men if I wanted any of this to work.

"Peter, let's not ruin the night. James is leaving. We can talk about this later." I placed a calming hand on his chest, trying my best to placate him.

"You're right, Gwen. Go enjoy the feast with your sister. We'll escort *Hook* out." He emphasized Hook, and I had to physically hold myself back from rolling my eyes. None of the Lost Boys had appreciated me calling him James. Apparently, it was getting under Peter's skin as well.

"Good night, James." I nodded my head in a cordial goodbye, knowing anything more would send Peter over the edge, and turned back to Mic.

Peter made to follow, but I put my hand up to stop him short. "Sisters only." It came out more firmly than I intended, but I had to be clear on what I needed. It was the only way this was going to work.

"Gwen"—Peter gently grabbed my arm, pulling me closer—"the last time I left you at a feast, I almost lost you to the very man who's sauntering about."

"Is that why you're upset? Peter, I'm not going anywhere. I promise. This isn't May Day." He peered over at Tripp, who had given Mic and I our space since she'd arrived, and his shoulders slumped. I knew he was giving into my needs against his better judgment.

"I won't be far away. Enjoy your time with your sister. Just know that I'll be watching." He kissed my lips chastely before releasing my arm. The beast princes looked uneasy as I stole Mic from their suffocating presence. I wondered if she could feel their stares burning into our backs as we walked away. I steered Mic toward the center of camp, avoiding the shadowed pockets where the Fae were celebrating the feast in other ways besides drinking and dancing.

"What the hell was that?" I asked.

"What was what?"

"Seriously, Mic. Did you not just see the king of the beasts jumping to your beck and call like you're Mary fucking Poppins snapping her fingers?"

"I have no idea what you're talking about."

"Don't play dumb with me, Mic. I know a whipped man when I see one. 'As you wish?' The Dread Pirate Roberts would be absolutely mortified."

"Gwen, that's an awful lot of movie references. I think you're letting your imagination run away with you. That's fiction. This is reality."

"Peter Pan was supposed to be fictional too yet here we are, so I don't think your argument holds much water. You're trying to avoid me. What happened while you were with the beasts?"

"What is this?" Mic completely ignored my question as she reached up to rub the exposed skin by my collar bone. I glanced down, only to realize the black veins were creeping down from my shoulder and on to my chest. Fuck. Tonight was supposed to be special. I knew if I told Mic about the deal I'd made with the bone faerie, she'd want all the scary details and it would cast a dark shadow over tonight's celebration. It was better to keep pretending it was nothing. Tomorrow was a new day. I'd explain everything tomorrow.

"It's just a bruise." I shrugged her off and tugged up my dress to cover the marks. "You're trying to avoid my questions."

"Nothing happened, alright." She huffed in irritation. "Do I find them attractive? Sure, of course. But any living, breathing woman would. And seeing that I was very nearly a non-living woman, you'll excuse me if I'm not quite ready to jump into a relationship right now. I'm still getting used to the idea of not being dead. I'm not anywhere near ready for men right now. You, on the other hand, have quite a bit to talk about. Like how you're managing to handle five men all at once? Have you told them about James yet?" Mic's face lit up and I had to stifle a groan. James was the last thing I wanted to talk about right now.

"He will destroy you," a dark voice hissed in my ear, and a chill ran down my spine. I'd heard that voice before. In the caves under the Temple Mount. I hadn't been in my right mind at the time, so I had ignored it. I'd forgotten all about it until now.

I whirled my head around, but no one stood out amongst the crowd. No one was even close enough to have whispered in my ear. No, no, no. I had enough to deal with and I was absolutely not going to give any credence to a voice that was apparently only inside my head. It had to be the bone faerie. I'd heard her voice in my head before, and although this one was different, it seemed like too much of a coincidence. Was this her way of toying with me? I physically shook my head to dispel the foreboding feeling.

Tomorrow I would deal with all of this. Tonight was for celebrating. I'd allow myself to wallow in my own denial for just a little bit longer. I redirected my attention to Mic. Focusing on her made my own issues fade to the background. Besides, I knew she was keeping something from me. She was moody and her shoulders were tense. I decided to wait her out, and I shot her a soul stripping glare. The silence between us was deafening.

"Fine," she huffed. "There is something I need to tell you."

"I knew it! Did you sleep with him? Poor Lu is gonna be so pissed if you slept with Nico!" My words came out in a rush, excited to hear the juicy drama that had absolutely nothing to do with my own fucked up situation.

"Shh! Will you keep it down?" she hissed, reaching up to cover my mouth as she scanned around to see if anyone had heard me. "No, I haven't slept with any of them."

"But you want to. Am I right? I know I'm right."

Mic rolled her eyes at me for a moment before her face became stoic. "I'm leaving, Gwen."

"Leaving? What do you mean by leaving? You want to go back home?" My heart rate picked up and anxiety bloomed in my chest. I'd finally accepted the fact that maybe I could have a happy life here in Neverland, and Mic was pulling the carpet out from underneath me. I hadn't considered what she would want once she'd been healed.

"No, I'm not going home."

"I don't understand. Where are you going?"

She took a deep breath before continuing, "I'm going with the beasts to the 2nd Realm." My jaw must have hit the ground, because Mic's worry lines grew even deeper as she stared at my face.

"I still don't understand. Why? Why do we need to go to the 2nd Realm?"

"*We* aren't going anywhere. You are staying here in Neverland. I am going to the 2nd Realm."

"No way. I just saved your ass from the Grim Reaper. You can't leave. You need me. We need each other. We have to stick together." My words almost sounded like a plea as my thoughts turned into a chaotic jumble inside my head. She smiled then, putting her hand on my face. "Sweetie, I will always need you in my life. But I don't need you to save me anymore. You've gotten me this far. I couldn't have done it without you, but I need to go the rest of the way on my own."

"What are you talking about? You're healed. There is no 'rest of the way.'"

"I'm healed, for now. But just like the faerie dust, the beast's magic is only temporary. Iver died before he could heal me permanently. I need to go to the 2nd Realm. Nico tells me they have the best healers in the cosmos there."

"And Nico's just going to take you there?"

"All of them are, save for Lucius." I was shocked yet again. The beast princes were leaving Neverland. This would be huge news for Peter.

"Why not Lu?" I asked, knowing that his affections for Mic were much deeper than he let on. I couldn't believe he would simply let her leave. The way he looked at her... that man would follow her to the ends of the universe if he could.

"It's complicated, and I don't really know the details. But apparently he's in exile here. He can never return home."

My heart broke for Lucius. He was a pain in the ass, but his grumpiness had grown on me and I'd developed a fondness I couldn't explain. Now, his grumpiness would be on a whole other level.

"Why can't I come with you?"

"You've already sacrificed so much for me, and I'll be damned if I let you walk away from your happy ending. You belong here, with these men. They complete you. I see it in your eyes. You love them— all of them."

I could hear the resolve in her voice. She was leaving and there was nothing I could do to stop her. "When?"

"The day after tomorrow."

"That's so soon! I thought we had time. I was looking forward to doing some normal, sister things for a change."

Mic peered around as the night's festivities surrounded us. It was magical. Pixies, satyrs and nymphs were mingling about, dancing to the melodic thrumming of drums, the air above them sparkling with faerie dust. "I don't think things will ever be 'normal' for us again, but I'm okay with that," she said, pointing out the obvious. "Plus, we have tonight, and I expect that you'll be there to say goodbye when we leave."

"We do have tonight.If this is anything like the last feast I attended in Neverland, I think you're in for quite a show."

"Will you do me a favor, though?" she asked.

"Of course."

"Keep an eye on Lucius for me. He's got a tough exterior, but really he's a big softie and I worry what'll happen to him when we all leave. He'll need a friend."

"You're asking me to willingly subject myself to his asshole-ish-ness?" I glared at her through squinted eyes.

"Oh stop, I know you enjoy the banter."

"Alright," I agreed, giving her a hard time even though I would have done it even without her request. "But you'll owe me big time when you get back."

"I wouldn't have it any other way."

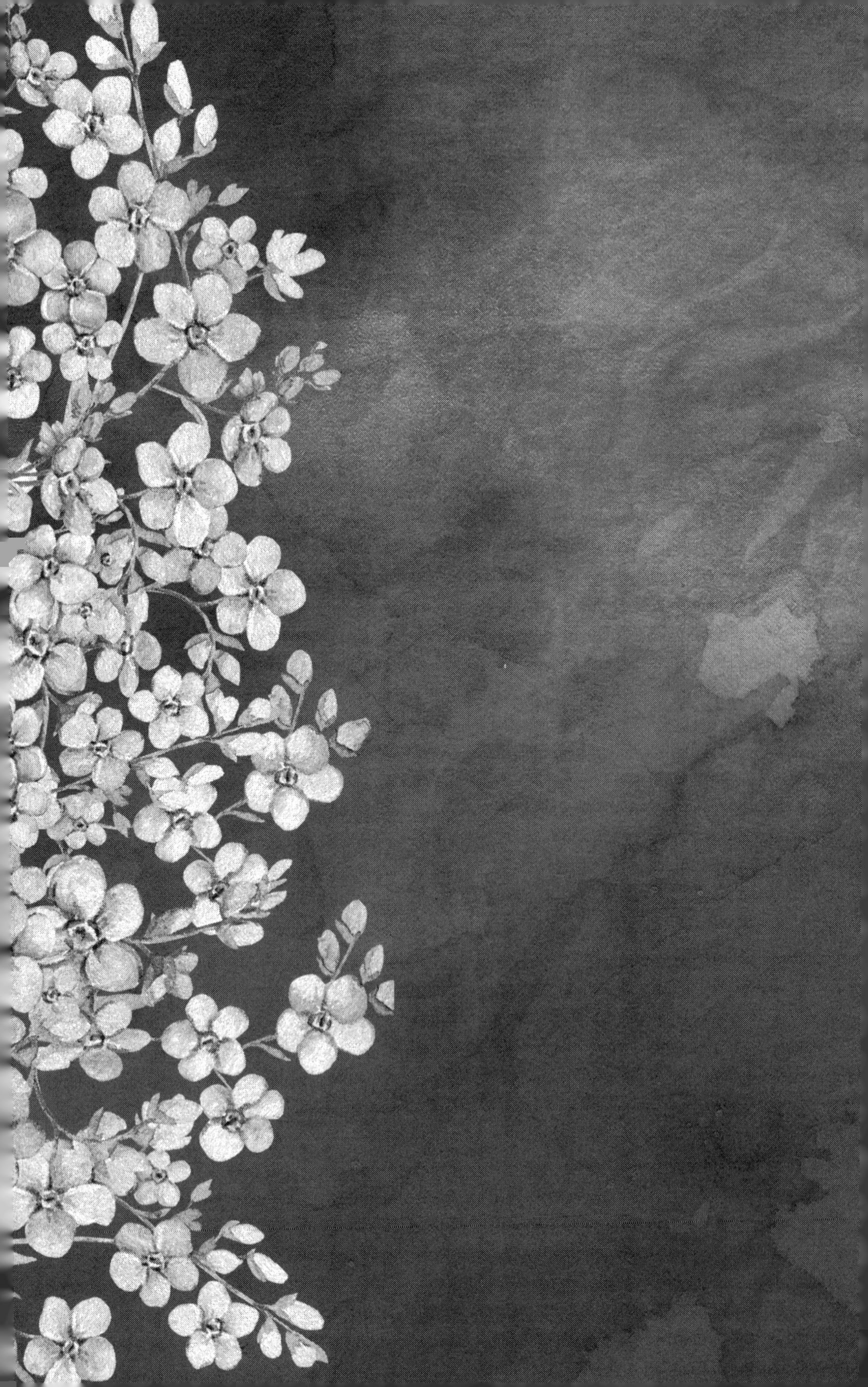

CHAPTER VIII
IT IS TIME
-GWEN-

Mic and I spent the night eating, dancing and drinking faerie mead. We ignored our men, making a conscious effort to focus on each other. It seemed we could never escape time. It was always fleeting, the grains of sand in the hourglass were always running out for the two of us. This time was different, though. This time, goodbye didn't mean forever, it only meant for now, and that was a much easier pill to swallow.

Without having to say a word, my boys gave me space. As if they could anticipate what I needed even before I did.

I felt their eyes on me, always on me. When I danced, I knew I was dancing for them. I'd lock glances with each of them, hoping they could read my dirty promises for later. The mead was making me bold. I finally had all my Lost Boys together again and I was ready to let them worship me.

"Excuse me, miladies," a jovial satyr approached Mic and I, interrupting my heated thoughts. "It's almost time. Please, let me fill your cups." He motioned to a ceramic vase in his hands that was ornately decorated and painted with symbols.

"Time for what?" Mic asked.

"The witching hour, of course."

"The witching hour?"

"The moon is reaching its zenith. A time when spiritual energy is at its peak. Pan will speak his words to life, and we will all celebrate with drink and devotion." He poured the warm liquid until our cups were overflowing before moving on, filling every cup as he went. I shot Mic a questioning glance, but before we could ponder everything the satyr had said, Peter was at my side. He smiled his cock sure smile at me as he slid his hand into mine. His piercing crow drew the attention of everyone at the feast. A hushed tone fell over the sizable crowd until all that could be heard was the snap and pop of the many bonfires. Peter paused dramatically, waiting until every eye was upon us. My insides were squirming with all the attention and I cursed Peter for not warning me about this. I had no clue what to expect next.

"Neverland... welcome. Welcome all. Man, Fae and beasts alike. I've brought you all here to unite us under one banner. For too long, we've been divided and I intend to bring us together. Tiger Lily was consumed by her own selfish interests. Neverland was never enough for her ideas of grandeur. But Neverland needs a leader, one who was delivered by the Divine. I was brought here to be Neverland's protector. Molded by the hand of the Divine, preparing me for this very moment.

It will not be easy, and we have a lot of work to do, but together with my leadership and your support, Neverland will prosper. So I'm asking you tonight, follow me into the future. Together, with my queen by my side, anything is possible! One leader. One land. Neverland forever!"

"Lies... all lies!" The voice was back inside my head, hissing its words into my mind. I tucked in a piece of loose hair, running a finger over the tender skin behind my ear where Eben's mark was still healing, hoping the rush of pain would dissipate the chill that brought goose bumps across my skin. This was not happening! I recited promptly to myself, dismissing the whole incident. Peter held his cup up to the crowd. "A toast! May the Divine bless us with love and abundance!" Peter called out. His eyes locked with mine, a triumphant smile on his face before he brought his cup to his lips and drained the contents.

The crowd erupted with cheers. "Long live the house of Pan!" they chanted back at Peter. Everyone tipped their cups back, sealing the toast with the ceremonial drink that had been passed out earlier. My mind was whirling with all the things Peter had just said. Most especially, the last part about me. Amara had coined me Queen of the Lost Boys, but I never viewed that as an actual reality. And now here it was. Peter would rule Neverland. I only had to decide how I fit into all of that.

Did I even want to be a queen? It was a preposterous thought. Only last year I'd been dreaming of going to university while I worked a dead-end job at a cafe. Hell, I'd barely been able to keep Mic alive and now the well-being of an entire realm was being placed at my feet and I was having a hard time wrapping my head around that. It felt like a fever dream at that moment. I tried to ignore the unease I felt and pulled the cup to my lips mechanically. As the warm liquid hit my tongue, recognition hit me. I'd know that root beer flavor anywhere. It was Lush Tea, and I'd just taken a large swig. I turned my attention to Mic just in time to see Lu snagging her cup before she put the mind-altering tea to her lips.

"I don't think you're quite ready for that yet, dove," he answered her questioning gaze.

"More like you're not ready for that yet," I snickered to myself. The Lush Tea swirled like a warm ball of fire in my belly and I was instantly light-headed. Lu growled at me, that paired with his over exaggerated scowl, and I couldn't help the giggle that escaped my lips.

"I'm sorry. Really, I am, but sometimes I just can't take

you seriously." My giggle evolved to a full-fledged laugh, and I was having a hard time reining it in.

"Think it's time for us to make our leave now. You still need your rest," Lucius said to Mic, his gentle tone completely different from the one he reserved for the rest of us.

"Yes, you're right. I'm exhausted. Gwen, sweetie, you'll come to see me off, won't you?"

"Of course. Wouldn't miss it for anything."

"Meet us at the den the day after tomorrow," Lucius grumbled. "Bring the atlas. Nico's fulfilled his end of the bargain. It's time to pay up, Darling girl," he sneered at the last part. Darling girl… he was such an asshole. But I wasn't totally convinced that he hated me. It was a love, hate relationship and I liked to think I was growing on him as much as he was growing on me.

"So now you're Nico's errand boy? Collecting his debts for him? That seems low even for you, Lu."

His glare would have knocked anyone to their feet, but I shot a smile back at him, getting some odd sense of comfort knowing that would piss him off the most.

"Not a minute past midday, or they'll be leaving without you," Lucius snarled, obviously butt hurt by my fit of laughter at his expense.

"Fuck off, Lu. Don't get your knickers in a bunch. I'll be there before noon. And I'll even bring the atlas because you asked so nicely."

I ignored the growl resonating from Lucius and

embraced Mic one last time. I pushed down the grief that was trying to bubble up inside me as she disappeared into the blackness of the Neverland night surrounded by her beasts. She would be back. This was only temporary. At least those were the thoughts I used to placate the sadness that would fill the void of her leaving.

As much as I didn't want to see her go, I could feel the tingle of the Lush beginning to take hold. I reminded myself that the last thing I wanted her to see was me losing myself to the tea and dancing naked before the fires. A warm breeze caressed my skin, and I shuddered at the sensation. Every nerve ending was firing, my body coming alive with the world around me.

I felt the warmth of someone approaching behind me, and his scent hit me. I pulled in a deep, contented breath as the cinnamon and leather undertones stimulated my senses. I moaned as Peter's body molded to mine. One arm banded around my middle while the other reached up to cup my breast. I closed my eyes and focused on the feel of his solid length behind me, slowly grinding my hips into his hardness.

"And how is the Lush, my queen?" he growled in my ear, the vibration of his words sending a shiver through me.

"Stimulating," I sighed. I opened my eyes to find my other Lost Boys were standing before me, their gazes ravaging me. Dark promises reflected in their eyes.

"How about we find," Peter started, his words interrupted as he kissed along my neck, "somewhere a little more private to enjoy the rest of the evening?"

I moaned my approval and Peter swept me into his arms. "Alright boys, let's show our queen a good time."

Peter walked out of the camp, all the Lost Boys in tow. The percussion of the drums fading to a slight hum. I paid no attention to where we were going. I could only focus on Peter. My fingers raked through his hair. The feel of the strands passing through my fingers was mesmerizing.

"We have a surprise for you," Peter whispered in my ear.

"Oh, I love surprises! What is it?"

"Then it wouldn't be a surprise."

"Well then, give me a hint," I begged.

"Okay, one tiny clue. We're headed to the Never Cliffs." As he spoke, I could just make out the sound of the ocean mixing with the distant thrumming of drums.

"The Never Cliffs? That doesn't help me at all."

Peter laughed. "Well, I won't keep you waiting." He placed me down on the ground in front of what appeared to be a half-finished house. "We'd hoped to have this finished, but I think it's rather fitting for tonight. This cottage is our gift to you. The place where our story begins." I took a step toward the structure that would eventually become my home. Now, it was nothing more than a shell. Four walls and no roof. A wave of warmth washed over me. I couldn't tell if it was a result of the Lush, but something pulled me to this place as if I belonged here. A certain sense of comfort that only comes from returning home and I felt tears prick my eyes.

"You did all of this for me?"

"Tripp put the most work into it. I think he should do the honors," Peter said.

Tripp swept me off my feet instantly and I let out a little mew in surprise. "I've got you, baby girl," he said as he nuzzled his nose with mine and my heart melted in my chest. He took one large step over the threshold. I was surprised to find that the interior was lit with hundreds of little candles and flower petals were strewn across the ground. He carried me to the back of the cottage into an enormous room that overlooked the ocean. The waves shone silver in the light of the new moon. He set me down on a large pallet, a makeshift bed of sorts, covered in pillows. My gaze drifted up to where the roof should have been, but it was wide open and the vast array of stars twinkled down on us. It was breathtaking.

"Welcome home, Hen," Ryder called from behind me as I stared wide eyed at the decorated space.

"How did you do all this?" I asked in wonder.

"Anything for our queen. We wanted to make tonight special. Let's just call it a fitting beginning to our happily ever after," Eben said.

"It's… it's beautiful." My words stuttered right along with my heartbeat.

"We plan to make some amazing memories in this place. Starting with tonight," Tripp said as he knelt down next to me, nuzzling against me and pushing my hair aside. Ryder joined us, taking up my other side, the two of them kissing up my neck.

"Holy fuck," the words escaped from my lips as the sensation of their delicate lips on my overly sensitive skin coursed through me. The Lush had taken hold of my body and I was ready to fall over the edge of ecstasy with my boys.

"Take off your clothes," Eben commanded as he watched Tripp and Ryder feasting on my neck. I slid to the edge of the bed, rising to my feet. Ready to please them in any way I could. Tripp and Ryder trailed their fingers against my skin as I rose.

"Well then, Eben, I guess you'll oblige me and undo my laces." I turned my back to him, waiting for him to come to me. I shivered as his fingers caressed the exposed skin of my shoulders, tracing down until he reached the laces. Instead of untying them, like any reasonable man would do, he pulled his knife, running the cold blade up my spine as he made quick work of the laces. He slowly dragged the dress down my body, his knife still clutched in his hand, grazing along my bared skin.

"Oh my Divine. Hen, you truly are the most stunning creature I have ever seen," Ryder breathed as he took in my exposed body.

I was surrounded, all of them converging on me like moths to a flame. Eben's hands curved from behind me until he was cupping and pinching both of my breasts in his rough hands. Ryder and Tripp flanked my sides, nipping and kissing at my neck. Peter stood before me, his hands clasping my face, running his fingers over my cheekbones before he pulled me in for a kiss. Not just any kiss. He was desperate, needy and passionate all at once. His tongue flicked along my lips, demanding entrance, and I granted it eagerly. Tripp's fingers grazed against my belly, dropping lower, and I groaned into Peter's mouth. My body was vibrating with need. The feel of my boys, the Lush tea rushing through my veins— I was desperate for more. There was a hunger inside me that had to be quelled.

When Tripp's fingers finally trailed along my clit, I broke from Peter's punishing kiss to let out a throaty moan.

"Yes! Please, don't stop," I begged, not needing to convince him. I knew if he stopped, I might shatter from the pent up desire inside me.

"Don't worry, Hen. We've got you," Ryder said as he tilted my chin towards him, claiming my mouth as he added his hand to Tripp's. While Tripp worked my clit, Ryder slipped a finger into my wetness. My body was literally weeping with need for them. Surrounded by my boys, my orgasm came crashing through me like a freight train. I came all over Ryder's fingers, shamelessly grinding on him as I rode out the waves of ecstasy. I felt limp as it receded and all four of them held me in place while I came down from the high.

Ryder brought his fingers to his mouth, still wet with my cum and licked them slowly, one at a time. "You taste divine," he breathed before laying back and positioning himself on the cushions. "Come here, Hen. I'm not finished with you yet." He beckoned to me. When I kneeled down over him, he grasped my hips, pulling me forward until I was hovering just over his face. He smirked up at me and then clamped his lips over my clit, his strong arms holding me in place as my legs trembled with the rush.

I felt the cushions dip and Peter positioned himself before me, unbelting his pants, pulling his hard cock in his hand as he watched me come undone on Ryder's mouth. His eyes locked with mine. "Open that pretty little mouth for me, my darling girl." The demand slipped sweetly off his lips and I immediately opened my mouth, reaching for him, pulling him closer. I wanted to be filled with my boys in every way. I took Peter's length to the back of my throat, but when I tried to pull back, I felt a solid body behind me and large, calloused hands slipped into my hair. "Take it all the way, my goddess. I want to watch you take it all for Pan." Tripp's sultry voice growled from behind me.

I felt lost in the moment, staring up at Peter as I pleasured him, tears leaking from my eyes, all the while I was coming apart for Ryder as he devoured me. It was a heady mix. I held it together as long as I could, trying to draw out my climax, but Ryder was relentless. I pulled off of Peter's cock with a pop and my moans filled the night air, joining in with the crashing ocean below.

"I get you first this time." Tripp was picking me up off Ryder's face as if I weighed nothing. A feral growl pierced the night, and Eben was beside us.

"And why should we let you have her first?" Eben challenged, violence dancing in his lust filled eyes. The two men glared at each other, neither one backing down. But my alpha males needed to learn to share.

"Don't worry, there is enough of me for all of you," I said calmly, placing a hand on Eben's bare chest and pushing him back a step. I turned to Tripp, feeling like it was my turn to control the group. I knelt before him, working his pants down, his cock springing free. I stared, getting lost in the sight of him. He was all muscle, beautiful tattoos scrolled across his body, his throbbing cock that was hard just for me, the tip glistening with his excitement. "Lay down," I commanded as I got to my feet, feeling a thrill of excitement as he complied.

"Come here. Let me own you," Tripp said, his voice husky with need. I climbed on top of him, rubbing his head through my dripping pussy and then sinking ever so slowly down every inch of his shaft until he was fully sheathed. I reveled in the sight of him, his eyes rolling in his head as his fingers dug into my hips. Before I started to move, I looked back at Eben, who stood behind me, stroking his cock as he watched.

"Now you," I said as I leaned forward, exposing my delicate opening to him. I felt a wave of panic— he was so big. Would the two of them tear me apart? But I trusted him to give me only what he knew I could handle. He bent down, running his tongue over my ass, getting me ready for him, and I moaned at the intrusion of his tongue. He spit in his hand and stroked his cock a few times before positioning himself behind me. He worked into me slowly, letting me adjust to the size of him, to the feel of them both filling me so completely. I tensed at the initial shock of it, but Eben stroked my back, rubbing his thumbs into my hips. "You take us in so good, baby. Just relax. Let the Lush take over." My body responded to his praise. The fullness of both of them inside me had my body tingling with pleasure. I wanted more. I wasn't done yet.

"Ry, I want you, too. Come to me," I called to my blonde Adonis. He'd been watching me take in his brothers, stroking himself as he took in the view. He cocked a half smile at me, but wasted no time, as if he already knew what I was planning. He knelt down at Tripp's head, holding his cock at the root. I shifted my attention to Peter, his dark hooded eyes watching the spectacle. "Watch me, King of Neverland. Watch as I make your men worship me." I saw his eyes flash with hunger before I eagerly pulled Ryder's cock into my mouth.

The feel of them, all at once, was overwhelming. My body was awash in sensation. Their bodies glistened with sweat as we began to move. Slowly at first. Eben pushed in behind me, shifting me forward in a chain reaction as I rode Tripp's hard length and took Ryder's cock to the back of my throat. The night was filled with their curses, moans and hisses of pleasure. A lusty symphony that was stimulating in its own way.

With each thrust of his hips, Eben sent a shock wave of pleasure through all of us. I tried to focus on pleasuring Ryder, swirling my tongue over his delicate head, hollowing out my cheeks and sucking hard. I wanted it to last. Ride on the edge of orgasm for as long as I could. Tripp and Eben fucked me slowly, teasing all of my sweet spots at once.

But when Tripp tilted his hips beneath me just right, it was my undoing. My climax ravaged me, every muscle clenching around my boys, and I knew I was taking them over the edge with me. I moaned through my orgasm with Ryder still in my mouth. With a curse, he spilled his hot seed down my throat. I heard my name carrying on the sea breeze as it swirled around us. We all collapsed on the makeshift bed, satiated and panting. The union of our souls had been bliss, and now we were back to being pieces of the same whole.

But the night wasn't over yet and Peter made damn sure I didn't forget. He swept me off the bed, pulling me away from the others and carried me to an opening in the stone foundation. One that would eventually be an enormous window overlooking the ocean far below.

"That's quite a show you put on for me, my queen. I never thought I could be so jealous and so fucking turned on at the same time." He dropped me to my feet and turned me around, bending me over the unfinished edge of the window, the rough masonry scratching at my stomach. "Now I'll have my revenge," he growled and slammed into me from behind. I let out a cry as his hardness met my tender flesh, but he didn't let up. One hand grabbed my hip, the other wrapped around my hair, pulling my head back. My vision filled with the endless expanse of the ocean. I was entranced by the view before me. The waves rippled like silver in the moonlight. Thunderless lightning skittered across the sky, as if jumping from one constellation to another. I was drowning in the beauty of this moment and I never wanted to surface.

"Our future is as endless as the sea. You. Are. Mine. Forever," he said each word as he pounded into me. Peter's pace quickened, the pleasure building until he was tearing another orgasm from my body and the two of us called out our pleasure to the Divine under the starry skies.

I'm not sure how I got back in the bed. I'd passed out at some point, my body pushed to its limits. But I found myself keenly awake. The glorious starry skies were gone, the candles long since burned out. I could barely see in the darkness. I felt my boys all around, random arms and legs draped over me, cocooning me. The warm weight of their bodies was almost suffocating.

"*Gwen..*" the dark voice inside my head hissed my name this time. It sounded so loud in the quiet depths of the night. I wriggled out from under my boys, doing my best not to wake them. I needed some air. I was too hot, that's why I was hearing voices, I lied to myself, fully indulging in my denial so I could stave off the panic attack that was brewing under the surface. The ocean breeze cooled my heated skin, and I sighed, feeling instantly better.

"*Listen to meee... It is time,*" the voice whispered, drawing each word out, and then my vision flickered. I wasn't in the cottage anymore. It was a bright sunny day, and I was standing in a meadow. I could make out two figures, a man and a woman, in the distance. They were talking, no, they were arguing. But I couldn't make out the words, only echoed sounds. The woman started to scream and thunder clouds rolled in, darkening the beautiful day. Her body began to glow and hum with power. She pushed the man to the ground with her magic and descended upon him.

"Hen—what are you—" Ryder's garbled words brought me back to reality. A reality where I was straddling Ryder, my hands in a death grip around his throat, the familiar feel of magic coursing through me.

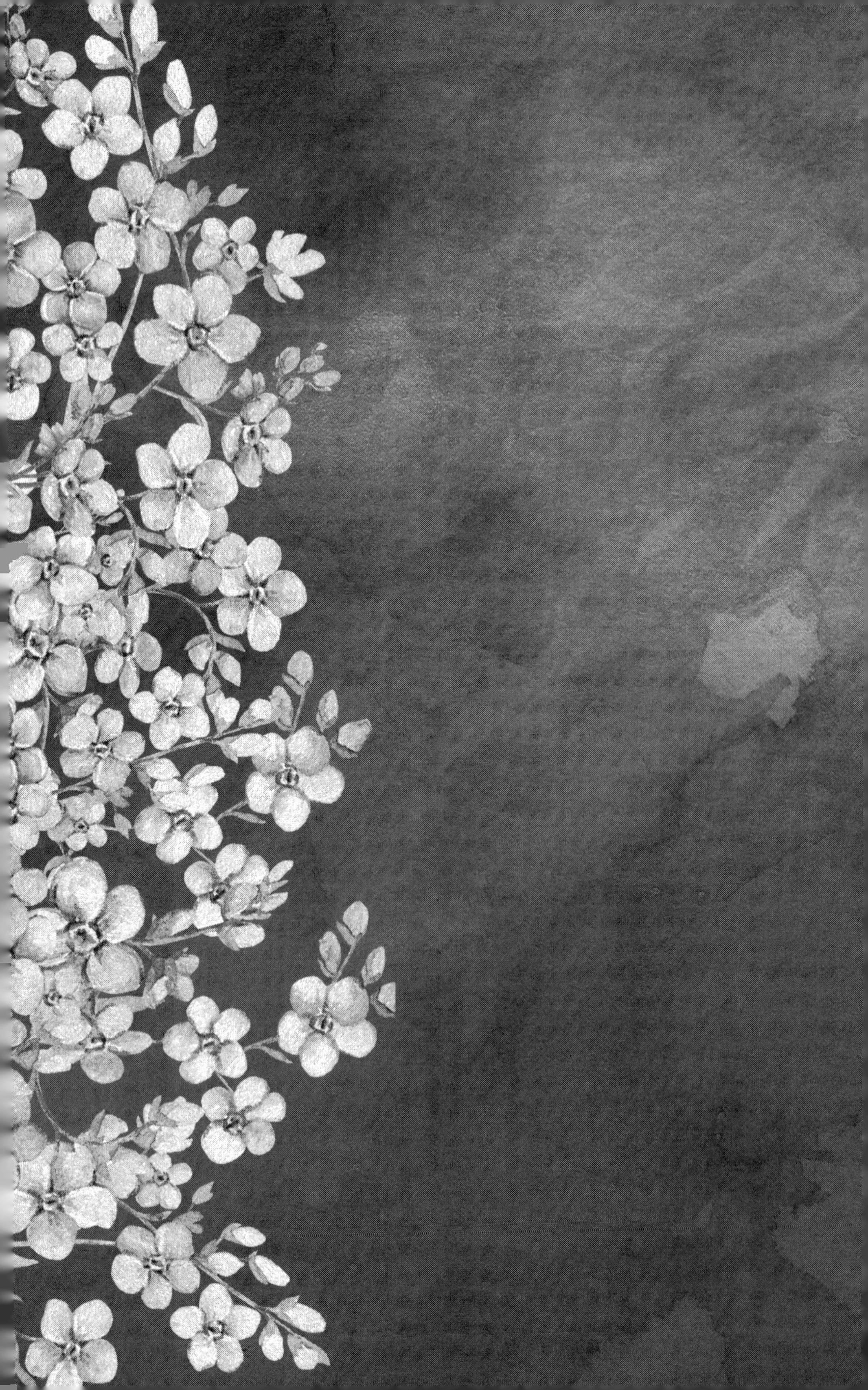

CHAPTER IX
THERE IS A PRICE
-GWEN-

I sat cross-legged on the makeshift bed while my boys paced the unfinished space of the cottage. Their faces were plastered with variations of the same emotion: fear. They were afraid. I wasn't sure if they were afraid *for* me, or *of* me. I'd lost myself somehow. Magic had taken hold of me and I'd almost killed Ryder. My cheeks were still wet from the tears that I hadn't been able to hold back once I realized what I was doing. What if I'd had a knife? I could have killed him while he slept and not even been aware that I'd done it. The magic I'd wielded that night under the Temple

Mount had been so powerful, it had consumed me. Now I was petrified of what I might be capable of.

Was that the price the bone faerie was trying to collect? Had my time unknowingly run out, and now my boys' lives were the payment due? Fuck! I had no idea what was happening to me. None of this made sense. I let my tear-streaked face fall into my hands. The feeling of helpless desperation threatened to consume me.

"I can't believe you didn't tell us! I thought we were supposed to be honest with each other," Eben seethed as he paced, his hands raking through his hair.

"I know… I mean, I have been honest with you. I was going to tell you as soon as the feast was over, I just didn't want to interrupt the celebration. I didn't think it was a big deal."

"You're hearing voices, and now you're trying to kill Ryder. I think that's a big fucking deal!" He was angry with me for keeping it to myself, but could I really blame him?

"I'm fine, Eben. She didn't mean it. It wasn't her. Cut her some slack," Ryder barked, jumping to my defense. Eben stopped short, looking deflated as he climbed on the bed with me.

"I'm sorry, that didn't come out right. I didn't mean what I said. I know it wasn't you." He took my hand in his, his dark eyes searching mine for forgiveness. "I just hate not knowing what to do. I don't know how to help you and it's eating away at me," he mumbled, his voice low, his words meant only for me.

"I saw something. It was like I was in a dream. A man and woman were arguing and then the next thing I knew, she was striking him down with her magic. What if that's an omen? A picture of what's to come." My voice wavered at the end and I felt disgusted with my own weakness. I couldn't control anything… my actions or my emotions.

"We need to find the Osakren," Tripp said, not giving any credence to the dire premonition I'd just shared. "We've put it off too long. The taint is spreading more quickly than we anticipated, and whatever is happening with these voices in your head, we can only assume it will get worse until your debt has been paid." He was matter-of-fact, hiding his emotions behind his planning.

"While we were arranging the feast, I sent men to the Temple Mount to search in case we missed it," Peter started. "They came up empty. But they also couldn't find all the bodies of Tiger Lily's guard. One in particular, Arion."

"That's probably our best lead. He's the only one of her guards who would have known its significance, and have the balls enough to take off with such a dangerous relic," Tripp added.

"He's disappeared. Not a trace of him yet, but I have men out looking for him. I need to get the morning update from Dain, see if they've heard any news. I instructed them to ask around during the feast. Maybe we got lucky and they have some leads." Peter nodded briefly and then ducked out of the cottage.

I felt utterly useless. A burden to the men I loved. Worse,

I was a ticking time bomb, and no one knew when I might go off. My first inclination was to run. I couldn't predict when the voices would return or when I might lose control again. I'd never forgive myself if I hurt any of them. I had been so stupid to believe I could simply ride off into the sunset of my very own fairytale. No, I was on a cosmic shit list for some wrongs I'd done in a past life and now I was meant to lead a life of suffering. The most loving thing I could do would be to walk away. Hell, I should curl up in a ball until the bone faerie's curse ran out, and she took my life as penance. Maybe that was mercy for all of us.

"Stop that shit right now, Gwen," Tripp's voice cut harshly, pulling me from my inner demons. "I know what you're thinking, and you just need to stop." He pulled me from the bed and left me standing in the center of the room. He pulled a pack from under the bed, opening it to reveal new clothes I'd never seen before.

"We will do this together, because that's what we've agreed to do. We belong to each other. We may not have made it official, but our souls are bound together. What happens to one, happens to us all." He pulled the clothing out and began to dress me, slipping on a pair of tight fitting black pants, a tunic top to match and cinched it all together with a leather bodice and knee-high boots. He reached under the bed one last time and pulled out Gage's sword. My sword. He placed the baldric over my head, settling it into place.

"I'm sorry, Tripp. I just don't want to hurt any of you."

"I promise I won't let that happen. Now it's time to be the warrior that I know you are. I need you to fight for me—fight for us. We'll figure this out, side by side." He kissed me solidly, and the doubt I'd been nurturing began to fade. Tripp was right. It may have been completely foreign to me, but this is what love looked like.

Peter returned with a tall Fae trailing behind him. "Gwen, this is Dain. He's my new general, leader of the Neverland Guard. One of the few Fae I can truly trust with my life. I think you'll agree." Peter made quick introductions and my mouth popped open in recognition.

"You! I know you. You helped me and my sister. You saved us from that plane. I never got a chance before, but… thank you," I said.

"Milady, it is good to see you alive and well," he said respectfully as he bowed.

"And… What news do you have? Any word on Arion?" Eben barked. His volatile temper cut our little reunion short.

"Nothing solid. Whispers of sightings have been reported from all over the island. It will take some time to follow up on all the leads," Dain reported.

"Rumors about him are spreading. He's become the phantom that's hiding in every shadowed corner of Neverland," Peter conceded.

"Fuck, so basically we have nothing." Eben stalked to the window, letting out an irritated sigh as he stared out at the ocean.

"We'll split up. We can cover more ground that way," Ryder offered, wringing his hands like he was chomping at the bit to get moving.

"Pan, there are some Fae that stayed behind after last night's festivities. They are requesting meetings with you today."

"Tell them that Pan's unavailable. We've gotta track down Arion and get the Osakren. That's priority number one. Gwen's running out of time," Ryder answered.

"I don't think it's wise that we tell anyone outside this room about Gwen's condition," Peter said.

"Is Gwen your dirty little secret now? Can't let anyone find out the leader of Neverland has a tainted mate?" Eben growled. Peter was instantly in Eben's face with a feral growl of his own in response.

"I will let that go only because I know you're not thinking clearly. But don't you ever fucking question my loyalty to her ever again, or I will slit your throat."

"Enough! Peter's right." I interrupted. "I don't want anyone to know about this. Peter should stay here. The last thing we need is for the Fae to turn on Peter. Neverland would get pretty damn hostile for all of us if that happened. The rest of us can go search for the Osakren."

"Spoken like a true queen," Tripp said.

"One last thing, Pan," Dain added. "Amara and her delegation arrived this morning. She is asking for…" His eyes darted to me, as if he wasn't sure if he should continue his report in my presence.

"Whatever you have to say can be said in front of Gwen. She is my equal in all things," Peter answered his unspoken question.

"She is requesting a private audience with the, the umm... Queen of the Lost Boys. I'm assuming she means you?"

My heart leapt at the mention of Amara. I'd missed her strength, her guidance, her friendship. I felt like she could truly see me, with all of my flaws, and still see the potential. I was eager to see her and tell her all about everything that had happened under the Temple Mount. Thank her for the Inalto. It had saved us all.

"There is a price for drawing on such magic." Her words of warning had been taking up space in the back of my mind and it nagged at me now. She hadn't mentioned what that price was. I hadn't told the boys about it, and I cringed. Yet another thing I was keeping from them. It wasn't intentional, at least at first it hadn't been. It just hadn't come up and apparently I was suppressing more of that night than I realized. Now I was just a coward. I didn't want to face the boys with yet another secret, especially Eben. I knew in my gut that secrets had a way of coming out at the worst possible time. Last night was a prime example, but I just couldn't bring myself to tell them.

"Yes. Where is she? I'll meet with her right away." My mood instantly brightened at the idea of seeing my friend again.

"Gwen, baby, we have got to find the Osakren. I'm sure

Amara will understand. Once we get this all straightened out, you'll have time to meet with her," Eben said.

"She says it's urgent," Dain was adamant.

"What if she knows something?" I tried to justify taking the time to meet with her, even though I knew Eben was right. Time was a luxury I didn't have right now.

"I'll meet with her, find out if she knows anything," Peter offered. "You go with the Lost Boys. They're best suited to keep an eye on you. And take Lill with you in case you need her magic to subdue Gwen." Peter tried to hide the pained look in his eyes, but I caught a glimpse before he slammed his mask firmly in place.

Tripp nodded. "It's decided then. We'll send Lill with updates once we've located Arion."

W₄ sᴘᴇɴᴛ the better part of the day hunting down every lead that Dain had on Arion. Each one a dead end. The man had simply vanished, and I began to get nervous that maybe he'd left Neverland altogether. We didn't have time to go on a wild goose chase, searching for hints of him around the entire cosmos. Even if we found him, there was no guarantee that he had the Osakren. The longer we searched, the more my thoughts turned negative.

"Cheer up, Hen." Ryder wrapped his big arm around

my shoulders. "We'll find him. I'll even let you castrate the bastard once we get our hands on him. The fucker deserves no less." I laughed at his outlandish plan, but then tried to rein it in. I didn't doubt for a minute that Ryder would offer up Arion so that I could part his balls from his body, and my stomach turned from the visual that played out in my head.

"Thanks, Ry. That may be the sweetest gift a man's ever offered me, but I think I'll pass."

"Mmmm, so close. Call the magic, take him down now before it's too late!" I stopped dead in my tracks, pulling away from Ryder's embrace, putting space between us. If the voice was back, I didn't know how long I had before it took over.

"Leave me alone!" I called out to the voice. I wasn't sure if the bone faerie could hear me, but the feeling of desperation made anything seem plausible at that moment.

"Yoooou know I'm right. Love has deceived you before. It will happen again. Love will break you."

"Stop it! Leave me alone!" I was begging now, desperately trying to cling onto my consciousness. My boys' lives depended on it.

"Gwen, baby, what's wrong?" Eben was by my side, his hand stroking my hair.

"Get away from me! I don't want to hurt you," I screamed at him, tears forming in my eyes as I pushed him away from me. I barely moved his solid frame and in the next instant, he was trying to pull me into his embrace.

"Love is a mirage. Don't be fooled again." The voice thundered in my head, shutting out every other sound. The

world around me faded and my vision doubled as the scene from the meadow tried to pull me into an alternate reality. My limbs felt heavy, and they began to move of their own accord. Fuck, I couldn't let this happen! My hand darted for Eben's belt, and before he realized I was no longer in control, I'd slipped one of his blades into my hand. The vision took over and again, I was standing in the same beautiful meadow, watching as the woman struck the man down.

No! This wasn't happening! I pushed against the invisible wall surrounding me. I pushed with everything I had until I felt it crack and the vision before me began to recede, just enough that I could regain some sense of my surroundings. Eben held me close to him, my arms wrapped around his neck, with the blade poised, ready to sink it into his back.

"You don't control me," I slurred the words through gritted teeth. I focused all of my energy and managed to deflect the blade in my hand, sinking it into my arm, saving Eben at the last moment. The world came rushing back to me. The pain cleared all traces of the voice from my mind. Eben jerked back when I started screaming, the blade solidly implanted into my arm.

"Holy shit! Gwen, baby! Are you alright?"

"Stay away from me! Please!" I clutched my arm to my chest as big fat tears ran down my face. The pain was immense, but my tears were for Eben. I'd almost lost control. I'd almost killed him. I reveled in the pain. It kept me grounded, kept me present.

"Gwen"—Tripp's hands were up as he approached me, as if I was some kind of wild animal—"let me look at your arm. Are you good? Are you with us?"

"Yeah, I'm here." I nodded at him.

"Will you let me take that blade out and get Lill to heal you up?" he asked, not moving, waiting for my approval. I glanced around at my boys. Panic colored Ryder's deep indigo eyes. Eben was still panting. I could tell he was processing the fact that I had almost killed him.

I took inventory of my body. The voice had gone dormant again, and the familiar twinge of magic had receded. I nodded at Tripp, afraid to speak, because I wasn't sure I could keep the utter terror out of my voice. Tripp's big hands gently pulled my injured arm away from my body. I winced as pain shot up my elbow, like fire burning my arm from within.

"Look at me, Gwen. Focus on my eyes." Tripp's words were soft and calming, exactly what I needed to hold my sanity together. I focused on his beautiful, moss green eyes. Focused on the love that reflected back at me. In the next instant, I was screaming. The pain of the blade being ripped from my arm was so overwhelming that my vision flashed white. Lill was nothing more than a flutter of glitter as my eyes flooded with tears. Tripp's hands cupped my face, drawing me back to him. "It's done. Take a deep breath. Let the faerie dust work its magic." I sucked in a breath, the pain subsiding. Once it finally became bearable, I risked a glance down at my arm. It was covered in blood, but where the knife had been only moments before was nothing more than a pink pucker of skin.

"Shit! Hen, come here." Ryder shouldered Tripp out of the way and wrapped me in his arms. "I'm so sorry this is happening."

"It should be me who's apologizing. Eben, I'm so sorry."

"You saved my life," he breathed. "I don't know what kind of dark magic the bone faerie put inside you, but you stayed strong. You fought it, and you saved me." Eben grabbed my good arm, pulling me from Ryder and wrapping me in a bear hug. "I love you so fucking much." He kissed the top of my head as he held me to his chest.

"I think the pain is key. My vision cleared, and the magic retreated once I sank the knife into my arm. Maybe it can buy us some time until we can get the Osakren," I said hopefully. It was a last ditch effort before I begged the Lost Boys to restrain me.

"I can't say I'm in favor of you hurting yourself. Let's try to avoid that as much as possible. But we need to keep moving. We're running out of options. I think we need to take a chance and head to the Mermaid Lagoon," Eben suggested, proposing a new direction for our failed search.

"The mermaids won't give us shit without Pan. He's the only one they are soft on," Ryder countered.

"Not true. You remember the time they tried to steal Tripp? I think they've been eyeing him for years."

Tripp chuckled a little. "I'm pretty sure they were trying to drown me, not seduce me. If it wasn't for Pan, my bones would be decorating their caves."

"It's worth a try. The sea carries all of Neverland's secrets. If Arion's still on the island, they'll know where he is," Eben pushed.

"Or we could die trying," Ryder pointed out.

"Well, I'm a dead woman walking at this point if we don't find Arion soon, so I say we go. Death by mermaid doesn't sound nearly as bad as facing the bone faerie's wrath." All the boys glared at me. "Alright, I get it. Death jokes suck. I think my family has a morbid sense of humor."

Tripp sighed, "Alright, let's give it a go. But at the first sign that they aren't willing to play nice, we're leaving. Understood?"

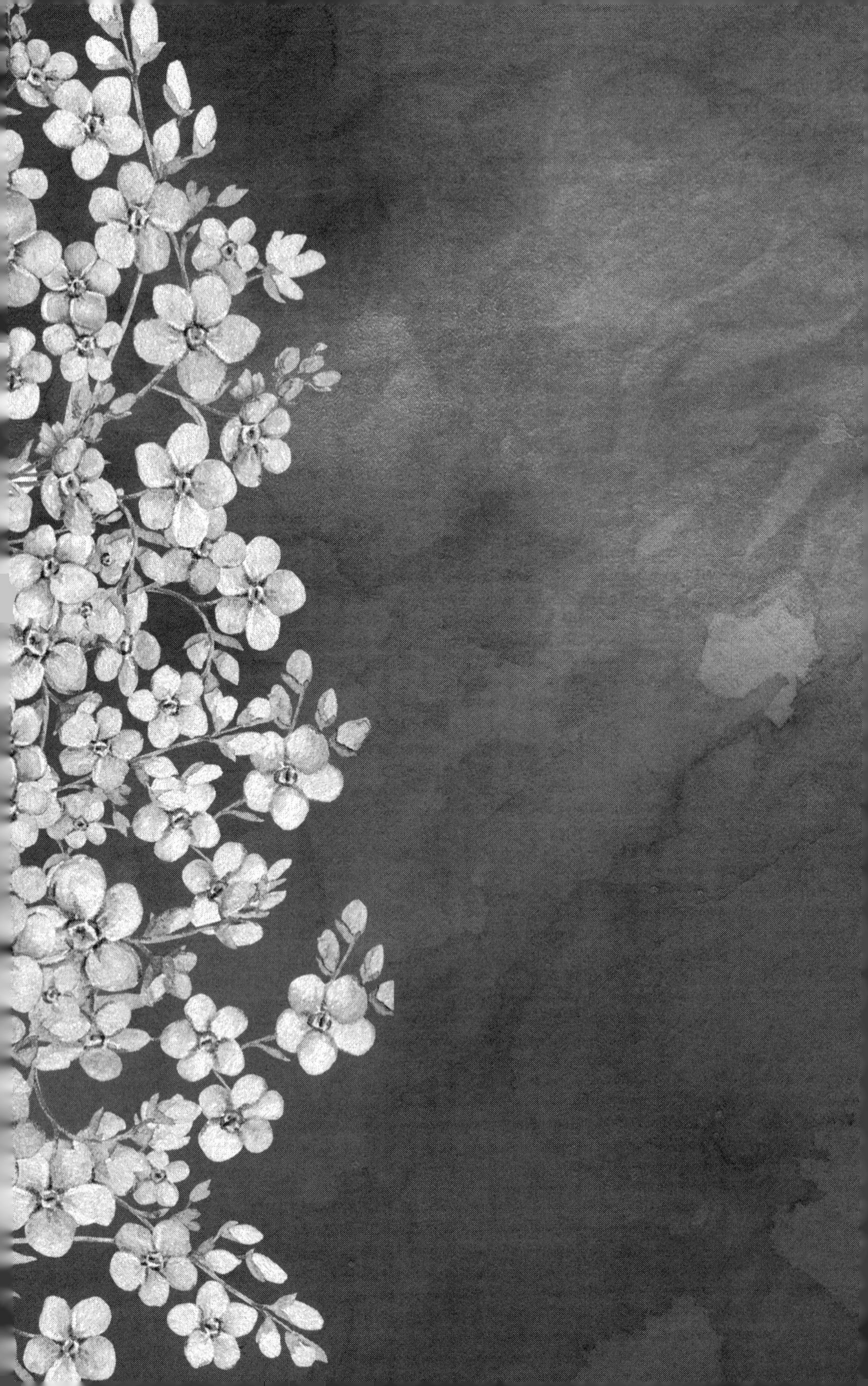

CHAPTER X
A MERMAID NEVER FORGETS
-GWEN-

The last time I'd been at the Mermaid Lagoon, it had been paradise— like walking into Eden. That was not the scene that awaited me this time. The smell was the first warning that things weren't right. The scent of death hit us before we even arrived. We'd all shared knowing glances and drew our weapons before we breached the forest and found ourselves on the beach. The pristine waters had receded, leaving a vast expanse of dead fish covering the sand. Lill began to glow blue, her tinkle of sweet melodic bells sounded almost melancholy as she spoke.

"Lill says that the mermaids are in mourning," Tripp interpreted her words for me.

"Mourning? Over what?" I asked, mortified at the death surrounding us.

"Mermaids are the goddesses of the sea. Like Peter is connected to the land, they are connected to the water. Something must have happened. A mermaid must have died," Tripp explained.

"I thought they were immortal?" Ryder questioned.

"They are, unless they choose to move on to the next life, or they're killed. Judging by the lagoon, this was not an intentional death." Tripp sheathed his sword as he scanned the desolate beach, looking for any signs of life.

"This is big. Pan needs to know about this." Eben's face was bleak as we walked along the beach, heading for the grotto.

"What would kill a mermaid?" I asked, feeling a chill run up my spine. Everything seemed to be falling apart. Could it be a coincidence that it was all happening at once?

"Only something vile. Something with powerful magic. We need to figure out what's happened and send word to Pan." Tripp led us into the grotto, stripping his clothes off when we reached the cavernous space. My cheeks heated at the sight of him and the memories of my first time with Peter came flooding back to me. What was wrong with me? The mood was somber and yet I felt a rush of wetness as I thought about fucking my Lost Boys in the grotto.

"We have to go into the mermaid caves. Lill, we need some dust," Tripp ordered. I followed suit, stripping my clothes off along with Eben and Ryder.

"Hen, wear my shirt. There is no way I'll be able to concentrate if you're naked. Even with my shirt, I'll probably still have to hide my hard on from the mermaids." Ryder tossed his shirt at me and I pulled in a deep breath of his scent.

"Well, how is that fair? I have to stare at all three of you naked," I shot back at him, trying to hide the smile from my face. This obviously wasn't a time to be smiling.

"Don't worry, we'll make it up to you later," Eben growled from behind me and I jumped.

"Gwen, my goddess, stop distracting the boys." Tripp winked at me. "Come over here and get some faerie dust."

"What's the faerie dust for?"

"Flying isn't the only thing it allows you to do. It also allows you to breathe underwater, and we've got a bit of a swim to get to the mermaid caves." Tripp caught me completely off guard, blowing faerie dust in my face. The tiny particles tickled my nose and coated my throat, sending me into a sneezing fit that had all the boys laughing.

"Fuck, Tripp! You could have warned me! My sinuses will never be the same!"

"I don't think I've ever heard a cuter sound," Tripp chuckled, pulling me in and kissing my forehead as if that would earn him my forgiveness.

"Stay close, Hen. The mermaids can be deadly, and they especially don't like women," Ryder warned.

"Gee, Ry, you're painting a really great picture," I retorted.

"He's right. They are dangerous, but as long as you show them reverence, you should be fine," Tripp added.

"You can be a submissive little thing, can't you, Gwen?" Eben smirked at me, conveying his lewd undertones. I shot him back a sassy smile of my own.

"Good girl," he purred. The cheeky bastard.

"Let's get a move on, before we lose all inhibitions and have an orgy in the damn grotto." Tripp reined us all in, bringing the mission back into focus.

Swimming with faerie dust wasn't as carefree as I envisioned it. I assumed I'd hold my breath and would have no need to take in another. I'd held my breath until I'd almost passed out, knowing that it would be just my luck that the faerie dust wouldn't work for me, and I'd stupidly drown in some underwater cave. When Ryder realized I was struggling, he showed me he was actually breathing in the water. It went against every instinct to pull the water into my lungs, but when I couldn't hold it any longer, I sucked in the water and it felt like taking in a deep breath. The cool water filled my lungs, as if I was sucking in a breath of crisp, clean air. I cursed the boys for not telling me how it all worked.

Once the initial panic subsided and I knew I wasn't going to drown, I could take in the beauty of the surrounding cave. Instead of being pitch black the walls were illuminated in bioluminescent algae, glowing in saturated blues, purples and greens. Fluorescent seaweed waved in the undercurrent and colorful fish swam in schools, circling around us as we went deeper into the cave system. We swam for what seemed like forever; the boys taking the lead.

I wasn't sure what to expect, but it definitely wasn't long, icy fingers wrapping around my ankle. In the next moment, I'd lost all sense of my body in space. It was as if a wave had picked me up and I was tumbling ass over tea kettle, my vision obscured by a thick blanket of bubbles. I couldn't see the boys anywhere. The only constant was the hand gripping me tightly.

The world finally came spinning to a stop as we broke the surface. "Breathe," a sickly sweet voice hissed in my ear. The cold hands pinned me to the solid body behind me, one wrapped around my throat, while the other held my wrists together. The arms constricted, tight around me, and with a cough, the sea water drained from my mouth and nose, glittering with faerie dust as it rejoined the ocean. It was almost painful to pull in that first breath of air. My throat was raw from the salt water, and oddly, the air felt foreign to me. I was completely disoriented, and it took me a moment to get my bearings. I was in an underground cave that closely resembled the grotto. The rock ceiling soared above my head, with countless crystalline stalactites that glowed in the darkness, giving the illusion of being under a starry sky.

The water before us rippled, and then my boys surfaced.

Their faces morphed into shocked expressions when they realized I was no longer following behind them, but in the arms of a potential threat.

"It was so kind of the Lost Boys to bring a gift with them. How thoughtful," the voice behind me spoke. It was definitely female, and her voice was as sweet as a bell as it echoed off the cavernous walls.

"We have come to give our condolences," Tripp spoke slowly, keeping any sense of panic from his tone.

"Those words are meaningless. They accomplish nothing. But an eye for an eye could help restore the balance," she hissed, her hand disappearing from my throat momentarily before I felt the sharp edge of a blade replacing the icy fingers.

Tripp's arm shot out just in time to stop a furious-looking Eben from advancing on us. He shot him a lethal glare, his look alone conveying more than any words could. "We are happy to offer you an eye for an eye. That is why we are here. But let us help you find the one responsible. She is nothing more than an innocent girl."

"Adira, bring the girl to me. She is no innocent— she is something more," an authoritative voice called out to us. The strong hands holding me loosened as the blade fell away. I twisted in the water, finally able to see my captor. The mermaid's face was so beautiful, it didn't seem real. Her hair was a dark blue, almost black, hanging in thick, wet waves around her pale face. Her eyes glowed turquoise in the muted light of the cave. Her blue tinged lips were pressed together in a hard line. These were not the docile mermaids you read about in fairytales. She was lethal.

Her hand wrapped around my wrist again, and pulled me further into the cave, bringing me to a shallow rock shelf where I was finally able to pull myself up. The cave was filled with different pools of varying sizes, circling around a centralized pool. The mermaids were all gathered around, their otherworldly eyes fixated on me.

They parted at once, giving way to a mermaid perched atop a small stand of stones. She was equally beautiful as the others, but she had an aura of authority that radiated from her. They all looked young, but I could see in her sage green eyes that she was ancient. This was the mermaid who would decide if we left these caves alive. "Bring the Lost Boys for your sisters. Their sorrows will be eased by feasting on the sight of them," she said, and I had to bite my tongue before my jealousy got us all killed.

"Come girl, let me look at you," her voice was as sweet as honey, luring me forward. Beautiful things in Neverland aren't always what they seem, and she was a masterpiece. Everything about her seduced you into her trap. Her brilliant orange hair curled over her ample breasts. High cheekbones, full lips and a multicolored tail was fanned out before her. I got to my feet, my legs wobbled as I put my full weight on them, and I took a careful step forward.

She closed her eyes, pulling in a deep breath of the salty

air. "Yes, I can smell the magic of the Divine. This girl has been marked. A favorite of the Divine. A heavy burden, to be sure."

"I'm not favored. I have never received any favors from the Divine."

"To be favored does not mean you are lavished with gifts, although I see the men she has gifted you are quite fine." My eyes flicked to my Lost Boys. They stood in a pool not too far away from me, cupping themselves as mermaids swam around them. I had no response for her. She was right. My boys were the greatest gift I'd ever received. "My name is Elordis, Queen Mother of the Mermaids. And you are?"

"I'm Gwen, Queen of the Lost Boys." The title slipped out before I had a moment to think about what I was really saying, I felt foolish the moment the words left my lips. Her brow raised in response. I'd piqued her interest, and I had a feeling that was something that didn't happen often.

"We've come to pay our respects. Can you tell us what happened?" I turned the conversation around. I was tired of her prophetical bull shit. Her riddled comments about a fate I apparently had no control over couldn't help me at all in my current circumstances.

"Welcome to our home, Queen of the Lost Boys. We are most humbled in your presence. We do not take kindly to outsiders, but I am willing to make an exception. I can see that Neverland depends on it. Come, let me show you." She beckoned me forward again and this time I went to her, confident that we were on equal footing, at least for now. As I approached the center pool, my eyes caught on a lifeless mermaid curled in a fetal position as she floated in a sea of flowers.

As I got closer, it became more apparent that she had died a painful death. Dark bruises covered her body. Gashes marred her perfect skin. A section on her tail was missing. I felt tears well in my eyes at the sight of her. Elordis clicked her tongue as she watched my expression. Her eyes missed nothing as she surveyed my character, and I felt almost naked in her presence.

She reached an elegant hand down to her fallen sister, pulling an iridescent shell from her hair. "You see, a mermaid never forgets," she started. "And we see everything the water sees. This was Alara, and this is her last memory. Would you like to see it?"

"It would honor me to see it." I felt a moment of awe. She was obviously offering me something sacred. Something only a few ever get to see. She gestured to a small basin beside her. Nothing more than a depression in the rock. She broke the shell open, revealing a perfect pearl that shimmered in her fingers. "Look. The water will show you." She dropped the pearl into the basin and the water began to shimmer. "What am I supposed to do now?"

"Drink." She nodded at me with expectant eyes. I had a moment of reservation. What horror would I see in this last painful memory? I let out a deep breath to calm myself… just go with it, I thought, as I scooped up a handful of the enchanted water and swallowed it down.

    I had been expecting to see a scene played out, like an underwater movie, but it was so much more. There were only fragments of images, sounds, smells and feelings cycling through my consciousness. Scenes flicked past my eyes so quickly that it was hard to focus. It was dark, but I could make out bound wrists, as if I was looking down at my own hands. There was blood everywhere. I felt her agony. Her fear gripped me. My heart was pounding in my chest. *"Tell me where she is and this will all be over,"* a deep, rich voice echoed in the memory. The next was a scream, followed by a scene that almost made me vomit. A beautiful man, dressed in white finery, used a jeweled blade to slowly cut the fins from her delicate tail, his sleeves pushed up so as not to get any blood on his fancy clothes. I rubbed my eyes, shaking my head until the vision dissipated, tears streaming down my face. The pain from the memory was so intense, it lingered even after the vision had left me.

    "That is… that was… awful," I breathed out. "Who is he?" I felt anger bubble up in my chest. What sort of person would do such a thing?

    "That is the bastard prince of the 1st Realm. Dorian," she drew out his name, venom lacing her words. I felt a chill run down my spine. It was as if I already knew that name. Somehow I knew it would plague me for the rest of my life.

    "Why? Who is he looking for?"

"The memory is eroded. That answer he has hidden within his magic. He's hiding behind the darkness."

"Do you know where he is? How can we help?"

"Eager to join into the battle of realms? I'm not sure you're ready. As it is, your soul is tainted. You have a parasite living within you." The way she said parasite made my skin crawl. I itched at the black veining that now covered my entire left arm and was curling its way down my breast and on to my belly.

"Another reason for my visit. I am hoping you could help me find something, or someone. I am looking for an ancient relic, it's a powerful—"

"I know where the Osakren is."

"You do?" I couldn't hide my excitement. "Please, I would be indebted to you if you could tell me where it is."

"It just so happens that we've been monitoring one wayward guard. Arion plans to make a trade for the Osakren. What a foolish Fae. You cannot barter with evil, and Dorian is evil incarnate."

"I need to get my hands on the Osakren. It's a matter of life and death."

Elordis dipped her hand into the pool before her, disrupting the still water. As the eddies reached me, I could start to make out an image. It was Arion, drinking from a stream, a dark forest reaching out behind him. Fear tingled in the pit of my stomach. I'd been here before. The sickly feeling of dark magic as it sunk its tentacles into you, spreading dread to the depths of your soul, was only something I'd ever felt in one particular place.

"He's in the Viridianwood," I breathed as the image of Arion faded.

"Hmm, you may not be as useless as you look, human girl. Yes, he is hiding right under the nose of the ancient one with the very possession she seeks. He's used her own cloaking magic against her. Quite genius actually. But he will not be there long. Arion is holding on to the relic, trying to sweeten the deal in his favor. But he's been given three days to deliver it, so your time to retrieve it is fleeting. Once the bastard prince has it, it will be lost to you forever. If he gets hold of it… all of Neverland will be lost."

"Where is Dorian now?"

"He is hiding, cloaked in his dark magic. He is stalking us in the In Between, a place both of this realm and not of this realm. But he will not stay there long. Neverland is ripe for the taking, Queen of the Lost Boys. Find the Osakren and then get your army in order."

I swallowed the lump forming in my throat. Just when life was supposed to be getting good, everything was falling apart. "Thank you for everything. And thank you for sharing Alara's memories with me. I hope she is swimming in peaceful waters with the Divine." Elordis cocked her head at me, still evaluating my character. Had she found me wanting?

"I have a gift for you." She pulled a shell from her hair and offered it up to me.

"Thank you. Is this one of your memories?"

"It is a blank slate. It's for *your* memories. Once you are gone, that is all that will be left of you. Fill it with the best memories, Queen of the Lost Boys, and you will have lived a worthy life."

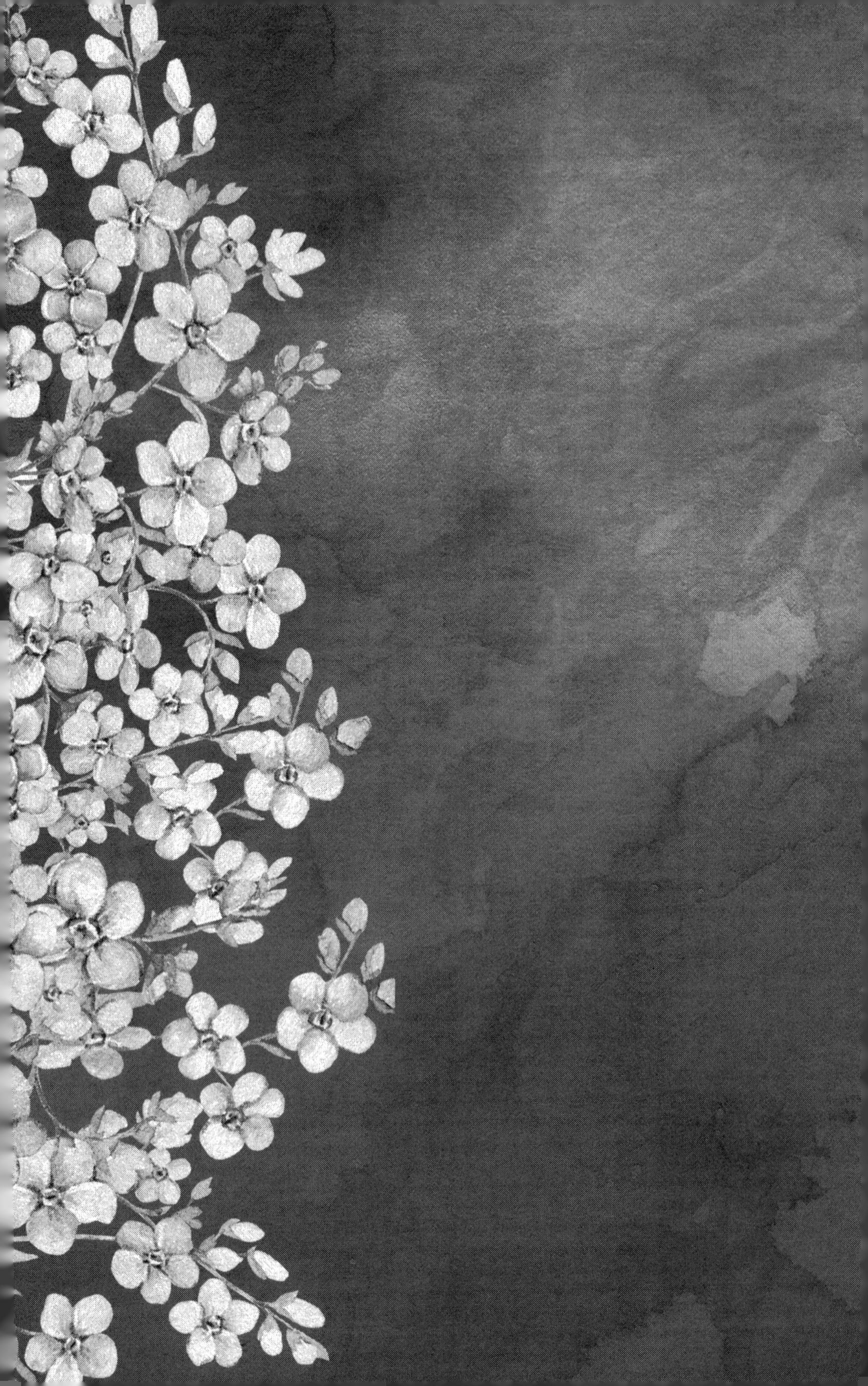

CHAPTER XI
PARASITE
-GWEN-

I watched as the night gave way to the gilded dawn. It felt peaceful in that moment before the night relented to the day. We'd returned to my half finished cottage after our encounter with the mermaids. It had been a long night as we updated Peter on all that we'd found. I listened intently as the boys made plans to extract the Osakren from Arion, and by the time my eyes began to droop of their own accord, we had a solid plan in place. I finally collapsed on the makeshift bed, surrounded by my boys. The lure of sleep was a tempting mistress, and I was eager to lose myself in her. But even with their comforting presence, it wasn't enough to ease my heavy mind and let me drift off into the oblivion I craved. I dozed on and off for a while, rolling around the bed in fitful sleep, until I couldn't take it anymore. I needed some time to myself, and the dawn beckoned me.

I sat on the precipice. My legs hanging over the lip of the cliff that dropped an easy five hundred feet into the roiling sea below. The undertow seemed to call to me, a peaceful alternative in the face of it all. It wasn't lost on me as the perfect metaphor. My fairytale life was hanging precariously on the edge and I knew clinging to the cliff, trying to claw my way to the top, would be the harder path. Today was going to be a rough day. Before we could take on the dangerous task of hunting Arion down, I had to say goodbye to Mic. Send her off to a whole new realm… without me.

I was losing the one person who really knew me. All of my past, all of my secrets. The one person I could talk to about this fucked up situation I found myself in. I was attempting to carry on a relationship with five men, two of which would rather kill each other than stay in the same room, all while trying not to die from a faerie curse.

And if that wasn't enough, I had to somehow refrain from killing my boyfriends because of a parasitic magic that I had no idea how to get rid of. Just an average day in the life of Gwendolyn Mary Darling Carlisle. I was exhausted, and yet sleep eluded me. I cursed myself for not being able to simply cuddle up and fall into a peaceful oblivion with the four gorgeous men sleeping in the house behind me. My mind was a fickle bitch, and the best I could manage was futile brooding over my problems.

"Greeting the dawn, my goddess?" Tripp's voice pulled me from my reverie. I turned and took a moment to bask in his glory. His taut muscles stretched away the sleep, his pants slung low on his hips. The morning light gilding his body in its golden rays.

"Couldn't sleep."

"It was Ryder, wasn't it? He treats you like his own personal teddy bear. I should tell him to cut that shit out."

I laughed at the casual conversation. I would love for my only problem to be that one of my lovers was too overzealous in his snuggling. "No... It's Mic." He sat down beside me on the cliff's edge, wrapping a supportive arm around me.

"Today's the day. Not ready to say goodbye?"

"No. I've never been ready to say goodbye to her. That's how I ended up in Neverland again, because I couldn't let her go."

"You know, you're strong enough to be your own person without her."

"That's a bit harsh," I said, bristling at his words.

"They aren't meant to be. You've never seen yourself clearly. I wish I could show you all the beauty you possess. Not just the physical, but your soul. Being a sister, a lover, those things don't define you, they only compliment the perfection that you are."

I huffed at his beautiful words. "No one's perfect, Tripp."

"To me, you are."

"Do you have any idea how much I love you?"

He pushed an errant strand of hair behind my ear, his moss green eyes piercing into me. "I think I have an idea. Maybe a fraction of how much I love you, but that's still a lot." He smirked at me, and I nudged his shoulder. I guess all that I'd suffered had somehow been payment enough for these men, and they were exactly what I needed to be whole. To finally believe in myself.

"Come on, let's give your sister a proper sendoff."

I'D TAKEN my time getting ready. Dragging my feet, hoping time would slow down and delay me from a farewell I wasn't sure I was ready for. All of my procrastinating bit me in the ass, because it was almost midday and I still wasn't ready.

Lucius's warning burned in my mind, *"Not a minute past midday, or they'll be leaving without you."* If the beasts took my sister before I had a chance to say goodby, no amount of time or space would save them from my wrath.

We made a quick stop at the camp. I'd stashed the atlas

at Peter's place, and I had to make good on my bargain with Nico. He'd come through for Mic, and it was something I'd never be able to repay him for, but I could start by returning the atlas. I barged through Peter's door while the boys waited for me. My heart nearly jumped out of my chest when I realized the room wasn't empty.

"Oh my god, Amara! You gave me a shock. I wasn't expecting you here," I breathed out, clutching at my chest. Amara rose gracefully from the chair she'd been sitting in, a warm, motherly smile on her face.

"It is good to see you again, my dear child." She grasped my hands, squeezing briefly before she pulled me in for a hug.

"It's good to see you, too. I've been meaning to meet with you. I've just been so busy. So much has been happening."

"I know, but we need to speak. It cannot wait any longer," she said firmly.

"I have to go send my sister off right now, but we can catch up as soon as I get back."

"You know they have ulterior motives for bringing her to Hiraeth."

"Hiraeth? What are you talking about? I don't understand."

"Hiraeth, land of the beasts, the 2nd Realm. They are taking her there because Neverland is no longer safe. The balance has been disturbed."

"Mic is going to the 2nd Realm to heal."

"That is only part of the truth."

"Well, if Neverland isn't safe, then all the more reason she should leave."

"There is so much that we need to discuss. Things are happening, and the Resistance cannot stand alone against the evil coming for us. But first we need to talk about the Inalto. I know you used it." Her tone was grave, and I felt an instant sinking feeling in my stomach.

"How did you know? I mean, I was going to tell you. There just hasn't been time."

"I can feel his presence again. I can feel it even more strongly now that I am here with you."

"Amara, you're not making any sense."

She let out a deep sigh. "I should have explained it better, but there wasn't any time. An Inalto is incredibly rare. When a Fae is killed in a particular way, the Inalto blooms from their remains. The fruit essentially contains their magic and a piece of their soul. When you consumed it, you borrowed that power and welcomed that foreign soul into yourself." The pieces of the puzzle began to click into place. *"You have a parasite living within you."* That's what Elordis had said. All this time I'd thought it was the bone faeries doing, when ultimately, it had been my own.

I swallowed hard. "So what does that mean now? You said powerful magic has a price."

"It's complicated. The price is different, just as every kind of magic, every soul is different."

"You know whose soul is hiding within me, don't you?"

I tried to catch her gaze, but she shifted her eyes to the ground. "I do," she admitted, her voice sounding guilt ridden.

"Who is it, Amara?" She didn't automatically respond, and my nerves got the better of me. "I deserve at least that much!" I shouted, feeling a bit desperate as the weight of everything felt unbearable.

"His name was Kían. He was my mate."

I tried to keep my jaw from hitting the floor. "Your mate? That can't be. The voice inside my head is... vengeful. It's evil. How could you have been mated to someone like that?"

"It's a long story, and I know that sounds like an excuse to keep things from you. I promise to tell you everything some day, but right now those details aren't important. I know you must see your sister off. But I had to warn you. I believe he's trying to relive what happened between us, only he's trying to create a different outcome. He will try to use you as a surrogate to accomplish that task."

My head was spinning with all that was going on. The scene at the meadow flashed in my mind's eye. "The meadow. That was you. That's when you killed him," I whispered as it all seemed to come together. I shook my head and pinched the bridge of my nose to clear my thoughts. "Let me get this straight. You killed your mate in some lovers' quarrel and now he's trying to exact his revenge by making me kill mine?"

"There's so much more to it than that. I always loved

him, even to this day my soul pines for his, but I had no other choice.

"What do I have to do? What is the price I have to pay to rid myself of his spirit?" My voice wavered as I waited for her to spell out what fate I would have to face to get rid of this parasite.

"I'm not completely certain. Like I said, Inaltos are rare. I've only ever read about them in books. An Inalto only blooms when a Fae is betrayed by their own mate. The spirit cannot rest until balance is restored. From what I can gather, either he'll fulfill his vengeance and one of your Lost Boys will die at your hands, or you'll prove him wrong. Prove that love is a sacrifice."

"A sacrifice? So either this spirit forces me to kill one of my boys, or they have to sacrifice themselves for me? Sounds like either way, I'm losing one of my boys and that is not acceptable. I will never let that happen."

"I'm sorry. I tried to warn you that there was a cost to using magic. But I don't regret it. I had to ensure that you and Peter survived that night. You are too important. May the Divine surely cast me into the underworld for all of my sins, but I would gladly sacrifice one of your Lost Boys, if it means that you survive." She sighed deeply as she took in my face. Could she see my soul cracking with the weight of her words?

"My dear child, I am sorry. You are a chosen of the Divine, and that is no easy burden to bear." Her face fell, but not before I saw the tears spill from her eyes.

"A chosen of the Divine," I huffed at the absurdness of it all. "First the mermaid queen and now you. Why are you telling me this now?"

"Because it is almost time. The Divine has gifted me with the sight, and I've seen that you are the catalyst that can bring balance back to Neverland."

"Amara, I don't care who you think I am or what role you think I have to play, but I won't allow one of my Lost Boys to die for me. There has to be another way to get rid of his spirit. I have to go see my sister, but I promise I'll figure this out. Do you know how long I have?"

"I don't know for certain. His soul will continue to feed off of yours, corrupting you. He will eventually become too strong for you to control. You must tell the Lost Boys."

"No! Absolutely not. They are never to know about this. Promise me, Amara."

"I cannot promise that. They are impacted by this. They must have a choice in how it all plays out." She stared at me, incredulously, as if I'd completely lost my mind.

"If they knew, one of them would run off and sacrifice themselves in some senseless act to save me. I won't allow that to happen. There has to be another way and until I can figure that out, you must keep this between the two of us."

"I don't like it, Gwen. If one of them dies by your hand, even if it's not you who wields the blade, it would be much worse than the alternative."

"The Divine gave them to me. I am their queen. Allowing them to become a martyr for me isn't acceptable. I will find a way to deal with this. Please, I'm asking you to keep this a secret for now. I promise I will find a way."

She huffed in resignation, "Go and see your sister. I will keep your secret for now. I will start searching through the old texts and see if I can find any alternatives."

"Thank you, Amara. Is there anything I can do to keep him at bay? Weaken him so he cannot take over my body?"

Amara tapped her finger on her chin. "His spirit is like a leech, feeding off of your magic. There is a plant. A cursed plant the Divine has spread across every realm. It weakens magic. Maybe it could buy you more time."

"Yes, that's exactly what I need. What's it called? Where can I get it?"

"Moonflower. But it should not be taken lightly. I can't even guarantee that it would work. It will make you physically sick, alter your mind. And you can only take it for so long before it affects your magic permanently. If you take enough of it, it will destroy you."

"I can handle it. I'll be careful. I have but a few grains of magic anyway. Losing it wouldn't make any difference."

"It will, my child. Your magic is still growing within you. It's more a part of you than you realize. You won't be the same person if you lose it."

"It's a chance I have to take. Anything to buy us some more time."

"Because of its properties, it is destroyed the moment it blooms in most realms. It isn't something that's used in polite society. I suspect that your Captain Hook could get some for you."

Damn. That would complicate things. James would want to know what it was for. Would he give it to me if I insisted on keeping the details a secret? Would that cast a dark shadow over our budding relationship? I felt like I was being cornered into deceiving all the men in my life, and the feeling of helplessness threatened to take over.

"Are there any other options?"

"None that would be quick."

"I'll work on it. But Amara, I have to go. I can't be late to see my sister off."

"A word of warning. Until you get that root, try to stay away from anything with magical properties. They will only feed his corrupt magic and make him stronger. There are many things that contain magic here in Neverland, from tea leaves to simple fruits. That means faerie dust as well."

Perfect. I had a million things on my plate and now I'd be slowed down without being able to fly. "It can't be helped today. I'll never make it to the den in time if we walk. The last time he tried to take over, I sank a blade into my arm. It shut him down immediately. Could my pain have an effect on him?"

Amara cringed at my admission. "It's possible. He needs a healthy host. If you die, he dies with you," her words trailed off, and I could hear a certain sadness within them. A chill ran down my spine as what she said began to take shape in my mind. She'd just given me my failsafe, and she knew it. If I couldn't fix this, I could take my own life and end it all.

"But that is not an option, my child. If you die, Neverland will be plunged into darkness." Her words were stern, but all I could give her in response was a sad smile. If it came down to my life or one of my boys, it was a simple choice. She took a tentative step toward me, placing a hand on my cheek. "I'm so sorry, Gwen." Her eyes searched mine, as if she was looking for any sign of her jaded mate inside me. "Kían… I know you're in there. I know you can hear me. I need you to know that I'm sorry. I had no other choice," she said pleadingly.

I could feel the foreign magic begin to tingle in my gut. Amara had stirred the sleeping dragon within me, and for the first time I recognized it as the parasite that it was. It was evil. Before I could stop it, my arm shot out, grasping her slender neck in my hand. I could feel my fingers digging into her skin, but I couldn't get my hand to release. I stared at her in abject horror, as her bewildered eyes began to bulge, the edges of her lips turning blue as I cut her airway off. Her nails scraped down my arm.

"Gwen?" Peter's voice calling for me was enough of a distraction for me to take back control. I promptly released Amara's throat before Peter entered the room, and she doubled over, coughing and sucking in deep breaths. "Gwen, is everything alright?" He took a couple of strides toward me and Amara.

"No, Peter," Amara spluttered through coughs, holding

her hand up to stop his approach. "I'm fine. Just a little tickle in my throat is all."

Peter looked her over warily. "Gwen, are you ready to go? We'll be cutting it close if we don't leave now."

"Yes, Amara just wanted to say hi, and I lost track of time. Let me grab the atlas. Amara, I'll see you soon."

"Do be careful out there, my child."

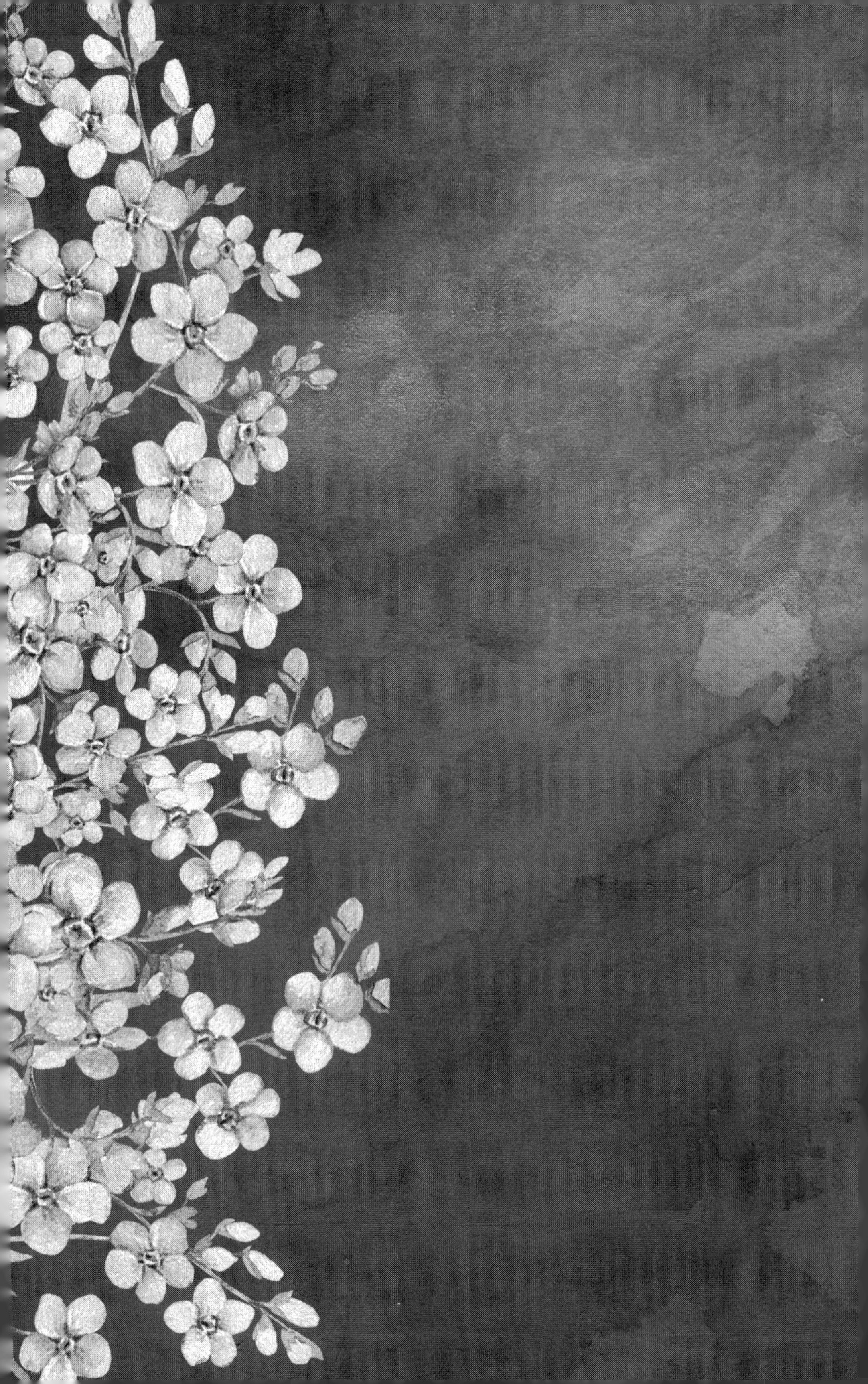

CHAPTER XII
LOQUENTES CARTIS
-GWEN-

I retreated into myself as we flew to the den. My mind was whirling. Everything was a fucking mess. Too much was happening all at once. I was so overwhelmed that I felt paralyzed. I didn't know where to start. If the Divine was trying to test me, I felt like she was probably sorely disappointed with her so-called 'chosen one'.

I'd palmed a jagged rock before taking my ration of faerie dust, crushing it in my hand until it pierced the skin. The pain cleared my head and kept Kían at bay for the moment. I wasn't taking any chances since the faerie dust could lure him out. I hid it from the boys, letting them think that my somber mood was nothing more than my sadness over Mic's departure. They remained my ever steady companions, staying strong while I was obviously falling apart. But even that was tainted now. I couldn't keep them close, not while I knew I was a danger to them.

I was desperate to get to Mic. It was bitter sweet knowing that I had to keep all of this from her. If she knew, she'd never leave, and I wouldn't let her sacrifice her healing for me, not after coming this far. But being in her presence for what little time we had, would soothe my soul, the part that still belonged to me.

The dark, moss-covered walls of the den rose out of the mountain, its soaring towers disappearing into the thick mist. Lucius awaited us, standing stoic at the massive wooden doors of the castle. I gasped when I looked at him. He was dressed in finery, his dark hair styled away from his clean face. He wore polished black boots, with twill breeches, and a long, black military style jacket with crimson lapels and embroidered gold accents. It was the first time I'd ever seen him look like the prince he was.

"You're late," Lucius growled.

"Nice to see you too, Lu," I said sarcastically. "It's about time you took a bath and put on some new clothes. You clean up nice." I smirked at him, delighting in the dark scowl he shot at me.

"Wish I could say the same for you. I can still smell the stench of too many men on you," he grumbled.

"Fuck off, Lu. I'm not here to see you anyway. I see they've reduced you to the butler these days. Really moving up in the world." He growled at me and I had to hide my shit-eating grin. Trading insults with Lucius somehow calmed my nerves. It felt like being in the presence of an old friend, and it was comforting.

"After you, Queen of the Lost Boys," his deep voice raised in pitch to a falsetto, mocking my title, and I burst out laughing.

"Thanks, Lu. That just made my day."

"It's Lucius. Luuu-ciusss! Not Lu."

I let it go, knowing he secretly loved that I called him Lu. But I think he loved giving me a hard time about it just as much.

"What will happen to this place after they leave? Are you getting an upgrade?" I asked as we walked the grand halls of the castle, noting that everything had been covered in sheets.

"Not my scene. It will be closed up and kept shuddered until the princes's return."

"Seems like a waste. Maybe we can throw the next feast here. What do you say, Lucius?" Ryder asked, excitement clear on his face at the idea of a party in the grand space. Lucius responded with a dismissive growl that reverberated in the hallways, effectively shutting down any further conversation.

We walked the rest of the way in silence, passing through countless corridors for an absurdly long time.

Lucius led us through another set of outrageously large doors, opening up to a magnificent garden. Lush, neatly trimmed hedges splayed out in geometric patterns along the ground. Vibrant flowers were blooming all around. The courtyard was buzzing with various animals, and at the center of it all was Mic.

She looked like a princess in her hunter green dress. Her chocolate hair was braided away from her face. I smiled as I looked at her. I wanted to remember her exactly as she looked right now. A flurry of birds fluttered around her as she smiled in awe, a slight blush to her cheeks. I felt like I was watching a scene from a Disney movie.

"Gwen! Sweetie, I'm so glad you're here," she squealed when she saw me. She ran across the garden, barreling into me with her exuberant embrace.

"Come, I made tea. Let's sit and enjoy the garden for a bit." She grabbed my hand and pulled me to a long table that was set with tea and snacks. The rest of the beast princes joined us, and the garden seemed to get very small, very quickly. Mic didn't seem to notice, but each of the seven princes had one eye on her at all times.

"Sit down, have some tea. I'll be right back. I've got a present for you." She kissed my forehead quickly and rushed out of the garden, Lucius following discreetly behind her.

"Pan, daughter of Wendy, we're pleased you all could make it," Nico said, bowing slightly to us in a warm greeting. Something about his typical harsh demeanor had softened.

"I would have hunted you down if you'd taken my sister before I'd had a chance to say goodbye."

He chuckled a little. "I don't doubt that one bit. But we have things to discuss in Michaela's absence, so I'll get right to the point. I know you're still seeking the Osakren, and I would bet that underneath those long pants and sleeves, the bone faerie's mark has all but covered you. As a consideration for Michaela, I've done my best to locate the relic for you. I've stumbled across some grave news that I must share with you all. But before I go into the details, you must promise me to keep this between us. It's imperative that Michaela does not know, and I think you'd agree that's in her best interest."

"Let's get a few things straight, my sister's health and well-being are my number one concern. I know she'd never leave if she knew the trouble I was in. But you're not being honest with her. You're fleeing Neverland. You're taking her out of harm's way."

"Gwendolyn—"

"I'm not faulting you for that, Nico. But I need to know why. I need to know why you and your brothers have such a vested interest in a frail human girl. Can I trust you with her safety?"

Nico's brow furrowed and his typical scowl returned as if I'd just insulted his honor. "No one can protect Michaela like we can, I promise you that." He stalled for a moment, his eyes darting to each of his brothers while he contemplated what he would tell me. "There is a prophecy.

A founding prophecy that dates back to the dawn of Hiraeth. I won't go into detail, but there's mention of a woman. A woman who's pivotal in the future of our realm. I believe Michaela is that woman."

I had to stop myself from rolling my eyes. What were the odds of both Carlisle sisters being woven into the fate of not one, but two realms? "Are you fucking with me, Nico? I know she's beautiful. If you're looking to start a relationship, you have my blessing. But it's bad enough that you're lying to her. Don't lie to me, too!" I banged my fist on the table, my irritation simmering to the surface.

He glared at me for a moment before producing a small, leather-bound book from the inside pocket of his jacket. He flipped through the pages rapidly and slammed the book on the table. One side contained text in a language I'd never seen before, while the other contained a startling image. A woman sitting astride a bear, flanked by six others. Blue lines of magic connected the group. It was a beautiful depiction, but what chilled me to my bones was that the image was the exact likeness of Michaela. There was no mistaking that it was her.

"I told you once, I'm a man of my word. I would die for her and so would everyone of my brothers. I give you my word that she will be safe."

I nodded slowly, still staring at the picture of Michaela. Feeling insignificant in the shadow of the cosmos. I didn't need any further proof that our lives weren't our own.

"Now that that's settled. I have news about the Osakren."

"It's in the Viridianwood," I said stoically.

He cocked an eyebrow at me. "You never cease to surprise me, daughter of Wendy."

"We have a plan to retrieve it." Peter started. The boys had let me lead the conversation as it pertained to Mic, but I could tell they were eager to see what news the beasts could offer in our quest to recover the Osakren.

"We're going after Arion the day after tomorrow. He's set to make a trade. Once he leaves his hiding spot, we'll make our move," Peter concluded, laying out the core details of our plans for the beast prince.

"A word of warning, Pan. That trade must never happen. The bastard prince is lurking in the shadows of the In-Between. He's been waiting a millennia to sink his claws into one of the realms. He's been looking for a seat of power, and Neverland awaits to be conquered."

"I won't let that happen," Peter snarled.

"Don't underestimate this Fae. He has your advantage in every aspect. The strength of his magic far exceeds what you're capable of. If he gets his hands on the Osakren, then all is lost, and you'll need to get Gwen out of Neverland." Nico's words were harsh, and I could see Peter's jaw clench as he absorbed the gravity of his warning.

"What can you tell me about this bastard prince?"

"Dorian is an elusive fucker. A demon biding his time in the shadows. There are only a handful of texts, they contain little more than whispers. Many believed him to be a legend. I will give you what I have. But you must prepare the island. Dark days are coming."

"And what about the beasts? Can I count on the beasts as an ally in this fight?"

"Lucius will command the beasts on the island. This is their home as well, and they are prepared to fight to the death to protect it. One of my most trusted comrades has been stalking Arion, keeping tabs for me. I am assigning him to you, to help recover the Osakren. And for an extra pair of eyes on Gwen to help keep her safe in our absence." Nico snapped his fingers, and in a moment, an enormous white wolf padded into the garden. The sound of fluttering wings filled the air as the animals scattered with his arrival.

"Alo!" I called out to the wolf, a smile tugging at my lips as my heart warmed to see him again. He whined in response, and I felt his greeting poking at my mind as if he'd spoken it aloud. He wasn't just a typical wolf, he was so much more.

"Alo will be your companion while we are gone. Michaela insisted, and Alo here has a soft spot for her. I guess it's fitting, though. Wendy, herself, had a wolf. And, of course, Lucius will offer his sword to the cause."

"Thank you, Nico," I said, sincerity ringing clear in the words. "I have something for you as well." I pulled the pack off my back, opened the flap, and pulled the ancient atlas from the bag. "I should have given this to you sooner. Consider our bargain fulfilled."

Nico's eyes lit up as his hands curled around the worn leather cover. "This atlas has been in my family for thousands of years. It was a pleasure doing business with you, daughter of Wendy. Best deal I ever made."

The beasts shifted their focus as Michaela rushed through the giant doors, clutching a package to her chest. Her face flushed as she hurried back to me. She plopped herself in the chair beside me. "A month ago, I couldn't even get out of bed without help, and yet it's still annoying when I get winded running across the world's largest castle." We both laughed, breaking the tension. She handed me an ordinary wooden box tied with a gold ribbon. She looked at me expectantly, her eyes wide with excitement. I could see that she was about to burst with the secret she was keeping.

"Go on, open it!" she prompted, a broad smile stretched across her face.

I pulled the ribbon and lifted the lid from the box. My heart promptly migrated into my throat. I stared in disbelief, tears welling in my eyes. I'd promised myself that I wasn't going to cry today, at least not in front of her. I was determined to hold it together for Mic's sake. I had to take a steadying breath and blink away the tears. Nestled inside the box was a perfect replica of my throwing knife.

"I promised I'd get this back to you one day," Mic said softly as she pushed my hair from my face.

"You took it. In the stairwell. You took the remnants of my blade." I recounted. My mind was transported back to the MSV Estrella, in a cold stairwell. *"I'm going to give you this blade back whole."* I'd dismissed the idea, not entirely sure we'd survive the night. But Mic had made good on her promise. I ran my finger along the blade, the vein of faerie dust sparkling in the afternoon light, trying to rein in my emotions before I made a fool of myself in front of all these men.

"I had to get this back to you. You sacrificed so much for me. It's the least I could do. Everyone pitched in. Lill provided the faerie dust, Eben and the Lost Boys helped with the design. Lucius even helped to forge it."

"Mic, this is… this is perfect. Thank you so much." I pulled her in for a hug, still choking back the tears. "I have something for you as well. I can't really say it's a gift, since it's already yours." I reached back into my pack. Trying to distract myself from the well of emotions that had me teetering on the edge of being a blubbering fool. My hands slid over warm metal, and I curled my hand around the familiar object.

"You're the oldest. It belongs with you." I placed the heirloom locket around her neck. I grabbed the gilded acorn, opening the locket to reveal the miniature photograph of Mic and I when we were children. The edges were still singed and splattered with blood, but I felt like it was somehow fitting. We'd clawed and scraped every step of the way to get here, and it made the moment that much sweeter. The saying engraved within, "To die will be an awfully big adventure" seemed to take on a whole new meaning for me now. Would my next adventure be to die for those that I loved? When it was officially my time, I couldn't think of a better way to go than dying for those I loved the most. "Will you please hold on to it this time?"

"I'm going to miss you so much, sweetie," Mic crooned. Her own tears spilled down her cheeks.

"Whenever you miss me, just know I'm right here," I said as I touched the acorn locket. "This kept me grounded. Kept your memory bright in my mind when I needed you the most."

Lucius cleared his throat, interrupting our emotional moment. "I have a gift as well."

"Holy shit, it must be fucking Christmas! Lu has a gift," I snarked at him, trying to stem the tide of tears that were threatening to break the promise I'd made to myself.

He glared at me for a moment, but apparently he could see through my mask. I must have looked like an utter mess because he didn't bite back. "It's not from me, actually. This is courtesy of Captain Hook." Lucius pulled two rolled pieces of parchment from his jacket and placed them on the table before us. "These are the Loquentes Cartis, the talking scrolls. They're paired scrolls that are embedded with magic. Whatever is written on one shows up on the other. Hook wanted to be sure the two of you could keep in touch."

My heart melted in my chest, despite the growl I heard from one of my boys. I ignored it, because this might have been the single most thoughtful gift I'd ever received. I missed James with a vengeance, especially now. I hoped he hadn't been lying when he said he'd arranged time for us. As much as Peter and the Lost Boys would be against it, I knew I had to see him soon. If nothing more than to say thank you. My libido chimed in that she expected much more than mere words at our next meeting, but I had to shut down that line of thought in an effort to hide the telltale blush that was hiding just below the surface.

"These are amazing! Lucius, please tell James thank you for me." Mic gushed.

"You promise you'll write?"

"Of course, sweetie. I'm sure we'll both have so much to share."

"Michaela, it's time," Nico interrupted us, his head turned toward the sky, judging the position of the sun. Michaela pouted exaggeratedly for a moment before she rose to her feet.

"I wish I could say that I was ready and that my nerves weren't getting the best of me, but I guess that's life. You can't grow if you don't push past your fears." Mic sighed deeply, lifting her chin a little. I'd always admired her bravery. She'd snubbed her nose in the face of cancer. Accepted her own death with the courage of a voyager, looking over the horizon for the next big adventure. I let her courage envelop me, as if I might be able to tap into it in my time of need.

We followed Mic and the beast princes back into the castle. My curiosity was piqued. To get to Neverland, we'd had to fly across the Veil. Now the princes walked casually into the castle, no indication that they would be flying anywhere.

My eyes darted to Lucius. He was holding it together, but I could see the tension in his jaw, his movements seeming almost mechanical as he forced himself forward. We stopped at a set of wooden doors. These were ornately carved in a woodland scene. Nico pressed his palm against the wood, and the doors swung open of their own accord. Nico waved us into what I could only assume were his private quarters. The room was massive, containing an equally massive four-poster bed, an adjacent library, and a long dining table rounding out the room.

The princes all congregated around an enormous full-length mirror, trimmed in a deep mahogany wood. One by one the brothers clapped arms with Lucius, patting him on the back briefly before turning to the mirror and simply walking through.

"What the…"

"It's a portal to Hiraeth. You didn't think we'd actually fly across the Veil, did you?"

"I didn't realize there were other ways. That would have been awfully convenient," I looked on enviously as the last of the princes disappeared into the mirror.

"You have a lot to learn," Nico chuckled as he walked to the bookshelves, dragging his hands along the countless tomes. He pulled a thick book from the shelf, a flurry of dust particles floating into the air as if it hadn't moved from its spot on the shelf in hundreds of years. He handed the book to Peter. "Immerse yourself in knowledge, Pan. The mark of a good leader is one that is well studied." Nico's words were veiled in front of Mic, but Peter accepted the book with a respectful nod of his head.

"May the Divine bless you in your journey, daughter of Wendy."

"I think we're at the point in our relationship where you can call me Gwen. I'm entrusting her welfare to you. Don't let me down." I glared at him, hoping to convey the severity of my convictions.

"Gwen, sweetie, I'll be fine. Don't worry. I'll write as soon as I get settled," Mic tried to comfort me.

Lucius came forward, a small, neatly wrapped package in his hands. "For you, dove." Mic took it tentatively, and started to untie the twine. "No, don't open it here. Next time you think of me, open it then." He placed his large hands over hers, and the two locked eyes for a moment before he leaned in, whispering something into her ear. The moment between them was so intimate, I felt like an intruder. I averted my eyes, shifting my gaze to my boys to give them as much privacy as I could. Each of them smiled warmly, each of them giving me the unspoken support I needed to hold it together in this final goodbye.

Lucius wrapped Mic in a hug. She looked so small with his big frame wrapped around hers. When he finally stepped back, I could see the raw emotion on his face. Letting her go was tearing him up inside. He managed to get his typical brooding scowl into place quickly before he stalked out of the room. Mic's eyes trailed after him. She wasn't able to hide the look of longing as well as Lu had. She shifted her gaze to me. I was the last loose end to tie up before her big adventure.

"You boys take care of her, okay? She's something special." Mic's eyes stayed firmly on mine as the boys all voiced their agreement. She pulled me in for one last hug, her arms crushing me against her in our final farewell. "Maybe... maybe I should stay. Is it cold in here? I just got such a terrible feeling all of a sudden."

"Mic, are you alright?" I held her at arm's length. Her brow was furrowed, a worried expression plastered on her face.

"I just feel like I shouldn't leave you. I think there was something I needed to tell you, but I can't remember. Death isn't the curse... It's the answer? I don't even know where that came from, but does that make any sense?"

"Mic, it's just your nerves getting the best of you. It's not every day that you walk through a mirror and enter a completely different world. It's okay to have some reservations. I'll be fine. We'll both be fine. And when you're done healing, maybe we can make a girl's trip back home, just the two of us and we'll hit up all our favorite pubs."

Mic let out a soft laugh, shaking her head as if she was trying to dislodge the anxiety that was holding her back. "You're right. Of course you're right. Just promise me you'll keep that blade on you at all times."

"Of course I will. It will remind me of you every time I see it."

"I'm not going to say goodbye, because goodbyes suck. How about 'see you soon.' Let's manifest that shit happening. See you soon, sweetie."

"See you soon." We kissed each other's cheeks. I placed her hand in Nico's, and with one final look over her shoulder, she walked through the mirror, leaving me behind. The moment she was gone, the warmth went out of the room. I could physically feel the loss of her. I sank to my knees as I stared at myself in the reflection. The tears I'd been holding back let loose, streaking down my cheeks as a sob escaped my lips. My boys joined me on the floor, each of them placing a hand on me, holding me together while I fell apart.

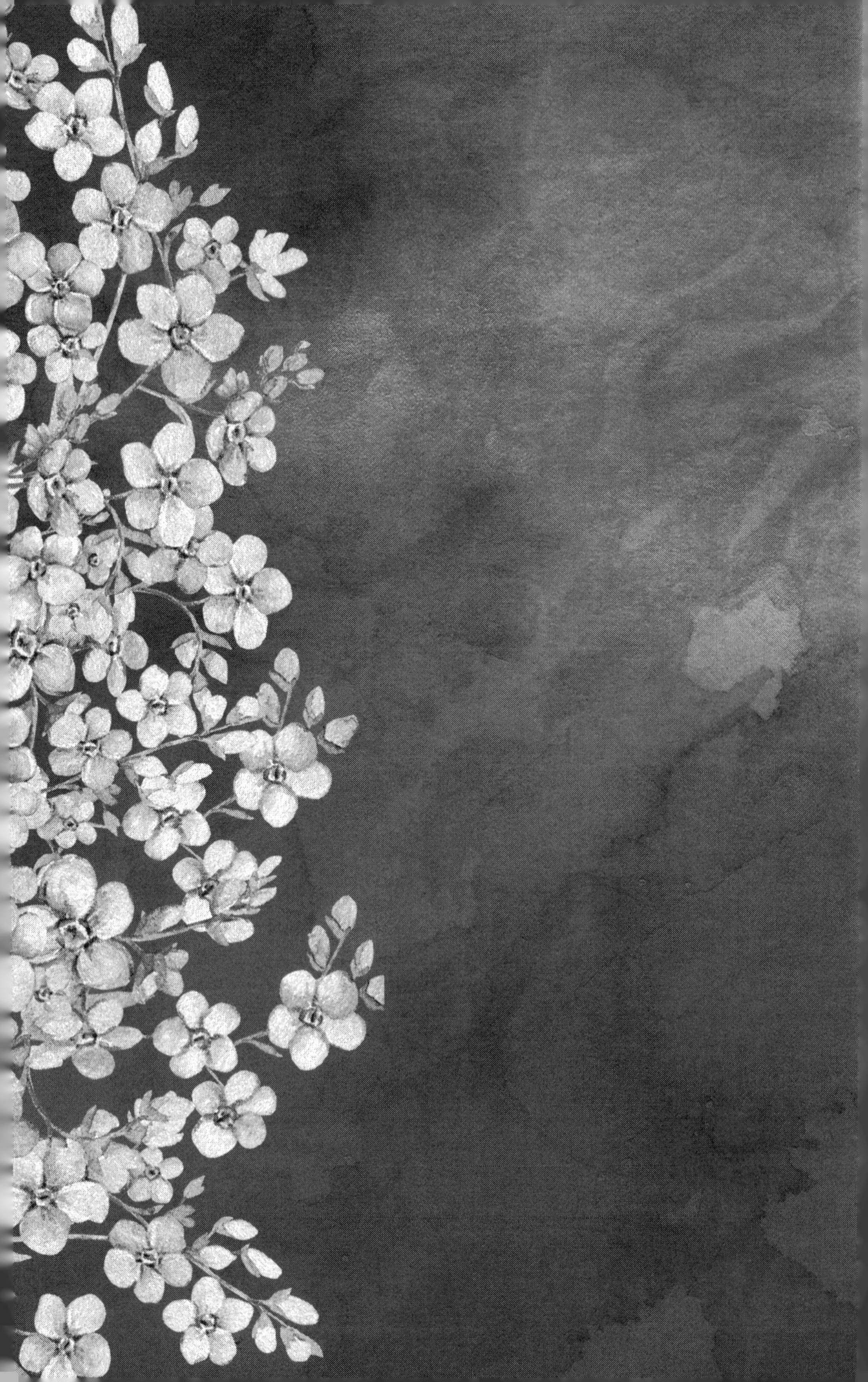

Chapter XIII
Revelations
-Gwen-

I had spent the better part of the day training with Eben. Keeping my body in a constant state of stress and pain had served two purposes: diverting my mind's attention away from Mic, and ensuring Kían remained buried within the recesses of my subconscious. I had to get my hands on some Moonflower. At some point, my boys were going to start to question why I was constantly "getting hurt".

Peter had informed me that James had called in his debt and I was expected to be delivered to him before sunset. He would be escorting me to the Jolly Roger this afternoon.

None of my boys were happy about it, and had no issue making it known. I, on the other hand, was giddy with excitement. I missed my dominating pirate. Plus, the timing couldn't have been better. I needed to confess to James what was going on with Kían. As it was, I'd have to use faerie dust to get to the Jolly Roger, and I wasn't sure how much longer I'd be able to keep my dark tormentor buried.

"Gwendolyn, love, I've been expecting you." Hook smiled as he reached his hand out, gently guiding me down to the deck of the Jolly Roger. Peter hesitated, hovering in the air before landing on the deck with a thud. The last time I was here, I was going home to Mic. A heartbroken shell of a woman, desperate to save her sister. I'd had no idea how to salvage what was left of my shattered life. I was lost. But things were different this time. Fulfilling a debt, sure, but being here with James was no punishment. Not only did I need his help, I craved his company. My sister was thriving and off with her beasts. And I was finally allowed to live… for myself.

"James, I've missed you." I smiled, wrapping my arms around his neck. He smelled like sin, excitement and dangers untold. I'd never tire of it. A heady mix of musky thrall, sea salt, and leather intoxicated my senses. I could feel my body responding to him already. This man stirred something deep with-in me.

"You look ravishing." He leaned into my embrace, pressing his lips to the sensitive spot behind my ear. He was charming and gentle with me in a way that was contrary to how he behaved with others. "Come, I've arranged for us to watch the sunset." Grabbing my hand, he led me towards the bow of the ship. "Smee!"

"Yes, Captain." I jumped as Smee appeared out of nowhere. He was always lurking just out of sight. Waiting for a command, like a dog starved for attention.

"Escort Peter off the ship, and see that he makes his way back home."

"That won't be necessary," Peter quickly retorted. "You said I had to deliver her to you. I've done that." I knew Peter was still leery of James. He had begrudgingly agreed to the relationship, but the history between the two was centuries long. If the story books were true, it was a longstanding rivalry. Getting them to trust each other was going to take some time.

Smee stood his ground, staring wide-eyed, waiting for orders.

"You never said I had to leave her alone with you." Peter smirked as if he had just won an epic battle of wits. "Call off your dog. I won't be leaving."

"Peter, really, I'm safe here. You don't have to stay." I made a feeble attempt to diffuse what was quickly becoming volatile.

"I'm not leaving you alone with him. Not until I'm certain he won't hurt you."

James pulled me back behind him. Effectively putting himself between Peter and I. "I assured you she would be safe with me. If my word means nothing to you, after all this time, then by all means Peter, stay." His eyes darkened, and a sinful smile crept across his face. "Watch how a real *man* treats a woman."

"James," I chided. I began to wonder if this was going to work. Could these two make peace for my sake? I hadn't thought about the logistics of loving arch enemies, let alone at the same time. I had the feeling this evening was about to turn into a pissing contest.

"Darling, I'm simply offering what he's asking for. He clearly thinks you are in danger. Let the boy chaperone. Maybe he'll learn a thing or two."

I turned to look at Peter. "You two need to learn to trust each other. Or this isn't going to work. This ridiculousness needs to end."

"Smee, set an extra plate at my table. Peter will be joining Gwendolyn and I for dinner."

"Aye, aye Captain." He scurried off, leaving the three of us.

"Come, love, time waits for no one. The sky is already beginning to blush with the evening's seduction." James continued to lead me up to the deck at the bow of the ship. Peter flew up into the rigging and perched like a bird. I had never seen him more like the boy from the story books. I chose to believe he was trying to give us some space and not just get a better vantage point to watch us from afar.

The Jolly Roger had been anchored facing the shores of Neverland. Her vibrant greens were quickly darkening into silhouette. The sky transformed into spectacular shades of orange and red as the sun began its journey behind the peaks and valleys of the beautiful island. James stood behind me and wrapped his arms around my waist, pulling me back against him.

"Neverland is most beautiful at sunset. She puts on a show before shrouding herself in darkness." As the sun set deeper into the blossoming night, the clouds shifted to a smoky purple. And the sky was ablaze with fiery light.

"James, this is the most beautiful sunset I have ever seen." I was in awe of Neverland's beauty. At this very moment, it hit me, this was my home now. I was living my very own, very real fairytale. Aside from the issues with the Inalto and the looming debt with the bone faerie, my reality truly was better than my dreams. My heart warmed with the thought. For the first time since I could remember, I was looking forward to the future.

"She was dazzling — alight; it was agony to comprehend her beauty in a glance."

I turned to look at James, shocked to hear him quoting Fitzgerald. Only to find him staring at me intently. I felt my cheeks heat as I realized he wasn't talking about the sunset. "You read Fitzgerald?" I asked, trying to shift the tension building between us.

"The Beautiful and the Damned seems a fitting tragedy for a man like me. I quite enjoyed it."

"Michaela gave me the scroll. They told me it was from you. I can't thank you enough. It means the world to me."

"I know how much she means to you." He reached up and tucked a piece of hair behind my ear. "With the scrolls you will always have a direct line of communication. I hope it helps ease the pain of her being so far away."

He was right, having the scrolls meant I could check in any time I wanted. It was the closest thing to having a cell phone that Neverland could provide, and his selfless act would not go unnoticed.

"Thank you for sacrificing your personal means of communication for me."

James slid his hand behind my neck and gently pulled me in, his lips mere millimeters from mine. "For you, my love, I'd give the world." He sealed his lips to mine, kissing me with a scorching heat. His tongue sensuously explored my own with a tenderness that sent my heart into a frenzy. This man was not the big bad villain that everyone thought they knew. He was deep and caring. At least with me he was.

"Ahem," Peter cleared his throat. I had forgotten he was perched above. He'd never seen James and I kiss. Though he had agreed to my relationship with James, I knew it was going to be hard for him to actually see it. "Ask him about the naked lady on the bow," he said smugly.

I looked out at the figurehead carved into the bow of the Jolly Roger. A beautiful woman, her arm outstretched, holding a glowing lantern, illuminating the undulating sea below. Her Victorian bustled skirt seemed to melt into the bow of the ship at her knees. Her tiny waist was accentuated by a corset that framed the underside of her bare breasts. There was a sadness to her beauty. A warning in her frozen gaze. Like a siren, alluring you into your inevitable demise.

I looked back to James, my eyebrows lifted. "What's the story behind the woman?"

"That's a story for another time." His demeanor shifted. I could tell there was something there he didn't want to talk about. "Peter is just trying to goad me."

"What's wrong, Hook? You don't want her to know about your past? Afraid she might not like the real you?" Peter dropped from the rigging with a thud. He could have glided down gently, but his landing was hard and intentional. He was provoking Hook.

"The story of my figurehead is not something Gwendolyn needs to be afraid of. You house quite a few skeletons in your own closet. Shall I start exposing the real Peter Pan?" James took a step towards Peter closing the distance between them and driving the tension to near breaking. If I didn't do something, there was going to be a bloodbath.

"Enough!" I stepped between the two and pushed them apart. "You two need to call a truce."

Peter huffed and crossed his arms.

"Can't I invoke parlay or something?" I had no idea

what that really meant, but I had heard the term in reference to pirate code somewhere.

James chuckled. "That's not exactly how parlay works, love."

"What's the story here? Why are the two of you mortal enemies?"

"If we are going to have this conversation we are going to need a lot of rum."

Peter's eyes went wide at the suggestion. He was hiding something. I could see it in the concern plastered all over his face. "Gwen—"

"Peter," I interrupted, not giving him the chance to negotiate out of this. "We are having this conversation."

"Smee!"

"Captain." I jumped as Smee popped out from behind me. Where the fuck did he come from?

"Go into my private reserve and bring several bottles of rum to my cabin. Alert the cook. We are ready to eat."

"Aye, aye."

As we made our way back to James's private quarters, I paused to look up at the night sky. I made a wish on a particularly bright star that the evening would end well. No blood would be shed and peace would be possible. If nothing else, I was about to hear the story of a lifetime. No one seemed to know the history between these two and I was about to dive in deep.

James's cabin looked exactly how I remembered it. The crocodile, still chained to the wall, closely watched our every move. The thing was massive, and I was certain it was plotting its revenge. The large table at the center of the room where I penned my goodbye letters, once covered in scrolls, had been cleared and set for a proper romantic dinner. A dinner that was intended to be private. A third setting had been hastily added to the far end of the table to make room for Peter. Who was still standing idly staring at the crocodile, not quite sure what to do. Candelabras spread about the room added a soft, warm glow to the atmosphere. A shiver ran through my core, imagining what this evening could have been.

Being in this room brought back memories. The window, his lips, the table, the cold thrill of his hook, the large four poster bed draped in crimson. The velvet touch of his tongue. I felt my cheeks heat as I remembered just how much I enjoyed giving in to the fear and charm of his seduction. James unlocked a darkness in me that night, and I was grateful for it. I craved it.

"Please, my love, have a seat." James pulled out a chair, ever the doting gentleman.

Peter stood with his arms crossed, clenching his jaw. "Gwen, this is pointless. I have no clear memories from back then. I just know we're enemies." It's true, Neverland made you forget, but was it complete amnesia, or did you have flashes of the past? I looked at James. Wouldn't his memory be altered as well? What was his angle here? As if he could read my mind, he offered an explanation.

"I wear a magical talisman to protect my memory. It

keeps me from making the same mistake twice." He pointed to his forearm. There, tattooed on his arm, was an elaborate design. Three swords piercing a heart. Not exactly an anatomical heart per se, but a heart shape made of aubergine and crimson muscle. Veining and arteries entwined at the top created an almost root like appearance. I had never seen a tattoo move on its own accord, but drops of aubergine blood appeared to actually be dripping in rhythmic time from the center sword's tip. It was grotesquely visceral, yet poetically beautiful.

"This tattoo has been enchanted to preserve my memory. I remember every graphic detail of my preternatural life." He reached across the table, grabbed a candle, and lit his cigars before pouring three glasses of rum. "The good and the bad." With the back of his hook, he slid a glass to me. Mischief sparkled in his eyes before turning his attention to Peter. "Do you still want to stay, Pan?" He raised an eyebrow in question as he slid a glass toward Peter. "Or are you too afraid to hear stories of the past?" He paused, surrounding us in a dramatic silence.

"To truth." James raised his glass.

"To truth." I followed suit and looked to Peter. "For us."

He thought for a moment. "Fuck it!" He snatched the glass. "To us, and the truth, whatever it may be."

It was a start. This was a step in the right direction. I slammed the shot back, excited for the future possibilities. Before I could catch my breath from the burn of the alcohol, James was pouring another round.

"Where to begin?" He paused, stroking his beard. "I had the unfortunate honor of being the first Lost Boy. Back then they called me Jas."

Peter's eyes lit up as if the memory had suddenly resurfaced. "Yeah we called you Jas, until I fed your hand to that slimy croc." He actually smiled, as if he was proud to have given Hook his moniker.

James furrowed his brow, shooting Peter a sinister look. "I was enamored with him, as they all are. Young boys with no desire to grow up. No responsibilities, no parents to reprimand them. He promised eternal youth. Only he couldn't keep that promise, could you, Pan?" There was a bitterness to his tone. Decades of festering wounds came flooding back to the surface. Unforgiven broken promises made to a young, impressionable boy.

Peter's jaw flexed before he gulped down another shot of rum. "How was I supposed to know you would grow old? I didn't."

James continued on, ignoring Peter's remark. "We did everything together. And for a while, things were wonderful. Neverland was our very own Shangri-La. Things were different back then— simpler. But time was not at a standstill for me, like it was for Peter. Eventually I grew into a teenager, surpassing the very boy who'd promised me eternal youth." James paused, mindlessly ashing his cigars.

I couldn't believe what I was hearing. James had been the first Lost Boy. This was the story I was waiting for. So what was the catalyst for their falling out? There had to be something salvageable between the two of them. Something I could use to help restore the peace.

My thoughts were interrupted as Hook's cabin suddenly came alive with crew. They brought in tray after tray of the most delectable food. James had gone all out for this evening. "Please, my love, indulge yourself. I had my cook prepare his best just for you." He pushed an unopened bottle of rum towards Peter. "You're gonna want this. We're just getting to the good part."

I filled my plate and my belly while James continued on.

"In the end, it was my inevitable aging that led to our demise. Peter, ever fearful of growing up, wanted to rid himself of anything that couldn't follow that simple order." I remembered the old weathered sign at the entrance of the Lost Boys camp. It was written there in the rules, never ever grow up.

"The rules were simple, Hook. Never ever grow up. Look at you, you're an old man."

"He's mature," I chided. "And from the sound of it, you are just as old, if not older."

"Thank the stars I don't look like it. I still have my youthful charm." Peter snapped back.

"I find James quite alluring." I looked at him and bit my lip. He may have been old enough to be my father, but I couldn't deny the animalistic attraction I felt toward him.

"And I you, my love." He reached across the table, pulling my hand in for a chaste kiss before sneering at Peter.

"You made rules no man could abide, and yet I was punished for it."

"You were punished? For aging?"

"Myself and many others after me."

"Your hand?" I was starting to wonder who the villain was in this story.

"Ha!" Peter exclaimed before taking another pull of rum. Clearly irritated that I would assume the worst.

James ignored Peter's outburst. "No, my love. That came many years later after my return."

"Wait, what? You left Neverland?"

"Not by choice. I was returned to Earth. Much like yourself, with nothing but the clothes on my back."

Peter's smile softened. He was all too familiar with being abandoned. I wondered if it was hitting home? Was he realizing he caused someone else the same pain he had suffered?

"He left me, a naive teenage boy, alone in the streets of Charles Town, South Carolina. I suffered unmentionable horrors at the hands of many. With no other choice, I became a pirate to survive. Peter is the reason I am who I am today."

My heart sank thinking of what he had possibly endured as a young boy.

"Edward Teach took pity on me and offered me a position as a powder monkey on the Queen Anne's Revenge."

"Edward Teach? You worked for Blackbeard? The most

infamous pirate in history." I was awestruck.

"I did. He was a vile, wicked man." He paused to numb his thoughts with more rum. "I made my way through the ranks and eventually became quartermaster."

"But how did you get back? To Neverland."

"I'd like to know the same thing," Peter interjected.

"I discovered Blackbeard was actually a Fae living in hiding. In exchange for my service and my silence, I was given passage back across the Veil."

I had so many questions. "Blackbeard was Fae? How long were you in service? What was it like—"

"I'm done offering up my past." Hook interrupted my rapid fire questioning. I had struck a nerve. He clearly didn't want to talk about what happened while he was back on earth. "The details aren't important. I spent my days plotting revenge on Peter. He was the reason I lived a nightmare."

My eyes lit up as the pieces started to fall into place. "The age gap." It was all making sense. "You aged while back on earth."

"He came back an old man." Peter chuckled. His emotions seemed to be all over the place.

"Your crew, are they—"

"All Lost Boys who aged out." James interrupted, confirming my suspicions. "I've spared them the horrors I endured. I give them a home when *he* won't."

There he was, the man I knew, hiding within the rough facade. My James painted my Peter in a very different light.

"I've changed!" Peter slammed the bottle on the table. "The Divine has taken my ability to defy age. I no longer bring boys across the Veil. Doesn't that count for something?" He reached across the table for my hand. "My family is whole now. He's the one holding a grudge."

"Aren't you both tired of all the fighting? It clearly hasn't solved anything. You can't change the past. Holding a grudge just soils the future. You don't have to like each other, but you need to learn to trust the other when it comes to me. At the very least, can't you two call a truce for my sake?"

"I've accepted that you love Peter. Without him, I wouldn't have you." He turned to look at Peter. "He is the one insisting on chaperoning."

"A truce?" Peter huffed.

"Truce or not, I will continue to see Gwendolyn for as long as she'll have me. Leave, or stay and watch, Pan. I don't care. I've grown tired of this conversation." Hook stood up from the table. "He has stolen enough of our time together." James grabbed my hand, pulling me up from my chair. "My love." He reached into his pocket and presented me with a small box. "A gift for you."

It was an old blue velvet box with a gold latch at the front. The edges had been worn, but the original charm showed through the years of wear. I slowly opened the box and gasped. "James…" Inside was a stunning diamond encrusted ruby pendant. I had never been given such an extravagant gift. I was utterly speechless. "It's beautiful."

"A queen deserves to be draped in jewels." He took my hand and led me to a full-length mirror across the room. Standing behind me, he reached for the box and gently placed the pendant around my neck. "I want to see you wearing nothing but this." He whispered into my ear, sending a shiver down my spine. The ruby was large, shaped like a teardrop, and rested perfectly between my breasts. I was mesmerized by its beauty.

I watched in the mirror while James swept my hair to the side, draping it over my shoulder. His tongue slid up the smooth skin of my neck before he stopped and growled in my ear. "Are you a good girl, Gwendolyn?"

His mere words caused a flood of excitement to pool between my legs. I looked at him through the mirror, his eyes locked on mine. "Yes," I whispered.

"I want you to watch while I undress you." His hand coiled around my neck, giving a gentle squeeze before he nipped at my jaw. My breathing hitched as I became intoxicated by his heady seduction.

I looked back at Peter. He was intently watching from the table. His eyes glued on me. I couldn't tell if he was enjoying the show or if he was disturbed to see his enemy worshiping his girlfriend. I could feel the heat of his gaze watching our every move, and it made it feel even more taboo. My dark side was enjoying every moment of it. I closed my eyes and leaned my head back, savoring the feel of James's lips on my neck.

"Eyes open," he demanded. "I told you to watch." I had

never been shy, but watching James and myself brought a whole new level of intimacy. It made me feel vulnerable. "Do as I say, and I'll give you what you're too scared to ask for."

I opened my eyes and stood transfixed as he removed my shirt, exposing my breasts. His hand trailed across my back before reaching around and cupping my breast, my nipples hardening with his touch. He growled again in my ear as he drug the tip of his cold hook slowly down my sternum, leaving a red welt in its wake. He paused for a moment before hooking my pants and pulling them down, leaving a puddle of fabric on the floor and me in nothing but my wet knickers.

James smiled before dropping to his knees, sliding his hand and his cold hook down my sides and over my hips. I could feel his hot breath between my thighs. "I can smell your desire."

I felt my face blush. My body was craving his touch, and his slow seduction had me dripping with anticipation. He slid off my knickers and held them to his face, inhaling deeply and growling before tossing them at Peter. "She smells like the sweetest sin. Does her pussy weep for you like this?"

Peter's gaze was intense. I couldn't tell if it was lust or anger. He grabbed my knickers from the table and held them to his face before tucking them into his pocket.

"Spread your legs." The order was firm. Before I could obey, his hook was between my legs, nudging them apart.

Ever so gently, he positioned himself so that the tip of his hook skimmed my sensitive clit, drawing out a mew of fear and excitement. "It turns you on, doesn't it? Knowing I could hurt you at any moment."

"I... I..." My words stammered. I still wasn't ready to confess just how much fear and danger excited me. He flipped his hook and slid the cold metal along my wetness. I moaned shamelessly, giving into the sensation, throwing my head back.

"Eyes forward." He stood up and slowly licked my desire off his hook. "You, my love, are exquisite." He looked me up and down, admiring my nakedness. "It's better than I had imagined." He smiled, pleased with himself. "The ruby rests perfectly between your beautiful breasts." His eyes shifted to the black veining. I could see the concern he was desperately trying to hide. He traced the lines along my arm. It had spread across my shoulders and was beginning to creep down my belly over the top of my hip. "I do love the color of rubies. Like the blood I'll spill of those who dare harm you." It wasn't a direct threat against the bone faerie, but it was implied that he was keeping watch.

He turned to a chest of drawers that was just to the side of us, pulling out two small metallic devices. "Do you know what a safe word is?"

I nodded yes as the fear of needing a safe word flooded my thoughts.

"Your word is ruby. Do you understand?"

"I do."

He leaned in, kissing me hard. His tongue explored my mouth before dropping to my neck and trailing further to my taught nipples. He pinched my nipple between his fingers and placed a clamp over the sensitive skin. He slowly adjusted the tension until a groan escaped my lips. "Good girl," he purred. It was a strange sensation, somewhere between pleasure and pain. But it was causing a rush of desire to flow through my body. He repeated the process on the other side before admiring his work.

"Peter, look how beautiful our girl is when she's delirious with need." My heart quickened. Could I have them both at the same time? Never had I even considered it a possibility until now. Would they be willing?

James took my hand and led me over to the table where we had just been. The weight of the clamps tugging on my breasts with every step heightening the foreign sensations.

Peter stood, not sure what to do. A massive erection straining beneath his pants. "Fuck, Gwen. I—"

Before he could get the words out, James cleared the table with one sweep of his arm. Sending everything on the table to the floor in a loud crash. Peter took a step back, unsure of what was about to happen. James scooped me up and gently placed me on the table, leaning me back and placing my feet close to my body so that my legs were bent, exposing my now dripping core.

"That's right, show me that pretty pussy." Silently, he circled the table, stopping behind my head just out of sight. He grabbed my shoulders, sliding his hand and cold hook down my arms before grabbing my hands and pulling them over my head. I felt the familiar sensation of ropes binding my wrists before being pulled taught, anchoring me in place. The tension, causing my back to arch, pushing my breasts up and increasing the pull of the clamps. My mind was awhirl with fear and excitement of the unknown. "Isn't she pretty, with her tits pushed up to the sky. Begging to be touched. Dripping with need."

Peter began to circle my now displayed body. Stopping to linger at my exposed core. "She's stunning," he whispered. I could feel their eyes on me. Staring at my most intimate parts. My body on display for their pleasure. Or was it mine? I felt dirty, and I liked it. I wanted them to touch me, to use me for their pleasure. I began to writhe about seeking some form of friction, but all it did was cause the clamps to tug at my nipples, sending my need to higher levels.

"Please," I begged.

James came back into view, this time with his shirt off. His masculine physique a delight to my eyes. "Please what?"

"Please, touch me." I rubbed my thighs together, hoping for some relief before James forced them apart. Taking a seat before my spread core, he leaned in, dragging his velvet tongue up my slit, pulling an animalistic moan from my lips.

Peter appeared over my head, hunger in his eyes. He traced his hands down my arms before caressing my breasts and leaning down to kiss me from behind. James's tongue worked my clit while inserting his fingers, one at a time, until he was gently stretching my opening. I couldn't keep from moaning into Peter's mouth. I was lost in the pleasure, on the brink of climax when James abruptly stopped and stood up. I whimpered at the loss of his touch.

"Taste her honey. I've made her ripe for you."

Peter wasted no time. His tongue began to slowly explore my most sensitive parts, bringing me back to the edge of pure bliss.

"Eh eh eh, not so fast. Just a taste. We don't want her spent yet." James pulled Peter from the table before repositioning himself between my legs. I couldn't see what he was doing, but I could feel the familiar sensation of cold metal pressing at my opening before sliding in deep, filling me to the brink. He stood and rounded the table while the weight of whatever he had put in me tugged with my movement, sending me mad with need.

"Watch this," James boasted to Peter before flicking the clamps on my nipples, sending me completely over the edge. I lost all control, my core clamped around the foreign object placed inside me as I cried out, blind with pleasure. Lost in the throes of an orgasm.

"Good girl," James purred. "You're so pretty when you cum." He removed a large silver phallus from me and brought it to his mouth growling as he tasted my release. He rounded the table again, positioning himself behind me before leaning down to kiss me. I could taste myself on his tongue as he explored my mouth. He removed the clamps from my nipples, causing a painful rush of blood to my now sensitive skin. I groaned in protest and he quickly sucked them into his mouth, soothing them. James released my bindings, placing delicate kisses on the now chafed skin, before leading me to an ottoman at the foot of his bed. "On your hands and knees." I obeyed his order, placing myself on display once again. I could feel my release starting to drip down my legs.

SMACK!

I flinched as the familiar sting of Hook's hand took hold of my ass and I moaned with desire.

SMACK!

I yelped this time as the sting drove deeper, heating my skin. My pussy growing wetter with each slap.

"Peter, put your cock in her mouth and keep her quiet."

SMACK!

"Oohhh" I gasped as Peter appeared, stroking his cock in his hand. The tip glistened with his own excitement. I quickly took him into my mouth, savoring the taste of him as I bathed him with my tongue.

"Fuck, Gwen. That feels amazing." Peter began to thrust his hips, fucking my mouth.

James's cock pressed hard against my opening, sliding in agonizingly slow and deep as I pushed back, matching his thrust, burying him to the hilt. "That's my good girl. Your greedy little pussy is dripping for my cock."

I moaned shamelessly as I was filled by both my men. James thrusting from behind pushing Peter's cock deeper down my throat. I was lost in the act. A slave to pleasure.

I couldn't tell where one of us ended, and the other began.

"Do you remember your safe word, Gwen?" I turned to look back at James and nodded yes. "I'm going to give you what you're too afraid to ask for." My heart began to race with thoughts of what was coming. A sinister smile crept across his face before he pulled out leaving me wanting. Fisting my hair James pulled me up from the ottoman and ordered Peter to lay down in my place. "Straddle him. Slowly."

I wasted no time, and as I was asked, I slowly dropped down on Peter's cock. He groaned in approval. James gently pushed me forward so that I was chest to chest with Peter. His hand roaming down my back trailing fingers down between my spread cheeks before inserting a finger into my already stretched opening right alongside Peter's cock. I stilled at the sensation. Unsure of what to think. It was on the verge of pain but oh so pleasurable. "James, I—"

"Shhh, my queen, you were made for this. You and I both know there is pleasure in a little bit of pain." Before I could protest, he slid in a second finger, increasing the stretch and drawing out a cry of pleasure from both me and Peter. "That's right, my love." He gave my body a moment to adjust before gently sliding out his fingers and moved behind me, positioning his cock against my opening.

"Wait." I panicked. There was no way he was going to fit with Peter inside of me.

"What's your safe word, Gwen?" he asked calmly. "If

you want me to stop, use your word." I hesitated, wanting to have them both, but afraid of what that would entail. Slowly, he began to push in and I was blinded with pleasure and pain. An animalistic cry escaped my lips as he slid in alongside Peter. "That's my good girl. You take us so well. Your pussy was made for us." It was unlike anything I had ever felt, and James's praise only drove me deeper into the madness.

"Fuck," Peter cried out as James began to move in and out, pleasuring us both at the same time. Peter flexed his hips in rhythm with James, driving me to the precipice. When I thought I couldn't take anymore, I fell over the edge, taking my men with me. The orgasm ripping through my body, crashing in waves as all three of us finished together in a symphony of moans. My body was spent. I collapsed onto Peter, exhausted. James slid out of me gently and helped me off of Peter before carrying me to the bed. He spread my legs, inspecting me for injury before gently applying a warm, soothing cloth. "You did good tonight, my queen. Now rest, you earned it."

I WOKE DELIGHTFULLY sore in James's bed with Peter passed out next to me and cold ruffled sheets on the other side of me. The sun had still not risen and the soft glow of moonlight filtered into the room. James was standing at the large window looking out to the sea. I crossed the room and joined him, stroking his enchanted tattoo. It wasn't the first time I had seen aubergine blood.

"I dreamt once that my blood was this very color. It was after the attack at Amara's camp. While I was recovering from injury."

"Those who have been altered by magic sometimes bleed aubergine. It doesn't happen to everyone. Has yours changed yet?" He paused, waiting for an answer that wasn't coming. My blood was in fact still red, but James knew me better than I thought. "Back at the temple mount, I saw dark magic in your eyes. Gwen, I'm not a fool. I know something has happened."

I sighed. "Please be quiet," I pleaded. "I don't want Peter or the boys to know."

His brow furrowed with concern as he turned to face me.

"Amara gifted me an Inalto to help defeat Tiger Lily. I tried not to use it, but I had no choice. She had the upper hand. I had no idea the cost would be so high."

"My love," he sighed. "Whose magic have you consumed? Whose soul?"

"Kían, Amara's mate. And he wants me to kill one of my boys, to achieve vengeance. Amara said it's his way of changing the outcome of his fate? All I know is I keep getting possessed by his soul. James, I've already tried to kill them."

He stared at me silently, listening. "When was the last time you tried?"

"He used me to try to kill Amara just yesterday." I was mortified speaking it out loud. "I have discovered that pain seems to keep him at bay." I dropped my head in shame. "I've been secretly hurting myself to keep him away. I assume it's why he hasn't come to the surface tonight."

"My love—"

"James," I interrupted. "I can't. I *won't* kill one of them. I'd choose death over losing any of you ever again." Tears welled in my eyes. "Amara said you might have a way to suppress him. Something called Moonflower?"

"My love, Datura, or as you called it Moonflower, is extremely toxic. There is no guarantee that it would even work. In fact the only guarantee is your death, or worse. I can not give you this."

"But I have no other choice. I won't survive if he succeeds. I need to try."

James wiped the tears that were now streaming down my cheeks before pulling me into an embrace. "We will find another way, my love, but I can not aid in your death." He leaned down and kissed me softly. "We *will* find a way. Even if I have to keep you tied up and spanked for the rest of your days." A sinister grin crept across his face.

"I can think of worse ways to spend my days." I smiled and leaned in, resting my head on his warm chest.

"Rest, my love. Tomorrow is but a few hours away. We will figure this all out soon. I give you my word."

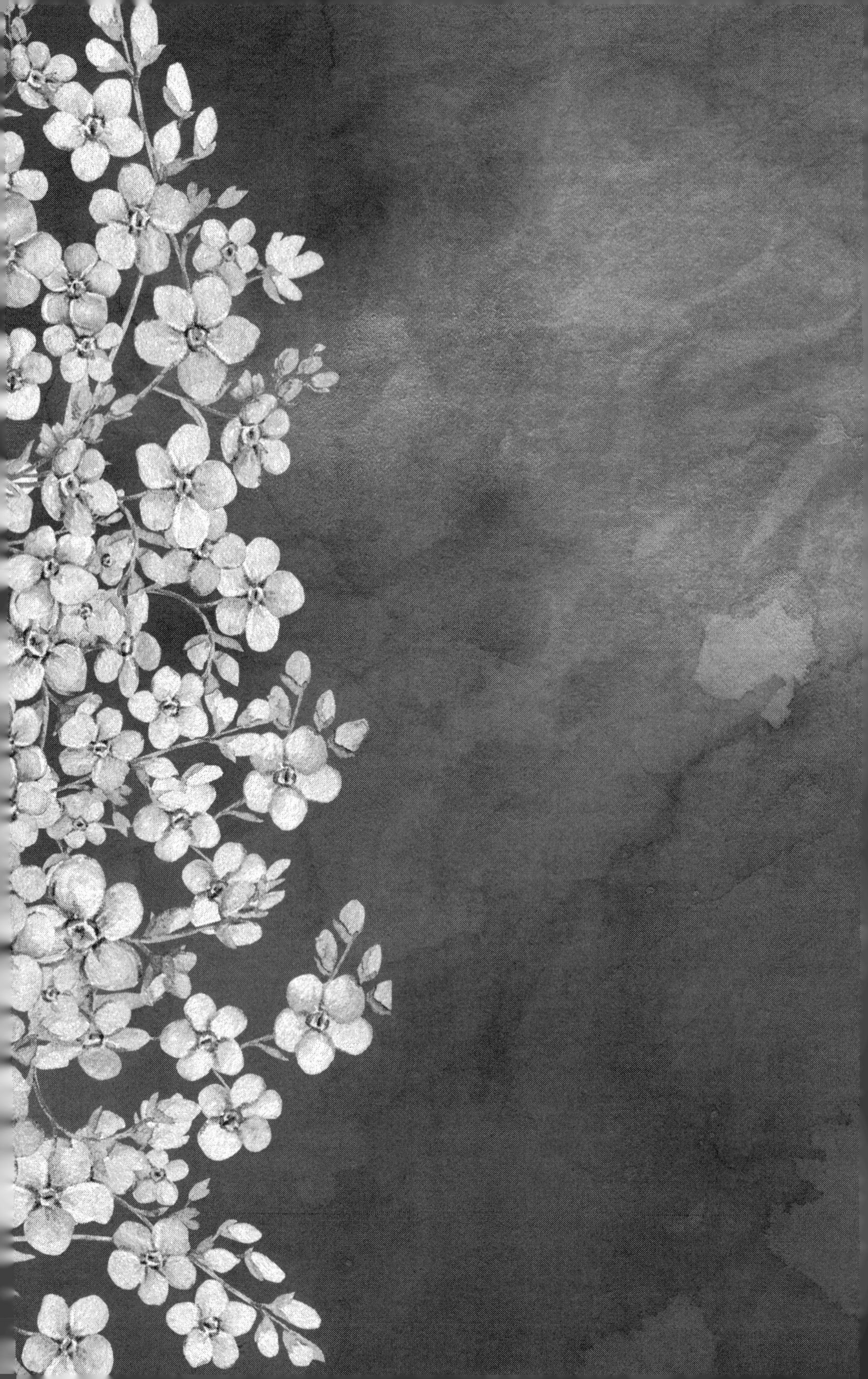

CHAPTER XIV
ALLIES
-PETER-

"P*eter… Just because I'm dead doesn't mean I don't still own a piece of your soul.*" Tiger Lily's sultry laugh echoed in my mind as my body jolted out of the dream.

I cracked my eyes open in a panic and instantly regretted it. The morning sun filtering in from the window seemed violent, blinding me with its overzealous rays. I felt like my head was about to split in half. Fucking rum. I swore to myself at that moment that I would never drink again.

Where the hell was I?

Once my eyes finally adjusted to the morning light, I

found myself in a massive bed. Gwen lay sleeping next to me, her chestnut hair fanned out around her. Silken sheets covered her lower half, but her perfect little breasts were exposed. My already hard cock twitched against the sheets. The previous night came rushing back to me all at once and I groaned.

I rubbed my hand over my face, trying to wipe away the visions that danced in my head. It had been so erotic, so taboo, so fucking hot. And the fact that I'd shared that moment with Hook made the shame rise from the pit of my stomach and start to eat away at me. I wasn't ashamed of Gwen, more so of the filthy things we'd done to her together. I'd allowed Hook to corrupt me, and I hadn't cared. Where did that leave us now? Still arch enemies? I don't think there was a rule book, but I doubted fucking the same girl at the same time was something one did with a mortal enemy.

I sat up slowly, letting my throbbing head adjust as I moved. I searched the cabin for Hook. He stood, his back to us as he stared out the window, silently taking in the sea as the day dawned. Part of me wanted to pull Gwen into my arms and flee the cabin, leaving the bastard behind, but I couldn't. Gwen would have my balls if I did and, as much as it pained me to admit, I needed something from Hook.

He didn't turn to face me when I rose from the bed, but I could see the change in his stance. He stiffened, every muscle in his body tense. Was he just as confused about our shared night with Gwen? Would we ever be able to put the past in the past and move forward?

I guess last night had been a start, and now I was about to take a leap of faith. Go against everything I believed in, and I didn't hesitate because I would do anything for Gwen. And now that I knew the truth, so would he.

"Do you think it's possible to bury the hatchet after so many years?" I whispered as I came up beside him. I didn't want to wake Gwen, and this conversation between us felt private.

He stood stoic for a long time, and I began to wonder if he'd even acknowledge me at all. He swirled a glass of rum in his solitary hand. How he managed to drink after the night we'd had was beyond me.

"The way the sun shimmers along the water as it journeys into the sky, that's something I will never tire of seeing. I pull myself from the comforts of my bed every morning because I never know if that day will be my last." His voice was raspy as he spoke, stopping to take a sip of his rum. "Once upon a time, I would have welcomed an honorable death. But she has changed all of that for me. I want to spend an eternity pleasing that woman in every way possible. If the hatchets and the guns and the swords and even the crocodiles," he paused and his eyes flicked to the beast that remained chained in his cabin, "are to be buried, it would be for her. I will never trust you. Never let my guard down around you, and I would happily kill you if you put her at risk. But I don't know how many sunrises I have left, and I won't squander them for the likes of you any longer."

I nodded, taking in his words. They resonated with my own sentiments, and I knew some new sort of truce had been struck between us. "I need your help." It felt strange to say. Never in my life would I have ever envisioned myself saying those four words to Captain James Hook.

He took another swig of his rum, his gaze still settled on the rising sun. I wasn't about to grovel at his feet, but I got the feeling he would not make this easy on me either, the fucker. Even though his face remained emotionless, I was sure that his inner demon was grinning ear to ear. I continued on, confident that once he knew the details, there was no way he'd sit on the sidelines, not where Gwen was concerned. "I've located the Osakren. Arion has it and he's been holding up in the Viridianwood. You know as much as I do, that Gwen is bound by death to return it to the bone faerie. I'm planning a mission to relieve him of the artifact. He's planning to trade the relic with the bastard prince—"

"Wait... Did you say the bastard prince?"

"I did. Apparently he's a—"

"I know who he is," he barked, interrupting me yet again.

"You've heard of him?"

"We crossed paths a lifetime ago. May the Divine have mercy on our souls if that's the Fae who's hunting Neverland."

"He's attempting to barter with Arion to get his hands

on the Osakren. According to the beasts, it's game over if that happens."

He tapped his hook against his chin, a deep furrow now present on his brow. "You need more than just my help, Peter. We need a goddamned miracle. This Fae is the worst of their kind. A soulless demon, with no compunction for the sanctity of life. His only pursuit is power."

"What… Are you afraid of a little challenge now? Old age getting the better of you?"

"Fucking hell, Peter! Haven't you been listening to me? No! You never listen. I tried to warn you about all of this, but you and your pride laughed in my face. You still have a lot of growing up to do, boy."

"Are you trying to be my father now?"

"I am trying to be your goddamn ally," he growled, before shooting back the rest of his rum and slamming the glass down on the windowsill to accentuate his point. My ally? That's what I'd been asking for, and yet his words still stopped me cold. I was torn. This man was a master of deceit, and yet I felt inclined to believe him.

"What's changed? After all these years, what's changed?"

"That"—he turned and pointed to Gwen, still sleeping in the bed—"that right there. I *burn* for her. She has reforged the shattered pieces of my soul, and I've emerged as a different man. She has changed the very fiber of my being. I no longer live for myself. I exist to make that woman happy.

It isn't rational, I cannot explain it, but I will do everything in my power to bend fate in her favor."

"So you'll help us then?"

"My path leads wherever she goes. But let's get a few things straight. I am not one of your Lost Boys. This"—he pinched the bridge of his nose before shaking his head—"this alliance doesn't mean that I answer to you. Understood?"

"Agreed." I offered him my hand to seal the deal in good faith. He peered down at it briefly, then returned his gaze to mine, looking unamused by my offer.

"Tell me your plans," he demanded, leaving me hanging.

"He has until sunset to deliver the Osakren to Dorian. We lay in wait, and when he makes his move, we'll intercept. But I want to take Arion alive. I have plans for him. What he did to Gwen cannot stand, and I plan to make him pay severely for his error in judgment."

"That's it? That's your grand scheme? A bit too much left in fate's hands, don't you think? And she is quite a vindictive bitch if you give her the chance. I think we can do better than that." A sly smile parted his lips and I could almost make out the devil dancing in his eyes.

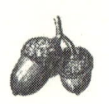

I took a moment alone to compose myself before I faced my Lost Boys again. When we got back from the Jolly Roger, I'd managed to update them on the new plans for Arion, before I'd run out on them. I needed some time alone to process. The truth of who I'd once been was eating away at me. Hook had brought it all to the surface and I couldn't hide from the actions I'd long since forgotten. He'd tried to paint me as the ultimate villain. And maybe I was the villain in *his* story. But he'd done awful, sinister things, too. Revenge had been his poison of choice. And he'd been relentlessly pursuing that revenge for years, with no regard for anyone who stood in his way... except for Gwen.

I had been an arrogant little shit who thought the sun and moon revolved around me. A spoiled brat with no care for anyone but myself. Visions of my own grandeur blinded me to the lengths I'd gone to achieve it. But the villain? The idea didn't sit well with me. I'd always questioned why the Divine had brought Wendy into my life. And now, just maybe, I had the answer. Wendy had started a chain reaction. Made me feel something for the first time. Something other than my own narcissistic admirations. And when she'd been ripped away from me, I hadn't handled it well. I'd handled it like the petulant child I was.

That had been the last straw for Neverland. She could no longer abide the selfish brat she'd helped to create, and it had been trial by fire. I was starting to realize that I was always meant to grow up. I'd just needed a really long time to get there. I wished fervently that I could go back and give my thirteen-year-old self some advice. Tell him that growing up wasn't all that bad. Maybe tell him how fucking good it felt to be balls deep in the girl that your soul burned for. That right there would have made all the difference. I felt my cock stir in my pants at the thought. But today was about the battle for the Osakren. Only after we'd secured it, and I laid vengeance at Gwen's feet in the form of Arion's corpse. Only then would I let myself indulge. When Gwen was finally safe from the bone faerie, then we'd all have our turns with her.

My mind drifted to thoughts of Tripp, Ryder, and even Eben. We'd grown so close over the years. Growing up side by side had forged an unbreakable bond between us. Something I never had with the previous Lost Boys who'd inevitably grown up and left me behind. And now Gwen rounded out our rag tag family. Hook had been right about fate. She'd dragged me through the mud, but man had it been worth it.

I would never admit it to anyone, but Gwen had softened me. I could feel the rivalry between Hook and I begin to ebb. We'd never be friends, like we'd been as boys. But we could be respectful allies. And I think I could live with that.

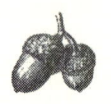

Everyone was busy preparing at the arms cellar when I joined them. Eben was strapping a plethora of weapons on Gwen.

"Shit Eben, she's not going to be able to move with all those weapons. I think you're just getting your rocks off by strapping them to her," Ryder teased.

"Fuck off, Ry. Apparently, I just care about her safety more than you do," Eben shot back.

"Or you have a weapons fetish. Keep an eye on him, Hen. He just might try to fuck you with the hilt of his knife." We all laughed, and Eben lunged for Ryder, pulling him into a headlock. I smiled at the sight. Everyone had been on edge. Today's mission was possibly the most important mission of our lives. My gut reaction had been to reject the plan that Hook had laid out, even though I could see the tactical aspects behind it were sound. But Gwen had been all for it, and I knew I was letting my emotions hold me back.

Everything was set. Now was the moment just before battle when adrenaline was running high, and your nerves were on the brink of getting the better of you. But Ryder had a way of easing the tension. Each and everyone of us added something to the group that was necessary, and I knew I would die for any one in that room.

"How about you save some of that for our enemy," I said. "It's time to move out."

We spent the morning flying over Neverland, each of us lost in our own mind as we made our way to the

Viridianwood. Lucius and Hook were waiting for us at the edge of the forest when we arrived. I had to still my hand from pulling my blade on the white wolf, Alo, when he came bounding in out of nowhere, butting his head against Gwen as soon as she appeared.

"Stop being a kiss ass," Lucius grumbled at the massive wolf. "Michaela's not even here for you to impress."

"Maybe he's not an asshole like you. Maybe *he* actually likes me and isn't using me to score points with my sister," Gwen shot back at him. Even though her words were crude, she was having a terrible time holding back her grin. An unlikely friendship, but it was clear that she had a soft spot for the wayward beast prince.

"My love, you look ravishing," Hook interrupted, "or maybe it's that you look ravished."—the corner of his lip curled with a knowing smile—"I think it's a look that suits you well," he purred as he pulled Gwen in and kissed her deeply. Apparently, he was no longer hiding his relationship with Gwen.

Eben cleared his throat, interrupting the display. "You had your fun last night, Hook. Now she needs you to focus on the mission." Eben sneered, not at all hiding his own feelings.

"Do you have the potion?" I asked, brushing off the alpha male display from Eben. Today wasn't the day for petty jealousy to get the better of us. Hook pulled a glass bottle from a pouch at his belt. "It's tough to come by in large quantities. This is probably the largest batch in the entire cosmos, but I have enough for each of you, save for the wolf, but he has no need of it."

Lucius took a step toward Hook, obviously ready to intervene on Alo's behalf. "Remember who we are fighting," Hook cautioned, not backing down from the hulking prince. "We must play on their weaknesses. They won't pay any mind to ones they believe to be lesser Fae. He'd just be another wild beast of the Viridianwood and no threat to them." Hook was quick to explain and Lucius grumbled his agreement. "One swig will render you invisible, to the untrained eye at least." Hook handed me the bottle. Its contents looked like nothing more than pond water. A dark green liquid with particles floating about.

"And how long will it last?" I asked.

"It varies. We'll have no more than two hours, possibly less."

"Are you sure this isn't some plan to off the rest of us so he can keep Gwen for himself?" Eben charged.

"Eben, stop," Gwen groaned in obvious irritation. I grinned in surprise. Watching her put Eben in his place was hot as fuck. Eben simply stared at her, and my normally mouthy Lost Boy remained silent. She went to him, placing a hand on his cheek. "I know you don't trust him, but I promise James is not here to poison you. Do you trust me?" Eben closed his eyes for a moment, before nodding his agreement.

"Now that's settled, Gwendolyn, my love, your bindings await you," Hook beckoned her forward, a length of rope in his hand. "Reminds me of the night we first met. We may have to role play the rest of the scene later."

"James," she scolded, but I could see her telltale blush. She liked being restrained, and I made a mental note to get some rope of my own. She stopped by each Lost Boy, taking a private moment with each of them. When she made it to me, I pulled her in, crushing her to my chest.

"Don't do anything rash today, okay," I murmured in her ear.

"Me? I have more protectors than one girl could ever need. It's you I'm worried about. Stay safe. All of us come back from this or none of us do." She pulled back and kissed me, hard. All of her restrained emotions let loose on that kiss and when she pulled away, I was breathless.

"I love you, Peter." And with that, she turned and walked to Hook, presenting her wrists to him.

"Down the hatch, boys," I called out before I took a swig of the potion and handed it to Eben. My heart stuttered in my chest. The last time I'd drank a potion, I'd lost my free will. My anxiety rippled through my body as my skin began to tingle. I held my hand in front of my face and watched as my fingers disappeared into the ether. When I looked up, only Hook, Gwen and the massive wolf stood at the edge of the forest, the rest of us now cloaked in dark magic.

"Remember, my love." He lifted her chin with his hook until she was looking into his eyes. "Any words that I say out there, they aren't real. It's all a façade, and it must be perfect for this to work. So know that I am already sorry, and I will make it up to you once this is all over."

We trailed behind. Gwen's hair swayed back and forth as she hung over Hook's shoulder. The sight of her bound wrists threatened to take my mind completely off the mission and into much more hedonistic territory and I had to force my eyes away altogether. At some point, Smee had joined his Captain. The sneaky bastard seemed to materialize out of nowhere.

I watched as the enemy sentries began to surround them. One very useful advantage of being invisible. My hand instinctively went to the pommel of my sword, and I had to remind myself that this was all part of the plan. I did my best to stay close to them. It was crucial that I could hear everything being said. Hook stopped abruptly, tossing Gwen to the ground like a rag doll and placing a boot on top of her. My teeth clenched in response, but I held my ground.

"I know you're there. Why don't you stop wasting both of our time and show yourself?" He pulled a white handkerchief from his sleeve and waved it in the air. The hidden sentries remained in place, quietly watching, waiting for some signal. "I have a deal to make," Hook continued, "I know you're in league with the bastard prince, and I have a gift that he'll be very pleased to get his hands on."

It was then that Arion finally showed himself, sauntering out of the woods with a cocky swagger that had my blood boiling. His dark hair was pulled back into a thong, and he was fully dressed in black leather armor. He'd obviously been preparing himself to show off his strengths to Dorian and beg at his feet for some scrap of attention. I couldn't wait to get my hands on him, but I had to be patient.

"Hook, I never expected to find you this far inland," he said warily.

"These are desperate times. And you're not the easiest Fae to find these days."

"And what is the nature of your business with me?"

"It's times like these that require alliances, and I'm in the business of picking the winning side. I know you have connections to Dorian, and I'm looking to gain an audience with him. The tides are turning, and according to my calculations, Neverland will fall within a fortnight. I am here to make a deal. I'm offering my allegiance in exchange for a lucrative position within his new kingdom, and to sweeten the deal, I have Pan's little whore. I think that's enough to buy my way into his good graces."

"You're a goddamned leech, Hook. Fucking pathetic." He sneered at Hook and my pulse quickened. Hook had to sell it better than that. I watched as Arion's outer ring of sentries began to fall. One minute they were standing poised, the next they were slowly falling to the ground with their throats slit by an invisible Grim Reaper. My boys delivered them a silent death, and with all eyes on Arion and Hook, no one sounded the alarm. "And why should I trust you, anyway? Word has it that it was you who took out Tiger Lily," Arion accused.

Hook chuckled, "If you really believe that, you're more

incompetent than I originally assumed. Of course Pan blamed me for her murder. He had to keep his hands clean to take control of the island."

"I saw you that night. I watched you follow her into the caves. That's the last time anyone saw her alive."

"Tiger Lily and I had an agreement. She committed heinous acts against her own people, and I was a convenient scapegoat. All for the price of turning a blind eye when it came to my dealings. Now why would I ruin such a favorable deal?"

Arion scratched the stubble on his chin, obviously contemplating his words. Hook could see the shift too and he continued, trying to capitalize on his indecision.

"I just need you to arrange an audience with Dorian." Hook stooped down, yanking Gwen to her feet by her hair. She let out a clipped scream, and I ground my teeth so hard I was surprised they didn't crack.

"She's the perfect bargaining tool. Pan and his Lost Boys will fold the moment they realize he has her. Once Pan is compliant, it will make subjecting the natives to his will that much easier. Not to mention, she is beautiful. Has the makings of a perfect little plaything."

Arion sneered. "Dorian is a pureblood Fae. He'd never spoil himself by putting his cock into a lowly mortal."

"Well, you know what they say, once you've fucked a human…"

"No, actually, I don't know what they say."

"Right. Well then, never mind that. Let's get to business,

shall we?" I could see Hook's eyes flick to the side almost imperceptibly, attempting to check our progress at taking down the outer ring of sentries. There were more of them than I had expected, and we never would have been able to take them all on in direct combat. We were running out of time. Arion was surrounded by a small group of what I assumed were his best fighters. There was no way we could take them out without Arion knowing what was happening. The best chance I had was to take him out myself and watch as my boys slaughtered the rest. There would be no prisoners here. None of them would leave this forest alive.

Arion took a step toward Gwen. Hook was still holding her bound wrists from behind. His predatory eyes raked over her in a way that had my blood boiling. He grabbed her cheeks in his firm hand.

"For a human, this one is awfully hard to kill. Maybe I'd been going about it all wrong. Maybe something a bit more drawn out would be a better choice. See how loud she can scream." His face transformed into a sinister smile before he leaned in and took a deep inhale of her hair.

"Fuck you, Arion," she growled even as his fingers dug into her cheeks, and then she spit in his face. I would have laughed, if not for the seriousness of the situation we were in. The look on Arion's face was priceless. His smirk was gone as he reached up to wipe the spit from his cheek. In a flash of movement, his hand whipped out, backhanding her, causing her head to whip to the side. It took every ounce of strength within me not to gut him right there. I heard a rustle of leaves and I said a silent prayer to the Divine that my boys held it together.

"Now, now... I won't have you bruising the fruit before I have a chance to present it to the prince," Hook scolded, doing his best to save her from any further abuse.

"How about you leave her with me? I'll make sure she gets to Dorian"

"When you say you'll make sure she gets to Dorian, what I'm hearing is that you plan to take credit for my prize and leave me with nothing. That's not how this works. You arrange the meeting and I bring the girl."

"I expected more from you, Hook. But you've walked into the lion's den with nothing more than your bosun and you're standing between me and my prey." Arion grabbed ahold of Gwen's arm, and pulled her forward, dislodging her from Hook's grasp, and that was the final straw. The idea of her falling into enemy hands tipped me over the edge. A loud crack of thunder reverberated off the trees, and a brilliant flash of lightning split the sky. Arion and his guards startled, their attention pulled to the darkening sky. I could feel the rage pouring out of me, burning off whatever magic was keeping me invisible, and when their eyes dropped from the skies, they landed on me.

It was chaos in motion. All of them sprang into action, reaching for their sword, and they were met with steel that had been hiding amongst them. The white wolf leapt into the fight, tearing a throat out with vicious teeth, covering all of us in a spray of blood. Arion was the exception.

Instead of pulling his sword, he reached for a pouch at his belt.

Hook grabbed for Gwen, pulling her out of the way. Leaving me open to stalk Arion, knowing she was safe in his arms. I saw a hint of fear in his eyes as he fumbled for whatever was in his pouch. Could he see his death dancing in my eyes? He backed away from me, but I closed the gap between us. I could almost taste the fear radiating from him. When he finally managed to open the pouch, my eyes caught a flash of white and I registered he was holding the Osakren a moment before a blast of energy shot out of him, knocking me flat.

The blast of power from the Osakren laid out everyone in close proximity. Every bone in my body ached, but I scrambled to get to my feet in time to see Arion disappearing into the woods. I wouldn't lose him, not this time. Gwen would die if I didn't get that god forsaken skull. I let the enormity of that wash over me. A vision of her lifeless corpse flashed in my mind, her vacant caramel eyes staring through me.

Something snapped inside me. A shift, a change, a metamorphosis of sorts and for the first time ever, I could feel the power from the island. It pooled like electricity, sparking around my feet. It had always been there, just waiting for me to access it. Waiting for me to be pushed far enough to awaken the power that had been dormant within me. It was like opening a floodgate, and I let the power surge into me, crawling up my legs, into my chest. Miniature bolts of lightning crackled around my hands. This was it, the power that had been promised to me, my destiny finally manifesting. Coming to my aide to protect that which belonged to me.

I grinned and started after Arion. He was no match for me, even with his feeble attempt to use the Osakren. I stalked him into the forest, making up ground quickly. I knew exactly where he was. The land fed me his location through our connection. He couldn't hide from me. I took to the trees, silently following him from above. With a resounding crack of thunder, I dropped from the trees directly in front of him. He skidded to a halt moments before he collided with me. The look of fear in his eyes was delicious, and I was hungry for more. He began to lift his hand, the Osakren clutched in his palm. I lashed out, grabbing his wrist, sending a bolt of energy into his arm until he dropped the skull to the ground.

"That's better," I growled. "You're too weak to wield that kind of magic. But I'll give you a chance to redeem yourself. Fight me like a man."

I pulled my sword from its scabbard, beckoning him forward. He pulled his sword and circled to his left, knowing he had no other option. He made the first move, lashing out, steel kissing steel, the sound was like music to my ears. I toyed with him, enjoying the lethal dance far too much. The thunder cracked as our swords met, lightning flashed, reflecting off the silver.

"You know you can't beat him, Pan. He will take the

realm. All you have to decide is how much suffering you want to endure before you submit."

"That's always been your problem. Choosing the losing side. And here you are again, only this time, your life will be payment for your poor decisions."

We continued to dance together, sword against sword. I drew out the moment, reveling in the fact that I was merely playing with my prey.

When I'd reached my fill and the need for vengeance became too much to bear, I whirled on him, my sword connecting with his leg, severing his hamstring. He fell to the ground, and with a flick of my blade, I relieved him of his sword, letting it skitter to the ground. The next arc of my blade had it poised at his neck, but that was too easy of a death for all the havoc he'd caused. Now it was time to give my girl the revenge she deserved.

Arion chuckled as he kneeled, unarmed and at my mercy. "He's coming for you, Pan. Killing me now accomplishes nothing."

"Says the desperate man. Now get up. You have a date with the Lost Boys."

"I can't walk."

"Then you better start crawling."

I DROPPED Arion to the ground at the Lost Boy's feet. I'd had to carry him the last bit of the way. The gash in his leg had saturated his clothes, his blood dripping down my back. I'd spared a pinch of faerie dust to partially heal his wound so he wouldn't bleed out before I had a chance to exact my vengeance. The Osakren, even for its slight weight, felt heavy hanging from my belt.

I stood over Arion, his body sprawled on the ground and the sense of power was overwhelming. My Lost Boys, along with Lucius and the wolf, had laid waste to the rest of the traitorous Fae and the euphoria of our victory was palpable. Gwen stood, still in the arms of Hook, her wrists now free.

"Gwen, darling, I've brought him to you. When it's all over, you can rest easy knowing that he's dead," I said, offering him to her as some morbid gift that might ease some of the trauma she'd suffered at his hands.

She left Hook's embrace and took tentative steps toward Arion. "String him up," she commanded, her voice as cold as ice, her face expressionless, a hint of a bruise beginning to form where he'd struck her.

Eben and Ryder grabbed him under the arms, ignoring his groans as they strapped him to a tree. Gwen pulled the blade her sister had given her, her hand shaking as she approached him.

"I hope you feel the same fear that I felt, that my sister felt. I want you to feel that desperation crawl into your chest and consume you. I hope you burn in whatever hell exists after this life." Arion remained silent, his eyes downcast. He knew his luck was up and he wouldn't give Gwen the satisfaction of begging for his life. She held the blade to his face, her chest heaving with emotion, but she hesitated. Tripp came up beside her, running his hand slowly up her back.

"Gwen, beautiful… It's okay. You don't have to do this."

"I can do it. I have to do it. He tried to kill me. Tried to kill Mic." Her words trembled with the weight of her emotions.

"I know you can do it, but you don't have to. Let us be your protectors. We want to feel his blood on our hands. We want to extract the revenge that is owed. Will you let us do that for you?" His hand traced up her arm, closing his fingers around hers, pulling the blade down from Arion's face. She crumpled into his arms, nodding her agreement.

Each of us took our turn with Arion, reveling in the screams we inevitably pulled out of him. We tortured him in unspeakable ways until he was nothing more than a bloody corpse sagging against the tree. We were all covered in his blood, and none of us made a move to clean it off. It was a mark of pride to wear our enemies' blood. A stern warning to anyone who thought to cross us. Gwen had watched every gory moment, never averting her eyes. Only when it was done, when he took his last ragged breath, did a tear fall from her cheek.

A slow clap jolted us all back to reality. "Bravo, boys, bravo! I do so love a good torture session. It always gives me a tremendous cock-stand that I'll have to address later." We all whirled to find a man stalking toward us, and instinctively, I pulled Gwen behind me. He emerged from the shadowed depths of the forest, too handsome to be a mere mortal. He bordered on pretty, dressed as he was in all white. Tight breeches covered by a long tunic coat that hung almost to his knees, trimmed in gold and silver embroidery. He wore unique armor under his coat, a rib cage made of silver and encrusted in jewels encased his broad chest. Hair that was so pale, it almost looked silver, hung to his shoulders. But what really drew my attention was the massive expanse of feathered black wings spread out behind him, a stark contrast to the pristine white clothes he wore.

"Who are you?" I growled at the beautiful stranger. Now that Arion had been taken care of, we had to see about the bone faerie. I was in no mood for distractions.

"How depressing," he mused as he fidgeted with his nails. "I was sure my reputation proceeded me. I endeavor to do better next time. Allow me to introduce myself. I am Dorian, Son of the House of Einar, Fae Prince of the First Realm. A true blood descendent of the Divine." There was a collective silence as we all took in the demon that now stood amongst us. "Ahhh, so you have heard of me. How lovely."

"You are not welcome here," I said, turning to face him head on, shielding Gwen, my Lost Boys fanning out around us. Even Hook stood his ground beside me.

"Don't you know the proper etiquette for welcoming royalty into your realm?" he tsked. "A word of advice for

Neverland's self-proclaimed king, never let anyone see your naivety, it leaves you vulnerable."

"Don't misjudge my bluntness for naivety. I don't care whose son you are, I don't make a habit of inviting demons into my home."

"If you truly are the great king you profess to be, then allow me to negotiate a trade. You hand over my birthright, and I won't slaughter your friends." He said it so nonchalantly that it took me a moment to process his words.

"Birthright? I have no idea what you're talking about."

"Oh don't play coy with me, Peter Pan. I know you have the Osakren, and it belongs to me. It is the only gift my father ever gave to me, and it was wrongfully stolen from me. Now I expect you to return it, and I will happily allow your friends to leave this forest with their lives. An honest trade don't you think? Or do their lives have no value to you?"

The bastard had me between a rock and a hard place. If I showed any emotion for Gwen or my Lost Boys, they would all have targets on their backs from here on out.

"Let's say I can offer you this birthright, then I expect you will leave Neverland the moment it's returned to you?" I stalled him, trying to drag out these so-called negotiations. He was simply toying with us now. I had to get the Osakren to Gwen and get her out of here. Buy her time until she could get to the bone faerie. Maybe the old hag could offer her some protection.

"I do believe I've offered you quite a generous deal. It

would be a shame to slit her beautiful little throat over a simple memento. My offer stands. What say you, King of Neverland?" He pulled a small dagger from his belt and began picking at his nails with it. He looked utterly bored with the entire situation. I used his momentary distraction to slip the small skull out of the pouch at my side and placed it in Gwen's hands behind me. The moment her fingers touched the bone, I felt the pressure of magic breathing down my back. Before I could even register the danger, Gwen was ripped away from me.

Chapter XV
A Wrinkle in the Fabric
-Gwen-

I clutched the Osakren to my belly, the pronged antlers digging into my skin. I held on to the small skull for dear life as her gnarled fingers curled around my neck—long nails scraping along my jawline. The smell of rotting flesh enveloped me and I knew the bone faerie had come to collect on our bargain. Her tongue clicked in my ear as she sucked in a breath. I blinked rapidly, staring out at all of my men. Each of them covered in Arion's blood. They were all that stood between me and Dorian. Now, we were caught between two evils. My mind was desperately trying to play catch up. It had all happened so fast. The situation with Dorian had been on the precipice, moments away from falling into violence. Peter had placed the relic in my hand, preparing to make a stand, to give me the precious time I needed to escape the demon before us. The moment my fingers skimmed the smooth surface, I'd felt the strange tingle of magic, and she'd materialized behind me, yanking me away from Peter and my boys.

Now, I was firmly tucked into her taloned grasp, her membranous wings cocooning around us. The look of sheer terror on their faces must have mirrored my own. Alo whined, crouching down on his haunches as he attempted to get closer to me.

"Well, if it's not my dear sister," Dorian said, drawing out the words with an air of refinement. The word sister coming off his lips with a sneer. His predatory eyes fixated on the old hag. Sister? There was no way the sinfully handsome features of the bastard prince shared the same bloodline as the bone faerie.

"I cut that bond a millennia ago," she hissed, and spit on the ground at my feet.

"Oh Peytra," he tsked, "you cannot sever the blood ties that bind us. I've told you that a thousand times. And yet you go to such lengths to defy me. Such a pity." The condescension was thick in his eloquently spoken words.

"The blood that connected us was purged long ago. I am something altogether different now."

"You are exactly what I intended you to be. A stepping stone. You thought you could run from me, dear sister. Thought you could steal what was rightfully mine? It was an amusing game, I must admit. But now that I have you firmly under my boot again, you know there will be consequences to your actions. It's only fair."

"*She* is long dead, Dorian. Crushed under your *boot*, but what arose from the ashes is a force you cannot control."

"Give me the relic, Peytra. Give it to me now and I'll let you scurry back into the shadows where you belong."

"A fork, like the serpent's tongue, tickles fate. The chance has eclipsed you, bastard prince. The blood of the old ones is a seductive whore, but a chosen daughter is an awfully fine prize indeed. The fates have set this path. I have seen it in the bones."

"Sad, really. Sad that you think the remains of a few dead animals can save you from me. I don't sleep in the fates bed any longer. I make my own fate, and it will be glorious. This is my last warning. Give me the Osakren."

"I am here to take the star," her raspy voice hissed in my ear. "The fate of worlds hangs in the balance. The Osakren belongs to her now. Raise arms against me and I will destroy it. And you'll have to wait until the birth of a new universe to exact your revenge."

"It's mine, Peytra!" he snarled, losing his composure for a moment. He ran a hand through his silken locks, and firmly returned his calm, collected mask back into place. "You know I will just find another way and it will be all the more painful for the natives here. That will be on your conscience, not mine." Dorian glared at her, a sliver of the evil within him still shining through.

"Bone faerie!" Peter's booming voice demanded her attention, drawing the unlikely siblings from their war of wits. "That wasn't the bargain! You wanted the relic, she's brought it to you. Now take it and go."

She hissed at him, baring her black, rotting teeth as she backed away, pulling me with her. "The Divine forbids it. Our strings may not tangle, only when the last grains fall."

"You cannot have her," he growled in response.

Her whole body shook with a wicked cackle. "Fools! You cannot stop what is already written."

"I will not let you take her from me." Peter drew his sword and shifted into a defensive pose, each of my Lost Boys following suit.

"How about we make a deal, Peter?" Dorian interjected. "A first between rulers. You get the Osakren. I'll let you have the girl. An act of good faith to get you in my good graces."

A loud crack of thunder reverberated in the air around us. Neverland, herself, reacting to the fury swirling in Peter's eyes, reiterating his answer without a single word spoken.

An audible click pulled my attention to James, his pistol resting on his hook, the barrel trained on the bone faerie. "I'll put a bullet through your skull before the beat of your wings even rustles the air, old one."

"Oh dear, this day is giving me a headache." Dorian

reached up to rub his temples as though the volatility was nothing but a simple inconvenience.

"Have they eaten your soul like a rotten, wormed apple yet, my little star?" The bone faerie stopped and took a deep breath, inhaling my scent. "No… it's something else that eats away your soul, a wicked doppelgänger. He will sever the bonds that hold you together if you don't come with me now." She laughed again, and it sent a chill down my spine. I could feel the blood drain from my face. I'd been keeping this terrible secret from my Lost Boys and I couldn't risk them hearing the truth of it now.

"Interesting. This insignificant girl is quite the opposite of what she pretends to be. I am thoroughly smitten." Dorian stroked the clean lines of his pretty face as he looked at me with a whole new set of eyes.

"Time to tie off your strings, little star. Tie them tight so they will be here when you return." I made up my mind. I had to let her take me to keep my boys safe. The moment Amara laid it all out and told me I was a danger to the men who gave meaning to my life, I knew leaving them might be the only way I could save them. Now the Divine was presenting me with an out, and I had to jump at the chance. And if the bone faerie knew of a way to rid me of Kían, then I would follow her to the ends of the cosmos and pry the answer from her dying corpse if I had to.

"She's right. I have to go."

"Hen, don't you dare." Ryder glared at me.

"Ry, I have to. There is so much more at stake than just us."

"You don't even know what she's saying. Her words don't always mean what you think they mean," Eben growled.

"Let her go now and she may never come back. Best to keep what is yours under lock and key, lest she fall into… more seductive hands." Dorian raised an eyebrow, trying to use me as a pawn to convince them to retrieve the Osakren. Something about his hesitancy was telling. He fully believed the bone faerie would destroy us all if he moved against her.

"Gwendolyn is quite capable of making her own decisions. Just do be careful, my love," James winked at me, his way of saying goodbye. He already knew my decision.

"The offer is once and the bones are restless. The Divine has made it so. Refuse me now and nothing will deliver you from the maelstrom. I will read the birth of a new cosmos in *your* bones." Her words may have been riddled, but her meaning was clear. She was my last chance. Our last chance to save Neverland from the darkness that was stalking her.

"You have to let me go with her," I called to them, tears leaking from the corners of my eyes. I drank them in, my gaze settling on each of them in turn. I'd made my decision. I could already feel the ties severing between us and the longing take up residence in my heart. I wasn't one to pray for much of anything, but I found myself saying a silent prayer to god, the divine, the universe… anyone who would listen. I prayed this wouldn't be the last time I laid eyes on my boys.

"Don't come after me. I will come back to you. I promise." I had no way of knowing if I could uphold that promise, but they needed to hear it. I needed to put it out into the universe. But my decision to leave was final and I could tell the bone faerie knew it, too. With the next beat of my heart the world around me began to disintegrate. A blur of white fur lunged toward me, and the sound of them calling my name was the last thing I remembered.

I DON'T KNOW how much time passed from the moment I was ripped away from the Viridianwood. I could feel my body moving through time and space, but I had no control. I couldn't make out solid forms. And then I was simply staring at my hands as they lay in my lap. I didn't know how long I'd been staring at them. It occurred to me at some point that the black veining was gone. I smiled at the oddity of it. I'd grown accustomed to the dark lines that cut across my skin in an intricate web, covering me like an ominous tattoo. Now the creamy skin of my hands seemed almost foreign.

An incessant buzzing pulled me from my trance. The flutter of tiny wings caressed my face, pulling my attention from my hands. I absently swiped at whatever it was that was trying to pull me from the quiet oblivion that seemed so comforting at the moment. A cold nose and a warm tongue lapped at my face, accompanied by a gentle prodding in my mind. Was I alright? That seemed to be the question, and yet I had no answer.

The incessant buzzing returned, threatening to break the peace I was straining to hold on to. I swatted at it, more forcefully this time. "Ouch! What the f—" Pain seared through my pinky finger and I pulled it to my mouth, tasting blood as I sucked on the offended finger.

My eyes darted around wildly to find whatever danger was flying around my head. I settled on what looked like a... pixie? Or at least at one time it had been. The tiny body was nothing more than bones that shimmered gold, as though they had been gilded. Its face, although there was still some discernible flesh, was pale and sunken in, outlining the tiny skull beneath. Empty black pits where the eyes should be were focused intently on me. It was oddly beautiful, even in death. Because although it was flying around my head, it was most definitely dead.

"Porthos! Do not touch what the Divine has claimed. That finger is key." The bone faerie's raspy voice brought reality crashing back to me. I swiveled around, my eyes landing on her repulsive figure. More black eye sockets stared back at me, but hers had much more depth, as if I was staring into the abyss of hell itself.

I chanced a look around, attempting to get my bearings.

We were in some sort of swamp. Stunted trees grew up from the ground like gnarled hands, thick moss covered the branches, like curtains hanging from their wicked fingers. There was no sun. What little of the sky I could see looked like a sickly gray. We sat at the entrance to a large cave. The bone faerie sat before me, draped in thick black robes, with her hands resting on a rudimentary wooden staff. Tucked into my side was Alo. His piercing amber eyes trained on me. He was the one pushing the question of my well-being into my mind.

"I think I'm alright, Alo. But where are we?"

"Nowhere." The bone faerie croaked. "Tis the beauty of it. Just a wrinkle in the fabric. A spot in the cosmos where we exist and don't exist at the same time."

"So... we aren't in Neverland?"

"Primal desire is a distraction even the Divine cannot control. Your strings pull you too tightly into their beds. Your time is fleeting. The safe heaven that was once Neverland is no more."

"I take it that's your brother's doing?"

"Neverland is a tasty morsel that can offer him redemption. But vendettas lead down a futile path. Nothing but death is in that direction, and yet death is the answer."

"If time is fleeting, then get to the point. What can you tell me about this... parasite? How can I get rid of him?" The crone raised to her feet, turning toward the entrance to the cave without answering my question. "You told me you could help me! I'm here! I've done everything you've asked of me. I cannot be the chosen with this... this thing inside of me. The Divine owes me at least that much!"

"Owed? She's owed, Porthos!" She cackled to herself as the zombie faerie circled her head. "You are here because the Divine wishes it to be so. You are alive because it is the Divine's whim. Nothing more is needed."

"You promised me answers!"

"Mmm... anger. I feel its power running through you, but you must point it in the proper direction."

"What the fuck was I thinking coming here? You don't know anything!" I threw up my hands in frustration. "You're just an old crone whose magic is nothing more than parlor tricks." She was right. I was angry. She'd been my last hope. I'd stupidly thought the Divine was finally throwing me a fucking bone. Now I was trapped here with no way to strip this stain from my soul. I'd left my boys to face Dorian without me, and I had no answers. I was completely useless.

"A daughter of Wendy. Ha! The power gifted to the first race ran thicker than blood in my veins. The House of Einar had a daughter, a diamond. But it took the weight of everything evil to make it so. Fair and beautiful... That was my veiled gift. The Divine works mysteriously. A great gift? Or truly a curse in disguise."

The air around her began to shimmer, like heat rising from a blacktop in summer. Her image flickered and where the crone had been, a beautiful woman stood. Long, platinum blonde hair hung in lustrous waves around a shapely body. Stunning amber eyes locked onto mine, conveying so much in her stare. Could it really be so? Had this hideous creature truly been the beauty before me?

"Come, the sand runs through our fingers. You must see with eyes that you do not yet possess." Her form flickered for a moment and the beautiful woman was gone, leaving only the old crone and her urgent tone propelling me forward. Alo was right on my heels, a low growl rumbling from his chest. He was obviously on edge here in this surreal world of the bone faerie's making.

I followed her into the dark cave. What else could I do? I had to find answers any way I could, even if she wasn't forthcoming with the information I needed. My eyes glued on her as she pulled the Osakren from her robes. At some point in time, she'd taken it from me. Somehow, she'd managed to pry it from my death grip without me even knowing.

The skull drifted up from her palm, as though invisible fingers held onto it, and in a flash of movement, the skull slammed against the wall of the cave, shattering upon impact. I gasped aloud as shards of the magical relic clattered to the ground.

"What are you doing?" I shrieked. "You were willing to take my life for that! And now it means nothing?" I was irate. I'd been through hell trying to get that bone back to her, and now it was little more than rubble at her feet.

"Mmm... No vision. Look harder. Just because it is changed doesn't mean it contains any less magic. Change is the lifeblood of the universe. The Osakren blurs the lines of change between the world of the living and the world of the dead. A master of that which is to come and those that have already been. Come, I will show you."

She beckoned me forward, and I felt compelled to go to her, my body moving of its own accord. The moment I was within her reach, her boney hand snatched my wrist. She slammed my palm against the cold stone of the cave wall—the very place the Osakren had shattered. Alo's growl filled the cave, baring his teeth at the bone faerie, who paid him no mind.

"The Divine has asked me to give you a gift," she hissed. I could feel the well of panic begin to rise in my chest. Being a chosen had never served me well, and the last thing I wanted was to see what kind of gift the Divine had in store for me. "Now it is up to you to discern its meaning." A glint of silver caught my eye as a hatchet swung toward me. I had no time to react until it was done. The sound of metal on stone reverberated in my ears. I heard the sound of it first and then the pain came, shooting through my hand like a lightning rod. My eyes told me that my finger was gone, but my mind was having a hard time processing what had just happened. A scream bubbled up from the pit of my stomach, breaching the silence as I looked at my hand. Blood poured down my arm, spurting from the place where my pinky finger had been. What the fuck was happening? My mind was in utter chaos. The intense pain shut out any other thoughts. I couldn't process what I was supposed to do next. Alo barked incessantly, his warm body pressed against my side. It was the only comfort I had to hold on to.

The bone faerie dropped my arm, and I pulled my hand to my stomach. I was afraid to look at it. I couldn't even bring myself to staunch the bleeding. I was in shock. The bone faerie circled her skeletal hand, the shattered remains of the Osakren lifting from the ground, a warm light surrounding them. The shards began to mutate, taking on the form of four delicate bones, glittering in the light as if they had been coated in faerie dust. When they connected, a skeletal finger emerged from the pieces.

The hag snatched my hand again, my blood oozing between her clenched fist. She paid no mind to the sound of my sobbing as it echoed off the cave walls. Carrying on with her work as if nothing happened. Once again, I was useless. Staring at her with no idea what would happen next. She could have severed my skull from my body, and I would have sat there and let her do it. I watched in horror as she levitated the bone finger to the gory stub that was all that remained of my own. The bones clicked into place, fusing to my body, sending a shockwave of pain through me. My scream was so primal it was silent. The bones rendered from the Osakren felt like a hot coal, burning through my soul as if to purify me from within. Once the bones made my skeleton whole; tendons, muscle and skin manifested and my finger was restored. Only this one had all the markings the Osakren had carried. Black runes were now tattooed on the finger, wrapping around and trailing up the back of my hand.

Once the transplant was complete, the pain subsided. Knowledge flooded my mind like a tidal wave. My knees hit the ground with the weight of it all. Visions overwhelmed me, flashing in my mind's eye, from the very first day of creation forward. Everything that had ever been, every being that had ever lived, every magic known to the universe. The Osakren unlocked it all for me, giving me a glimpse at the enormity of it all. It was rapture, to see the beauty of life and all that it contained. The small kernel of magic that had rested in the pit of my stomach expanded until it coursed through every vein, rippled over my skin, waiting to do my bidding.

"The answers are at your fingertips, my chosen." An ethereal voice filled my head and tears trickled down my face. The words of the Divine filled me with a peace I'd never felt before. I wanted to bask in this light for the rest of my days. *"But you cannot stay here."*

"No, please, don't make me go. I want to stay. It's too hard. I can't do it all," I sobbed at the idea of leaving the peace that surrounded me.

"You would stay and forsake that which makes you whole?" Visions of my men began to flash inside my mind. Tripp, Ryder, Eben, Peter, and lastly, James. Their handsome faces cycled through my mind. I felt their missing pieces, my soul incomplete without them. And for the first time, I could see how we were one. Each of us making decisions that brought

us together, our souls tugging us along, lonely sojourners wandering through time and space, desperate to find one another.

"No," I breathed out as the realization overwhelmed me. "I made a promise to them, to me. I won't leave them. We belong to each other. I won't sever that tie. Not now, not ever."

"*A worthy chosen, just as I knew you would be. Now go, there is much to learn.*"

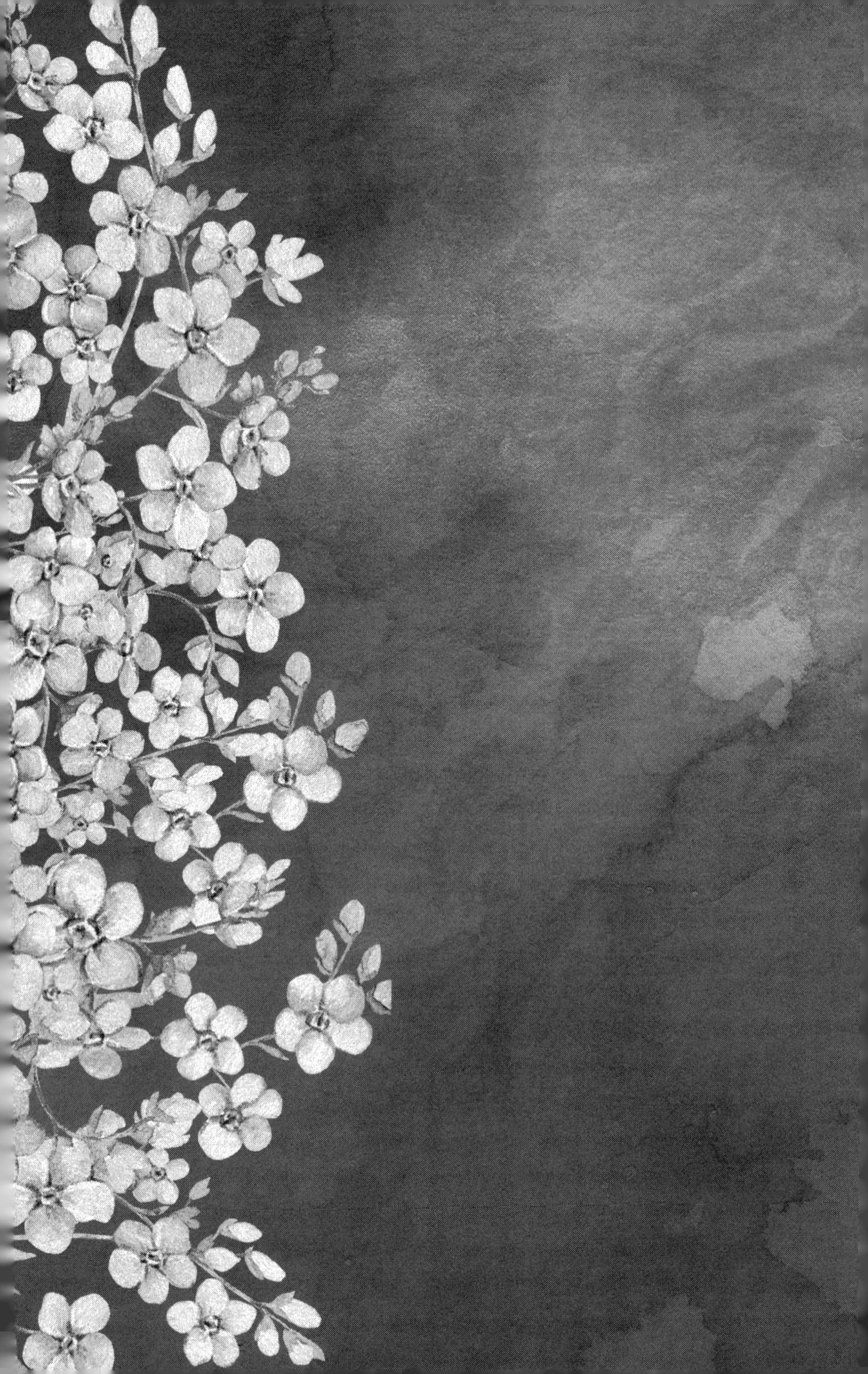

Chapter XVI
MEMORIES
-RYDER-

I rolled over in my empty bed. Another fucking night of tossing and turning. I think even my damn pillows were starting to feel violated. But nothing could make up for the loss of her. I was a goddamn mess. I would have given anything to have one of Pan's dreams. At least he got to see her, even if it was only a figment of his mind. I'd have slept the days away if it meant I could see her smile one more time. She'd been gone a month now, and I was petrified that I was starting to lose that vision of her. I held onto it with everything I had, determined not to let Neverland take those memories from me.

She'd asked us not to go after her, promised that she would come back to us. We'd waited, impatiently, for a week before we caved. We scoured every inch of the Viridianwood. Pan used every resource available to us, and we'd come up completely fucking empty. She was gone. And I think if we'd taken a moment to rein ourselves in from the fear and the anger, we would have known. I could feel the absence of her. As if someone had cut out half of my heart and the damn thing was pounding away at an irregular rhythm, each beat more painful than the last. Fuck, I was being so sentimental. Next, I'd find myself in a puddle of my own tears. And I wasn't looking forward to explaining that shit to my brothers while still holding onto my balls. It didn't help that my last words to her had been harsh, forbidding her to leave me, and yet she had anyway. Her life has been one travesty after another. Even though she tried to hold it all together, I could tell things were getting too much to bear in the days leading up to her disappearance. It made me worry about her even more.

Without her, I simply existed, going through the motions. Each morning was a repeat of the days before. I got dressed, strapped on any number of weapons, and fumbled around for any friendly drop of mead, or whatever was potent enough to take the edge off the day.

I entered the arms cellar to find Pan and Tripp already

in deep discussion. Dark circles had taken up permanent residence under Tripp's eyes. He'd been assigned the night watch, but it didn't matter. He hadn't been able to sleep either. Instead, every moment he wasn't following Pan's orders, he was working on Hen's cottage.

"The southern colonies are demanding I meet with them today," Pan huffed. "They've been hit hard this past week. Twenty-three have gone missing and they want answers. Not that I blame them, but the fucking timing is terrible. Neverland's crown is barely rested on my head and now this. They are starting to lose faith in me. Can you believe there's talk of crowning a new leader? Replacing me with a native born." Pan's voice was harsh and frustration radiated out of him. Neverland's problems were a good distraction, requiring every bit of his attention day in and day out.

I leaned against the cold wall of the arms cellar, waiting for Pan to get on with the morning report, which was always abysmal. Every day, things got worse. Reports of natives going missing were constantly flooding in. No one was safe. They simply vanished without a trace. No one ever came back, and no bodies were ever recovered. Pan made it a point to list the names of everyone who'd gone missing, and the list kept getting longer. I guess it was his way of honoring those whom he'd sworn to protect, and it felt like right now we were doing a piss-poor job of it. We all would have preferred a tangible threat. A head-to-head battle where we could take our opponent down. Dorian hadn't been seen since Hen disappeared. He'd popped out of existence a moment after the bone faerie had taken her. We all knew he was behind this, but we'd never had to deal with an enemy we couldn't get our hands on. It was infuriating.

"Any news from Eben?" I asked Pan, interrupting his rant about the unstable politics he was trying to rein in. It was the same question every day. Eben had truly lost his shit when we realized Hen was no longer in Neverland. He'd insisted on expanding his search into the realms. Pan had ordered him to stay, knowing we needed all the manpower here. But Eben was done taking orders from Pan. He'd allied a few sentries to his cause and he'd been crisscrossing the Veil from one realm to the next. I wanted so badly to join him, to feel like I was actually doing something to find our girl, but I had to think of Gwen. She would have wanted me to stay here. Help in any way I could and be patiently waiting for her when she finally returned. I reminded myself of this constantly. It was the only thing keeping me sane.

"Got word last night that he's checked her home, school, anywhere that had a connection to her, but he's come up empty. He's planning to check the 10th Realm next. It's the most remote. It's possible the bone faerie has taken her into hiding there." Pan sighed, running his hand through his disheveled hair.

I nodded absently. Pan had used an awful lot of words to

tell me that Eben had absolutely jack shit for all his efforts. "What's on the agenda for today?" I asked, moving down the list of my daily questions.

"Amara wants one of us to bring her a specimen of the Fae hounds." The mention of the hellish creatures sent a chill down my spine. While we'd been searching for Gwen in the Viridianwood, we'd stumbled upon a whole new nightmare. Lurking in the depths of the dark forest, we'd found a new breed of Fae that we'd never encountered before. A grotesque beast of sorts. They were large, rivaling the size of a bear, only with sleek hairless bodies that were as black as the midnight sky. Their faces were long, with a muzzle that tapered into the lethal beak of a predatory bird. Even the skies weren't safe. Although they preferred to hunt on all fours, they had membranous wings, and they would swoop in and pluck you out of the sky like a vulturous gargoyle.

They were feral creatures that prowled the darkness, guarding the perimeter of the wood, attacking anyone who tried to venture too far into the forest. They worked in packs like dogs. Unnaturally fast, picking soldiers off one at a time. The damn things were difficult to kill, the vital parts of their bodies covered in natural armor. Swords and arrows just seemed to glance off of them. We'd lost so many men, we had to abandon the forest altogether.

"She wants to see if she can figure out which realm they originated from. Maybe we can find a more efficient way to kill them," Peter explained. It wasn't any simple task he was laying out for me.

"Make sure you take a crossbow with you. Seems like that's the best weapon against them. Hook has provided us with a potent poison. Should help take them down even if the bolt doesn't pierce their armor," Tripp added. Ever since Pan had taken Hen to the Jolly Roger to fulfill our debt to him, the two had tolerated each other. Hook had even offered his assistance with the missing natives. Pan refused to discuss what happened, but leave it to Hen to mend bridges even across the most violent of rivers.

"Take a group of men with you. Pick the best among us. It's crucial that we get Amara a specimen." Pan was to the point, barely glancing at me as he doled out his orders. Ruling was taking its toll on him. He thought this new power that had awakened within him when we destroyed Arion somehow meant that he couldn't fail. But sometimes he was so fucking arrogant, he couldn't recognize his own flaws. He had absolutely no idea how to control this new power, and I worried his blind faith could be our downfall. Between that and losing Hen, I worried I might never see my friend again.

"Anything else, your majesty?" I snarked back at him. My own temper easily roused these days.

"Nope. Just get it done, Ry. Report back to me when it's finished." Pan shot me a dark glare, but that was as much as he could spare for me, before turning back to the piles of reports before him. Bastard.

I slung the damn crossbow over my shoulder and left the arm's cellar without so much as a goodbye. Once upon a time, we'd been like brothers. Sharing literally everything. But losing Hen was destroying us all. I never felt so alone as I did at that moment. Each of them had something, some way to keep occupied while she was gone. Someway to be useful to her even in her absence. Except me. I had nothing to offer besides the damn pining in my chest. I was the least useful of her lovers, and the truth of that festered in my mind.

Before I set out for my assignment, I found myself at the threshold of Hen's cottage. Yet another redundancy to my day that I couldn't shake. I let myself in and made a beeline for her room. I had to be in and out before Tripp made his way over to find some minuscule detail to obsess over. The cottage had been done for the last week, but he couldn't leave it alone. He preferred to suffer in silence. That's why he'd volunteered for the night watch. Fewer people to deal with. I'd thought about confronting him, seeing if he needed someone to talk to, but I got the distinct impression that if I tried to hug it out with him I'd lose an arm.

I walked into the massive closet that Tripp had designed. Apparently, girls like large closets. At least that's what Tripp says, and I wasn't about to question him about it. It had been filled with countless dresses. None of which she'd ever worn. And I had a hard time picturing Hen dressing up in the stuffy gowns on a regular basis. She was much more practical. A pair of well-worn jeans and a T-shirt seemed to fit her better. Although I had snuck in a few of my shirts. Hoping she would surprise me one day and wear them. The thought of her in nothing more than my shirt had my cock instantly hard, and I groaned. It was painful at this point to get hard at the thought of her, and have nothing more than my wholly inadequate hand to finish the job.

At the back of the long closet, her pack hung from a hook. It was the only thing of hers that we had. I visited everyday, hugging the lumpy bag to my chest, inhaling her scent. Which only served to further harden my cock uncomfortably against my pants. I'd never opened it. Never ventured to look inside. It felt like a violation of her privacy to go through her things without her here. But just holding onto it somehow made me feel closer to her. Damn, I was such a fucking sap. If anyone had walked in, seeing me holding onto a backpack like it was the hottest woman I'd ever seen, I think I'd probably die of shame, but fuck if I could stop myself from doing it. I lingered as long as I dared, rubbing the rough canvas against my stubbled cheek as I let visions of Hen flood through my mind.

"Wish me luck today, Hen," I said to the inanimate pack, feeling more like a loser in that moment than ever before. I went to place the bag back on its hook, but my mind was so overwhelmed with thoughts of her, I missed the hook entirely and the pack fell to the floor, spilling its contents.

"Fuck!" I grumbled, stooping down to collect

everything, until my eyes settled on a picture. A familiar face I hadn't seen in so long I'd almost forgotten. A small, black-and-white photograph of myself as a boy peered up at me.

"What the..." The picture had come from a beige envelope labeled Lost Boys. I picked it up, torn between opening the file and putting it back in her pack. Why did she have a file on me? She hadn't mentioned anything about it since she'd returned, and for the life of me, I couldn't think of a reason why she'd keep something like that a secret. My curiosity got the better of me. The file was about me, after all. At least that's what I told myself, so I wouldn't feel so guilty for snooping through her private things.

The first page was basic information, my birthdate, the names of my parents. The hospital I was born at. It even included a clipping from the paper with my birth announcement. I flipped the page. This time I was confronted with the headlines, "Local Boy Gone Missing." And, "Prominent Family Offers Reward for Missing Son." I slogged my way through the articles. I wasn't great at reading, and it took for fucking ever, but Hen had made it possible.

My heart ached for my parents. I knew it was going to be rough for them at first, but I figured after some time and more children, they'd have the picture perfect life they always dreamed of. I flipped to the next page, and this one was an editorial. A full page spread in the paper and it was written by my father a year to the day after my disappearance. More money was offered for news of my whereabouts, more pleas to the public for any leads. I could feel my emotions stick in my throat as I read the words.

Memories of my parents, that Neverland had hidden away, shifted to the surface. The more I concentrated, the more I could picture their faces in my mind. Each page that followed was another article from my father, marking the anniversary of my disappearance. After about five years, I found a different article from the paper, an obituary for my mother. Abigail S. Ryder, age 37, died at Hanwell Asylum having suffered depression and hysteria after the loss of her son. She leaves behind husband, Preston D. Ryder II.

My hands trembled as I tried to hold the pages together. Tears began to leak from the corner of my eyes as I read the words in disbelief. That's not how it was supposed to happen. They were supposed to have more sons. Many strapping sons that would carry on the family name. They were supposed to be happy. Instead, she'd died. My father's next entry stated that she'd died of a broken heart. I couldn't read anymore after that. I flipped to the last page. The final words my father had written shattered my heart.

"As my days grow short, I am comforted by the notion that I will finally be reunited with my son and his smile will warm my soul once again."

The last clipping in the folder was my father's obituary. Preston Daniel Ryder II, age 74, passed away at his home. He's preceded by his wife, Abigail and son, Preston D. Ryder III.

It felt like I was in a nightmare of my own making. I'd sacrificed my chance at an amazing life so they could have everything they wanted, when in the end, they'd only wanted me. And I'd single-handedly destroyed them. I gently closed the file and placed it back in Hen's pack. I couldn't decide if I wanted to destroy everything around me, or curl up on Hen's bed and fall into a deep depression.

I'd been an awful son, and now I was an awful lover. I had nothing to offer Hen. I'd likely just destroy her too, like I did to my parents. And she knew it. She'd had the proof in her pack this whole time. Maybe she'd never return, doing to me exactly what I did to my parents, and that's exactly what I deserved. The only thing I could do now was be a good soldier. I could follow Pan's orders. I could put my life on the line for the greater good, and if I didn't come back… Well, I'd kept my father waiting long enough.

After I'd put Hen's cottage back exactly the way I found it, I headed out on my own. I decided to take on this mission solo. A slight deviation from Pan's orders, but I was feeling reckless, and I refused to put anyone else at risk. I landed just on the outskirts of the ominous forest. The trees swayed and creaked in a non-existent wind. The forest swallowed up the light, and beyond the first row of trees was an engulfing blackness. The Viridianwood always disturbed me. A current of dark magic cursed the place, and it was something I wanted no part of. But I couldn't turn back now. It felt like the forest was watching me— waiting to see if I'd cross the line.

I took a deep sigh in an attempt to dispel my reservations, and crossed the boundary. I didn't allow myself to think too much about it, or else I might very well change my mind. I stalked through the woods, the crossbow poised. I had it tucked against my shoulder, my finger resting on the trigger. I turned abruptly when the foliage rustled behind me, but nothing was there. I kept pushing forward. The only way I'd be able to lure them out was if I encroached on whatever it was they were attempting to guard. My heart was hammering between my ears. No matter how hard I tried to control my response, I couldn't stop the knot of anxiety from tightening in my chest. This was a bad fucking idea. Possibly the worst decision I'd ever made.

Nothing seemed amiss until I felt eyes on me. I stilled, waiting for some tell, some sign that the final blow was about to drop on me, and not some figment of my overactive mind. The forest was completely silent, too silent. When my instincts told me to turn, I didn't question. I spun on my heels as the black death descended upon me. The Fae hound was mid lunge, its wings spread wide, when I pulled the trigger on the crossbow. I'd aimed for the flash of pink in his gaping mouth, his rows of teeth poised to rip my throat out. The poisoned bolt hit true. The thing let out a brief whimper before it crashed on top of me, pinning me beneath its hulking form.

I struggled to take a breath, the dead weight crushing down on me. Thick, purple blood poured from the carcass, covering my chest and face. I could even taste the silver tang as it got into my mouth. I flailed underneath it, desperate to push it off of me, until I heard the low rumble of a growl. I froze. The rest of the pack had found us. I lay completely still as two other hounds circled us, sniffing at their dead companion. They nudged the dead beast a few times, and I held my breath as the body rocked on top of me. When it didn't move, the group let out a collective whine. Their mourning was cut short, the two remaining hounds looking up as if something had called to them. And thank my lucky stars, they bounded off into the forest. I watched as they went, taking note of where they were going. One minute they were running, the next they completely disappeared into thin air, as though they'd leapt through a portal. I could still see a glimmer of magic as the boundary sealed itself off again.

Well shit. I knew there were many unexplained things in the Viridianwood, but I'd never heard of something like that. After a monumental struggle and a slew of indelicate curses, I finally managed to push the fucker off of me. I was covered in its stinking blood. I could only imagine the look I'd get from Hen if she saw me like this, and I chuckled to myself.

I stared at the dead hound, feeling conflicted. I'd accomplished my task. I had the specimen Amara needed, but I'd seen where they went. This could be our only chance to figure out what they'd been guarding. A warm tingle began to take up residence in the pit of my stomach. I spat quickly, remembering all the blood I'd swallowed. My saliva was still tinged in purple, and I could tell the blood was starting to affect me. A shot of whiskey had nothing on this. The magic that had been coursing through its blood was being metabolized in my gut. The magic heightened every one of my senses and it rippled across my muscles. There was no better time to go after the remaining hounds than right now, with their borrowed magic strengthening me.

I felt a certain thrall. Something was calling to the magic, and I decided to follow, letting it guide me to my prey. I approached with caution. I could feel the static charge of the magic barrier. The dark forest before me was nothing more than a mirage. I walked through, feeling the pull of the barrier as it tested me, determining if I was allowed. I don't know if it was the borrowed magic or the blood covering me, but I met the demands and the barrier let me pass.

On the other side, I found myself at a familiar juncture. A cleft in a massive rock. The entrance to the bone faerie's home. We'd been here before. We scanned the whole area when Hen had gone missing. This boundary definitely wasn't there before. The thrall continued to lure me forward, and I let it direct me into the stone passageway.

When I exited the other side, I was wholly unprepared for what I saw. The small glade where the bone faerie's cottage had been was gone. The trees had been cleared, leaving a massive expanse of land. At the center was the beginning of a castle, the black stone of the walls shined like obsidian. All the native Neverlanders that had gone missing were slaving away, carrying the stones in long lines and building the castle from the ground up. Hundreds of them, all walking stoic, like mindless zombies fulfilling their task.

"It's quite beautiful, don't you think?" I whirled at the sound of the smooth voice. There he was, sitting atop the stone I'd just crossed through, his black wings splayed out behind.

"Dorian," I snarled, and attempted to draw my sword.

"Ah, ah... I don't think so. That's awfully rude to come into someone's home with swords drawn," he tsked at me, with a look of disappointment on his perfect face.

"What is going on here? What do you want?"

"Come, let us find ourselves a more suitable place to talk." He jumped down from his perch, landing right in front of me. I couldn't pull my eyes from his calculating stare. He snapped his fingers once, and Neverland disappeared. I found myself in a dark, concrete room. It was empty save for a metal bed and a woman, who sat in a wheelchair with her back to me, facing toward a tiny barred window, the only one in the room.

"There, this is better. Much quieter here," Dorian said as he walked around me, his predatory eyes looking me up and down.

"Where are we?" I asked, staring at the woman, wondering who she was and how she was connected to Dorian. Trying hard not to focus on the fact that I'd fucked up royally, and the chances of me getting out of here alive seem to be getting smaller by the minute.

275

"It still surprises me to find the most useless species in all the cosmos here. And as guardians, no less. The 9th Realm places altogether too much faith in the likes of humans. So weak, no magic, so... mortal. It's one of the many wonders that still plague me." He tapped a long, elegant finger on his chin as though he was deep in thought, pondering the answers to his own questions. I think the narcissist in him just liked to hear the sound of his own voice.

"If I'm so weak and helpless, why don't you just get it over with now? Go ahead, kill me, and then we'll see how much you've underestimated Pan."

"Another ridiculous human notion I can't wrap my head around. To die for the greater good. So many jump at the chance to martyr one's self for a cause. And what does that really accomplish? You're dead and I have one less enemy to kill. Maybe you can explain it once I've broken you. It would make for an intriguing conversation."

"Go to hell!"

"Feisty little thing, aren't you? I like that in my pets. It makes it more of a triumph when I finally break you. An accomplishment really."

"I'll never be your slave. I'll kill myself before I let that happen."

He laughed, holding a hand to his mouth, covering his sinister smile. "When I'm done with you, you'll gladly sink a blade into that pretty little girl of yours when I ask it of you."

"I'll kill you first," I snarled at him, struggling against

the invisible bond that held me in place. I put every ounce of energy I had into it and got nowhere. The fucker just stood back and watched me struggle, an amused expression on his face.

"If you're quite finished." He raised an eyebrow at me. I was panting, and beads of sweat dotted my forehead. "First lesson about me. I never take threats lightly." He turned and walked toward the woman still sitting in the wheelchair. "Oh and by the way, Preston, that seductive temptress that has you wrapped around her finger, she's been lying to you. I'll enjoy telling you all about it during our time together."

My anger boiled to the surface, but he wasn't wrong. Gwen had been keeping secrets from me. I pushed the doubt out of my mind. I couldn't afford to lose my wits. When Dorian reached the woman, he turned the chair around, and the shock of recognition hit me, my mouth gaping wide as I took in her familiar features.

"Preston, is that you?"

"Mum?" My voice broke as I took her in. She was always put together, her blonde hair was never out of place, pinned perfectly around her glowing face. Now she was gaunt, her hair disheveled. The innate spark of life had disappeared from her eyes.

"It is you! You've been gone so long. Why did you wait so long to come back to me?"

"This isn't real. She's not real. My mother died years ago." I tried to sound confident as I watched tears begin to fall down her cheeks.

"Are you certain?" Dorian questioned. His long fingers brushed her hair off her neck. "Could it be that we've simply gone back in time? Hmm, that is quite curious. Let's find out, shall we?"

He turned his raptor gaze to the metal bed, and I watched as the dirty sheets began to move, twisting together, and then sliding off the bed as if it were a snake. The animated sheet made its way toward my mother, sliding up her leg, twisting itself around her neck.

Her desperate eyes never left mine. "Come to me, Preston. I've been waiting so long." She reached for me, paying no attention to the sheet that was coiling around her neck.

"What are you doing? Stop! Leave her alone," I barked at him, my voice wavering.

"Oh, but this isn't really happening. Isn't that what you said… Preston?" He mocked my given name as he leaned nonchalantly against the concrete wall, picking at his nails.

"Mum, I'm sorry. I'm so sorry," I called out to her as tears ran down my cheeks.

"Come to me, Preston. Please! You're breaking my heart." Her hand remained outstretched, reaching for me. I tried to get to her. I tried so hard, but I was no match for the magic holding me in place. I watched in horror as the end of the sheet wrapped itself around an exposed pipe in the ceiling and began to tighten. My mother's body was pulled from the wheelchair, raising her up until her feet hung a foot from the ground. One hand held the sheet around her neck while the other still reached for me.

"Stop! Please let her go." I began to beg as her face started to turn purple, her lips still mouthing my name.

"You brought this on yourself. Threatened my life and expected there to be no consequences? There is a lot for you to learn, my little pet. I am not a lenient master."

"She's innocent," I pleaded.

He chuckled to himself, the sound vile as it rolled off his tongue. "Dear boy, that's never deterred me before." He continued to be distracted by his fingernails. Not at all swayed by my mother as she flailed, her legs trembling as she succumbed to death right beside him. I tried to close my eyes, to blink several times and wake myself up from this nightmare. But my vision settled on her unmoving body, swaying from the sheet around her neck. A part of me died in that room, right along with my mother.

"One day," I growled, "I promise—"

"If the next words out of your mouth are yet another empty threat against my life, then let me show you what that will cost you." His hand whirled in the air, smoke erupting from his palm. A vision of Hen appeared in the smoke, her beautiful face smiling as if I'd just told her a ridiculous joke. My heart caught in my throat, and swallowed the threat I'd been about to make.

"Ah yes, he can be trained." He clapped his hands as he stalked over to me, his shoulder brushing past my mother's corpse as he approached. "Preston Daniel Ryder III, such a pretentious name for an illiterate excuse of a son. You are useless. You've always been useless. A burden to bear. But I can offer you solace. Provide meaning to your futile existence. All I require is your allegiance. Submit to me, willingly be my slave and I promise you, the simplicity of that life will be your redemption."

CHAPTER XVII
LET IT RIPEN
-GWEN-

I felt the rush of wind rustle the hair that had fallen out of my braid, as the arc of my sword sliced through the air. Eben's words echoed in my head, guiding me through this lethal dance as beads of sweat ran down my forehead, stinging my eyes. I pushed myself harder, doing my best to master the blade in my hands. I refused to let myself be idle while I waited, impatiently, for the bone faerie to return. Since the Osakren was now officially a part of me, it had unlocked my magic, feeding it until I was more powerful than I ever dreamed possible. And when the bones had fused with my body, it brought along all the knowledge I needed in order to use it.

Controlling it was something that would only come with practice, or at least that's what Peytra kept saying. I was a good student, trying to master it quickly so I could get back to my boys. I could feel the connection that bound us to one another. It had always been there, now I just knew how to access the bridge that tied us all together. I could feel their anguish, their loneliness, their anger. That was the only thing that kept me going. Even when I was exhausted, I pushed further.

But Peytra would only take me so far before she'd vanish. Leaving me alone in this void of a place. I was thankful I had Alo with me. He was my loyal companion. And now that the magic had been awoken within me, I could speak with him telepathically. It wasn't quite like talking to a human. He was blunt and to the point. He was a good listener, but not much for in-depth conversation.

Porthos, Peytra's reanimated pixie, kept me company as well. I could finally understand the pixie chatter. When he spoke, it was as if he was talking in plain English, the sound of bells now only a melodic tone that accompanied his speech. He was always drunk on Fae wine. How a dead pixie could get drunk was still beyond me, yet he was constantly drinking, slurring his words and fluttering into things in his altered condition. He was a devious little fucker, too. Tying my hair in knots, brushing his wings in my ear every time I was deeply concentrating on my magic, and he had an obsession with biting. I tolerated him because his drunken antics were about the only amusing thing in this never changing place I was stuck in.

I had no idea how long I'd been here. The sky was always the same putrid gray. No sun ever rose or set. I slept when I was tired, ate when I was hungry, and just randomly existed at Peytra's behest. She wouldn't be pushed. She would instruct me only until a certain point, and then she'd leave. It was the same every time. I'd beg her to stay, and swear that I could keep going. But she never changed her mind.

"The seed has sprouted, but the fruit is still hard and green on the vine. You must sleep on it— let it ripen. The magic within you is sentient. Only when there is nothing will it come to you." She always made some ridiculous fruit comparison mixed in her riddled speech. None of it made any sense. And then she'd simply disappear, leaving me alone to pick apart her words until I was about to lose my sanity. It was infuriating that she could leave and I couldn't. But she'd shown me what Dorian was capable of. I'd pulled bits and pieces of his history from her riddled warnings, and the picture she'd painted gave me nightmares.

Born the bastard son of the immortal king, he'd been raised in the shadows of the 1st Realm as the king's dirty little secret. But as he grew older, so did the darkness within him. His appetite for vengeance was insatiable and Neverland was the stepping stone he needed. A stronghold from which to crush his opposition. Bring down each realm in succession, until he could destroy his father, taking absolute power for himself. If we had any chance to stop that from happening, I needed to be his match in the magical sense. A way to even the playing fields. There was no way we could win this war with brute strength alone. But as my mastery of the sword improved, that too brought me comfort. I wouldn't allow myself to be vulnerable ever again. I would be a well-polished weapon in every sense of the word when I returned to my boys.

"Little star," she greeted me warmly when she finally reappeared, not at all noticing the perfect resting bitch face I was wearing. "The bones are impatient. They've whispered that you are ready to breach the spiritual element."

"Finally! What took you so long?" I barked, wiping the sweat from my brow as I tried to catch my breath.

"Ungrateful! Ungrateful little star, thinking she burns so brightly that we all revolve around her. Mark me, I am not one of your strings," she hissed.

I huffed at her harsh words, "This is taking too long. I thought we had no time, yet you refuse to push through. I can handle whatever you give me."

"Still a sprout. No fruit. You must learn patience. The bastard prince has been patiently waiting for this for a millennia. Well honed evil with wide jaws that will swallow your restless soul. The viper lies in wait to strike."

"Easy for you to say, you're thousands of years old. And might I remind you, we don't have a millennia to *hone* my skills." I grumbled, trying not to piss her off too much. I couldn't risk her leaving again. "We're wasting time we don't have. Let's get started." I waved her on as I sank my sword into its scabbard.

"Wind, fire, water, land... You've mastered the basic elements of the cosmos. But it is the spirit element that is most important. When all the others are gone, all that is left is the spirit. The soul is slick and runs through your hands. By design, it is hard to manipulate. But when you mold it to your whim, legions apart will rest at your fingertips. Come now, your stain makes for a perfect partner. Go within yourself and find him."

I spent what felt like hours trying to master control. I retreated into myself, searching my own spirit until I'd found him shuttered up inside of my soul. He'd become dormant since I'd entered this place between worlds. His whole reason for existing now was to exact revenge and return balance to his own soul. But without my lovers near, he'd remained quiet, waiting patiently for an opportunity to rise again.

I knew I'd found him when the litany of memories I'd been wading through began to change, and a memory that was not my own began to materialize. A familiar scene took shape around me. I was in the meadow, watching as Kían relived his last moments with Amara over and over again in nightmarish purgatory. I felt a pang of guilt for what he must have gone through, but I couldn't let it cloud my judgment. I began to lock him away with the new magic that I now possessed.

As the scene around me began to fade, I pulled back in abject horror when a half decomposed figure appeared inches from my face. A skull partially covered in flesh cocked back and forth, its movements jerky and unnatural. *This is only a figment of my mind!* I repeated this over and over as his eyeless sockets bored into my soul. *"You cannot be rid of me forever."* The raspy voice hissed through a jaw that was hanging on by a few fragments of putrid skin. *"When the mating bond is set, no amount of chains can keep me from my vengeance."* The disgusting figure of Kían chuckled in my face as the smell of death filled my nostrils. I ignored the talking corpse before me, picking up my speed as I closed him off, feeling my whole soul tremble with fear. The idea that that thing was living inside of me made me sick. I promised myself that I would never allow him to exact his vengeance out on my boys, and so I made my magical barriers thicker.

"Good, little star. Good! Ruthless, that is how you must act when it comes to Dorian. He is a master of the spiritual element, weaving terror from your own thoughts, warping your memories. Fear is his ally. He will strip you naked and dissect your fear to use as a weapon. You must be strong, partition your mind so he cannot see what you are truly afraid of."

I listened intently to her words. Using magic to explore my soul, finding ways to wall off all of my fears. I'd envisioned a metal box to handle all of my volatile emotions my whole life, but now I had a much better understanding of how to manipulate things within my own spirit, and now I was building a fortress.

I stumbled in my concentration when I felt a searing pain across my back as if my skin had been flayed open. I was jolted back to my conscious thought. What the fuck was that? I was still in the void. Only Peytra, Porthos, and Alo were present. But a lingering pain nagged at me, nagged across the bridge between me and my boys. I closed my eyes, focusing my attention until a searing pain radiated into me, and then Ryder was before me with his wrists tied, blood pouring down his back, the crack of a whip resounding in my ears as the scene of Ryder left me.

I blinked my eyes rapidly. The images of Ryder felt like they were burned into my vision. I tried to pull in a breath, but I felt like the wind had been knocked out of me.

"My star? What is it the Divine has shown you?" Peytra questioned.

"I...uh"—I managed to suck in a breath—"I saw Ryder. I felt his pain as if it was my own." My body was still shaking from the vision.

"Ahhh, a burden for those with bonded souls. The strings between you carry more than just emotions. A price extracted for a soul's true love."

"So what I saw is real? That's really happening to him right now?" I couldn't keep the urgency out of my voice as fear began to leach out of the fortress I'd been in the process of building.

"Mmm, your strings are coveted."

"I have to go to him. You have to take me back right now!"

"It's not your time. Your magic is still ripening. Leave now and you shall wither on the vine. Everything you have learned, all that you have been shown, will leave you if you're premature in your departure. That is the way of it. You will return to Dorian as a mere mortal, your magic cloaked in darkness."

"I don't care. I'll figure it out. Please! I have to go to him," I begged. I sank to my knees before her, pulling on her tattered skirts.

"Maybe there is grace in this outcome."

"Grace? You're saying I should leave him there? Let him die? Because if he stays where he is, that's what will happen. I can feel it."

"You have four other strings to keep you tied up. And by cutting one, the balance will be restored, the stain will finally wash from your soul."

"I'm not sacrificing Ryder. I will sacrifice myself before I let that happen."

"A mother bear will kill its own cub to give the others a better chance at survival. It is but nature, my little star."

"That's not an option!"

"If Neverland falls, the chain fire starts. All the realms will fall, and you, my little star, are the catalyst. Your story either lights the spark or snuffs the flame. The Divine has ways to test a chosen. Do not choose the wrong path." She rose from her seat and I began to panic.

"No, don't leave. You have to bring me back!"

She stopped then, whirling on me in a flurry of ragged skirts, cocking her head and clicking her tongue. "Sleep on it. Let your decision ripen. And remember, death isn't the curse, it is the answer, and it is an awfully big adventure. The bones speak the answers. You only have to be quiet enough to hear them." And with that, she vanished.

"No!" I screamed at the empty space before me, pounding my fists on the ground of this prison that she'd left me in.

"It will be alright, girl," Alo's words echoed in my mind as he butted his head against me, his tongue lapping at the tears that had fallen down my cheeks.

I stayed that way for a long time. Opening up the tie to my boys, letting Ryder's pain and fear take over my body. Even though he didn't know it, I was with him. I pushed myself into that dark, cold room and my soul laid beside him.

"I won't break, I won't," he mumbled as he rocked back and forth. "He can't have her. He can't take her from me…" His breath choked out as the sob he'd been holding back broke through. "Fuck! Gwen!" He screamed out my name over and over again. "Please, Divine… Why? Tell me why?" he pleaded with the Divine and it broke me. I sat with him in the depths of his own private hell. Feeling what he felt, crying out with his pain, letting it tear me up inside until I couldn't take it any longer. I had to find a way. I stumbled to my feet, wiping my tears away with the back of my hand.

"We're getting out of here, Alo. Ryder needs me. I have to figure out a way."

"Porthos," was the only response he sent to me.

"Agreed."

I marched over to the dilapidated bird cage where Porthos lived. Shaking the cage to get his attention.

"I know that you have the answer, Porthos!" A full bellied laugh mocked me, and I had to stand on my tiptoes to see into the cage. He lay strewn across a tipped over bottle of Fae wine. "Tell me how I get out of here." I demanded.

"And let the fun flee with you... preposterous," he slurred the word 'preposterous' so much that it was barely intelligible. I glared at him through the cage. "Stop, the weight of your eyes crushes my bones!" He rolled over, his skeletal arm draping over his nonexistent eyes in a ridiculously dramatic display. "You're some all powerful chosen, why don't you do it yourself? Oh wait, yes, you cannot do it alone. That will not work. My mind escapes me sometimes." He giggled at his inside joke and it deteriorated into fits of laughter.

"You know something," I said as I reached into the cage and plucked his tiny body from the wine bottle. He still convulsed in laughter, having a hard time pulling it together. "Tell me what you know!"

"Now listen here"—he hiccuped as he pointed his skeletal finger at me—"my feelings are a deep river, and you pay them no mind. Splash in my waters with nothing to offer me. No love, no witty conversation, no friendly drop of mead. I think I might cry."

"Porthos, you have no eyes. You can't cry. I'm sorry, I don't mean to be short with you. I will conjure up whatever you'd like if you could just tell me what you know."

"No. It's no use. You've spoiled my inebriated bliss. There is nothing I want anymore but to be left to wallow in my melancholia."

"I don't believe that. A new bottle of Fae wine? How about some mead?"

"Nope, nope. Nothing will do," he sobbed and dropped his head into his hands.

"How about some Lush tea?" He stopped his pretend sobbing then and perked up.

"Lush tea, did you say?"

"Of course. I'll make you a whole cup and you can celebrate like it's May Day."

"Ooh, how I remember. The dancing, the orgies… Oh, what a time. Yes, yes. The Lush, give me the Lush and I will tell you what you need to know." The little skeleton of a pixie kneeled in my hands, his fingers clasped together as he begged for the Lush tea.

"It's a deal then." He flew up to my face, kissing my ear before he promptly bit it and I had to swat him away. "Don't test me, Porthos or I'll make you the weakest version of Lush tea you've ever had." He zipped around my head, waiting for me to get on with it. I pulled a cup from the cave where I stashed all the human items the bone faerie had provided me while I was here and filled it with some water from the marsh, cringing at the sight of the murky water. That had been my first test. Peytra had provided me with no clean drinking water, and when I'd asked, she'd told me I would have to tap into the water element and clean it with magic. I'd finally managed it, but not before I'd had to drink several cups of the putrid water out of desperation.

I pulled a handful of moss from one of the trees and began. My hands glowed as I tapped into the elemental magic, cleansing the water, morphing the moss into Lush tea leaves and brewing them until there was a swirl of steam rising from the cup.

Porthos darted for the cup, but before he could reach it, I clasped my hand over the top. "Not so fast. You owe me information. Spill it, and then I'll let you have your Lush."

"Fine," he barked. "To return to the realm of the living, you must have the faerie dust. Now give me the Lush."

"Faerie dust? Really? That's it?" It seemed too simple. One of my first lessons had been to turn a handful of dirt into faerie dust, imbued with my own magic. Pixie shed it like skin, but the rest of the Fae had to create it themselves, and only a few were powerful enough to do it.

"Not just any dust. You really are a stupid chosen, aren't you?" His words were so sickly sweet, as if he'd meant them as an endearment and not an insult.

"Well come on then, out with it. What kind of faerie dust do I need?"

"The dust of the dead, of course. Why do you think that old hag has kept me around so long? She needs me."

"You? You're the key back?"

"Don't look so unimpressed. It hurts my feelings. Yes, yes, the faerie dust from the dead allows you to travel the spiritual world. It is quite potent. So many possibilities. Mixed with your borrowed bones, the dead would be kneeling at your feet," he rattled on.

"Before I give you the Lush, you're going to have to give me some dust."

"How dare you! Rude! Such an egregious offense against me. Never in my life have I been treated so poorly—"

"You're dead, Porthos," I reminded him, interrupting his rant.

"Hmmm, touché."

"Come on, Porthos. The tea is getting cold. It would be a shame for me to dump all of this into the swamp. What a waste."

"No, no, please! Don't throw it out. Fine! I'll give you the dust. Just give me the Lush."

He hovered over my hand, his whole body vibrating so rapidly that he appeared to blur and a fine coating of dust fell into my hand. It sparkled like faerie dust, but it was so black that it appeared to absorb the light around it.

"There. Are you happy? I gave you a little extra too, for all the good it'll do me."

"Thank you, Porthos," I said as I pulled the corpse of a pixie to my lips and kissed him.

"Be sure to be happy. Think of your anchor. The one thing strong enough to pull you back to the land of the living," he cautioned.

"Don't worry, Porthos. I have five of them. Now have your Lush. Enjoy the night. And if you can remember when she returns, tell her I'm sorry. Tell her I had to do what I know is right."

I wasn't sure if he heard me or not, because he dove right into the cup of Lush tea as though it was a bathtub, splashing around in fits of laughter in between taking big, slurping gulps.

"Come on, Alo. We don't have any time to waste," I said as I poured the black faerie dust into the pouch on my baldric.

"You're going into war like that?" he asked, drolly.

I peered down at the jeans and T-shirt I had on. They were a little worse for wear, since they were the only clothes I brought with me. But Alo was right. I had no idea what I would be returning to, and if I would be closed off from my magic once I returned, then I needed to prepare now.

"Right, got it. I'm supposed to be going back as a warrior. Even if I'm not that, at least I can look the part." I summoned the magic inside me, reminded of the time Amara had made me a dress from a simple flower, and let the energy flow into the clothes on my back. I could feel the loose shirt pull in against my skin, changing from soft cotton to a resilient leather bodice. Heavy, studded gauntlets encased my arms. My whole body was covered in black leather armor from head to toe. Tall boots laced up my legs and belts crisscrossed my waist. An assortment of weapons that even Eben would be proud of manifested until I was armed to the teeth. I spun around as I looked at my new outfit. I felt like Cinder-fucking-rella in my very own fairytale spin off. Only instead of a dress, I was decked out in armor fit for a warrior queen. Now I was ready.

"Are you sure, girl? What will you do when you have no memory of the magic you need to protect yourself?"

"I'll have to figure it out as I go."

Chapter XVIII
Home Sweet Home
-Gwen-

The world around me was a blur. I buried my face into Alo's scruff, trying to hold onto images of my boys while still holding down the contents of my stomach as we tumbled through time and space. I had no idea how long it lasted, and I couldn't really pinpoint when it ended. It was Alo's soft whining that brought my attention back to reality, and then the cold set in.

I pulled away from Alo to find myself in the Viridianwood. The very same place I'd last seen my boys. Only *so* much had changed. A swirl of snow whirled in the air around us. Neverland had returned to the frigid tundra that had enveloped everything when Peter had been taken by Tiger Lily.

I scanned the landscape, processing the vast differences from the last time I was here and I began to panic. How long had I been gone?

"This doesn't look good, Alo. Can you lead us out?" I waited for his response, but got nothing. I turned to him, thinking maybe he hadn't heard me. "Alo?" I stared into his amber eyes and he whined. I could feel the slight nudging at my conscious thought, but there was nothing. I couldn't tap into the magic I needed to communicate with him.

"Dammit! It's gone. My connection to my power is gone." Everything I had felt in the void, all the knowledge I'd possessed, was simply gone. Like a thought that lingered just outside your reach, but you couldn't quite grasp it. Fuck. A part of me had hoped that the bone faerie had been lying to me. Trying to scare me into staying in the void to continue my training. But the proof of her words was sobering, and I felt an unexplainable sadness at the loss of my magic. But there was no time to mourn. If I'd learned anything, it was that lingering in the Viridianwood was asking for trouble.

Alo and I wandered the frozen forest, trying to make our way out. The unease sent a chill up my spine. My instincts warned me that things were very wrong here. Neverland wasn't herself, and I was desperate to get to my boys and find out what had happened in my absence. It wasn't until we stumbled upon an enormous black castle, looming just past the tree line, that the fear truly sunk into my bones. There had been no castle in the Viridianwood when I'd left Neverland. And yet there it stood, a beacon of darkness hiding amongst the haunting depths of the forest.

"Alo, have you ever seen a castle here before?" I asked out of habit, forgetting that my constant companion couldn't answer me anymore. But his low growl was enough to tell me that he hadn't. I took tentative steps toward the castle. Something was drawing me in, pulling me forward. I tried to reach across the bridge that connected me to my boys, but it was gone, too. I'd been cut off from the direct connection to my strings, the other pieces of my soul. I stifled a sob that threatened to escape my lips. I felt lost. Now I could feel how incomplete I was without them, and it was devastating.

Alo's growl registered in my mind a moment before a hand clamped over my mouth and pulled me backward, away from the beckoning force pulling me toward the castle. I struggled against my captor, my hand instantly going to my throwing blade strapped to my thigh.

"What took you so long, goddess? I was starting to worry I might never feel you squirm against me again." Tripp's sultry voice resonated in my ear and I melted at the sound.

"Tripp!" His name sounded like bliss as it slipped out in a sigh. He loosened his grip just enough for me to turn in his arms and feast my eyes on him. His face was smeared in purple that was so dark it was almost black, his large body fully suited in leather armor. My white knight now appeared completely savage in the shadowed light of the forest. His moss green eyes raked over my face, and before I could get enough of the sight of him, he slammed his mouth on mine, his full lips hard against me, needy and wanting. His tongue demanded entrance, desperate to taste me, and I happily obliged. His strong arms crushed me to him, one of his hands finding its way to my ass and squeezing hard. My mind was swimming with a desire that had been stretched too thin. If he wanted to take me right here on the forest floor, I would have gladly rutted with him like animals. He broke the kiss off well before I was ready for it to end, leaving me breathless in the wake of it.

"Tripp, what's—" He held a finger up to my lips, silencing me.

"Keep quiet, beautiful. Let me get you out of here. These woods aren't safe." I heard him whistle a signal to whomever was scouting the woods with him and we turned to go.

We retreated from the Viridianwood at an agonizingly slow pace. Tripp was on high alert for any movement, stopping us several times to hide amongst the underbrush while unseen creatures stalked past our hiding spots. These woods had always been dangerous, but something told me things had changed since I was last here.

"Take a breath, beautiful. We're about to cross the barrier," Tripp whispered in my ear. I had no clue what he meant, but this wasn't the time for in-depth explanations. I sucked in a deep breath, and in the next step, I felt the current of magic wash over me, making my skin crawl. The air was thick, as though we were trying to wade through water. We stumbled out the other side, the barrier spitting us out.

"What the hell was that?"

"Dorian has a barrier around the castle he's building. Getting out isn't much of a problem, but only those with the right magic can get in," he answered.

"How were you able to cross?"

He pointed to his face. "Blood from the Fae hounds. Camouflages us just enough to get across."

"Fae hounds?"

"We've got a lot to catch you up on. But even past the barrier, we aren't safe here. We've gotta move."

Once we crossed the tree line, marking the edge of the forest, I could see Tripp visibly relax. He scooped me into his arms and spun me around.

"That's the last fucking time I'm letting you go," he growled into my ear. I could only nod, the weight of emotions threatening to turn me into a blubbering mess if I tried to speak. "Are you alright? Did she hurt you?" He held me at arm's length and scanned my body.

"I'm fine. Maybe… a little different from the last time you saw me. But I'm fine."

His eyes landed on the new markings on my hand, running his fingertips absently along the runes now embedded in my skin, trailing them all the way down to the tip of my pinky. When his eyes came back to meet mine, I could see concern flit across them. "You'll always be my goddess, no matter how much you've changed. You look every bit the warrior I knew you to be." He pulled my hand up, placing a kiss on the new tattoos, showing his acceptance of whatever I had become in our time apart.

"Gwen? Holy shit! Gwen, is it really you?" I heard Peter's urgent calls before my eyes settled on him. He was sprinting from the edge of the forest at a dead run, heading straight for me. I broke away from Tripp a moment before he came barreling into me. He crushed me to his chest, the momentum sent us colliding with the snow covered ground. His strong arms broke our fall, and in the next instant his mouth was on mine, equally as violent, like he was trying to consume me. Drink in my soul after all our time apart. I wrapped a leg around him, unable to get close enough. I could feel our bond snapback, the recoiling of a band that had been stretched too tight.

"Thank the Divine. I was starting to... I worried maybe..." he stumbled over his words.

"I know. I'm sorry I was gone so long." He rested his forehead against mine and I reveled in the weight of him on top of me. An otherworldly howl echoed from within the forest, and Peter tensed.

"We've got to get you out of here. We're too exposed." He stood up abruptly, pulling me to my feet. Somehow the snow had melted from the ground beneath us. Small flowers were beginning to sprout from the vibrant green grass, a sharp contrast to the snow bleached landscape. Neverland was coming alive with our reunion and I swear the chill in the air felt just a bit less.

"Peter, where are the others? Where's Eben... Ryder?" I already knew something had happened to Ryder. I'd felt every agonizing moment when I was in the void, but I had to hear it from them, confirm the truth I already knew in my heart. Not seeing Eben here with them sent me spiraling. He shot a weary glance at Tripp and then his gaze dropped to the ground, unable to look me in the eye. The silence lingered until I was at my breaking point. I had to know. I grabbed his face in my hands, wrenching his eyes up to mine. "Tell me, Peter. Tell me what's happened to them!" I demanded.

"Eben's not here, but he's fine. He's been searching the realms, looking for you."

"And Ryder?" The mere mention of his name drew a pained look on Peter's face.

"Gwen... Dorian's taken him captive."

"How long? How long has he had him?"

"Just over a month now." A month! How had a month passed so quickly?

"Just how long have I been gone?" I was almost afraid to hear the answer.

"It's been two months and fourteen days."

Two and a half months. It took a moment to let that resonate in my mind. I was expecting a wave of fear to come and drown me now that I knew for certain Ryder was in enemy hands, but only a small trickle settled into my chest. It was imperative that I kept my fear under wraps. I couldn't allow Dorian to use them against me.

"We have a plan to get him back." Peter rushed to tell me, obviously taking my silence as a mini mental breakdown. "That's what we were doing in the Viridianwood. Don't worry, Gwen. We'll get him back."

"I know we will," I confirmed, already starting to mentally prepare myself for the coming battle.

Peter turned from me, nodding his head, as Dain, Captain of the Neverland guards, approached. "Welcome back, my queen." He bowed slightly toward me, his hand to his heart before turning back to Peter.

"Send a messenger to Eben. The fastest one you have. Let him know that she's returned," he barked his orders. Dain saluted and was gone, a small battalion of Fae following behind him.

"What's your plan?" I asked, not wanting to waste a moment of time. Every minute that passed was another moment of torture for Ryder and the thought was making me physically sick.

"Not here. The forest has eyes. Let's get back to camp and we'll talk more."

I parted ways with Alo, sending him back to his pack. I hugged him longer than was socially acceptable, but I knew I'd miss him. We'd forged a friendship that was unbreakable, but now we had to see to our families.

As we flew over Neverland, the enormity of the changes

became clearer. Smoke rose from several locations around the island. Patches of the fertile land had been scorched, and massive depressions peppered the land as if bombs had been dropped at random. Neverland was a war zone. We landed outside of camp just before nightfall, a massive wall now surrounded our home, and I felt anger bubbling up in my chest. I'm not sure when it happened, but at some point, Neverland had become my home, and I wanted to slaughter Dorian for trying to destroy it.

It was eerily quiet at camp. Only a handful of lanterns were lit, just enough for us to see by. The normal chatter of pixies was gone, and the camp seemed almost vacant.

"Where is everyone?"

"Those that can fight have stayed, but the rest have been moved to a stronghold below the Never Cliffs. It's the only place we could keep them safe. Dorian's been kidnapping Fae since you've been gone," Peter explained.

I could only nod. Words escaped me as I took it all in, digesting what my new reality was. No more paradise. No more fairytale. We were in a battle for our very existence.

Tripp and Peter led me toward the coast. "Where are we going?"

"I have a surprise for you," Tripp answered, flashing his million dollar smile at me. We walked, with his arm draped around my shoulders, until I stood before my cottage. Not the unfinished shell that it had been when I left. The white façade of the quaint little cottage was covered in creeping vines. Window boxes were overflowing with exotic flowers.

A stone chimney ran up the side, smoke curling from it as if they'd been expecting me.

"I know I did this before, but it wasn't finished, so it didn't count." Tripp swept me into his arms, carrying me through the arched door. He had painted it to match his eyes, the perfect shade of moss green. He set me down on the wooden floor. I was speechless as I took in the space. Bookshelves covered an entire wall. Carved wooden furniture, covered in comfy cushions, were positioned around the room. A large table sat at the center, six chairs set around it. Large windows, overlooking the ocean, filled the entire back wall. The setting sun filtering through, lit the room ablaze in fiery light.

"Come on, let me show you the best part." Tripp took my hand and led me into the bedroom. The room was large, yet it still felt cozy. The biggest bed I had ever seen was positioned to look out of yet another window. Judging by the size, I could fit with all of my boys, and possibly still have room for James. I walked over to the window, a chaise lounge nestled underneath it, and peered out. The Jolly Roger was anchored below and I felt a tug in my heart for my salacious pirate. I wanted to ask about him. See if the boys had any news, but it would have to wait just a little longer.

"This place… it's perfect."

"It's not a palace," Peter started, "but it seemed fitting."

"It's more than I could have ever asked for. Thank you." I felt my eyes begin to water, my emotions getting the better of me. "Tell me the plan. When are we going after Ry?" I asked, changing the subject before I turned into a blubbering fool. I needed a level head. I had to think rationally, so I dawned a new persona. Queen. A mask that I wasn't even sure I wanted to wear, but it seemed useful at the moment.

"Gwen, you just got back. Do you think now—" Peter started to placate me, but I was having none of that.

"Yes, I do. We. Have. No. Time," I ground out the words. "I won't let Ryder suffer any longer than necessary, so we will do this now."

Peter sighed. "Black Lake Castle is formidable, but we've managed to get spies into Dorian's ranks. We don't have enough blood from the Fae hounds to get an army past the barrier and storm the main entrances, but there are slave quarters under the castle itself. And according to our intel, they clean out the dead from the dungeons once a fortnight. That is the only weak point we've found. Honestly, I'm not really sure how much of a weak point that is, but it's the only chance we've got to get Ry back. There will be a cleaning in two days time. We'll take a small contingent of warriors with us, and infiltrate the castle. Ryder's being held in a special cell, away from the others, so we'll have to venture into the castle." Peter concluded.

"It's risky, but it's the only shot we've got." Tripp tried to sound confident, but I could tell they were just as desperate to get Ryder back as I was, and this plan was a Hail Mary.

I nodded slowly, my tactical mind going over all the

possibilities. "Do you have any schematics of the castle? How is it laid out? Do you know the pattern of the guards? Or even how many we'll be facing—"

"Whoa, Gwen. You don't need to worry about all that. We've got it covered. I'll arrange for Amara to collect you in the morning and bring you to the stronghold. I'm sure she'll be pleased to see that you're alright," Peter said.

"Wait, what? No... I'm coming with you."

"Darling, I'm not about to let you walk into the monster's lair after we just got you back. We can't risk it. I *won't* lose you again." Peter was stern, and I could see the fear in his eyes.

"No! You need me. Ryder needs me. I've been training with the sword. I can be useful to this mission. I have magic... I just don't know how to access it at the moment. But it will come back to me. In our time of need, it will come back to me." I tried to keep my words from sounding like a plea from a useless damsel in distress, but I was royally fucking it up. I contemplated telling them about the Osakren. Telling them I *was* the Osakren. But I needed them to have faith in me alone.

"A lot has changed since you've been gone. The day we took out Arion, something awakened inside me. The power the bone faerie prophesized, it's finally come to pass. I can protect you now. You've been through so much already. Let us take care of you."

"We take care of each other, Peter. That's where our

strength lies," I countered. I wasn't meant to be some kept woman. The only way we can defeat Dorian is together.

Peter raked his fingers through his hair, obviously frustrated with the corner I'd put him in. "Think about it, Gwen. If something happens to me, Neverland needs a leader. You are her queen. You have to stay behind for that very reason alone."

"We are not mated. I am not Neverland's queen. I won't sit on the sidelines while awful things are happening to Ryder, and they *are* happening. While I was with the bone faerie, I could feel you, each of you. I could feel what was happening to him…" My words trailed off into a sob.

"Don't cry, beautiful. It's going to be alright," Tripp crooned.

"Tripp's right. Tonight we should be celebrating your return, not arguing over the war. Dorian has taken enough from us, I won't let him ruin this night as well. Tomorrow we'll figure everything out," Peter sighed, looking deflated.

Tripp pulled me into him, my back settling against his solid chest before he circled my waist in his muscled arms. "Once we get all this war business taken care of, we'll be able to start a life here. All of us," he whispered in my ear. I tried to let my mind envision it, the beautiful future he was trying to paint for me, but the visions were clouded. I couldn't stop thinking about Ryder.

Peter stalked toward me, slipping his big hands along my jaw, his fingers weaving into my hair. His warm umber eyes peeked out from the camouflage paint that still covered his face, studying me for a moment before he dipped in for a kiss. This time, his kiss was slow and soft. When he pulled away, he rested his forehead against mine.

"It's been so hard without you. Nothing could fill the void. I've hungered for you in ways I cannot explain, and now I am a starved man. Can we have this moment? Can we forget for just this night that the world is falling in around us? Because I need you. I need you to make all of this worth it. I want to drown in you until I have to face reality with the dawn."

His words were my undoing. We'd all been through hell. As much as it killed me to indulge in a moment of pleasure while I knew the cocky Lost Boy who owned a piece of my heart was being tortured, we all needed a moment to forget. To just exist in the pleasure of each other's bodies.

I leaned forward, brushing my lips over his, biting his bottom lip. It was all the consent he needed and I could feel the shift in both him and Tripp. Greedy hands stripped my leathers off, both of them pulling at belts and straps, dropping all my weapons in a pile at my feet, until I was standing completely vulnerable before them. I watched as they drank in all of my curves. The look in their eyes alone had my cheeks heating, and wetness slicking my thighs.

"Goddess… you take my breath away." Tripp cocked his head as his eyes continued to rake over my body. "Beautifully crafted perfection that speaks to each of us." He bit his lip as his intense gaze settled back on my eyes.

"Now it's my turn. Let me look at the both of you," I

commanded, feeling needy myself. They began to strip, leaving their own piles of weapons and armor at their feet. All of us shedding the desperation of the soldiers we'd been forced to become.

They stood before me, taught muscles covering every inch of their large frames. Neither of them made any attempt to conceal their massive erections. The camouflage paint on their faces gave them a carnal, animalistic look. The intensity of the moment had me feeling feral. I licked my lips, my throat going dry with the sight of them. They were mine.

Tripp circled behind me, wrapping his arms around me, pulling me against him, his hard cock digging into my ass. He pulled my braid to the side, kissing my neck, as Peter approached from the front, caressing my breasts and rolling my nipples in his fingers while he kissed me. My body instantly responded to their touch, and Peter swallowed a moan as I pressed into his hands.

"Don't be gentle with me," I breathed, encouraging Peter to pinch my nipples harder, sending a surge of wetness between my legs.

"You've always liked being caught between us, haven't you?" Peter crooned.

Tripp pulled on my braid, snapping my head back, before feasting on my neck, sucking the blood to the surface, marking me.

"Answer him, beautiful. You want to be caught between the two of us?"

"Yes," I moaned out, letting their roaming hands stoke the fire that burned in the pit of my stomach. Tripp dropped to his knees behind me, spreading my cheeks wide before his tongue darted between them, sliding over my delicate opening, sending a shockwave of pleasure to my core that I wasn't expecting. Holy hell, did that feel amazing.

Peter's mouth began to work his way down too, suckling on my overly sensitive nipples, leaving a trail down my stomach with his tongue. I was nearing my breaking point. Whatever magic Tripp was doing to my ass with his tongue was edging me closer and closer. Peter started to lap at my clit, pulsing in quick little bursts.

I was ruined, and I fell happily over the edge into oblivion. My hands pulled hard on Peter's hair as the orgasm hit me. It felt like it had been years since my boys made my body sing. The echoes of pleasure coursed through me, as my boys stood firm, holding my wilting form in their strong hands.

"Come on, beautiful. I want that perfect peach riding on my cock." Tripp took my hand, and led me to our enormous bed. I was at their mercy, my mind drunk with euphoria. I would do anything they wanted me to at this point. He laid down on his back, his strong arms positioning me so that I was facing away from him, reverse cowgirl style. His hard length slid between my cheeks, coating himself in my wetness. His strong hands bracing me, holding all of my weight, and slowly, I sunk his cock into my ass. He let out a hiss when I'd taken him all the way.

"That's right, beautiful. You take it so good. The way your ass looks, with my cock inside you, it's the hottest fucking thing. Fuck!" He grunted out the last part as I ground my hips against him, my body urging me on, wanting more.

"Wait, Darling, or you'll make him blow his load before we're done," Peter cautioned as he crawled up the bed towards me. He pushed me backwards until I was lying on Tripp's chest, his cock still buried in my ass. The position had my pussy on perfect display for him, and he continued his ministrations, his talented tongue lapping at my dripping core, sucking my clit into his mouth and grazing his teeth over it. I wriggled under him, feeling Tripp's hard length caress spots I never knew were so sensitive. The unearthly moans that came from my body were almost shameful. When Peter sunk two fingers into me, I detonated around them both. The climax hit me like a freight train.

"Don't you cum, Tripp. Not yet," Peter scolded at Tripp as I rocked out the rest of my orgasm on him.

"Easy for you to say," Tripp growled out as his fingers dug into my hips, halting my movement.

Peter crawled over me, lining himself up and slamming into me. My sensitive spots screaming with the friction, all of me still tingling with the last orgasm. I felt the fullness of them both as I was sandwiched between them. I was lost in an abyss of pleasure, and I never wanted to find my way out. Every nerve ending was firing, my senses heightened. I could feel their heavy breathing on me. Their hands roamed my flesh as their cocks punished me so sweetly from within. It was almost too much.

"Come on, beautiful. Cum for me one more time. I want to feel you tighten around me as I spill my soul inside you," Tripp moaned in my ear.

Peter adjusted ever so slightly and I was seeing stars. I could feel barriers cracking inside me. A tidal wave of pleasure crested over the barrier to the other half of me, the magical half that had remained shrouded in darkness. A literal snarl came from my lips as my body tensed and I came again, clenching around them, milking them both as they cried my name, falling into the abyss with me.

I had no idea how long we stayed collapsed on top of each other. But when Peter finally pulled out of me, I whimpered at the loss of him. Tripp lifted me from his body and nestled me into his side, placing my head in the crook of his shoulder. I was spent, but my mind was still reeling. For a moment, I had been able to feel my magic again. The barrier had fallen back in place, but it didn't seem so sturdy this time.

"Let me get you something so I can clean you up. And I'll make you some tea," Peter said as he got to his feet, walking out of the room in all his naked glory.

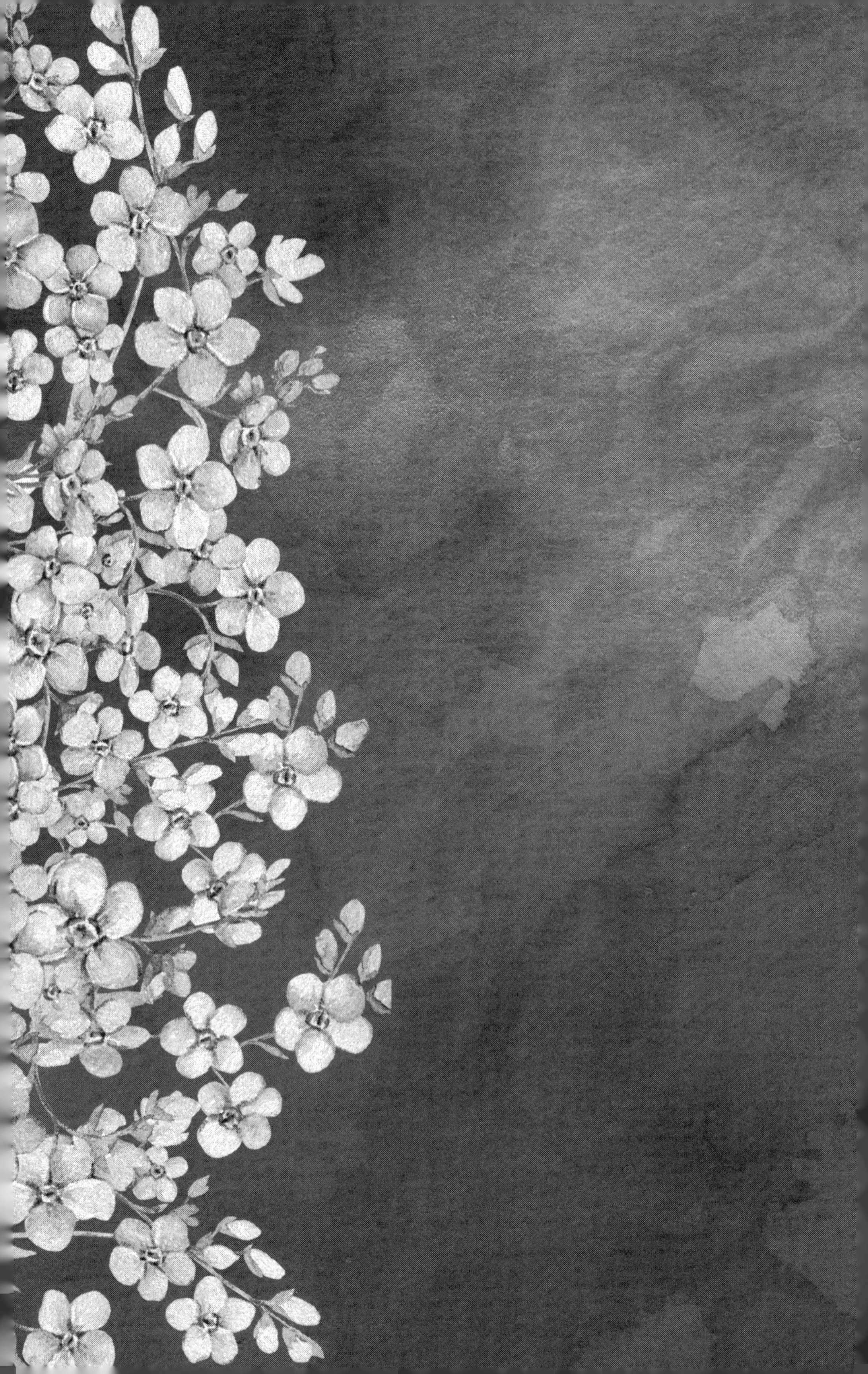

CHAPTER XIX
REGRET
-TRIPP-

"Is she asleep?" Pan asked, staring at our girl as she snuggled into my side. Her breathing had slowed, and she'd fallen asleep shortly after we'd had our way with her. She'd been through so much lately. It pained me to think that so many of her struggles started when she'd met us.

"She's out," I whispered, almost afraid to break the peace of the moment. My girl, safe and sound, tucked into my arms. Nothing could be better than this. But I could tell by the look in Pan's eyes, he had something to get off his chest and whatever it was would end this perfect moment.

"We can't take Gwen on the mission tomorrow."

I let out the breath I'd been holding and banged my head against the headboard in frustration. I'd known this was coming, but I'd been avoiding it, because there was no good answer. My mind was at war with itself and the indecision was starting to eat away at me. A big part of me wanted to protect her, put her somewhere safe until this whole war with the bastard prince was over. I couldn't stand the thought of losing her again. I was beginning to hold a grudge against the Divine. We'd been tested, separated more than once, and each time we'd clawed our way back to each other. Even death hadn't been able to keep us apart. Hadn't we proven ourselves? But I knew that we weren't finished yet. All the more reason to side with Pan on this one.

I'd seen the devastation in her eyes over Ryder. She wanted to be there, not only to rescue him, but to exact her vengeance in his name. Could I deny her that when my own soul was calling for blood? And we were a team, at least we were supposed to be. I knew if we left her behind it would crush her.

"Hear me out. You saw how he looked at her when we took out Arion. She piqued his interest. She's a shiny new toy he's desperate to play with. What if he gets his hands on her? It's bad enough knowing what he's doing to Ry. How are you going to handle it if he's doing that to Gwen?"

I couldn't hold back the low grumble elicited by the thought of Dorian with Gwen. Pan knew exactly what to say to sway me to his side. With thoughts of Dorian's hands on my girl, I slowly moved her off of me. She let out a slight moan at being disturbed, but then snuggled back down into the covers. "When do we leave?"

"Right now. Get geared up and we'll be chasing the dawn before she even knows we left."

I stepped back into my leathers, becoming the warrior once again. I was having a hard time reining in the indecision festering within me. Before Gwen, the last time I'd allowed my emotions to get the better of me was when I'd left my mum behind. Maybe that's why I could still remember vague details from my previous life. It was the last truly emotional connection I'd had, until Gwen turned my world upside down.

I'd left my mum for the very same reasons. I'd been trying to protect her too. She had been forced to sell her body in order to keep food on the table for me. I refused to be the reason she had to go to such lengths. I couldn't stand to see the marks covering her every morning. But the devil that lurks inside us all continued to cast doubts on my decision to leave. I had always feared that maybe I was no better than the deadbeat excuse of a man who'd been my father. He'd shirked his responsibilities and left us to toil in the gutters of society. Was I no better than he was? I'd left my mum all those years ago and to this day, I still don't know if it had been the right decision. Now, I had another choice to make. Would leaving Gwen behind now be the right decision, or would it haunt me for the rest of my life?

I stood in the doorway, armed to the teeth. A lethal weapon, fully ready to accept whatever might happen. I was prepared to do whatever I had to do to save my girl… my family. Even if it meant leaving her behind.

I watched Gwen, still asleep in the bed, her hair in a chestnut cascade around her. She'd been so worried about Ryder that it was a relief to finally see the crease in her brow smoothed out, replaced by a look of peaceful serenity in the depths of sleep.

"You know I'm right," Peter said as he came up beside me, gazing at our whole world lying in the bed. "Choosing to protect her will never be the wrong decision."

I let out a huff. "I can't argue with your logic, but why does it feel like we're making a mistake?"

"Don't worry. She'll forgive you. The moment she sees that we've brought Ryder back all will be forgiven. That's all she wants. Plus, I think she'll have her hands full trying to bring him back from whatever hell Dorian's put him through."

I hesitated, still conflicted, but I had to make a decision, and Pan wasn't about to let this go. "Come on. Dawn's about to break. If we get moving, we'll be back before nightfall. Let's make a bet… the Lost Boy with the most kills gets to make it up to her first." He punched my arm, a cocky grin on his face before he blew a kiss at Gwen and turned to leave.

I would have given anything to be back in Gwen's bed again. Instead, I found myself wading into the putrid water that surrounded Black Lake Castle. The darkness of the water rivaled the castle with its inky depths. Six of us had infiltrated the Viridianwood in the shadowed light of the dawn. Only four of us had made it this far, as two of our comrades had been taken out by the Fae hounds at the edge of the barrier.

Now, we planned to lie in wait. When they opened the back gates to dispose of the dead slaves, we'd make our move. We decided to take our chances with whatever was lurking in the shadowed lake surrounding the castle and hope for the best. It was easier to face obscurity rather than the demon who was most certainly waiting for you.

My gaze landed on Peter. He nodded at me and we both inhaled our ration of faerie dust and sunk below the surface. We waited, barely able to make out the castle through the murky waters. This was nothing like the Mermaid Lagoon. Inhaling this water felt like inhaling thick black smoke. My lungs burned, and I knew we wouldn't be able to remain too long in this hiding place.

When the drawbridge finally started to lower, I said a silent thank you to the Divine. But maybe it came out all wrong. Maybe I offended her, because in the next moment, I felt something wrap around my ankle. Shit. I pulled a dagger from my belt, maneuvering in the water until I could sink my blade into the tentacle that was trying to drag me down. It recoiled enough that I freed my leg, but Pan wasn't faring as well. I could feel the tingle of his magic, but it only seemed to spur the creature on. All of his limbs were immobilized. I had to do something. We needed a distraction. I took a chance and surfaced, finding a few guards pushing wheelbarrows of dead bodies across the drawbridge. I managed to fly out of the water and land before them. I was outnumbered, but with the adrenaline rushing through my veins, it only took me a moment to draw blood. I pushed the bloodied guards into the black lake, toppling their pallet of dead bodies in with them. I dove back into the water, swimming down further and further until I found Pan making his way back to the surface. The beast of the deep had been drawn to the fresh blood, seeking easier prey. I grabbed a hold of my brother, pulling him back to the surface with me. Once we crawled our way onto the drawbridge, we realized only the two of us had made it out.

We pushed forward into the now unmanned door with no time to even catch our breath. The stench of death and decay was thick within the castle. The dank corridor was lined with cages, filled to capacity with the unkempt bodies of slaves— Neverlanders that had been captured over the last several months. I swallowed hard to keep the contents of my stomach down. Pan and I broke open every cage we walked past, liberating the prisoners. But it was no use. Many of them stood there, nothing more than vacant zombies. Only a few recognized their own salvation, weeping as they grabbed others, trying to lead them to freedom. The cages seemed to go on forever as we made our way deeper into the bowels of the castle, questioning anyone who seemed like they could answer, but none of them could give information on Ryder.

The sound of the guards' voices echoing off the walls led us forward. We must have looked like the devil incarnate, emerging from the shadows of hell. One minute they'd been talking and laughing, fully secure in their control, and the next they were scrambling. We took a few of them down, but several of them managed to escape.

Fuck! Now we were on borrowed time. The entire castle would be on alert, and they would be coming for us. I gave chase, running one of the guards down, slamming him into the wall, my knife poised at his throat. "Where are they keeping Ryder?" I barked.

"I don't know. None of them have names. They are simply slaves," he hissed with a condescending grin on his face.

"The Lost Boy. Tell me where the bastard prince is keeping him?"

"I'm not telling you anything."

"I hoped you'd say that." I grinned as I pulled my knife from his throat and slammed it into his thigh. He let out a howl of pain, but didn't answer my question.

"We can keep going," I growled as I twisted the blade.

"He's... they're keeping him in the west wing of the dungeons. That's where the prince keeps his private stock," he groaned out the words. It sickened me to hear him talk about Ryder as if he was nothing more than a prized animal. But I didn't have time to take out my anger on this fucker, and he earned himself a quick death. I dropped his limp body at my feet, and trifled with his belt, stealing the ring of keys.

Pan wasn't too far behind me. We headed west, moving as quickly as we could. When we reached a heavily armored door with a myriad of locks, I knew that had to be it. The stolen keys proved invaluable, gaining us access to a darkened hallway. A total of four cells were contained here, two on each side. Each door had only a small slot to pass food through. The first three cells were empty, small black rooms with no windows and chains embedded in the walls. A sinking feeling filled me. It was as if each of these four cells had our names on them, simply waiting to be filled.

We found Ry curled into the fetal position at the back of the last cell. His back was bloodied, covered in weeping wounds. A torn pair of dirty pants covered his sickly skinny form. I could make out every rib. Pan and I locked glances and I could see the fear in his eyes. Could he ever come back from this kind of torture?

"Ry... brother. We're here," I called calmly to him as we approached.

I placed a hand on his shoulder and he flinched, peering

up at me with his arm shielding his face.

"Stop. Stop tormenting me." His chapped lips trembled as he looked at me.

"We're here. It's really us," Pan said as he picked up one of Ry's hands and placed it on his chest.

"No. You can't be here. This is where I belong. This is what I deserve. This is my redemption."

"It's time to go home to your girl, Ry. She's waiting for you. She's worried about you," I said, hoping the mention of Gwen would be enough to bring him around.

"Leave!" he bellowed, trying to turn his body away from us.

"Tripp, we don't have time for this. We'll just have to carry him out. He's too weak to fight the two of us. We'll have time to deal with him when we get him home."

I nodded my agreement, and we grabbed an arm, pulling his weak body off the ground.

"No! You don't know what you're doing. Dorian's my savior. He's shown me what I am. I need to stay, please," he begged as he tried in vain to fight us. My heart broke at his words, but Pan was right. He'd have time for healing once we got him out. When we reached the hallway, Ryder was snarling like a captured beast, still trying to get away from us, slowing our forward progress. That's when things shifted from bad to worse. Ryder started screaming. "Master! They're here! Save me!"

Fuck! That was the last thought I had before the walls of the dungeon began to melt away. The feeling of Ryder in my grasp disappeared, and was replaced by cold hands that circled around my throat. A firm body pressed at my back. Before I could register the threat behind me, I was lost in the vision before me.

I now stood in a darkened closet, looking through a tattered sheet into a familiar room that I knew all too well. The stench hit me first— stale beer, sweat, and sex filled my nostrils. This was the small room that my mother had rented out. The filthy place had been the only home we'd been able to afford after my father left us with nothing. The sound of my mother's bed creaked as some low life scum fucked her. Her face was turned toward the curtain I was standing behind. Her eyes vacant as she waited for her client to finish his business and be done with her. She looked as though she'd aged at least ten years from the version I'd held of her in my memories.

"What the fuck is this?" I breathed out as I watched. It was a goddamned nightmare that I'd lived as a child, come roaring back to life.

"This is what you wanted to know," the refined voice of Dorian tickled my ear as he spoke. "You always wanted to know if leaving was the right decision."

"It was the right decision. This isn't real. You're just fucking with me," I barked out. I attempted to shift my eyes from my mum, but for some reason I couldn't turn away.

"Funny. Preston said the same thing. But I would guarantee that if you asked him now, he would disagree with that statement."

Preston? Who the fuck was Preston? And how the fuck did the bastard prince know about my mother, about the fears that had plagued me all these years?

"I see the stain of it on your soul," he answered the question that was burning in my mind before I'd even had the chance to ask it.

"Watch, we're about to get to the good part," his voice rising in pitch with his excitement. My mother began to whimper as the man grew rough with her. When she tried to push him off, he backhanded her and kept pounding away. She continued to fight, even though she was no match for him, but that only seemed to turn him on more. When she tried to scream, he covered her mouth and pulled a knife from a belt in his pants that were still wrapped around his ankles. I tried to move. I tried to go to her, but my limbs were frozen in place. Dorian's hand felt like a vice around my throat, and his magic kept me rooted in place. When the man's arm swung, sinking the blade into her chest, I managed to wrench my eyes away. But I couldn't escape the sounds. The bed creaking, her muffled screams, his groans of pleasure, the sucking sound the knife made every time he pulled it from her body.

"If you'd only been there, this may never have happened. But you left, just like your father, and she paid the ultimate price for your decisions. That pretty little thing you left back in her bed… that will be another regrettable decision. You're always leaving the women who love you when they need you the most."

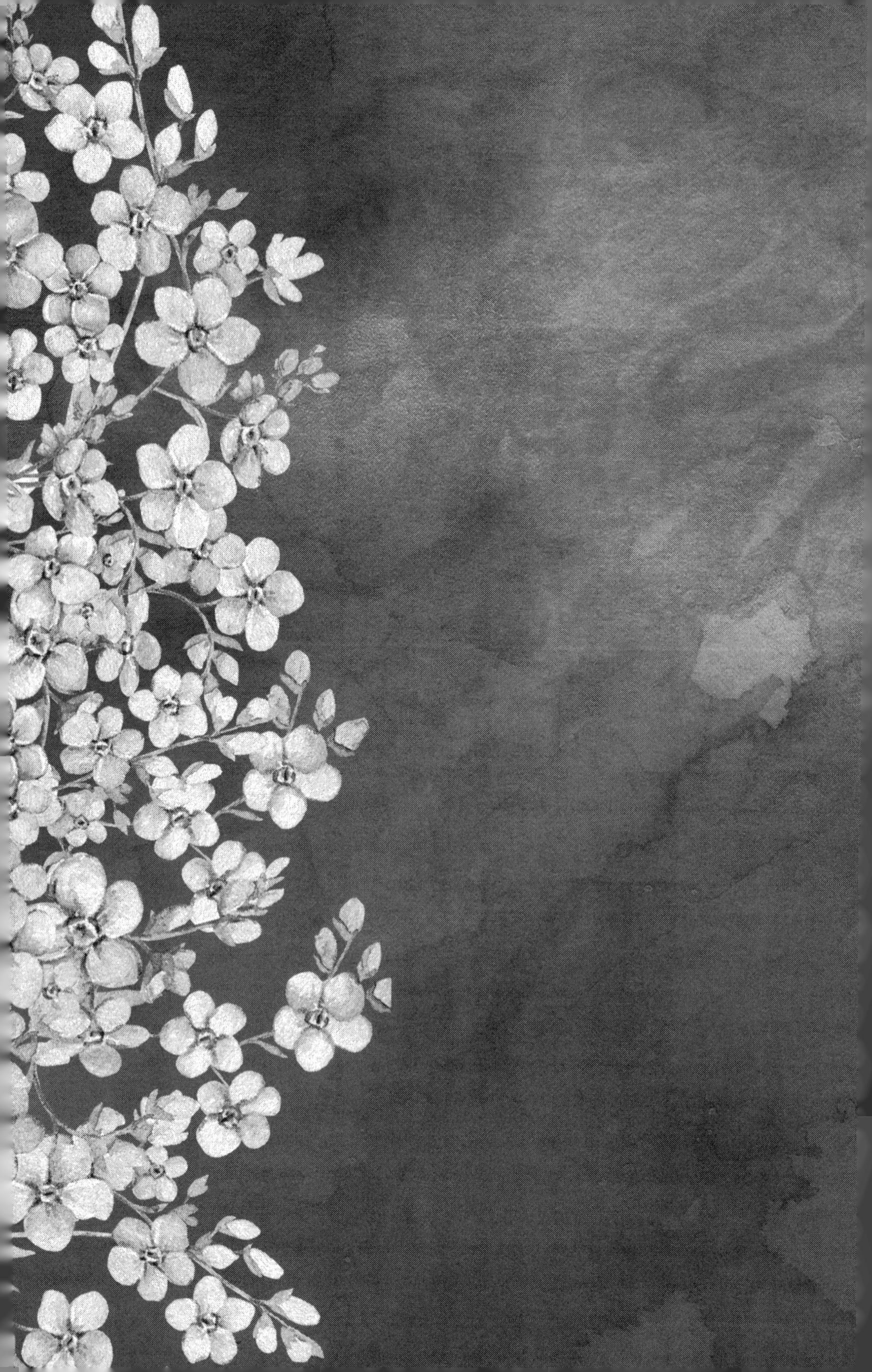

CHAPTER XX
ALL THESE WOES SHALL SERVE
-EBEN-

My hands trembled as I read the message from Pan. She'd returned. Thank the fucking Divine she had returned. For the first time in months, I felt my heart pound in my chest. The urgency to get back to her was overwhelming and I've never traveled home faster.

Neverland was barely recognizable. Peter had been out of sorts, with Gwen missing and the threat of Dorian looming over his head. I had expected bad weather but this was something else. Neverland looked like a war zone. Lil and I had only been gone a few months. We had searched

Gwen's home and every possible realm we could find. Only to come up empty-handed. I'd refused to give up on her. I prayed to the Divine to keep her safe. I had failed her once and I was determined to never do it again. Without her, I was nothing. She was my reason for living. I couldn't lose her again.

It was early. The sun was just beginning to rise above the horizon painting the sky with a delicate pink glow. I had seen Lill to the strong hold under the Never cliffs and gone straight to Gwen's cottage.

She was sleeping soundly. I watched for a moment, and thanked the Divine for bringing her back to me— to us. She appeared to be at peace, the weight of her worries gone from her beautiful face. The cottage was quiet, but for the soft coo of birds waking up off in the distance.

We were alone, my brothers were gone. Probably out preparing some extravagant breakfast for our beloved. It angered me that they had left her unprotected after all we had been through. Regardless, it left perfect timing for what I had in mind, and I wasn't in the mood for sharing. She had been missing for far too long and I wanted nothing more than to worship at her temple. I hated the idea of waking her, but the need to touch her outweighed all others.

Trying not to disturb her, I slowly pulled back the bedsheets, exposing her bare breasts. My cock stirred at the sight of her. She was perfection. I didn't deserve her... None of us did. Her pretty pink nipples pebbled in the cool morning air, begging to be touched. The black veining that had marred her porcelain skin was now gone. I breathed a sigh of relief. Her debt had been paid. Never again would I allow her to risk her own life for the sake of ours. This would be the start of our happily ever after. And just like a fairytale, I would wake my queen with a kiss.

I silently stripped off my clothes and crawled up the bed, straddling her sleeping body. Placing gentle kisses from her navel to her clavicle. She moaned softly as I dragged my tongue from her sternum to her neck.

"Sin from my lips? O trespass sweetly urged! Give me my sin again." I cooed into her ear. A smile spread across her face as she roused from her sleep.

"Romeo, is that you?" She stretched, arching her back. "Eben,"—her eyes still heavy with sleep—"I've missed you so much." She wrapped her arms around me, squeezing tight.

"Not nearly as much as I've missed you." I pressed my cock against her core, the bed sheet straining to keep us apart. "I need you."

"Lucky me," she giggled, kissing my neck.

I continued my assault of kisses, this time trailing back down her belly and pulling down the sheets to expose her warmth. Without a word she spread her legs, opening herself up to me. I paused for a moment to admire her body. The way she bloomed like a flower, spreading her petals just for me. Her scent intoxicated me as it drove my need to consume her body and soul. A possessive growl sprang from my throat. I couldn't wait any longer. I needed to taste her, devour her, and make her scream my name while I feasted on her desire.

Slowly, I ran my tongue up her glistening slit, teasing the sensitive skin and drawing out a moan of approval. The sweet taste of her arousal had me hard as a rock. "You're so wet for me."

"I've missed your wicked tongue," she mewed, spreading her legs wider.

Teasing her clit with gentle flicks, I began to worship her sex with my mouth. I could spend all day with my face buried between her legs. Listening to her lost in the throes of pleasure. I circled my fingers around her opening, gently massaging the slick skin before pushing in two, then three. She gasped, arching her back. Her body tightened on my fingers before relaxing into the sensation. Pumping my fingers in and out, I continued my assault on her clit with my tongue. She began to grind her hips, riding my fingers, searching for release. Her breath quickened— she was on the edge.

"I'm gonna cum," she cried, grabbing my hair and wrapping her legs around my head, completely lost in her orgasm. Her hips bucked against my face. The sounds of her pleasure were driving me mad with desire.

The need to be inside her took over. I quickly made my way back up her body. Pausing briefly to kiss her sinful mouth, before sheathing myself in her warm heaven. "Fuck, Gwen. You feel amazing." I tried desperately to take my time, but I lost all control. She had been away for far too long. Her cries of pleasure grew louder with each punishing thrust, testing my restraint.

"Eben!" she cried out as her sex clamped down around me, climaxing again. The sensation of her pulsing core threw me over the edge. I came, blinded by pleasure, before collapsing breathlessly on top of her.

"Don't ever leave me again," I whispered in her ear. "I'm utterly lost without you."

"I am yours, and you are mine. That will never change." She smiled, "All these woes shall serve / For sweet discourses in our time to come."

"Romeo and Juliet may be a romantic notion, but let me remind you, it is a tragedy."

"Our story will have a happily ever after," she promised, lacing our fingers together.

There— on her hand— were new markings. I hadn't noticed them before. Delicate runes where there used to be black veining stemming from her pinky finger. My heart froze as I assumed the worst. "What is this?" I asked calmly, inspecting the new markings.

"It's a long story. I..." She hesitated. "Basically, I'm now the Osakren." She answered with a sigh, as if a heavy burden had lifted from her shoulders.

"You're the Osakren? Should I ask the how, what and why?" This revelation had me concerned. Was she now at risk of becoming the object of Dorian's obsession? That bastard had a hard on for the talisman. Could we not have a moment's peace?

"It's complicated and quite honestly, I'm not sure I understand all of it myself. Peytra— sorry the bone faerie— said it was a gift from the Divine. Something to do with awakening my magic? Where are the others?" She asked, quickly dismissing the topic.

"I'm not sure. I assumed they were out getting breakfast? I'd like to talk more about how *you* are the Osakren."

Gwen's brow furrowed. "Wait, no one is here?" She jumped out of bed, grabbing one of Ryder's shirts and pulling it over her little frame. "Is there a note?" She began frantically searching the room.

"Babe," I spoke calmly. Reaching for my clothes. Our reunion was over. Her demeanor had changed. She was clearly unsettled.

"Gwen!" Hook's desperate voice echoed through the cottage, followed by his heavy footsteps.

"James!"

"Gwen!" He barged through the door and pulled Gwen into his arms before kissing her with a tenderness that I wouldn't have believed had I not seen it myself.

"My Love, I came as quickly as I could. Are you okay? Did she hurt you?"

"I've missed you so much. I'm fine."

I couldn't watch them fawn over each other. I started searching the cottage for the note she'd been so desperately searching for. I agreed to accept Hook's presence in Gwen's life. I never agreed to enjoy watching the bastard put his hands all over her. Something had spooked Gwen. My brothers weren't ones to leave notes, but maybe she knew something I didn't. Sure enough, on the table in the next room was a note from Peter.

GWEN,

Please, try to understand what I'm about to tell you. After much thought, Tripp and I have decided we can not put you in harm's way again. You have done enough for our little family. It's our turn to man up. You are our everything. Without you there is no reason to continue on. Tripp and I have gone after Ryder. Do not try to follow us. Dorian is more dangerous than you realize. We just got you back. We will not lose you again. We will return, with Ryder at our side. Until then, take your place as queen. Watch over Neverland and her people.

All our love, Peter & Tripp

FUCK. My brothers had been busy while I was gone, and it looks like Ryder had gotten himself into a mess. I made my way back to Gwen's room with the letter in hand. "Babe, I hate to interrupt your reunion, but..." I held up the letter.

"What does it say?" she asked, the panic beginning to rise in her voice.

"Here, you should read it." I handed her the letter and prepared for the worst.

"Oh no. Oh no no no." Her face went from fear to anger in the matter of seconds. "They've gone without me."

"Darling?" Hook interjected.

"How could they go without me? Without us? How could they risk it? Ryder's life is at stake." Tears began to well in her eyes. "I'm not a useless little girl." She turned to look at me for answers, shaking her head. "I should have told them about the Osakren. We have to go after them."

"Gwen, I'm gonna need you to take a breath." I reached out to touch her, to offer some sort of calming support. She was trembling and I was certain she was on the verge of a meltdown.

"Could someone please tell me what's going on?" Hook was losing patience.

"I think we could both use an update. Come, let's sit and talk about this."

Gwen spent the hour telling us how Ryder had been taken as a slave to Dorian while on a reconnaissance mission. And about Peter's plan to rescue him. She explained how she had changed while she was in the void with Peytra, and could now feel a physical connection with us. She was certain that Ryder had been enduring hours of torture. She went on in graphic detail about how she had imbibed the magic from the Osakren but did not possess the memories to call upon it. A lot had changed since she had been gone. Our girl had become a badass magical relic.

"I know in our time of need my magic will take over. We have to go," Gwen pleaded.

"Gwen... babe, how can you be so sure? You said yourself you don't possess the memories to call upon it." It was risky going in after them hoping that all would sort itself out at the appropriate time. I wasn't so sure.

"For once could you trust her instincts?" James chided. "You boys are always underestimating her abilities. Not once have I seen you give her the choice that is clearly hers to make. Has she not proven herself to you? Have you not figured out that you don't own her? Allow her a chance to fall and she very well may fly."

I knew Hook was right, and his words cut deep. My instinct was to scrutinize every word out of the man's mouth, but he'd torn away the blindfold and I couldn't deny the truth of what he said. We were so caught up in keeping her safe that we lost touch with the fact that she was indeed a capable woman. She had proven time and time again that she was stronger than we gave her credit for. We allowed our own fears of losing her stifle her abilities.

Gwen smiled and wiped a tear from her cheek. "I can do this. Trust me."

I sighed. We were diving into the black waters of the deep end. Would we end up like Icarus? Flying too close to the sun with wax wings?

"We're going to need an army of help. I'll request an emergency meeting with Amara."

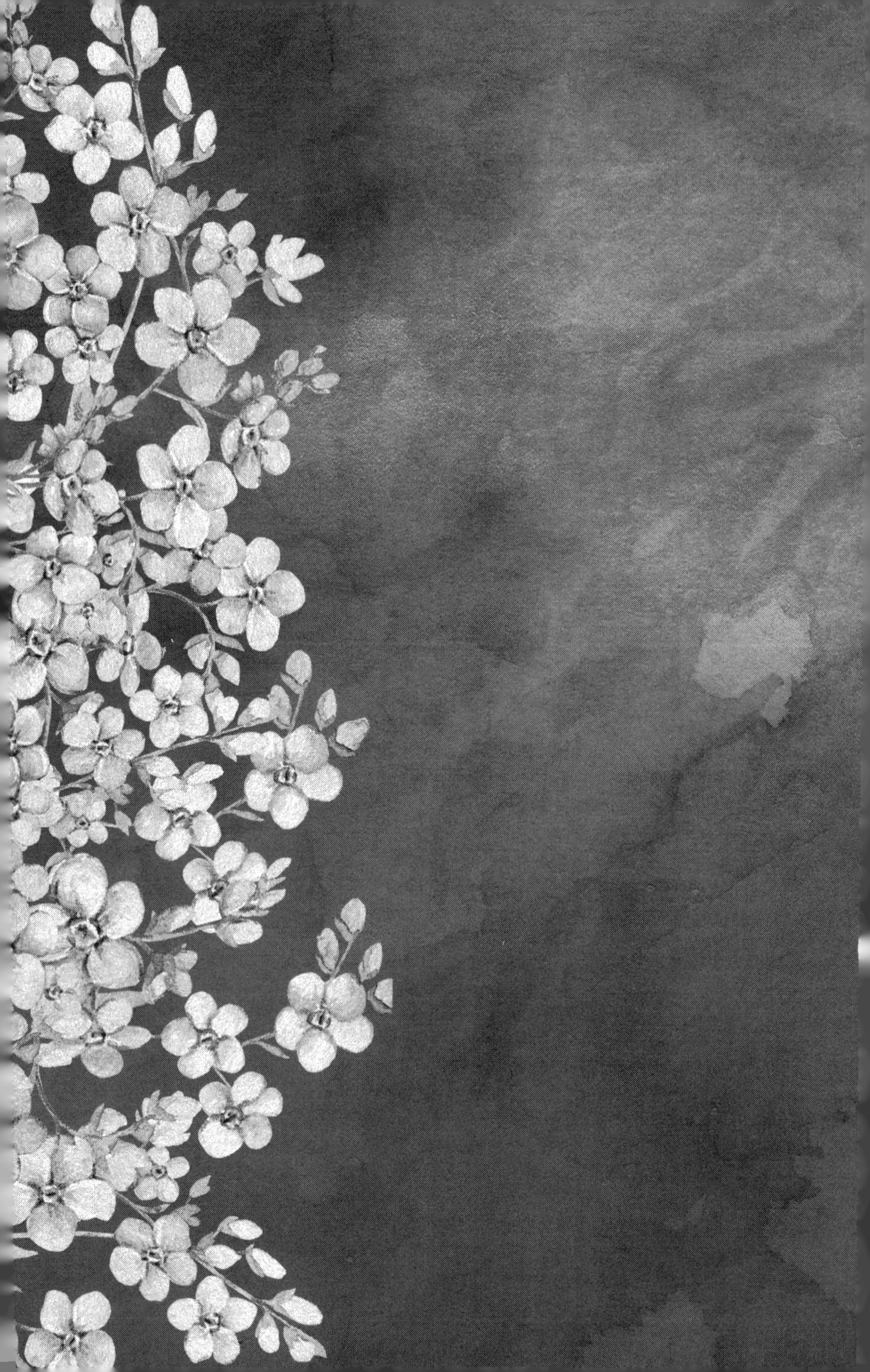

CHAPTER XXI
FROM NOTHING THEY RISE
-GWEN-

I bit my lip incessantly while we waited in the arms cellar for Amara. I was desperately trying to keep it together and not lose my shit. A part of me wanted to scream, let my fists connect with something, anything. I could feel my sword strapped to my back, and I itched to drive it through our enemies. I was still trying to wrap my head around everything that was happening.

Peter and Tripp left me. As pure as their intentions may have been, they had let fear get the better of them. They had let their fear separate us. I held my anger to a low simmer, embracing the emotion. Because the moment I had realized they left me behind, blind rage had burned through me, taking another shot at the barrier that kept my magic hidden from me. The rawest emotions seemed to bring me closer to being whole again.

Eben paced the cellar that had been transformed into a command center. A brooding scowl was plastered on his face while he carefully selected weapons and added them to his belt. James, on the other hand, sat at the war table, studying a detailed map of Neverland. The very picture of the cold and calculating captain he was.

It was a relief when Amara finally joined us, because my patience was beginning to falter. I needed to be doing something.

"My child!" The look on her face was sobering. Her normal composure slipped away, revealing a well of emotion in her glassy eyes. She pulled me in for a hug, gripping me tightly in her motherly embrace. "You made it back to us. You don't know how happy I am that you've returned."

"I missed you too, Amara." She held me at arm's length, scrutinizing me for a moment. I was worried she'd forget her promise to keep Kían a secret, and the last thing I needed was Eben going off half cocked if he found out I'd lied to him all this time. Her eyes shifted to the runes on my hand, a smile spreading across her face as she ran her thumb over them.

"You carry the change with every bit of grace." she whispered as she nodded. Somehow she knew that I'd become the Osakren. "We have much to discuss. We have a war to win."

Amara, James, and Eben spent the morning going over different tactics. Weighing in on every possible angle. I sat quietly, listening to everything until they seemed to reach a stalemate.

"Gwendolyn, you're awfully quiet, love. The Divine has made you a chosen for a reason." James raised an eyebrow at me as he tried to include me in a conversation I felt I had no business being a part of. But that's what had always lured me to James. He wanted to hear my thoughts, gave credence to my ideas, supported my decisions, and didn't handle me like a fragile porcelain doll.

"I'm feeling… a bit out of my league here. I don't know anything about waging war," I admitted.

"That's because you are." A familiar voice grumbled and my heart lightened as Lu squeezed his massive size into the arms cellar. "But you don't seem to have any problems getting men to rally around you, so maybe you're not completely useless."

"Lu!" I jumped from my seat and threw myself at my friend, wrapping my arms around him. He indulged me for a brief moment before pushing me off. Alo pushed past him, nearly knocking him over to get to me. The enormous wolf jumped up, placing his paws on my chest, licking at my face and whining in his exuberant greeting.

The beast prince rolled his eyes at our affectionate reunion. "It's Luu-ciuus," he reiterated. "Looks like you haven't learned a whole lot of anything since you've been gone."

"Nice to see you too, Alo," I said, ignoring his jab and cutting right to the question that I was burning to have answered. "Have you heard anything from Mic? I haven't had any time to check the scrolls."

"Not yet, but you don't have to worry. She's in the best hands." His brow creased with the mention of Mic and I could tell the silence from his brothers was eating away at him too.

"At least she's not here. Thank god we got her out before all of this started," I said, grateful to have *one* thing that was going right. "Amara was just saying that she thinks the only way to stop Bastian is with a full-blown attack?"

"Yes," she reiterated. "He's still working to build his empire. He's a harbinger of evil. Whispers of his dark plans are spreading fast. Attracting every malicious Fae from across the cosmos, drawing them here, to Neverland. His army will only grow with each passing day. We have to take him out now, while he's still vulnerable. He doesn't yet possess the Osakren. Without it he's not able to unleash the full assault he's planning." Her eyes flicked to mine, unsure if that was yet another secret I was keeping from the men in my life.

"It's okay, Amara. They know that I am the Osakren."

"Keystone? Chosen? Everyone is constantly telling me what I am, what I have to become. And no one wants to tell me what it all means. You're resting the weight of the realms on my shoulders, yet all you can give me is meaningless titles," I barked, my frustrations pouring out of me through my words.

"You are a chosen yes. But more than that, you are the keystone. The conduit to channel all the power and become a ruler truly worthy of the realm. I know you can feel it, the draw you have on your men. Each of them brings a part of the greater whole. Only together can you manifest the destiny the Divine has offered to you. Unfortunately, Peter is blinded by his own self importance."

"That, my dear lady, is the understatement of the century," James added, a smirk crossing his lips. Eben snorted a laugh, unable to hold back his reaction to James's words.

"I'm sorry to put this burden on you, but it really is on your shoulders. I am but a humble servant and I will help you in any way I can. Even you cannot do it alone."

I got up from the war table, kicking the chair out behind me as I got to my feet, joining Eben in his pacing. The weight of everything felt crushing, making it difficult to think of any solutions.

"Just so I'm getting this straight. I have to find a way to create an army out of nothing, march against a madman who's power far exceeds my own and find a way to protect

Lucius let out a low whistle, "*Really* moving up in the world. You can now add old bones to your list of unimpressive attributes." Both James and Eben glared at him, but I brushed them off with a look of my own.

"Fuck off, Lu. You're just jealous that I have some seriously badass powers now. Not to mention that Mic *and* Alo love me best," I teased him back.

Eben rolled his eyes at our ribbing banter and continued, "We can't launch any kind of offensive with his barrier in place. We only have a small amount of blood left from the Fae hounds. It's not enough to get a large army across."

"What army?" Hook barked. "Dorian's been purging Fae, man, and beast alike from the moment he got on the island. Even if we could put an army together on such short notice and storm the castle, we don't have the numbers. With every fight against these bastards we lose more men."

"What about Peter? He mentioned some new found power. He told me that now he has the ability to protect us all. Is that true? Can he pull this off on his own?" In my heart of hearts, I had serious doubts that Peter alone could liberate Neverland.

Amara raked her fingers through her hair and shook her head briefly. "It's true, Peter is a chosen and he has finally managed to tap into his gifts. But he was never meant to be the soul savior of Neverland. It is you, my child, who is the keystone."

everyone I love. And if I fail, every realm will fall to Dorian's darkness? But no pressure— really!" I threw up my hands in frustration. "I don't understand any of it. I don't know what it means to be a conduit? I know that I am bound to these five men in ways that I cannot explain, but how do I use that to become a weapon to defeat the bastard prince?" I ranted to myself as I continued to pace, every statement making me feel more trapped by the perilous situation we found ourselves in.

"I can only pass along what the Divine has shown me," Amara sighed. "I am only given a glimpse for a reason. The how and the why of it, you must figure out on your own. All will be revealed in time. Have faith in yourself my dear child."

No one in the room spoke as each of us tried to hide the defeated looks on our faces. My mind continued to cycle through everything that was mounted against us. Where was I supposed to find an army to fight this war? Amara expected me to do the impossible— create an army out of nothing... Nothing?

The words stuck in my head for some reason. Something Peytra had said was nagging at me now. A memory that was trying hard to surface. Many of our conversations were still firmly tucked behind the barrier that shrouded my magic. That's when the idea hit me. Elordis had given me a gift, a pearl to hold my memories. I wasn't sure if the damn thing would be defective after my time in the void, but I had to try. I needed to remember. I pulled the pearl that I'd kept safely tucked into my baldric.

"The Queen Mother of the Mermaids gave this to me. It's supposed to hold my memories. I know Peytra gave me answers. If I could just remember. Her riddles have more meaning than we realize. Maybe the pearl can show me that?"

"Elordis gave you a pearl?" Amara asked, awe in her voice. "You must have made quite the impression. To my knowledge, no pearl has ever been gifted outside the order of mermaids."

"Quick! I need some water," I turned to Eben. He grabbed a cup, filling it to the brim before handing it to me. I dropped the pearl into the water, watching as it turned the contents into a shimmering liquid. I took a moment to focus on my time with Peytra, or at least as much of it as I could remember, and downed the water.

Visions swirled in my mind's eye, whisking me back to that awful void.

"The magic within you is sentient. Only when there is nothing will it come to you." Her raspy voice echoed in my ears. What was she trying to tell me? This was my time of need. I had nothing left, I had to keep searching, sifting through memories, looking for clues.

"The soul is slick and runs through your hands... But when you mold it to your whim, legions apart will rest at your fingertips."

Legions of souls at my fingertips? Could that be possible? It was all starting to come back to me.

"Death isn't the curse. It is the answer."

"That's it! I know what to do!" My body was already in motion, carrying me out of the arms cellar.

"Gwen? Wait! Where are you going? What happened?" Eben called after me.

I had a plan. I had no idea if I could pull it off, but it was the only thing I could think of and it seemed as though the Divine was trying to lure me down this path. I had to be right about this. Storm clouds were rolling in and a frigid wind had picked up, whipping my hair around my face. I pulled my sword and before I could think it through, I ran it across the palm of my altered hand. Trusting my instincts to lead me down the right path. I pulled the last remaining dust of the dead from my baldric, saying a silent thank you to the besotted little pixie. I poured it into the well of blood pooling in my hand. I watched as the black dust absorbed into the wound. I could feel its power radiating up my arm, finding the barrier blocking my magic and pounding at it. I curled my bloody hand around the pommel of my sword, ready to become whatever weapon the Divine needed me to be.

It was a start, but I needed more. I needed to feel something profound. It was the only way to bring the barriers down. I searched my soul for the bridge that connected us all, reaching out, trying to access the pathway once again. I could feel James and Eben with me.

"Gwendolyn, my love. I'm here for you. We're here for you." James reassured me as he placed his hand on my shoulder. I felt a strange sensation. I couldn't say I'd never felt it before, but more that I'd never fully recognized it. The feel of magic that wasn't my own, but yet familiar, seemed to radiate into me. It was James. He was unknowingly feeding me his own magic, supporting me. I felt the barriers beginning to slough away with the two of us combined.

I sucked in a gasp when Eben placed his hand on my other shoulder, adding his own brand of magic. It was a heady mix surging through me, pushing past the darkness that had been hiding the bridge between us. I felt it now, connecting us all. I could feel Tripp and Peter. Their unwavering determination came through in waves, covering the underlying fear they felt. I pushed past them until I reached my last string. Ryder was holding on by the thinnest of threads. Pain, darkness, fear… the emotions tore into me, a scream escaped my lips. I could feel James and Eben's fingers digging into my shoulders, refusing to let me go. I felt Ryder losing all hope, I could feel him starting to give up. The thought was front and center in his mind. Hopelessness was the only emotion emanating from him. That's what broke me down. I could lose him. I would burn the realms to the ground for any one of my men, and that surge of emotion brought down the last barriers. My magic reared up inside me as it was finally unleashed in a surge so strong that it dropped me to my knees. Then the whispers started. Otherworldly sounds ringing in my ears.

"Passed the tests."

"She is worthy."

"The Divine has chosen well."

The grating voices flooded my mind, like demons hissing in my ears.

"Call us and we will answer. Call us and we will answer. Call us and we will answer."

All of the voices spoke at once, each of them saying the same thing, growing louder until it was deafening in my head. This was it. We had nothing left, an army from nothing. With James and Eben at my side, I drove my sword into the ground. I let the magic flow through me, calling on the spirit of the island itself. A roll of thunder cracked above and lightning split the sky, a blinding fork racing to the ground, exploding in a brilliant flash upon impact.

A rumble began, low at first, then increasing until the ground erupted. Skeletal hands burst through the surface as an army of skeletons clawed their way out of the ground. They weren't corporeal, their transparent bones glowed in various shades of blue and gray. Bits of deteriorated clothes clung to them, along with rusted swords and weapons strapped to their bodies. An army of dead stood before me, all of them staring at me, a faint yellow glow radiating out of their eye sockets.

"W-what do I do now?" I stumbled over my words as I looked over to Eben. He stood wide eyed, staring with his mouth a gape.

"I don't know, baby. You summoned them. Maybe they will follow you?" he stammered out.

"They need a queen," Amara announced. I whirled

around to face her. She stood tall, a carved stone box in her hands. "The time has come, my child. Our lives are planned out with a series of paths. The Divine offers us choices. I am lucky to have had the chance to watch you choose the right path time and time again, and now you are here."

"Amara, I'm not sure I—"

"You can," she interrupted me. She slid the top from the stone box, and removed a stunning golden crown adorned with spires of delicate leaves. It was simple and elegant. The crown seemed to glimmer, even though the dark clouds hid the sun, finding light in the darkness. "This is the crown of Neverland. Only the true ruler can wear it. It is not given. It is not a birthright. It is earned. And that is why it has not been worn in many, many years. Now it's yours. You must take what you have earned."

I knelt before Amara, my limbs seeming to move of their own volition. I was still balking at the idea of being queen, but my family needed me. They needed me to be the best version of myself. And if that meant I had to accept the weight of the crown, so be it.

I closed my eyes, letting go of all of my worries. My insecurities melting away as I allowed myself to fully embrace what I was to become. Amara placed the crown gently upon my head. It felt light as a feather, settling perfectly on my brow.

"Rise, child, as the new Queen of Neverland." Amara's voice was full of pride as she announced my title. But it just didn't seem right. It wasn't me alone who would lead Neverland to victory.

"No, not the Queen of Neverland," I corrected. "I am Queen of the Lost Boys and *together* we will rule."

Eben and James offered me their hands and helped me back to my feet. The army of dead parted, clearing a path. A towering skeleton, draped in patches of half destroyed chainmail and a spectral crown that mirrored my own, came forward. I had a moment of panic that he might plan on challenging me, considering I had no idea if the spirits I'd summoned were friend or foe. But before I could contemplate my next move, he sank to one knee.

"My Queen," he rasped out in a deep, grating baritone and the rest of the army began to speak in unison with him. "We have no hearts to offer you, but we give you all that we are: our unwavering loyalty, and unrelenting devotion. In this hour of battle, we pledge fealty to you. We will fight by your side until our bones crumble to dust. We will obey your every command, for you are the light in the darkness. Your word is law, and your will has given us purpose. May the Divine smile upon us as we enter this battle. May our oath of fealty to you, guide us in the heat of battle, and may it bring us victory in your honor. We swear this oath upon our bones, we pledge ourselves to you, now and forevermore. So mote it be."

The army of the dead echoed a response cry, the deep resonance of their voices shook my bones. Patiently, they stood, waiting for my command. It was now or never, and Ryder needed me now.

"We march on the Viridianwood," I called to the army of dead before howling a battle cry of my own. Raising my sword above my head, I made a silent vow to Ryder. His vengeance would be mine. "I will part the bastard prince's head from his body by nightfall!"

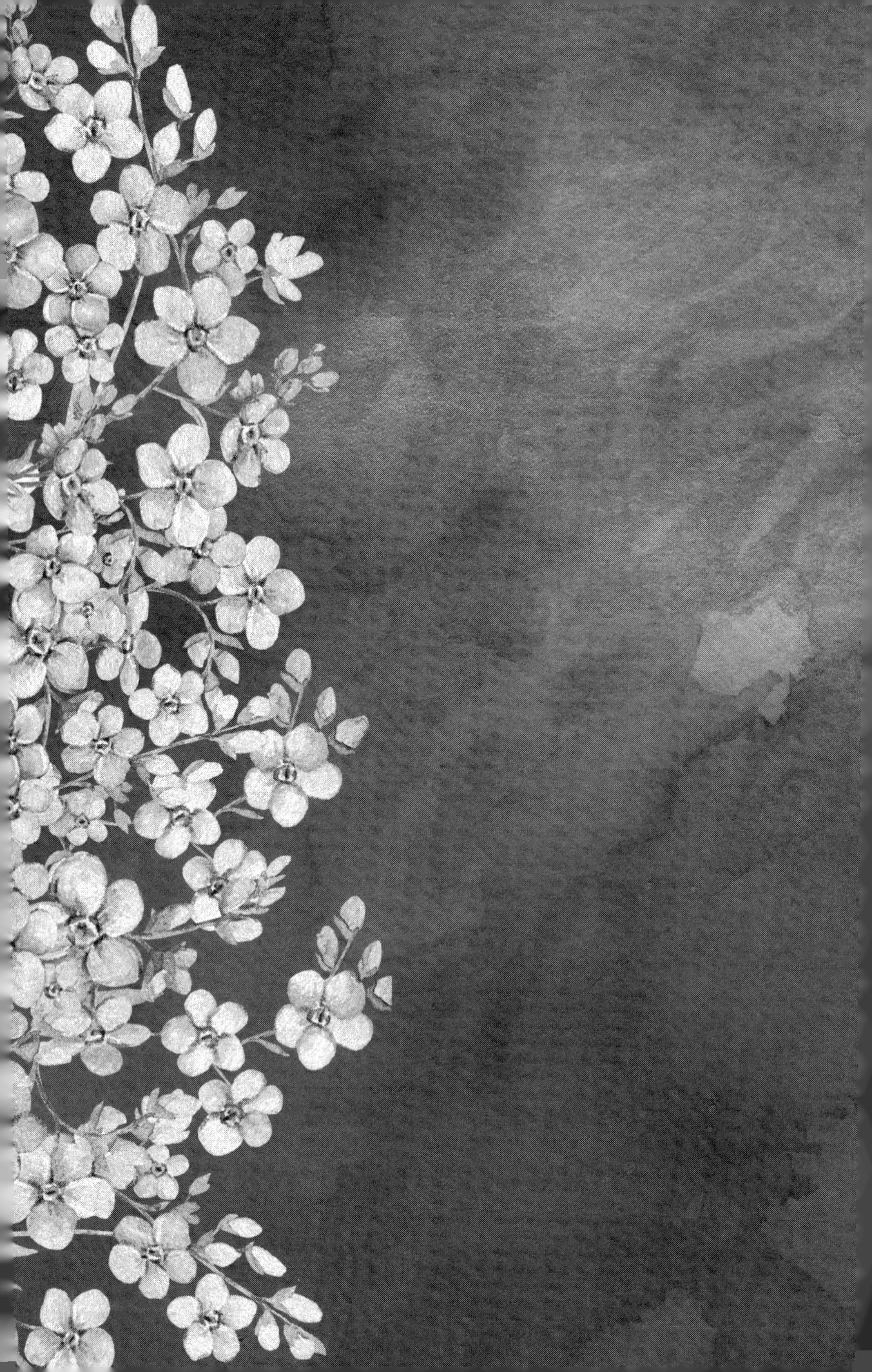

CHAPTER XXII
I WILL HAVE MY VENGEANCE
-GWEN-

We marched across Neverland, our tattered banners whipping in the relentless wind. The island was frozen, as if it were stopping time, waiting to see who would reign victorious. But the bitter cold wouldn't stop us. We crossed the scarred land in reverent silence. Our beautiful sanctuary was a casualty of the war Dorian had brought to our shores and seeing the reality of it strengthened our resolve.

The spectral army never wavered, never tired in their

march toward Black Lake Castle. Fae, beasts, and even pirates began joining our army of dead as we crossed the land. Each of them called to take up swords against our enemies and fight for survival. Fight for a home that was worth dying for.

By the time we reached the Viridianwood, we'd grown in numbers, swelling to a formidable legion. The current of dark magic had always run through these woods, but now it was vibrating with it. The trees groaned in the wind, carrying the sound of baying Fae hounds, the sound growing louder as we approached the barrier. A large pack of Fae hounds stood guard, meeting us with gnashing teeth and taloned claws. But they were no match for my summoned soldiers. With no flesh to sink their teeth into, they were rendered powerless, falling quickly to the soldier's blades.

Barely missing a beat, the skeletal soldiers continued their march straight through the barrier, disappearing once they'd crossed over. None of them were affected by the magic that the living had to conform to, which left the remaining Fae hounds to be taken down by our own men. Eben was the first to charge in, the need for bloodshed clear in his dark eyes. Just a taste— something to whet his appetite. I watched in rapt interest as his body moved in the lethal dance, a satisfied look on his face. This was his element, and he was stunning in his execution.

"We can use the blood from the Fae hounds," Eben

panted. "But we've grown in numbers far beyond what we can safely get across."

"No. We need everyone. We all deserve the chance to fight for Neverland. I don't know what kind of magic we'll face from Dorian. He's a master of the spiritual element. He may be able to take out the dead army with one swipe. We have to be prepared for anything," I demanded.

"My love, how about you impress us all with a display of that new found magic? Show Eben here just what you're capable of. I think the both of us will unlock a new kink to further enthrall us with your beautiful soul," James encouraged with a sly lift of his brows.

I smiled back at him, the heat in his words not lost on me. I felt a heady rush as the magic welled up inside me, flexing, waiting to be unleashed. It was time to finally show them the weapon I had become. Show them the real me. Because I finally felt whole in my skin for the first time in my life.

My eyes locked on Eben, who cocked a brow at me and crossed his arms over his chest. "Why do I get the feeling that James is right? You know I have a bit of a weapons fetish."

I stared at Eben, my mouth popping open in surprise. He'd used James's name. There was no condescension in his tone. It had simply slipped out without him even being aware.

"James?" I repeated.

Eben shrugged. "Leave it to the brink of battle, the

moment when death is breathing down your neck, to finally see the truth right before your eyes. This isn't the time to get into it, but I'm starting to realize... we aren't all that different, he and I."

"Once this is all over, there are many truths that need to be spoken between us all," James reiterated as his eyes flicked to me. He was the only one of my men who knew about Kían. But as Eben had said, now wasn't the time. Especially since I'd locked Kían away, cutting him off from my magic and my lovers. He wasn't a threat to us anymore. But I'd have to broach the subject with James before I buried the secret for good.

I turned to face the barrier. The eyes of all our forces rested on me. I faltered for a moment, wringing my hands as doubt tried to gain a foothold in my mind. I didn't know what I was doing. This wasn't a scenario that I'd played out in my training with Peytra. But I had to believe that she'd given me the foundation I needed. Now it was up to me to follow my instincts. They'd led me down some bumpy paths, but here I stood. The Divine had tested me. Torn me down to my very core. Everything had been stripped from me in an attempt to break me. And yet I got up. I kept getting up. I would always get up. I was a queen. A warrior queen, and I would have my vengeance against those who dared to take what's mine.

I closed my eyes and focused. I held the image of Ryder in my mind, letting the magic flow as it pooled in my chest. I began to pull magic from the ground, adding to my own reservoir.

The magic from the island felt ancient, invoking an arcane emotion that I couldn't explain. It was a balance— love and hate, joy and fear, wonder and disappointment. It filled me and kept me centered. I could feel the static charge in the air around me, tickling my skin as I gathered strength. But I needed more. I was holding back, fear and doubt were still blocking me. I allowed my emotions to run unchecked and unfiltered. Everything I'd ever felt for Peter, Eben, Tripp, James, and Ryder. I didn't back down from it. It was fuel to the inferno and it was ready to be unleashed.

I placed my hands on the barrier. I could feel the web of magic trying to recoil from my touch. Just when I felt like I couldn't hold the power any longer, I released it into my hands, tearing through the web. I could feel each strand giving way. A loud crack, like thunder, was deafening in my ears, as the barrier split and collapsed in on itself. I sank to my knees, the discharge of power leaving a void in my chest. I opened my eyes, the scene before me unveiled. Where there had once been an endless forest, now stood a black castle, looming above the trees.

We reached the edges of the castle grounds as the full moon was rising, setting an eerie glow to the charred landscape that surrounded the massive estate. It was a beacon of darkness. Its ominous presence mirrored in the placid lake that surrounded it. The light from the day was waning, but it seemed apropos to wage this war in the dark. We were prepared to go to hell and back. Tomorrow, the dawn would break on a new day. I stooped to the ground, digging my fingers into the scorched land. I dragged my muddied fingers across my face, leaving a swath of black over my eyes.

I turned to Eben. "May the Divine bless us, may our blades sing with the blood of our enemies, and deliver us the vengeance owed," my voice was as solid as steel as I marked his face to match my own. He nodded, slammed a fist to his chest before kissing me savagely. I met him with my own passion for a moment in time before I turned to James. He eyed me a little more wearily. I knew pirates were a deeply superstitious bunch, but we needed any help the Divine would be gracious enough to give us.

"You can mark me, love, but it'll do no good. Your words will fall on deaf ears. The Divine abandoned me long ago."

"James, there is such a thing as redemption. The Divine brought us together so we could find it in each other's arms." His forget-me-not blue eyes sparked with shock as he took in my words and softened, before he pulled me in for a kiss of his own. His love was conveyed in every hard line of his body as the force of his lips pressed against mine. He owned me in that kiss. I felt the promise of forever in that moment, in that kiss. There was no need to speak the words 'I love you.' Our bodies said more than words ever could. Pulling away, he took my hand in his and brought it to his face, drawing the black lines together. "May the Divine bless us," he whispered in my ear before turning to face our enemy.

With the kisses of my lovers still tingling on my lips, I felt giddy. I pulled my sword from its scabbard, twirling the hilt in my palm, reveling in the sound of the blade as it cut through the air. I had pulled on a pair of leather gloves to match the full black armored suit I'd created in the void. I didn't want the Osakren's marks to be on display. It was better that I kept that bit of information to myself until the right time.

Dorian had dared to hurt my family. He'd tried to destroy our home. I wouldn't surrender my happily ever after to this bastard. I was counting on the fact that he severely underestimated me, and I would make him pay dearly for that fault in judgment.

I watched as Dorian's soldiers poured from the castle, immediately engaging us in battle, meeting my dead army head on. Primal war cries filled the air as we charged into the melee, steel clashing with steel. But this fight wouldn't end until Dorian was dead. And he had my boys. He'd done despicable things to Ryder, and I couldn't let that go. Hell hath no fury... And I was about to rain fire down on him.

James and Eben fought beside me. Lucius and Alo were right behind us. Together, we cut our way through the hoards. It was sweet bliss when my blade made contact. The blood of my enemies was splattered on my face, and a nefarious grin crept across my lips. My soul had been crying for vengeance for what they'd done to Ryder, and this was a start. Feeding the darker side of my soul, a laugh escaped my lips as I took them down one by one. We worked our way to the castle, my skeletal soldiers clearing the path for us. As we reached the enormous entrance, all opposition fell away. I had a choice to make. I wanted to stay here and fight for Neverland in the most primal way possible. But I had my own battle waiting for me. The Divine had chosen me for a reason, and this was it. My destiny lay beyond those doors. My battle lay beyond this field. I turned to Lucius, who was fighting beside us. His hulking form took out our enemies two, three at a time. Our friendship was an unlikely one, yet he was laying his life on the line beside me. I could feel the love I had for him well up in my chest. The most absurd place to be feeling emotional was here on the battlefield. I let it flow nonetheless.

"Lu, you got this?" I called to him over the deafening sounds of battle.

He caught my eye for a moment, cocking a rare half smile at me. "I've got you covered. Now go kill that son of a bitch and don't be gentle about it, either." With that, he turned back to fighting, calling orders to the men, pushing back the tide of our enemy. I looked at Eben and James. It was vengeance or bust.

The moment I crossed the threshold, and my boot echoed on the veined marble of the great hall, his sinister chuckle filled my mind. *"Come to me, Queen of Neverland,"* his silken voice hissed in my head. I could feel his magic pulling on my own, leading me through the castle. The domed ceilings soared above our heads, grand staircases spiraling into a labyrinth of hallways. It would have taken us hours to search the palace, but I knew exactly where he was. Dorian was summoning me.

We reached the end of a hallway. Heavy arched doors stood before us. My skin crawled. He was here, behind these doors, and so were my Lost Boys. I could feel the ties between us, pulling us together after our time apart— our souls desperate to be one again.

"This is it," I breathed out, taking a moment to look at James and Eben. Taking in the details of their faces in case this was the last moment of peace we would ever have.

"Allow me, my Queen," Eben said as he took up position on one side of the doorway.

"No less than a grand entrance for our Queen," James reiterated, grabbing hold of the other door and swinging them open. The sound reverberated in the space before a melodic tune drifted from the room. A large ballroom spread out before me. Fae of all kinds waltzed around the room. All of them were dressed in finery, twirling around the dance floor while a quartet played. The chilling sound of the stringed instruments sent a shiver down my spine. I stepped through the dancers, who seemed completely oblivious to the war raging just outside the castle walls. None of them showed an ounce of concern, and that had my blood boiling. I had to remind myself that this was what I wanted. I needed them to underestimate me. I had to play my hand just right if we had any chance of leaving this hell.

"Ah, yes! Our special guest has arrived." Dorian's silken voice cut off the music and everyone stopped all at once to stare at me. "It is our honored guest. The Queen of Neverland has graced us with her presence." Dorian clapped as he stood from a long table he'd been seated at and my eyes brushed past him to Peter, who was sitting to his right. He sat solidly in his chair and made no move to get up, a pained look on his face. Then I noticed the dagger, Peter's very own dagger, had been sunk into the tabletop right through his hand, pinning him to the spot. The sight of it made me gasp in horror before Dorian spoke again, pulling my attention from Peter.

"A glorious occasion. Come, join Peter and I, we shall feast in your honor." He beckoned me forward to a long table set for a king. Lavish foods were centered around the corpse of a satyr that had been laid out on a platter. His mouth was stuffed with an apple and his cloven hooves trussed up like a choice entrée. He'd been meant to be the main course, and sections of his thigh had already been carved up.

My stomach threatened to revolt as I watched Dorian settle back into his throne, a pile of raw meat set before him. I stood my ground. I wasn't here for pleasantries. This was all a ploy. He meant to give off an air of indifference, a diversion to elicit fear and doubt within me, but I wasn't buying it. The slight tick in his jaw told me I had sparked some modicum of fear within him and the darkness inside me purred. I had to meet him on a level playing field, and if that meant dredging up my own darkness, then so be it.

"Have you ever had Fae before, Gwendolyn?" He asked as he speared a piece of meat from his plate. I stood with my chin held high, refusing to fall into his petty conversation. "The magic gives the meat a certain saporosity that cannot be recreated. It's a delicacy, really. You must try some." He glared at me with his amber eyes, never breaking his stare as he took the meat from his knife and dabbed it into the blood oozing from Peter's hand before popping it into his mouth. His eyes closed, and he moaned as though the taste had been pure ecstasy. "Peter, you taste like nectar of the Divine. Now I can see why she likes to get her mouth on you. I can only imagine how the rest of you might taste." He glanced at Peter, licking his lips as a salacious grin spread across his face.

"Enough of your games. I am here to negotiate your surrender. I'll let you leave with your life if—"

Dorian barked out a laugh, interrupting me. The entire court followed suit. "Surrender? I do believe this is a negotiation, my dear Queen." He snapped his fingers and my eyes landed on Tripp as he was walked out of the shadows, a knife to his throat. My heart fluttered at the sight of him in enemy hands, but then it halted altogether when I saw the man holding the knife was Ryder.

He looked as though he'd been prepared, a valuable commodity that had been put on display to try to break me. His blonde locks were styled neatly away from his face, but they lacked the luster of health. His skin had been rubbed with oil and he was naked from the waist up, wearing only a pair of finely embroidered silk pants that hung low on his hips. But they couldn't hide the fact that he was skin and bones. I could make out every rib, and his face was gaunt. But what killed me the most were his eyes. His beautiful, indigo eyes had lost that spark and they looked flat and dull in the dim light of the ballroom.

I opened myself up to the bridge that connected us all. I could feel Eben's rage, using every ounce of self-control to hold himself in place. James was cool and calculating, trying to determine the odds of our survival. Peter was a chaos of emotion— pain, anger, and defeat mixed together with fear. Tripp's eyes met mine and I could feel nothing but love and regret pushing down the bridge to me. He'd accessed it too, and the love pouring out of him strengthened my resolve. When I reached out to my last string, there was nothing there. Ryder was a void. No emotion came from him at all. Dorian had destroyed my happy-go-lucky Lost Boy and left me with nothing more than the pieces of his broken soul. I could feel my fear begin to well up in response, but that wouldn't help him now, and so I pushed it back into my mental fortress.

"Let me introduce you to my new pet. This is Preston," he said with a wicked grin as he nodded to Ryder. "Preston, say hello to Gwendolyn," he commanded.

"Hello, Gwendolyn." Ryder's voice was mechanical, and it nearly broke me to hear him call me by my given name.

I ripped my eyes from Tripp and Ryder, and set the full weight of my glare on the bastard prince. "Poor form, Dorian," the sugar-coated condescension slid off my lips. "I don't believe you've properly introduced me. A misstep that I'm sure you won't forget next time. But allow me…" I paused for dramatic effect and caught a slight roll of his eyes as Dorian picked up his wine, seemingly uninterested in what I had to say. "I am Gwendolyn Mary Darling Carlisle. Daughter of Wendy, Queen of the Ninth Realm, Chosen of the Divine and Embodiment of the Osakren." My voice boomed in the large space, the audience utterly silent save for the subtle sound of Dorian as he choked on his wine.

He shot a glare at me, the true evil peeking out from behind his carefully constructed mask. "She wouldn't," he snarled as he rose from his seat, his fists firmly planted on the table.

"Oh, she would. And she did." I slowly stripped off the glove of my altered hand, flexing my fingers as the rune tattoos glowed with magic. "So let's revisit our prior conversation. I believe we were talking about the terms of your surrender." Dorian's head sunk, digesting the news while he tapped his nails along the table. This was my ace in the hole. The one thing he hadn't been prepared for. It caught me off guard when he began to laugh.

"I am thoroughly captivated by you, Gwendolyn Mary Darling Carlisle. Dare I say you are the most intriguing human I have ever met. I knew there was something special about you. But that's beside the point. This new development truly adds to the negotiations."

"I won't negotiate with evil," I hissed.

"Oh, my dear, you broke the cardinal rule of royalty. You can't truly be a formidable queen when you've given away so many pieces of your heart. It makes you weak. But let me offer my terms." He began to walk from behind the table, tousling Ryder's hair as he passed him by, and I almost lost my composure, my vision going red at the sight of his hands on him. But he wasn't wrong. The men in my life were my Achilles' heel.

"I will let your men live. They may walk freely, unmolested, out of this castle," he paused as he stalked toward me, circling me like prey. "I'll even sweeten the deal. I'll send them to another realm altogether and banish them from Neverland. So long as you agree to be mine. My obedient queen. A lovely and powerful decoration for my arm. You will do as I say, and they will be safe to live out long and happy lives. While you and I rule the cosmos. Just think of the sons you would bear me. The power I could wield with our combined magic would be unstoppable." He stopped behind me, sucking in a deep breath as he moaned, "Oooh the possibilities."

I heard a scuffle and turned to see James holding Eben back. "Don't you fucking touch her. She'll never be yours. It'll never fucking happen," Eben seethed with more venom in his voice than I'd ever heard. But James held onto him, keeping him from rushing to a futile death.

"And if I refuse?" I tried to sound confident, holding my chin high. Hoping my instincts would show me the right path.

"Let me show you." Dorian smiled at me, and the room before me morphed into an alternate vision. Tripp lay, unmoving, face down on the table in a pool of blood. Ryder was crouched into a ball in the corner. Both James and Eben were strewn on the ground in abnormal positions, covered in blood. Even though Dorian stood behind me, the vision showed him piercing Peter's heart with his sword, pushing it all the way through til the hilt met his chest. The gurgled sounds coming from Peter were so real, I could feel a tear slip from the corner of my eye in response.

"This isn't real. This is only one path. One possibility," I snarled at him.

"True... But if I were to wager, I'd bet that fortune favors the wicked." I could feel Dorian move up behind me, his breath hot on my neck. "You cannot beat me," he crooned. "You can try, but I promise if you do, one or all of your men will die today and you will become my slave. Wouldn't it be better to be my queen, and know they all survived, rather than be my slave and live with the fact that you cost them their lives? You don't want to know the pain of living after your soul mates have died." His words cut deep. These perfectly flawed men were all I cared about.

A wave of guilt washed over me. I was Neverland's Queen, and I was willing to sell out the entire realm to ensure the safety of my lovers. But if I got them to safety, I could get close to Dorian and bide my time. I would be patient and let the passing years nurture my darkness until my vengeance couldn't be denied. At least then we would have a chance. At least they would be alive, and maybe we could begin again.

Then it hit me. What I had feared all along was truly my destiny. I'd always known that I would lose them. That nothing this perfect could last, at least not for someone like me. Not when the cosmos had already painted a target on my back. I'd known it all along and I chided myself for forgetting it and being foolish enough to believe I would actually get a happily ever after. But I'd known true love, and I'd basked in its glory for just a moment. If this was the price I had to pay, I could say with no regret that it was worth it.

"Time is fleeting, Queen of Neverland," Dorian's words brought me back to reality. I was standing in the ballroom again, James and Eben at my side. Dorian had returned to his side of the table, staring at me intently.

"How do I know you're not bluffing?" I questioned.

"I admire your stubbornness. It will be all the more entertaining when I make you submit to me. Don't you agree, Preston?" His eyes flicked to Ryder.

"Yes, sir," he responded immediately, but not before a moment of panic flashed in his eyes.

"Preston, please show her that we are indeed not bluffing," Dorian commanded as he began picking at his nails.

In a flash of movement, Ryder took his blade from Tripp's neck and pulled it viciously across his chest. Tripp hissed in pain as the blood welled up from his severed skin and poured down his body.

"No!" The word escaped my lips and I started forward before I even realized I was moving. I felt strong hands on my arm, and looked back to find James holding me in place.

"Don't fall for his tricks, my love." James's words echoed in my mind, screaming across the bridge between us. Just as Alo had communicated with me telepathically in the void, now James had somehow figured out how to tap into our bond and speak to me. I hid the shock from my face. I couldn't let Dorian know we could communicate with each other.

"Do you believe me now, Gwendolyn?" he asked casually.

"What I meant," I said, as I straightened to my full height, "is that I need assurances. If I agree, what's to stop you from going back on our deal?"

"Gwen," Peter growled. "You can't do this! We won't let you do this!" It took every ounce of self-control to ignore him. I couldn't let any of them deter me.

"I want the deal sealed in magic," I insisted.

"You drive a hard bargain, Queen of Neverland. I love it. Blessed be the Divine, who truly knows your ruthless soul might cater very well to my own. Fine. I will agree to the terms. A death bond. Each of us will be bound by the terms or the magic will end the treasonous side."

Fuck. A death bond would protect my boys, but it would also hold me to my side of the bargain. It would make vengeance all but impossible.

"The sands are running out, Gwendolyn. Time to make your move." Dorian pulled a jeweled dagger from his belt, and sliced it across his hand. A glittering light erupted from his hand right along with the aubergine blood that poured from the wound and onto the table. "Your freedom? Or your boys?"

"Gwen! Don't do it! We'll always fight for you, no matter what deal you strike," Peter pleaded with me.

"Peter," his name came out as a sob. "I'm sorry," I whispered.

"You can't do this, Gwen," Eben said. "This will kill us, too. You're our anchor. We'll be adrift in a meaningless life that none of us want to live without you."

"But you will live! And that is all I care about." I'd made up my mind and I stepped toward the table. I pulled a dagger from my belt, slowly dragging it across my palm, feeling my magic well up.

"Tell me you have a plan, Gwendolyn. Promise me you know what you're doing!" James's words came barreling down our bridge, ricocheting inside my mind. I could only shake my head in response. The flare of his anger felt as if my soul was on fire.

"My goddess, we'll find a way. I'm begging you, please don't," Tripp spoke softly even as Ryder's blade dug into his throat.

"I promise… I'll find you. In the end, I'll find you." I took another step toward Dorian. "We'll meet there and pick up where we left off." My eyes flicked to Peter as I used the words he'd spoken to me in the grotto. It seemed like a lifetime ago now, but even then, he'd known what fate had in store for us. Now I was ready to embrace it. I could survive anything as long as I knew they were safe and alive.

I reached my hand out to Dorian, our magic ready to seal the bond and lock me into a life I was ready to accept.

"No!" The words from my lover echoed in the ballroom. A flash of silver was all I saw before a warm splatter of blood covered my face. I blinked several times until the scene before me finally registered in my brain. Dorian's hand lay dismembered from his body, fingers twitching. A shining blade embedded into the table. My eyes lifted to meet vibrant indigo blue eyes.

Ryder's white knuckles held the blade in a death grip. "I will never let you do to her what you've done to me," he growled at Dorian. The ballroom broke into chaos as Dorian's screams reverberated in the grand space. There are some things even faerie dust can't cure. At least that's what Gage had said to me, and I could see the panic in Dorian's eyes. The world around me exploded, and everything slowed. Peter managed to tear the blade from his hand and whirled to sink it into Dorian's gut. Now was our time, and the moment was fleeting.

I pulled on my strings, drawing us together. Drawing on their unique magic to fuel my own. All of my men stopped, their bodies arching, arms drawn back as I pulled energy from them. The feeling was euphoric as we combined together, each of us adding something. The power pooled in my chest and when I released it, a shimmering cloud clawed from my body. Our magic formed a demon with gnashing teeth that darted for Dorian, eliciting more screams from the bastard prince. It circled his head before slamming into his open mouth.

I tried to control it. The magic was so potent. I tried to focus on ending him, but he fought back. His own magic pushed against us and it felt like I was being gutted when his power penetrated me. At some point, my screams filled the room, but I wasn't about to give up. I could feel them all pushing every ounce of energy to me and I funneled everything I had into Dorian. But he matched me, no matter how hard I tried. Both of us weakened with the constant back and forth between good and evil— neither of us gaining an edge. Our dueling magic crackled in the air, the swirling energy was almost blinding in the ballroom. I started to panic. I had no idea how long we could keep this going. A flicker of magic caught my attention a moment before Peytra popped into existence. She descended on Dorian like a harpy, her membranous wings spread wide, toppling him to the ground in his weakened state. Her hand raised over her head, plunging a fist into Dorian's chest. The sickening sound of it turned my stomach.

"Just how I knew it to be, brother. Hard and shrunken. Now I will reap the treasures of a new era with the bones that are owed to me." Drool poured onto his face from her malicious grin as he stared wide eyed at her. Her arm jerked backward, his heart clutched in her taloned fingers. His dark heart pumped a few times, dripping aubergine blood down her arm beforeDorian went slack beneath her.

My magic recoiled back to my chest and the flow of energy from my boys stopped. I sank to my knees, breathless from the raw power that had used my body as a conduit. Peytra remained hunched over Dorian's placid form, tearing at his chest until she managed to work his breastbone free from the carnage. She removed the borrowed breast bone we'd given her, and slammed her brother's bone into her chest. A brilliant light flashed and a shock wave of power knocked us all on our asses.

When my vision finally returned, a beautiful woman stood before me. Her eyes were liquid gold, and they locked with mine, filling me with a sense of familiarity. I knew this woman. Thick, flaxen hair hung in heavy waves, framing out a picture perfect face with fair, porcelain skin and high cheekbones. Sleek, feathered wings of pure white stretched out behind her. A golden spun dress clung to her womanly figure, matching her eyes. Eyes that were so deep they could see into your soul. This was Peytra. This was the bone faerie's true form. She was now fully restored.

"My little star," her melodic voice called as she offered her hand to me. I took it and she pulled me to my feet. "I knew you would choose the right path. Love is always the right path." She cupped my cheek, her amber eyes looking deep into my soul. "You have been tested and you have not been found wanting. Now it is time to revel in the spoils. You have earned it, my little star. Go to your men. Lead a happy life and know I will be watching." She kissed my lips in a chaste, motherly kiss and in the next instant, she was gone.

Chapter XXIII
With This Kiss
-Gwen-

Three months had passed since the battle at Black Lake Castle. Three long months of healing and working to bring Ryder back from the edge. Neverland was just beginning to recover from Dorian's torment, but she would bear the scars of his offenses for years to come. With Amara as my advisor, I was learning how to be the queen Neverland so desperately needed.

After almost losing each other yet again, we decided to bind our souls and seal our fate in marriage. James would still spend most of his time on the Jolly Roger, while Peter and our Lost Boys would make a home in my new cottage. We had earned our happily ever after, and this was the first step. Together, we would bring Neverland back.

"Ouch!" I flinched as Mira stuck me with a hairpin.

"Sorry, Gwen. I just want it to be perfect." She continued to fuss with my hair, obsessively pinning loose curls on top of my head. Mira and Fauna had been relentlessly preening me all morning. "Lill should be here with your dress any minute now. Fauna! I'm just about done here." She stepped back, admiring her work. A smile spread wide across her face. "Yes! It's perfect. I'll go see what's keeping Lill with that dress."

Fauna quickly took her place and before I could protest, she began painting my face with a heavy dose of makeup. "Even a woman as naturally beautiful as you, should be adorned on her wedding day."

"Thank you Fauna." It did feel nice to be pampered. I closed my eyes and tried to relax. This was the day, the day I would be forever joined to my boys— all of them.

"She's here!" Mira came running back into the room. "Lill is here, *finally*."

With Mic away in Hiraeth, I had asked Lill to be my maid of honor. She had excitedly accepted, provided I allowed her to be in charge of obtaining my dress. Considering I wasn't familiar with Neverland's wedding traditions, and had no idea what would be appropriate, I'd agreed to give her full control. I still hadn't seen the dress yet. She had been keeping it a secret this whole time, promising me that I wouldn't be disappointed.

Lill entered the room in her human form, a vision in spring green. Her platinum blonde hair fell in soft waves across her bare shoulders. A delicate crown of lily of the valley sat nestled on her head. The sweetheart neckline of her dress accented her voluptuous frame and cinched at the waist before draping into a pool of silk at her feet.

"Lill, you look beautiful."

"Thank you." She smiled. "Are you ready to see your dress?" She bit her lip, giddy with excitement.

I was a bit apprehensive having no idea what to expect. Ultimately, what really mattered was at the end of the day, I was going to have five new husbands. My family would be complete regardless of the dress I was wearing. I took a deep breath and prepared myself for the worst. "Yes, please. I'm dying to see it."

"You are going to love it," she squealed. She snapped her fingers and in a burst of sparkling faerie dust, my dress appeared.

I was speechless. It was very much in the style of a traditional bridal gown only it seemed to be alive with flickering fairy light. It was made of ivory silk, with a classic V neckline. Delicate boning ran down the bodice accentuating the curve of the hips before dropping into the luxurious waves of the full skirt. The dress was adorned with living flowers and it smelled like pure heaven. White hydrangea blooms and campanula capped over the shoulders, dripping down the bodice. While ivy and lily of the valley joined in the mix, appearing to sprout from the waist line. It trailed down the length of the dress, nestling between the folds of silk. I had never seen anything like it. It was pure fairytale magic.

"Lill," I gasped. "This dress—"

"Is fit for a queen." She was proud of herself, and rightly so. I couldn't have imagined a more stunning dress.

"It's beautiful." I reached out, pulling Lill into a hug. "Thank you. Thank you for everything. It means the world to me, to have you by my side today. I truly value your friendship."

She squeezed me tightly. "I value you too." She dismissed me, pulling away. I was quickly reminded that pixies were only capable of one emotion at a time. Lill was all bridesmaid right now. There was no room for emotional conversations. She was on a mission. "Now, let's get you ready for a wedding. Fauna! Let's get her make-up finished, please. It's almost time."

With the help of Lill's magic, I slipped on the dress. Within moments, it began to tighten and mold itself to my shape. It truly was a living thing. It corseted up the back, accentuating my curves. The flowers and vines shifted along my body, highlighting all the right places. Balls of fairy light pulsed like fireflies ducking in and out of the dress collecting a pool of glowing flowers along the train.

A tear spilled on my cheek as I thought about Michaela. I had always thought my parents and my sister would be with me on my wedding day. Just like other girls, I had dreamt of this day and what it would look like. Mic was always by my side in those dreams. I wished she were here to see me in this dress. To tell me that Mum and Dad would have been proud of me and the choices I've made on this journey. I desperately wanted to share this moment with her.

"Have you heard news from Hiraeth?" I asked. I still hadn't heard from Mic. It had been months. I'd reached out countless times, begging her to make the journey to Neverland to attend the ceremony. The scrolls sat void of any response, and my anxieties were beginning to whisper words of dread.

"I haven't heard anything." Lill shrugged her shoulders, taking my hand in an effort to soothe my nerves. "Lucius doesn't seem worried, so neither should you." She paused for a moment, thinking. "I could be your sister." A smile spread across her face and her brow raised in question.

Lill and I, after all we had been through, had grown a bond. She was just as much a part of my chosen family as my boys. "I'd be honored to call you my sister."

Lill squealed with excitement, pulling me into a hug. Her skin glowing from within as she melted into the embrace.

"Sisters." She said it like I had just given her the most precious gift. "Okay, now back to getting you dressed." And just like that, she was back to her bridesmaid mission.

I chuckled at her flitting emotions. She was right. Lu didn't seem concerned with the silence from Hiraeth. They were his family. He knew them best, and if he wasn't worried, maybe I should follow suit. "Could you pass me my throwing knife?"

"You're getting married. Why do you need a weapon?" Lill asked, handing me the knife Mic had reforged.

"It's a symbol of my sister's love for me. I want it with me in her absence." Turning the blade in my hand, I thought of how everything circled back to this piece. "Eben gifted me this knife—well, the original one. Without it, I wouldn't be here today. I sacrificed it to keep Mic alive. It's what brought us back to Neverland." I slid the blade down the center of my dress and nestled it down between my breasts, as close to my heart as I could get.

"There's only one thing missing." Lill stood before me, the Neverland crown in her hands. "My Queen." She bowed before placing the crown on my head and stepped back, allowing me to look in the mirror.

I stood silently, taking it all in. The girls had worked their magic. I looked like a fairytale princess. Only this wasn't a fairytale, and I wasn't a princess. I was a queen. Queen of the Lost Boys, ruler of the Ninth Realm, and today I would crown five kings.

"My child, it's almost time." Amara's gentle words

brought me back from my thoughts. "You look beautiful. Your parents would have been proud to see the woman you have become." Amara had been a nurturing figure in my life from the very moment I met her. She had become my greatest confidante, and my dearest friend. It was only fitting that she perform the ceremony today. She had known I would be forever entwined with these men long before I did. "Are you ready?"

"I've never been more sure of anything in my life." I smiled as she took my hands in hers. "I'm ready."

"Before I go," she paused, as if deciding whether or not to continue. "I don't mean to cast a shadow on your special moment. The Divine has had a plan for you all along. And here you are, about to fulfill your destiny. You have earned your happily ever after. But I feel the need to remind you. Please be mindful of Kían today." Her face was wrought with worry.

Amara's words took me by surprise. I hadn't thought of Kían in weeks. My new powers had allowed me to silence him so well that I had almost forgotten all about him. "Amara, I assure you. You have nothing to worry about. I have Kían behind a steel wall. I haven't felt his presence in months." The Osakren had locked him deep within my mind. A sort of prison cell to spend eternity in. He was no longer a threat to me or my boys.

"I should have known you'd have him under control. My thoughts were heavy with worry this morning. You deserve a perfect day. I'm sorry. You are ripe with a magic that rivals my own. I trust your judgment." She smiled as a knock at the door took her attention.

"Ryder, no! You can't see the bride before the ceremony. I'm sorry." Lill shut the door as quickly as she opened it.

"Lill, it's imperative I speak with Gwen now. Before the ceremony." Ryder begged from behind the door. "We can speak with the door between us. Just give me a moment alone with her, *please*."

My heart stopped. I hadn't heard him use my given name since that day at Black Lake Castle. "Ladies, a moment, please." I hurried to the door. I could feel his uncertainty, his heartache. "Ryder, I'm here. What is it?"

"I just… I"—he stammered—"I can't marry you." The words hit me like a truck. Crushing my heart with his pain.

"Ryder—"

"No, Gwen. I'm not worthy. I'm not deserving of your love." His words trembled as his emotions took hold. "I make stupid choices. I almost got you and my brothers killed. Gwen,"—he sighed—"I read the files in your pack."

I had forgotten about the files. Nothing in those would have ever given me pause. They were stories of a heartbroken family searching for their beloved lost son. "Ryder, I didn't bring those to punish you."

"My choices hurt people. Dorian showed me the consequences of my choice to leave home. He showed me what really happened. My mom" —he paused fighting back tears— "she killed herself because of me. I won't be the reason you die."

"My sweet Ryder," I opened the door slightly, reaching my hand out. "Take my hand." His warm trembling fingers interlaced with my own. "Dorian was a master manipulator. He used mind control to twist the truth into your own personal nightmare. You can't blame yourself for what happened. You were a child when you left with Peter."

"I was weak when I needed to be strong. I almost killed my brothers."

"Dorian tortured you into submission. Your actions while under his thrall were not your own. And yet you *were* strong. Strong enough to break through when it mattered the most. Your love for me was no match for the bastard prince. Without you, we wouldn't have defeated him."—I squeezed his hand tighter—"Your choices don't hurt people. You are a brave and loyal man. You make selfless choices to help and honor your loved ones, and *that* is the reason I love you." In a lot of ways, Ryder and I were the same. We both put our loved one's first, above all else, including ourselves. "There is no greater love than yours. Your love is unconditional. That makes you more than worthy."

"Gwendolyn," he sobbed, kissing my hand. "I love you more than anything this life has to offer."

"And that my love, is why you are going to marry me today."

I heard him sigh. "I'm coming in."

"Wait! Lil will have your head if you try to come in here."

"I need a hug."

"I just agreed to be her sister. I don't want to have to hurt her." I wanted that hug just as badly as him. His hurt ran deep, and I wanted to take it all away. I felt his face on the back of my hand. His cheeks were wet with tears.

"The next time we hug, I will be your wife." I felt him smile. "I love you Preston Daniel Ryder."

"I love you too, Gwendolyn Mary Darling Carlisle." He kissed the back of my hand. "If I can't come in, then you better hurry up, Hen. Don't keep us waiting any longer. I want to hug my wife."

THE CEREMONY WAS BEING HELD in the forest behind our little cottage. We had chosen to keep it an intimate affair, only inviting a handful of friends. We would hold a proper celebration once Mic could attend. An aisle of flickering lanterns illuminated the path to my destiny. Amara and my men stood waiting before a large wooden arch decorated in white hydrangea, forget-me-nots, and lavender to compliment my bouquet. It was elegant and romantic, and all of my dreams come true.

It was time. Everyone was waiting for me. I gripped Lu's arm a little tighter and took a deep, cleansing breath. This was it, the beginning of my happily ever after. We had defeated the enemy securing Neverland's future. Nothing stood in our way.

"Everything good?" Lu asked under his breath.

"It's perfect." I smiled. "Thank you Lucius."

A grin spread across his face when he heard me use his given name. "For what?"

"For everything. Getting Mic and I back to Neverland. For saving her life. For being here today, and walking me down the aisle."

"Thank you for bringing me to Mic." His words were simple, but they spoke volumes. "Are you ready?"

I nodded yes and allowed Lu to lead me back to my men, yet again.

They were dressed in their finest. James stood at the center in a black velvet frock coat fully adorned with his sword at his hip. The boys flanked him on both sides, wearing matching black belted dress tunics, emblazoned with green and golden embroidery. I'd never seen them look more handsome. Their eyes widened, as they saw me in my dress for the first time. Dropping to one knee, they bowed their heads while Lucius escorted me to them.

"You may rise," Amara's words commanded attention. "As you stand here today, surrounded by the beauty and wonder of Neverland, reflect on the strings that bind you together. Through the twists and turns of fate, you have found each other and formed a bond that was woven into the very fabric of the universe.

With this ceremony, you declare your intention to join in matrimony, not only in the eyes of your loved ones, but also in the presence of the Divine. You pledge to honor the ancient traditions that have been passed down through generations of Fae, and to uphold them throughout your lives. With your hands bound together by the Divine, you vow to cherish each other, to support each other through trials and tribulations, and to stand together as one in the face of all challenges. These promises are not taken lightly, they will be imprinted on your souls, and will guide you through your journey together.

And so, with all the passion and enchantment of the 9th Realm, do you still intend to go ahead into matrimony?" Amara turned to look at me. "Gwen?"

"I do."

"Peter?"

"I do."

"Tripp?"

"I do."

"Ryder?"

He hesitated, but when his deep, indigo eyes met mine, all of his reservations melted away. A slight smile tugged at his lips as he said, "I do."

"Eben?"

"I do."

"James?"

"I do."

"Let your answers be heard by all who dwell in this

realm and let your love be celebrated in the timeless traditions of Neverland."

"Now, take each other's hands." Amara bound our wrists together, stacked one on top of the other, with a crimson rope. "Repeat after me: I vow to honor and cherish you, to love and protect you, to explore and indulge with you, in every aspect of our union. Let our love be blessed by the Divine, and let us be bound together forevermore."

We spoke the words in unison, sealing our fate. Binding our souls, knotting our strings in an unbreakable bond.

"May your love be as enduring as the magic of the stars, and as enchanting as the songs of the mermaids. As you kiss, let it be a promise of the pleasures and joys that lie ahead. May it bind your souls in a life of love, magic, and enchantment."

Ryder was the first to pull me into an embrace. Sealing our fate in a heated kiss. "My wife." He smiled, stepping aside for James, who dropped me in a dramatic dip before clashing his lips to mine.

He righted me, growling, "Mine," in my ear and handed me off to Eben.

"With this kiss, I thee wed." Ever the romantic, he kissed me sweetly, and stepped aside for Tripp.

"My goddess." His kiss was hard and laid promise of more to come.

Peter stepped forward, reaching out his hand. There, in the center of his palm, was an acorn.

"Peter, it's perfect." My heart melted as I took the 'kiss'

from his hand. He closed the distance between us gently cupping my face, pulling me into a heated kiss.

"Fucking bastard, giving you an acorn like he did Wendy on your wedding day." My thoughts were suddenly not my own. *"He'll always wish you were her. Kill him now!"* I saw myself slicing through Peter's neck, his blood spraying across my possessed face. The room was in complete shock as I smiled from ear to ear. Peter's blood dripped from my chin. *"I will have my revenge!"*

I pushed back from Peter's embrace, reaching into the top of my dress. I pulled out my knife. A puppet to Kían's strings. "Noooo! Peter!" the words spilled from my mouth in a garbled guttural cry. Peter's handsome face twisted with confusion. I wrestled with the compulsion to slit his throat, desperate to silence Kían's vile thoughts. Before he could succeed, I turned the blade on myself and plunged it into my heart. Gasping for air, my eyes widened as I realized what I had done. I could hear screaming and commotion all around me as I stumbled back into Eben's arms. "I'm sorry," I cried, begging for their understanding. With Peter's help, Eben laid me down on the forest floor. Cradling my head in his lap. "I'm sorry."

"Gwen, no, no, no. What have you done?" Peter was panicking. His hands were trembling, hovering over me, not knowing what to do. The blade still lodged in my heaving chest.

"Someone get a healer now!" I heard James firing off orders before I saw his beautiful blue eyes. "Gwendolyn, what have you done?" My boys were beside me, panic plastered on their faces.

"Kían." I struggled to get the words out. "He... can't." The room started to dim around me. Ryder had my hand in his. "He can't... hurt you.. now." I was struggling to breathe, coughing up blood. "I... lov..." I tried to tell them I loved them, but the words wouldn't come out. My time with them was over. Tears were streaming down their faces. Blackness fell all around me. Silence. Peace.

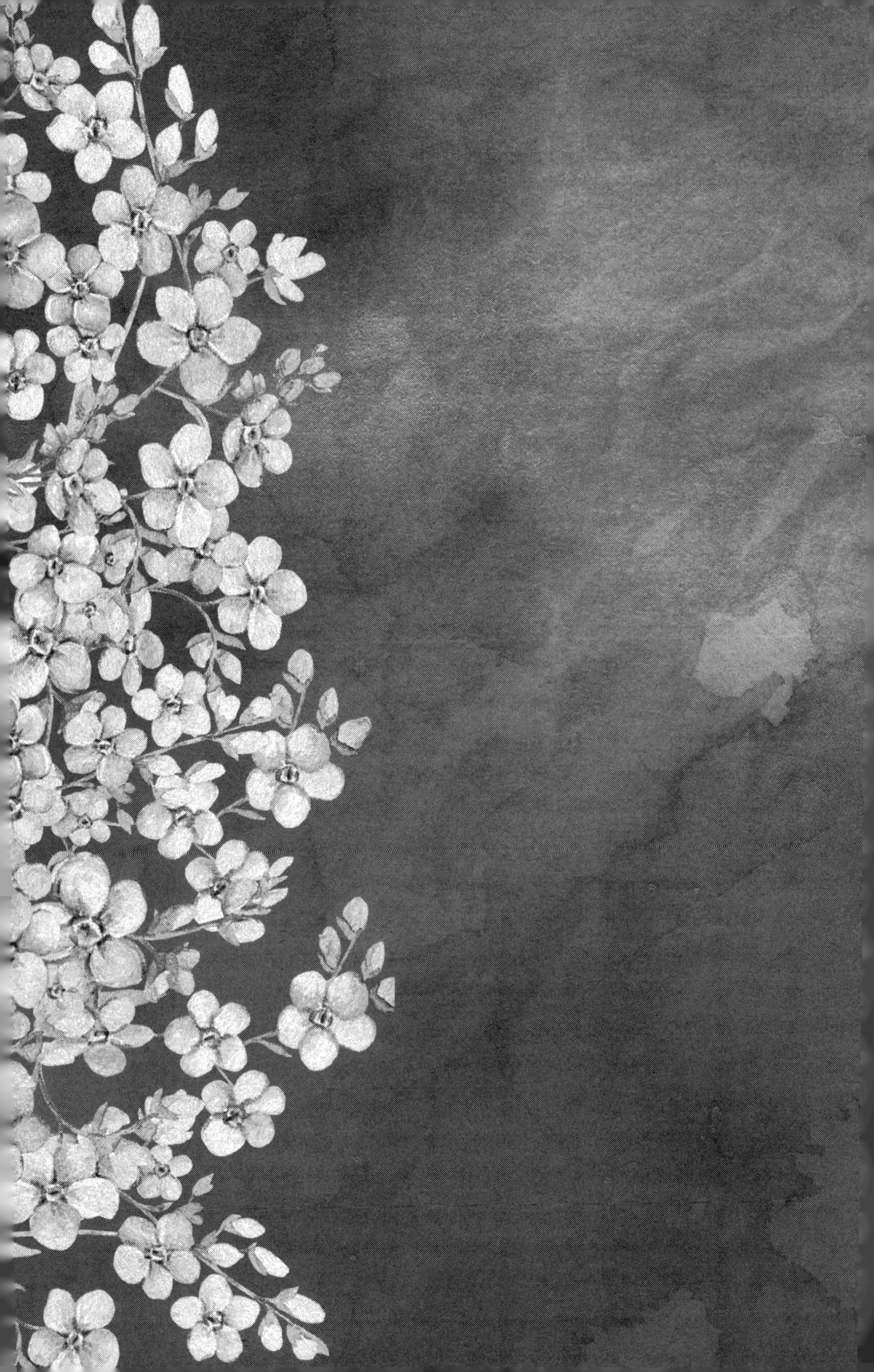

Chapter XXIV
Wherever She Goes
-Peter-

I could barely hear the loud crack of thunder that pierced the air the moment her eyes closed. The white noise inside my head buzzed so loudly that it drowned out the screaming. My mind was in utter chaos, preventing me from taking any rational actions. All of us, just barely her husbands, crouched around her, and none of us could do a fucking thing to help her. My limbs hung heavy, completely useless as I held her lifeless hand in mine.

"Lill! Faerie dust! She needs faerie dust now! She's not breathing," Tripp commanded, somehow piercing the veil of shock that was drowning me. His ever calm, collected demeanor was broken, and his words wavered with the weight of his emotions.

Gwen's head was pillowed in Eben's lap, and he incessantly stroked the hair from her face. His eyes fixated on her pale lips, all the color having drained from them. He reached over her, his hand gripping the blade still plunged into her chest. He jerked it from her body, and she didn't flinch. I was drawn to the crimson stain spreading across the fabric. The stark contrast to the ivory wedding dress was all wrong. This wasn't supposed to happen. My eyes lifted back to Eben again. The knife trembled in his hand, and I could see it in the black depths of his eyes. He knew. We all knew.

She was gone.

I could feel the loss of her, just as if someone had severed my arm from my body. Eben's hands were white knuckled on Gwen's blade and I knew he was not long for this life. He was preparing to follow her. I looked at Ryder. Tears poured down his face as he called her name over and over. He too wouldn't last in a world without her. Tripp held her bloodied hand to his face, shaking his head. Still not believing that she was dead. But once the shock of it passed, I had a feeling he'd be taking a long walk off a short cliff. My Lost Boys weren't mine anymore. They were hers. And they were truly lost without her.

Hook knelt stoically beside her. A streak, where a single tear had fallen, cut across his cheek. The man was ever enduring. And maybe that was the hell he'd earned for himself. To forever sail the universe with half of his soul torn out. And I... I too feared that this was some punishment I'd earned. An egregious act that I'd committed that was worth my very soul. Because losing her would surely destroy me. I wasn't infallible, but I'd done every damn thing the Divine had asked of me, and yet it was never good enough. She continued to take from me. Now I had nothing left to give.

Lill shouldered me out of the way, pouring a handful of faerie dust on Gwen's chest. Tripp and Ryder watched, hope flaring in their eyes. But I didn't have to look to know, the faerie dust had slid off of her like water. She was gone. Gone to a place that none of us could ever bring her back from.

Tripp elbowed Ryder out of the way and started pumping her chest in a vain attempt to get her pierced heart beating again.

"Peter! Help me! Why aren't you doing anything? Help me save her!" Tripp shouted. His tears fell freely, mixing with the blood on her chest.

"Tripp... I don't think... there's nothing..."

"Stop!" Eben screamed at him. "You know she's gone! She's fucking gone, Tripp! You feel it, I feel it, we all feel it!"

Tripp stopped abruptly, panting for a moment before jumping to his feet. Pulling at his hair as he paced.

"I did this!" Ryder's words choked out on a sob. "I don't know why she punishes me, but somehow I defied the Divine. I defied the stars... and Hen... she paid the price!"

Ryder was lost in his own hell again, rocking back and forth. His eyes were completely vacant.

Eben was eerily silent. Staring blankly at her lifeless body. Hook remained on his knees beside her, leaning forward to kiss her gently. He lingered there for a long time. He pulled away just enough to speak. "A last kiss that will forevermore haunt my waking moments. Until we meet again, my beloved." Blood still smeared her lips, staining his before he pulled away.

"What happened?" I snarled at him. Rage was easier to handle than the crushing acknowledgment that she was truly dead. I needed something. Someone to blame.

"The Inalto," Amara chimed in, her voice trembling with her own grief. "She took the Inalto to save you all from Tiger Lily. But it required a price. Balance to be restored. It required the life of a lover as payment. A payment she refused to pay with one of your lives, and so she paid with her own. I thought she could control it. She told me not to worry. I was so foolish… This is all my fault." Amara sunk into a crumpled heap, sobbing at Gwen's feet.

I instantly turned to Hook. "You knew, didn't you?" I growled. Feeling a deep-seated vendetta spring back to life because it was familiar and I wanted to pour all of this pain into something.

"I saw it in her eyes under the Temple Mount. She didn't want any of you to know. She didn't want you to worry. She thought she had it under control." He ground the words out, regret running thick in his tone.

"It doesn't matter, Pan. You can hate him all you want. It won't bring her back. You'll only be further staining her memory," Eben said. He shifted his eyes away from Gwen to meet mine. "It's been an honor to fight alongside you both. But I go wherever she goes, even if I have to follow her from this life to the next, then so be it." Eben lifted Gwen's dagger, poised and ready. I wanted to tell him no. I wanted to tell him to stop, but I couldn't. I was envious. I was so woven into the fabric of Neverland, duty bound so much that I could never take death into my own hands. No, I would remain, and he would be with her while I toiled on in a purgatory of my own making.

Before Eben could sink the dagger home in a fatal blow, a blinding light poured out of the mortal wound in Gwen's chest. We all stumbled back, Gwen's blade tumbling from Eben's hands. I forced myself to look into the light. Magic swirled in the air around her as her body lifted from the ground. Every inch of her body was enveloped in brilliant light. I could feel the energy surrounding her. A comforting heat drew me in, reigniting a hope that burned so fiercely in my chest that I felt like my heart might combust. All of us. All of her husbands drawing in around to watch in awe and wonder. The light began to build in intensity, illuminating the forest as if I'd crossed over to some spectral plane. All the fear and heartache melted away until all I felt was love. The feeling of coming home was overwhelming. Then the world came crashing back to me. Gwen was on the ground again, surrounded by all of us. She was propped up on her hands, head hanging low as she sucked in deep, gasping breaths, the sound of it like sweet music to my ears.

"Gwen!" I stumbled to her as quickly as I could make my body move. I grasped her shoulders, pulling her up until my eyes met the soft, caramel of hers. "You're alive! Thank the Divine! I don't know how… but you're alive!" I crushed her to my chest, letting all the emotions of the day pour down my face as I held my wife.

"Hen!" Ryder pulled her from my arms, taking his turn. Each of them passed her between them. All of us reveling in the feel of her, alive and well in our arms. The sound of family, our friends rejoicing filled the air around us.

"Peter? Peter, what's happened?" She stared at the tears streaming down my face with a look of confusion.

"What's happened? You had the dagger… and then you, ahh, you were gone. I could feel that you were gone. But now somehow, some way, you're back. Are you alright?"

"Yes, I'm fine. At least I think I am. I just don't know what happened. I remember the peacefulness. It was so serene, but it was wrong at the same time. Like I wasn't supposed to be there, at least not yet. I don't know why—"

"It was the ultimate sacrifice." A melodic voice cut in and we all turned to see the beautiful figure of Peytra, as she approached us, the setting sun shining around her.

"Peytra?" Gwen got to her feet, taking a few steps toward her.

"I told you, my little star, that I would always be watching. And I couldn't miss your wedding day."

"The ultimate sacrifice? I don't understand. The Inalto demanded payment. I made the payment. Kían is gone, I can feel it. So how am I here?"

"First lesson to be learned… You cannot bury the seeds of destruction within yourself. They will always grow, no matter how strong your walls. They will consume you. But when you were faced with the choice, you sacrificed yourself for those you love. There is no greater gift. Many have made such claims, but few have ever seen it through. That pure sacrifice, made in the name of love, was the single loophole. Unraveling the ties of payment. Giving you your life back in return."

"You mean I'm free? Free of his stain forever?" Gwen's voice wavered, but she couldn't hide the hope that lingered in the unanswered question.

"Forever after is at your fingertips my little star. However you choose to live it."

Gwen turned back to us, pure joy radiating from her beautiful smile as happy tears began to spill from her eyes. "Did you hear that, my loves? We're free! This is it. This is what we dreamed about. What we worked so hard for. This is the part where the happily ever after begins."

CHAPTER XXV
SINS OF THE FLESH
-GWEN-

We spent our first night bonded in matrimony, indulging in the sins of the flesh. Each one of my husbands worshiped my body in their own unique way, pushing my limits. It was a true test of endurance to satisfy five men in one evening. A test I was determined to ace for the rest of my life. We played for hours until I was spent. Delightfully sore, no longer able to keep up with their insatiable desires. We fell blissfully into sleep together, exhausted in a naked, tangled, sticky, mess of limbs.

The future was uncertain, but we had each other.

Nothing else mattered. We were bound eternally in the eyes of the Divine. There was nothing that could keep us from each other. Enemies would try, but we would prevail. Together, we were powerful, unstoppable. We would rule all of Neverland and restore the balance within its delicate system. This was our destiny— our happily ever after.

I ROUSED from sleep in the early morning hours before the sun rose. Ryder was standing naked at the window. The moonlight showcasing his perfect form. He was a feast for the eyes. I could stare at him for hours and never tire of it. Desperately trying not to wake the others, I untangled myself and padded my way across the room. I molded my body tightly against his, wrapping my arms around his chest. My cheek nuzzled into the space between his shoulder blades, pulling in his intoxicating citrus and cedar scent.

"You're up early. Is everything okay?" Ryder was still struggling with the effects of Dorian's torture. Witnessing my death, and believing I was gone hadn't helped matters. I knew it was going to take some time for him to fully recover, but his aloofness broke my heart.

"Everything is perfect, Hen," he whispered. "I was just reflecting on the last few days." He spun around to face me, tucking a stray hair behind my ear. "Are we really going to get our happy ending?"

"I already did," I smiled, reaching up on my tiptoes, kissing him sweetly. "I have you all. There is no happier ending than that." It was true. I had everything I ever wanted. The Divine had bestowed all of my desires. All that was left was for me to enjoy their gifts.

"I need to thank the Divine for bringing you back to me. For giving my life purpose." Ryder scooped me up in his arms, and headed for the door.

"Where are we going?"

"Outside, where we can be one with the Divine. I can think of no better way to honor their gift."

The blades of grass were wet with dew, and tickled my skin as Ryder gently laid me down in the meadow outside our cottage. "I want to make love to you here. In the grass, under the stars as the sun rises over us." Picking a single blade of grass, he began to trace it along my curves, drawing goose bumps in its wake. "You are perfection, Hen. Made for me in every way." I watched as he took his time, paying close attention to the subtle signs of my pleasure. Lingering on those places a little longer. He circled my nipples and brought them into tight peaks before dropping down my belly trailing the blade of grass between my legs.

Ryder gently parted my legs and placed a soft kiss on my tender flesh before dragging his tongue along my dripping slit. "Mmmm," he purred. "I'll never get my fill of you." There was a tenderness in the way he touched me. Gentle, not rushed, he was savoring the experience. My insides whirled with heated tension while Ryder's masterful tongue worked its magic. My mews became moans as the tension inside me grew. I ran my fingers through his tousled hair, gripping tightly, not wanting him to stop. The tension snapped and my legs wrapped around his head.

"Ryder!" I cried out as the orgasm took over, my body not my own. I was his and only his in this moment.

"I love it when you scream my name." He kissed me deeply, the taste of my release heavy on his tongue. He teased my opening with the tip of his massive erection. Pressing just hard enough to stretch my delicate skin.

"Please, Ryder. I want to feel you inside of me. I need to be one with you." I begged for him to fill the emptiness in my aching core. The sun was starting to peek above the horizon, painting the sky pink as if it were blushing at our raw display of love. He pushed into me slowly, pulling a gasp from my throat. Our eyes locked as we became one. I could feel the presence of the Divine within me in that moment. We were not only one with each other, but one with the land and all its energy.

"Can you feel that?" Ryder asked, clearly able to feel the same energy.

"It feels amazing." I rocked my hips gently. "Don't stop." The sensations were amplified. I had never felt anything like it before. There was something magical happening. Ryder's rhythm was slow and torturous, bringing with it a swell of pleasure. Building and building, the sensation was becoming too much to bear. Animalistic moans were escaping from both of us as we were lost in a trance.

"Ryder!" I cried out again, almost fearful, as the most intense orgasm of my life ripped through my body. My muscles spasmed uncontrollably as wave after wave of pleasure tore through me.

"Fuck, Gwen. You feel so good," he cried out, growling as he fell over the edge, joining me in ecstasy. His body jerked in spasm like my own before collapsing breathlessly on top of me. "That was…"

"Amazing," I giggled, answering for him.

"Incredible. I love you Hen."

"I love you too, Ryder." We spent a while cuddled together in the grass. Contented in each other's arms as we watched the sun rise over the Never Cliffs. The dawn of a new day, a new chapter unfolding.

"We should probably head back inside. The others will wonder where we snuck off to."

"Maybe they watched." Ryder smirked. Proud of his performance.

I giggled, shaking my head. I could feel the blush creeping across my cheeks.

"Don't worry. We'll just tell them we were practicing."

"Practicing? For what?"

"Have you forgotten? It's almost time for spring cleaning."

The End

EPILOGUE
-MICHAELA-

My Dearest Sweetie,
    I think I have read and reread your letter a thousand times. You would have laughed if you heard the squeal that came out of me when I read the news. It is bitter sweet though. I should have been there. We should have walked arm and arm down that aisle. I should have been there to give you away. You know I would have made each and every one of them grovel before I gave my blessing. Because you deserve a happy life. You've earned your

happily ever after, so you better damn well be enjoying every minute of it.

I want you to know how proud I am of you. After everything that happened, you never gave up. You've always been true to yourself, and you never lost sight of what's most important… love. I knew you'd find your way. Your light shines through, even down the darkest of paths. Never forget that, and make sure those boys remember just how perfect you are! I love you to the moon and back, sweetie.

I wish this letter could be nothing more than catching up and simple rejoicing, but I need your help. I know I was supposed to write the moment I got here, but things haven't exactly gone according to plan. The situation in Hiraeth is dire. While the princes were trying to establish a foothold in Neverland, their own kingdom was falling through their fingertips. Everything has been compromised. Not to mention that it didn't help their cause when the princes waltzed back into the realm with a human girl on their arm. My presence has taken a tense situation and poured fuel on the fire. I can't go into detail because I have no idea who we can trust, and I wouldn't want these scrolls to fall into the wrong hands.

I hate to ask for your help, just when you're finally getting to the good part, but I need you to convince Lucius to come home. I know he's not the easiest to get along with. And I swear I can hear you cursing to yourself all the way from here, but I need you to work your charm and get him to return. He'll say no. He'll tell you he can't come back—

that it's forbidden. But there is no other way. The kingdom and his brothers depend on it. He's more a part of this than he realizes.

Just remember, I need Lucius to come here. Not you! Are you listening? I don't want you to come here. Stay in Neverland with your husbands. I will return once everything has settled here and we'll have a proper celebration. I promise I'll be fine. Your life is just beginning! Go and live it… It's an awfully big adventure.

Love Always,
    Mic

The Neverland Chronicles

-Prequel-
Beyond the Veil
A Neverland Chronicles Novella
T.S. Kinley

-Volume I-
Second to the Right
The Neverland Chronicles, Volume I
T.S. Kinley

-Volume II-
Straight On Till Morning
The Neverland Chronicles, Volume II
T.S. Kinley

-Volume III-
Queen of the Lost Boys
The Neverland Chronicles, Volume III
T.S. Kinley

TSKinleyBooks.com

Also Available
The Smut Diaries

THE SMUT DIARY IS A READING JOURNAL FOR THOSE WHO LIKE IT SPICY. A QUINTESSENTIAL "BLACK BOOK" TO TRACK ALL YOUR BOOK BOYFRIEND AFFAIRS.

TSKinleyBooks.com